PERSPECTIVES ON T. M. DORAN'S WORK:

Toward the Gleam (Ignatius Press, 2011)

Kelly Scott Franklin, Author, WALL STREET JOURNAL book reviewer, Assistant Professor of English, Hillsdale College: "...part of the charm of Doran's book [*Toward the Gleam*] is that he populates it with wonderfully real historical figures: J.R.R. Tolkien, C.S. Lewis, Edith Stein, Winston Churchill, Agatha Christie, and my personal favorite, G.K. Chesterton. Of the lovable giant, Chesterton, Doran writes one of the best lines in the book: "The room was smaller when he left it." I never realized this before, but I've always wanted to read a novel with Chesterton as a character."

NEW OXFORD REVIEW: "[*Toward the Gleam* is] a grand saga in the heroic tradition...a complex tale bursting with spirited sideshows and memorable characters...[A] sequel to T. M. Doran's stirring new novel is most assuredly in order."

The American Chesterton Society's GILBERT MAGAZINE: "*Toward the Gleam* is a rousing salute to the culture of fandom, celebrating some of the major figures of twentieth-century literature and inserting them into an adventure revolving around a priceless historical manuscript, ruthless super villains, and the hunt for a lost civilization, possibly Atlantis...Doran's melding of minds and adventure is also a place I would like to explore."

Joseph Pearce, Author, TOLKIEN MAN AND MYTH: "Although [*Toward the Gleam*] basks in the reflected glory of *The Lord of The Rings* and conveys inklings of *That Hideous Strength*, it does not merely reflect the light that Tolkien and Lewis have shown; it refracts it in exciting new dimensions...*Toward the Gleam* rises above the level of parody or pastiche to reach the heights that few writers have achieved."

PERSPECTIVES ON T. M. DORAN'S WORK:

The Lucifer Ego, sequel to *Toward the Gleam*
(TMDoranBooks, 2018)

Stephen Mirarchi, Author and Editor, Associate Professor of English, Benedictine College: "Such deeply layered literary effects reward a second reading and distinguish Doran's work (*The Lucifer Ego*) as something more than one-off beach reading. And as with his previous novels, Doran uses these details to draw the reader's focus to the big picture: the big *eschatological* picture. At least one major character...will encounter the throes of redemption and the painful cost thereof."

John Granger, TIME MAGAZINE's Dean of Harry Potter Scholars: "A writer and story craftsman who thinks seriously and yet one who respects intelligent readers sufficiently not to have to draw out the moral of the story in painfully obvious fashion...*The Lucifer Ego* is worth every minute you give it because of that care and respect."

Mississippi Valley Archaeology Center (the protagonist in THE LUCIFER EGO is a paleo-archaeologist): "I was mesmerized by (the) incredibly imaginative story and, after several re-readings, *Toward the Gleam* remains one of my favorite works of fiction...*The Lucifer Ego* is a worthy sequel... and Doran's ingenious efforts might prompt one to re-read (or read for the first time) a celebrated trilogy written by another Oxford philologist."

Roger B. Thomas, Author and "Old Western Man": "If you like your intrigue brewed hot and your skulls well-duggered... then place your order for T. M. Doran's latest work, *The Lucifer Ego*...as rich and fast-paced as anything he's written so far, including his remarkable *Iota*."

PERSPECTIVES ON T. M. DORAN'S WORK:

Iota (Ignatius Press, 2015)

Lucy Beckett, Author, WALL STREET JOURNAL book reviewer:
"*Iota* is a gripping read...The atmosphere of tension, squalor, and fear is brilliantly sustained, and the plot has thrilling twists right to the end, with the "iota" finally explained. We are drawn into the moral and physical pain of the main character, while Doran's portrayal of the anguish of conscience inflicted by both Nazi and Soviet terror is entirely convincing."

Fiorella De Maria, Author: "This compelling story of a young man struggling to survive amid the horrors of the Soviet penal system reads like an eyewitness account. At times moving, harrowing, and genuinely terrifying, Doran's *Iota* asks unsettling questions about the nature of innocence, guilt, courage, and complicity. I simply could not put it down."

Michael D. O'Brien, Author and Artist: "*Iota* is a plunge into the darkest waters of human motivation and character. Set in a political prison at the end of World War II, the story of the "cage" is also a metaphor for the imprisonment of minds and souls in various forms of unbelief. It is ultimately about redemption, sacrifice, and mercy."

Mark Nowakowski, prize-winning Composer and Musician:
"A crisp and organized writer who nevertheless seems to revere the spiritual roots of language...Doran genre-jumps into pure historical realism with...a short novel entitled *Iota*. The narrative takes place primarily during November 1945, when Prague native Jan Skala finds himself suddenly kidnapped by Soviet operatives and imprisoned for reasons beyond his knowledge or control...True to the fine form Doran set in his previous book, *Toward the Gleam*, *Iota* provides us with a surprisingly satisfying conclusion, during which the meaning behind the book's title is finally revealed."

PERSPECTIVES ON T. M. DORAN'S WORK:

Terrapin (Ignatius Press, 2013)

StAR: "*Terrapin* conforms to some of (W.H.) Auden's strict categories, but also, as Auden says of Raymond Chandler, offers less genre writing than art...The portrait of this closed milieu of only apparent innocence, the working-class neighborhood, is the strongest embodiment of Auden's theory and the greatest achievement of Doran's creation."

NEW OXFORD REVIEW: "Doran's prose [*Terrapin*] proclaims that mortals drag their childhoods with them through life's long fight, and that each generation inhabits its own culture within the same country...the novel's imaginative ending demonstrates that fraudulent intellectual and moral gymnastics in any culture are no match for the ongoing, unmitigated ramifications on perpetrators and victims alike, ramifications that play forward in ways seen and unseen, whether or not they are ever acknowledged."

Sarah Reinhard, SNORING SCHOLAR: "I don't want to compare Doran's writing with other big name writers, because he really stands alone, at least with the fiction I end up picking up and reading for review. The words "impeccable", "clean", and "delightful" come to mind as I think of ways to describe it."

GALVESTON DAILY NEWS: "At first, the novel appears to be a tale about four friends coming to terms with the end of their youth...The novel proves a multilayered tale. Doran weaves in complex threads from both the past and present to yield a complex and subtle tapestry that works on several levels... *Terrapin* is a haunting novel, one that works as well as a study of human nature as it does a mystery."

KATAKLUSMÓS

KATAKLUSMÓS

T. M. DORAN

TMDoranBooks

2020

Kataklusmós, by T. M. Doran

Published by TMDoranBooks (tmdoran.com)

Printed by Kindle Direct Publishing

© 2020 T. M. Doran

The quotation from "What the Bird Said Early in the Year" is by C. S. Lewis.

The quotation from "The Secular Masque" is by John Dryden.

ISBN: 978-1-7324726-3-1 (print edition)
          978-1-7324726-4-8 (Kindle ebook edition)

Cover and title page illustrations © 2020 by Daniel Johnson (Artisticknack.com)

Editing by G. Miki Hayden

Always first in my heart, thank you, Sherry, for your many years of patience.

ACKNOWLEDGEMENTS

Kataklusmós is the conclusion of a fifteen-year writing adventure, beginning with a sudden idea, and then proceeding with deep research for the first book in this series, *Toward the Gleam*. On this journey, I've had the support and counsel of many talented people:

- For *Kataklusmós*, editor G. Miki Hayden, artist Daniel Johnson, and book production support by N. Mason.

- For *The Lucifer Ego*, editor Lisa Nicholas and artist Daniel Johnson.

- For *Toward the Gleam*, Ignatius Press editor Vivian Dudro, cover designer John Herreid, and cover artist Daniel Mitsui.

- My brother, Jim Doran, provided valuable critiques for all three books, and was the first to read an embryonic *Toward the Gleam*.

But all the while I sit and think
  of times there were before,

I listen for returning feet
  and voices at the door.

J. R. R. Tolkien

Kataklusmós:

κατακλυσμός, cataclysm,
deluge, a devastation

PART I
Sorrows

MARCH 26, 2019

Kampala, Uganda

B EATRICE ADAMS STEPPED OFF THE BUS and started down the busy avenue toward her apartment building, holding her breath until the smoke-belching vehicle had moved on.

After a full day of teaching at the university and three appointments at the free counseling clinic where she volunteered two days a week, Beatrice was tired.

Yet as weary as she was, Beatrice couldn't erase one case from her mind, an unwed mother with an abusive father. She had invited the girl to return to talk further, but would the father permit that? What else could Beatrice do?

She would have liked to have video-conferenced with Lyle that night, but her sister needed her, or so Maria had texted earlier in the day. And since Beatrice didn't have time for the slow bus to Maria's apartment, she would have to fetch her small motorcycle from her apartment building's garage. She didn't like to take the boda-boda out at night, but she'd make an exception for Maria and little Veronica.

After eating and visiting her sister, maybe Beatrice could sneak in a phone call to Lyle before he went to bed, as the hour was two hours earlier in Oxford than Kampala. They'd last seen each other three months before, and she missed him terribly.

Beatrice also liked sending Lyle handwritten letters because she could thoughtfully compose them over several days. She resolved to start a new one in the morning.

"Please excuse me," Beatrice said, barely avoiding an elderly couple exiting her building because she was so wrapped up in her thoughts and calculations.

She announced her arrival at the apartment entry-door speaker and was buzzed in. Management made a pretense of security here, but she was always on guard. The long-ago attack on her village and her family's desperate flight from the rebels had taught her caution. Beatrice had escaped the rebel *commandanté*, intact to the human eye, but not without an unforgettable scar.

Added to that experience was the recent and troubling conversation about the book that Lyle's uncle secretly sheltered inside his monastery. Beatrice understood how a certain psychological type might become obsessed with such a marvel because she herself had viewed the book once, though viewing was an impoverished word to describe the experience. She had sat and turned those wondrous pages with Lyle after he'd recovered the volume at deadly peril.

Though she hadn't seen the spectacular metallic cocoon where the ancient artifact had originally been protected from the ravages of time and the elements, she had a keen eye for beauty, and what she had beheld was transcendent magnificence unlike anything she had ever witnessed in a work of art or craftsmanship. Though the pages had been cut out of the book and hidden in an ordinary black binder, and though Beatrice hadn't understood a word represented by the rune-like figures or the meaning behind the many margin illuminations, her admiration had known no bounds.

If not new colors, here they had seemed to her what each color would be in its ideal state, as Plato had described what he called Forms. No wonder the relic had so strongly attracted Lyle, inspired archaeologist that he was, and no wonder he had struggled to part with a treasure he could have studied and plumbed for years without exhausting its mysteries. In Lyle's acquiescence to surrendering the pages of the book to his uncle immediately upon his return to England, Beatrice had perceived a heretofore unrecognized delicacy in Lyle's character that endeared him to her all the more.

Did Beatrice's adamant refusal to cooperate with the person who pressed her about the book mean that the matter was now closed? She hadn't been able to purge that confrontation from her mind.

"How are you, Professor Adams?" asked one of her neighbors as the woman headed for the street. The two paused briefly to exchange some friendly words before Beatrice went up in the elevator.

DID ONLY A FEW MINUTES PASS then before a startling, a horrendous explosion rocked the higher floors of the apartment building? Thousands of shards of glass hurtled like hail onto the people below, eliciting shrieks of horror and pain.

This shard-hail was soon followed by a gray cloud of fine debris.

On the street, pedestrians started to run, still screaming bloody murder. Soon afterward, shrill sirens howled.

APRIL 6, 2019

Oxford

L UCIA WAS TUGGING HARD ON THE LEASH as they made their way from the lift to the street door.

"One second!" Lyle Stuart scolded.

The rude halt to their forward motion wasn't well received by the impatient dog, but Lyle scarcely noticed because he saw he had a letter from Uganda to savor when he returned to the flat.

By late afternoon, when Lyle usually returned from his Oxford University office, Lucia was ready to put him through his paces, meaning a one to two-mile hike through town, going to all her favorite spots. Truth was, at forty-one Lyle wasn't as fit as he could desire—the scale told him as much, and these walks were as necessary for him as Lucia.

As standard poodles went, Lucia was a runt, though she pulled above her weight when she had a mind to, and the squirrel that crossed their path was ample provocation.

"Hey there!" Lyle shouted, to little effect.

His mind was apt to wander as they made their daily circuit: Developments in paleo-archaeology, his own research, Popa and the Lido site, and Beatrice—of course—circled through his thoughts.

Two years before, Beatrice Adams had left Oxford to help her widowed sister with a young daughter in Uganda, and since that time Lyle and Beatrice had only seen each other on a hand-ful of occasions in spite of good intentions and pledges to visit more often.

Lyle felt no different about her than he had when she'd left England. Though he couldn't imagine the rest of his life without her, he knew a more permanent arrangement would have to wait until matters were settled for her in Kampala. He'd pushed her as hard as he'd dared, but she wasn't one to budge when she made up her mind.

Lyle sometimes marveled at how their relationship had prevailed in spite of so many differences—she a believer to the core and he agnostic when he bothered to think about it; her interest in the human mind and heart and his in ancient cultures; she a person of action and he deliberative; she reared in African traditions and he as British as they came; she always on the look-out for someone in need, and he focused on his work. Even now, he couldn't quite put his finger on the reason for their attraction to each other. All he knew was he needed her to make him whole and yearned to have her in his life as he'd had when she'd lived and taught in Oxford.

The letter in the post rekindled memories of his most recent visit to Uganda, with Beatrice decorating every room for Christ-mas: tree, garland, crèche, candles, mistletoe, and wreath. Her apartment in Kampala was smaller than her Oxford flat, but the furnishings and appointments made Lyle feel as he had when he'd visited her in England, with the framed family photograph in the grotto, the turntable he'd given her for her birthday, the carved wooden giraffe, zebra, and other animals.

"None of that!" she had said to him on Christmas night, breaking away from his intended embrace. "We have dishes to wash and dry."

"I want to marry you, Beatrice."

She stopped what she was doing, giving him her full atten-tion. "Why?"

"Because you're...perfect" was all he could think to say.

"You know I'm not perfect. Far from it." She smiled. "Did you like Beni?" she asked him, referring to one of her friends.

"She quizzed me about Egypt. When I told her I wasn't an authority, she lost interest. I tried Lido—nothing doing."

"She's a bright girl who had a vicious childhood."

"Another lost lamb? Don't you have your quota?"

"There is no quota." She pointed to the high cabinet for the clean bowl.

"Plenty of lost lambs in England too," he offered.

She walked him to the mistletoe, kissed him, and said, "Happy Christmas, Lyle."

By the time he shook off that melancholy memory, he and Lucia were almost home, and he was sweating. Approaching the entrance, he heard a high-pitched voice say, "Hello, Doctor Stuart."

Surveying the landscape, Lyle spotted the bent-over elderly man with the walker who lived in the senior apartments across the street. Lyle had the hardest time remembering the man's name so a stout wave would have to do, and anyway, he was eager to hurry in and read Beatrice's letter.

Once inside his flat, he dropped the envelope on the table, put on his house shoes, and made himself a drink, stopping for a moment in front of his bookcase and rearranging several volumes on the shelf.

Wine glass in hand and on the verge of opening the letter, he noticed that the Kampala return address wasn't Beatrice's but that of her sister Cornelia.

Lucia, a clump of cocoa-colored fur, was resting under the window. Lyle, sitting in his usual armchair, opened the envelope, removing the half-sheet of blue paper and a newspaper cutting.

I am sorry for this news, Lyle.

The cutting, dated March 28, read:

Adams, Beatrice, age 37, victim of an explosion in her east Kampala apartment. Beloved sister of Cornelia Serwanga and Maria Azira, dearest aunt to Veronica Azira. Cause of explosion unknown. Private interment.

The drink glass fell from his hand to the floor, clanging like a tolling bell. Lyle looked around the room as if he expected to find himself somewhere else. Only one other time in his life had Lyle felt as he did at this moment, in the Russian consulate in Mainz with a pistol pointed at him, certain that death was imminent.

He kept looking at the notice to make sure it was real. He examined the envelope again—Cornelia's street number, the Kampala postmark.

Of course the cutting was real, as real as the night his mother died when Lyle was just thirteen years old. If he lived to be a hundred, this moment would remain as vivid as that terrible long-ago night.

He hadn't said a word, or done anything dramatic, but Lucia had sensed something was amiss and roused herself, coming to him, standing in the spilled drink and resting her head on his leg. Unconsciously, he reached down and gripped her fur.

His whole body tingled. A wave of vertigo came over him, so intense he thought he might be sick. Not moving an inch, he took deep breaths until the worst of it subsided.

Steeling himself, he retrieved his phone, punched in a number and waited with a desperation he couldn't have imagined when he came in from the walk.

"Sam?" he said at last.

APRIL 26, 1929

☻-☻-☻

Oxford
(90 years earlier)

"**D**UM TEE DUM, DUM TEE DUM TEE DUM...won't do, won't do at all," the man, sitting alone in his Oxford College office, said out loud.

A philologist working on a spectacular written artifact, a book in a magnificent metal box, John found much of the translation tedious—many words and phrases, linguistic thorns, resisting traditional techniques. Having no comparative texts for reference, he had to rely on deep experience, context, and an imagination informed by years of labor on this piece, this language.

Because he never failed to be moved by the book's beauty, the dullness could have been ameliorated if he allowed himself to work with the object itself rather than a utilitarian facsimile, but this thing was so precious he permitted himself to view it only when the door was locked and bolted, and he was copying the content for translation.

This month had been different, as he'd devoted himself to translating pithy songs by the most mysterious character in the chronicle, with this person—or whatever he was—singing his lively songs, doing marvelous things, and then abruptly exiting the story.

16

Translating this character's verses was both a challenge and a joy for John. He hoped to decipher them as precisely as different languages and thousands of years of separation from that world would allow. Much work was still to be done, and plenty of verses where he was dissatisfied with his translation, but these songs had turned out to be an oasis in a vast wilderness of hard hiking.

A knock on John's office door forced him to conceal the work.

He was more than a little surprised to see his wife enter, as her appearance on college grounds was rare.

Closing the door behind her, she said, "You were working on that thing again, weren't you? I can see it on your face."

"Am I that easy to read?" He smiled weakly and reached for his pipe.

E. M. gave him a penetrating look. "Only for me," she assured him. "So don't fret. Remember, not a page in the house, not even a transcription."

"I've kept my promise. You needn't worry." He had long understood her concern and had no intention of upsetting her by disregarding their agreement.

"Oh, I worry, but you know that," she said, tugging her ear as she did when distressed.

"To what do I owe the honor of this visit?" he asked, hoping to lighten the mood.

"You are lecturing today, aren't you?"

"Shortly. Would you care to sit in?" he asked, humor only she would recognize.

"Thanks all the same. But would you mind stopping at John's school this afternoon? His teacher requested a word. Constance has to leave early, so I'll be alone with Priscilla."

"Trouble at John's school?" the boy's father inquired.

"I have no reason to think so."

"Certainly, I will," he said.

"I won't keep you, but I wasn't sure I'd catch you on the telephone."

"You're always welcome here, E. M."

As she turned to leave, he said, "May I sing you a song?"

Her eyes narrowed. "Your own?"

"I'm afraid not. A translation." He cursed himself for giving into the impulse. He knew better than to speak to her about the book. Hadn't her little outburst just now been ample reminder? But sometimes his enthusiasm got the better of him. Moreover, to no one else could he even reveal the book's existence.

"You may," she said. He translated her unspoken words as *if you must*. The book had come to represent menace to E. M., a threat to her family, provoking more than a few cross words. "Well?" she said.

He'd spent enough time with the song to recite it from memory to a tune he'd devised himself.

Poor old Willow Man,
You put those roots away.
I'm in a hurry now;
Evening shall follow day.
I'm skipping home again,
Pretty flowers bringing.
Hey now, folderol, can you hear me singing?

"I'm not satisfied yet," he promptly added, still clutching the unlit pipe.

She smiled. "It's quite good, and your rendition was pleasingly dramatic."

If her response wasn't wildly enthusiastic, he had managed to defuse some of the angst the book invariably produced in her. "Thank you, my dear."

The door closed on the most beautiful woman in the world—his translation of what she was to him.

APRIL 6, 2019

Oxford

"I JUST TALKED TO HER LAST WEEK. She was fine. Are you listening?"

Sam Stuart's shoulders slumped and his eyes were lusterless.

"Who'd want to kill her?" Lyle said, more loudly than he'd intended.

"A dangerous country. You know that," Lyle's brother answered.

"One of her lost lambs, a lunatic. I told her…"

"Keep your voice down. It wasn't her fault. Remember that. She did what she needed to do."

"And see where it got her," Lyle said, gruffly.

"You don't know what got her." Pushing Beatrice's obituary across the table, Sam added, "Do you have any more information than this?"

"Not a thing." She wasn't dead, Lyle kept telling himself, the notice a mistake, a vicious prank, or a lying enemy. Then why, when he'd tried to phone her, had he received a message that the number had been disconnected?

Sam was seated opposite Lyle at a table overlooking a busy Oxford street. Lyle had wanted to meet in his own flat, but his brother had insisted on this location, the pub where Lyle, Sam, and Beatrice had first discussed the stolen manuscript over two years before.

Outside, a bright sky and warm air Lyle hadn't noticed on the way over. Actually, he remembered next to nothing about the drive.

As if Beatrice's death wasn't enough, Lyle couldn't ignore what he saw in his brother. Sam looked older than his fifty-one years. If he had shaved, he hadn't paid attention or used a mirror. Ten years younger than Sam, Lyle had always admired his brother, but this unkempt, sagging man didn't inspire much confidence. Sam had gained weight since he'd been forcibly retired from the government agency he referred to as *The Firm*. Several public incidents had convinced Downing Street that Sam was a liability rather than an asset. Lyle knew his brother had never cared for rules at any time and his defiant nature had finally caught up with him.

"I couldn't be more sorry," said Sam. "And not just for you. I thought the world of her." Sam turned to their waitress. "I'll have black coffee and he'll have a bottle of ale. Nothing to eat." Sam focused again on Lyle. "Before I came here, I called a Ugandan policeman I know. He confirmed the information you received."

"That's one policeman."

"A policeman I trust," countered Sam.

So much for Lyle's desperate hope that she wasn't dead, a vacuum that filled with rage in a rush.

"I need your help, Sam. As soon as possible."

Sam's expression wasn't encouraging. "What's the mission?"

"Track down whoever did it. Make sure they never do it again."

"What about school...your classes?"

"I don't care about that." So much emotion welled up he had to stop talking.

"Someday you will. I promise," said Sam, looking over his shoulder to make certain no one was listening. "What makes you think we can pull this off, with no authority, no intel, no backup... Where's that goddamn waitress?"

"I have *you*, that's why."

"You have a lofty opinion of me. Even in my salad days, I needed The Firm's resources to accomplish things." Looking

Lyle in the eye, Sam said, "I've never been a fan of sting-and-die missions, and that's what I'm hearing."

Lyle bowed his head. How weary he felt. He wished he were home, and he dreaded the idea of being alone in the flat. "You can decide how we do it. I just want the person eliminated."

"Is that all? Joseph Mutesi is the person I spoke to. He's with the Ugandan Internal Security Organization."

"I'm not ready to admit she's…"

"They never are, not when it's sudden like this. Have you talked to Cornelia?"

"I left a message," Lyle said, though how intelligible a message he wasn't sure.

"Cornelia and Maria are torn up too," Sam said. "You may not hear back for a while."

"I'll call every day if I have to."

"That won't make you feel any better, or them either. And the police may well apprehend the killer before we arrive."

"I'm going anyway…to make sure."

"To make sure she's dead?" Sam pressed.

"To make sure everything's being done to…that ought to be done. I'm going to blow his brains out!"

"Mind your tongue!" Sam whispered.

Their drinks arrived, Sam waiting until their waitress walked off to speak again. "Assassinate him while he's in custody? That's a tall order. Even if we find the person who did this, eliminating him won't be easy. The bomb proves he's no amateur or common criminal."

Much of what Sam said went right past Lyle. The words didn't register. Lyle said, "She didn't give up on me in Mainz."

"You were still alive. This is a different mission."

Lyle closed his eyes. "Agnes's centipede, get it up close to the bloody bastard."

"What are you talking about?"

"Agnes CurLio's diary, a lethal centipede that lives inside

a Mexican cactus. Attracted to hormones in the human body. Scolo...something or other."

"You're talking nonsense."

He *was* talking nonsense, his speech regulator scrambled by Cornelia's letter. He couldn't help noticing Sam's trembling hands, though why wouldn't his brother be distraught? His own heart hadn't stopped pounding since he'd read the obituary. "I'm getting this bastard, no matter what."

"You'll do as I say or you'll be dead or in prison in a month, and whoever did this will be free as a bird. That's how it works when amateurs go on crusades."

Ignoring his brother, Lyle said, "How long until you're ready?"

Sam reached across the table and gave Lyle's collar a hard yank. "Ready for what?"

"You know what," Lyle hissed.

"I have to be able to trust you. At this moment, I wouldn't trust you to hold an egg without dropping it. We're not going anywhere until this irrational phase passes. That's what they taught me, and it's kept me alive so far." He stared his brother in the eyes.

"We'll have another round, if you please," Sam called out to their waitress.

"We beat long odds with the manuscript," Lyle countered.

"We did, didn't we, but that doesn't make *these* long odds any less long. Friends at The Firm may help me if they can."

A piece of Lyle's heart ached for Sam too. His brother looked awful. "Thanks, Sam. You have to take care of yourself."

"You mean if I'm drunk, our odds'll be even longer." Lyle couldn't summon the energy to dispute his brother's observation. Sam said, "I'll make a list of questions for Cornelia and Maria."

After a pause, he asked, "What are you going to do next?"

Irritated by the question, Lyle took a long drink of beer. "What have we been talking about for the last hour?"

"You know what I mean. We've been talking about a monkey business op, not life. Whether we succeed or fail, in a few weeks you'll be back home."

"I'm not thinking that far ahead."

"I don't expect you to, but you need to think about it before the time comes, and in the meantime don't burn any bridges."

Shaking his head, Lyle said, "None of the women I've known held a patch on Beatrice. I can't find my way without her."

Sam's features softened. "I'm not surprised. She was the finest woman I ever knew."

"Maria and Veronica are my responsibility now," Lyle added.

"Thank you," Sam said to the waitress, waiting for her to step away before he said, "Don't get ahead of yourself. We already have one op. We don't need any distractions."

"Beatrice would see our op as the distraction and the girls as the main thing."

"That's why she was who she was, and we're who we are," answered Sam, staring into his cup. "In the meantime, I'm moving in with you."

"I have a one-bed flat," protested Lyle.

"I've slept on plenty of sofas, and you've seen my apartment. It's not as if I'm making a big sacrifice."

Lyle frowned. "You don't need to."

"What else do I have to do? I don't have a job. No girlfriend. No hobbies...healthy ones, anyway. I'll pack a bag and be over later."

"I have to take Lucia to the monastery," said Lyle.

Sam started for Lyle's collar again, but held off, folding his hands on his lap. "You're not listening. You realize this is going to end badly. At best, we'll come home empty handed. At worst— well, use your imagination."

"I don't bloody care!" Lyle roared so loudly that everyone in the pub took notice. This wasn't the impotent rage he'd felt when his mother died but a virile fury. Clutching the beer bottle in his bone-white hand, he hurled it at the window, shattering the glass and bringing the pubkeeper out from behind the bar with a mean-looking walking stick.

Sam stood with a raised hand. "I'll pay. He's in a bad way. Lost someone, sudden-like."

The bartender didn't move. Neither did the patrons. Everyone was staring at Lyle, whose forehead was pressed against the tabletop.

"Here," said Sam, putting a wad of money in the bartender's hand.

"He'd better be done smashing," the man growled.

"I'll see that he is," promised Sam. "His girl died."

The pubman returned to his post behind the bar, the stick in plain view on the counter.

"I didn't think you had it in you," Sam whispered.

"I'm sorry."

"Don't spoil it by apologizing. Bull's eye, dead center. Let's go clean up the mess."

Sam was halfway to the door when Lyle murmured, "Welcome to Mordor, Frodo."

APRIL 10, 2019

Oxford

"HELLO LUCIA," said the student in the hallway. "You too, Dr. Stuart." Lyle was always an afterthought when Lucia was with him.

Stepping through the door of the archaeology lab, Lucia in tow, Lyle made for his office.

"Not so fast," a piercing voice called as he passed Agnese Leone's door.

Agnese darted out of her office and commenced playing with the enthusiastic poodle. Lyle didn't interfere, as Lucia had been deprived of play in recent days.

"Come in for tea," Agnese suggested.

"I…"

"No excuses, my good man. Hustle along," she said, jerking at his sleeve.

As Agnese prepared tea, Lyle reacquainted himself with his colleague's office. Tucked away in the corner stood a battered secretary desk, while against the wall sat an out-of-plumb display case for gewgaws she'd picked up on expeditions. On top of the display case, a lab hotplate could be used for tea and sundry cooking—strictly prohibited. A moth-eaten housecoat hung from a hook on the wall, with pink house shoes on the floor beneath the robe.

Lyle had once overheard their department head refer to Agnese's office as a health, safety, and cultural hazard.

"Let her roam," Agnese said, referring to Lucia. "Have some Turkish delight." Without further ado, she popped a piece into his mouth before he could object.

A decade and a half older than Lyle, short and a bit rotund, Agnese Leone was an all-around agreeable person, something Lyle had learned by spending a month with her at a site near Mycenaean Pylos, scouring thief-ridden *tholoi*—stone beehive tombs—for the smallest treasure—digging digging, with Agnese singing.

As Lyle later discovered, Agnese was funding the schooling of a dozen indigent children in Oxford.

Today, she was attired in a mint-green frock, decorated with quarter-moons, looking like a Disney fairy without the wand. As always, she smelled of curry powder and pine—a purchased scent? Or something she had concocted on her own?

As bad as Lyle felt, he was glad she had invited him in. "Aggie, this isn't a camp. You need to replace that old desk with something more practical. It's seen better days, love."

"The same could be said of me," she rumbled. "Anyway, it's a hand-me-down from Sir Max. When we have time, I'll tell you a story about it. Needs the right mood, drinks in hand. The glow!"

Setting two teacups on her work desk and quite obviously restraining a sob, she said, "It's about time I expressed my condolences, but I didn't want to intrude. How are you faring, Lyle?"

He'd known this question was coming but that didn't make it any easier. "Day-to-day, getting accustomed to the new world. Lucia!"

The poodle was tossing one of Agnese's house shoes in the air.

"I've been looking for an excuse to replace those old things."

Lyle had only taken a few sips. "I really must be going, Aggie. I have a class this afternoon."

"My door is always open. Hot tea in a jiffy. Unless that cretin Dawson is about. Hold still," she said, straightening his collar and brushing something off the front of his shirt.

LYLE WAS COMPLETING DEPARTMENT PAPERWORK. Once rebelling against mundane tasks, he now took refuge in such prosaic activities, and he was indeed in a bad way if Agnese had to keep him tidy.

In former times, the archaeology graduate lab and library had been a haven, a place of rejuvenation. Not anymore. These days, the silence that once fortified him felt oppressive and the work that formerly anchored him seemed trivial. He couldn't glance at the skeleton of the Neanderthal girl in the corner without recalling how Beatrice had joked about it as her rival.

When he looked up from his work, another colleague, Andrea Fitzgerald, was seated across the desk. How long had she been there, and why hadn't Lucia alerted him to a visitor? As distracted as he'd been since receiving the news about Beatrice, he wasn't surprised he hadn't heard Andrea enter.

"I've been waiting until you came to the lab...were alone," she said, fighting back tears. "I can't tell you how bad I feel. I know how much you loved her, how much you must miss her."

Andrea had face, hands, and arms like alabaster—to go along with a keen mind. More than a superficial beauty, Andrea Fitzgerald was someone who dug deep after knowledge. No wonder the BBC had latched onto her.

"Thanks" was all Lyle could say. He found having a conversation about Beatrice impossible without stirring strong emotions he couldn't control.

Lucia was scrutinizing the woman, the poodle probably worried about losing the new toy she'd brought back from Agnese's office. Andrea said, "Concentrating on your work is wise. Productive distractions are healthy when grieving. I want you to know I'm here for you. I mean friendship, someone to talk to. Are you still going to Lido?"

"Not as soon as I'd planned. I haven't spoken to Popa yet."

"Don't rush. Take your time. You're human…a decent man."

Decent? What would she say if she'd seen his performance in the pub, the vulgar outburst and the broken window? He was a different man, the old Lyle Stuart conscious of his reputation, careful about what he said and did in public, while the new man didn't give a fig who'd seen or heard his eruptions.

"You'll be here until you travel to Lido?" Andrea said.

When he hesitated, she asked, "What are you planning, Lyle?"

Should he admit it? Andrea was a hard person to deceive. "I'm traveling to Kampala."

"When?" she immediately queried.

"A week."

She reached across the desk, gripping his hand. "Please don't."

Exactly the sort of thing he wanted to avoid. "I have to."

"Why?"

How much should he confide in her? "I have to see Beatrice's sisters. It's the least I can do."

He'd hoped this would satisfy her, but she was having none of it. "They wouldn't expect you to come so soon."

"I have to go, Andrea. I'm not staying long."

"That's the only reason you're going?" she probed.

He had a sense she could see inside of him—everything. "What else would I do there?"

"Remember the manuscript you recovered?" she went on, tacking in a different direction. "Whoever has it will let you borrow it for a few weeks. We could work on it together, or if it makes you more comfortable, you can work on it with Leone. That would be therapeutic. When you feel better, you can return it. The important thing is to give yourself time, and fill that time with something that excites you…not silly paperwork."

"Do you think that will make me forget her?"

She released his hand, leaving him feeling as if he'd been unplugged from a source of energy. "Of course not, but instead of thinking about her twenty-four hours a day, you might reduce that to maybe sixteen. And don't tell me she wouldn't want you to have productive distractions. I know she would."

The *manuscript*, a meager word for those luminous pages of runes, illuminations, gilding, foliate designs, and intricate maps he had recovered at grave peril. Those nighttime hours he'd spent in the Paris hotel paging through the manuscript were the most memorable of his professional life.

"You may be right," he admitted.

"Will you consider it?"

When Andrea got a bee in her bonnet, she was hard to resist. "Don't think I'm not grateful. It's this damn fog I'm in."

Looking down at the desk, she said, "I'm not the person I was two years ago. I said cruel things—I'm sure you remember—and I've never forgiven myself. I want you to know how sorry I am, bitterly sorry! Are you going to Kampala alone?"

To say anything about Sam would invite questions Lyle wasn't prepared to answer, and even admitting his brother was accompanying him would reek of mystery. Hadn't Andrea once been in contact with the wretched Caroline Desrosier, who knew all about his brother? What had Desrosier told Andrea about Sam?

He didn't like lying to Andrea, but what choice did he have? "Alone...to see Beatrice's sisters."

"This isn't an interrogation. You're not obliged to answer me."

"I'm not myself, Andrea. Put it down to that. Is Oliver well?" he asked her. Oliver Marks was their colleague who was handling day-to-day management at the world-famous Zeta2 site Andrea had discovered near Jericho. As the site's notoriety advanced, she had even changed the name from Jericho A72 to the jazzier Zeta2.

"He's soldiering on," Andrea answered. "Our camp is no oasis. Lyle, have dinner with me tonight. Please say yes."

"I can't..."

"Please say *yes*. I promise not to talk about…that."

He shook his head. He was tired, and tired of being on the defensive. "I'd be awful company. Sorry. I may not look it, but I'm grateful for the invitation." He smiled and grabbed at a change of subject. "I heard your series is confirmed."

A joyous smile lit her face. "Production starts in a few weeks."

"The sky's the limit for you, Andrea. I've always thought so."

"I'm not leaving Oxford. Trust me," she said.

APRIL 26, 1929

Paris
(90 years earlier)

"WHERE ON EARTH did you acquire this specimen, Dr. Rosman?" asked the man.

"A remote region," the woman replied.

"And on what continent is this remote region?"

"To be precise, an island in the Atlantic Ocean," she answered.

"I would be interested in learning the coordinates of this island."

"That can be arranged, Professor Alembert," said Rosman. She stood on the other side of the man's enormous desk. Wearing a navy suit and matching hat, she carried no pocketbook and wore no obvious makeup.

Visitors to Adler Alembert's office were invariably impressed, if not intimidated, by the two floor-to-ceiling window walls, twelve-foot ceiling with fine leather overlays, lacquered antique chairs, and his one-of-a-kind desk. This woman was unimpressed, or she disguised her awe masterfully, not even looking at the terrarium filled with live butterflies on her way from the door.

She placed the glass-encased butterfly she'd brought with her on top of the desk. The creature was as large as a salad plate and possessed amazingly long antennae and scarlet wings.

Holding the glass box up to the light, Alembert placed a magnifier over one eye, carefully inspecting the specimen. "I have never seen butterfly wings of this color anywhere, and I'm an expert."

"When I learned about your interest in lepidoptery, I thought you'd be intrigued," responded the woman.

Alembert was a negligible physical specimen: fleshy and round faced, with unruly white hair. He leaned over the desktop supported by two pallid hands, and said, "Surely, more than a desire to indulge a stranger's regard for butterflies brought you here. I don't often see people with whom I'm not acquainted."

"I'm aware of that, Professor."

"So you know something about me. Would you be surprised to learn I have discovered a few facts about you too, *Mademoiselle* Rosman? You claim to be an entomologist at a Spanish university, a false representation. You aren't teaching in Spain or anywhere else. As to your entomological credentials, they are bread crumbs that might satisfy most. Not me."

"That's why I brought you the butterfly. For access."

"So I surmised. What do you want?" Alembert demanded.

"A private conversation."

"The tariff will be steep. This specimen remains with me," he said, embers sparking in his ashen eyes. "And you will not have your conversation." Alembert seemed pleased with himself. "*Bonjour*, and be grateful the tariff for your deceit isn't steeper."

"I thought you desired coordinates."

Alembert glared at the woman. "I warn you not to trifle with me, *Mademoiselle*...whoever you are."

"You may not trust me, Professor, but I assure you I am not trifling with you."

"If I answer your questions, you will provide the coordinates?"

Rosman said, "We have more in common than you might imagine. This is an impressive office for a teacher of paleo-history."

"I have been fortunate in commerce."

"Your grandfather started the business, didn't he? Gorgo Alembert, though that wasn't his name when he set out to make his mark on the world."

Alembert's eyes narrowed. "Are you employed by one of the gazettes?"

"You know that I am not. My interest is personal. Whatever you tell me will remain with me. Gorgo Alembert attracted the interest of an author who modeled his detective's mortal enemy on your grandfather."

"Imaginative fiction doesn't interest me. Get on with it."

"What did your grandfather tell you about his parents—where he was born?"

Alembert took a seat, looking like a tow-headed child behind that massive desk. Instead of answering his visitor, he turned his attention to the butterfly, lifting the glass container once more and holding it close to his eyes.

"Your *curriculum vitae* may have been fabricated, but not this specimen. This creature is *bona fide*. Write the coordinates here," he said, pushing a notepad across the desk.

And what a desk. Displaying golden veins throughout, it was so masterfully assembled it appeared to have been sculpted from a single piece of wood.

She caressed the wood with her hand. "You haven't answered my question."

Alembert said, "I don't recall my grandfather ever speaking about his parents. As to his place of birth, southeastern Europe or southwestern Asia is the best I can do. A few years after his death, I made inquiries, but discovered nothing. Perhaps the endless tumult in that part of the world is responsible for a dearth of records."

"How did he die?" she asked.

"Heart failure. That's what was passed on to me."

"But you don't believe it."

He tore his eyes from the butterfly and pinned them on the woman. "Gorgo Alembert was in remarkably good condition for a man his age. I suspect a resourceful rival or a traitor within his organization eliminated him."

"Did you investigate his death?"

"I repay disloyalty and deceit in my own way."

"Were rumors, suspicions…fables connected to your grandfather?"

"Some believed he was a god," Alembert answered, disinterestedly.

"Did he tell you this?"

"Why does this interest you, *Doctor*?"

"I said my interest was personal—a family matter. I am now prepared to supply you with the balance of the tariff." She wrote numbers on the notepad and slid it across the desk.

"As you said, the Atlantic Ocean," observed the man. "Do you believe you are related to Gorgo Alembert?"

"I do."

"And you are interested in his property?"

"Trust me, I am not the least bit interested in his property. Many paleo-historians are collectors. And you?"

"On occasion…Pre-historical artifacts," he said.

"Books?"

He opened the drawer and produced a pistol, pointing it at her heart, and then returning it to the desk. She hadn't stirred. "A foolish question, Mademoiselle. How can a book be pre-historical?"

Rosman had not been invited to sit, nor had she. As she turned and walked to the door, Alembert said, "Will I be hearing from you again?"

"No further impositions on your time, Professor," the woman responded, without looking back.

He heard the click indicating the closure of the door. Removing calipers and color palettes from a desk drawer, Alembert attached his magnifier and spent the next hour examining, measuring, photographing the butterfly, after which he retrieved a map, locating the site of the coordinates the woman had given him.

No land was shown to exist at this location.

A KNOCK ON THE DOOR preceded the entry of a towering black man with ritual scars on his face. Attired in a dark jacket and tie, the giant approached the desk and waited. His hands were russet, gnarled like the roots of an ancient tree, large even for a man his size—two to three times the size of a normal man's hands.

"Well? I didn't expect you back so soon."

"We lost her," the giant said, in a deep baritone, meaning his employer's recent visitor.

Alembert sprang to his feet in an obvious fury. "You mean she lost you, don't you? What happened?"

"She went into a café on Garibaldi. Nadine followed her inside. I remained in the car. The woman visited the comfort room. She never came out."

"Clarity, Christopher."

"Nadine waited five minutes and went in. The woman wasn't there."

"Did anyone come out of the room?"

"No one."

"Did the room have any windows, or any other exit doors?"

"No, I checked myself."

"Sack Nadine at once." Alembert had intended to track the woman to her place of residence, to learn everything about her, then punish her, in one way or another, based on what he learned about her. He said, "You will locate her before clubbing tonight, or you will cancel your engagement."

"Helena is joining me tonight," the giant said.

"So you mentioned. Your Amazon will be disappointed, unless you locate *la Rosman* before the festivities commence."

The giant clenched and unclenched his pail-sized hands, bowed stiffly, and exited the room.

APRIL 15, 2019

St. Hugh's Charterhouse, England

"**O**UT, MY GIRL," Lyle said to Lucia. He didn't have to ask twice as the monastery was one of her favorite destinations.

Lyle had no doubt she'd be well cared for there, at least as comfortable as she was in town. He was worried about himself, though, not having her near when he couldn't summon the energy to talk to anyone else. The monastery was where she needed to be while he was away but the hole inside was already growing as he contemplated the ride home without her.

When he'd grudgingly brought her home after his Waterloo Creek Apartments neighbor William died, he'd expected a temporary arrangement. Lucia had kept her distance too, growling at him when pressed to do something she wasn't of a mind to do.

"The sooner you're gone, the better," he had said, and she clearly agreed.

In those early days, he couldn't have imagined how important she would become to him as his walking companion and his confidante—with him saying things to her he'd say to no one else. Now, he didn't know what he'd do without the dog he hadn't wanted. For years, he had come home to an empty house, convincing himself the aloneness didn't matter—until he'd experienced her greeting at the door, her reassuring presence.

"Would I have seen you if Lucia weren't staying with us?" Abbot Henry asked, a half-step behind his swifter nephew.

"Certainly."

"But perhaps not so soon. You've been on my mind constantly, Frodo."

Lyle's uncle was the only person who still used his first name with any regularity, or even knew Lyle's name was Frodo. A friendly faced man in his sixties with a prominent nose and more hair on his head than his nephew had, Abbot Henry said, *"I wish it need not have happened in my time...and so do all who live to see such times. But that is not for them to decide. All we have to decide is what to do with the time that is given us.* Do you remember those words of Gandalf's in the story? I can't properly express my sadness for your loss, Frodo. *My* sadness is grievous too. We corresponded more often than you know. A rare spirit."

"I'm lower than I've ever been, Uncle Henry," Lyle confessed.

A rabbit darted in front of them and off Lucia went, prompting his uncle to say, "The rabbits have free run of the grounds. We don't trouble them—except for our brown sentinel, Lucia, that is. But when the question comes to our garden, we build a fortress to keep them out."

Lyle was happy to see his girl racing about, better than tearing a friend's house shoes apart. "Are you successful in keeping out the rabbits?"

"We build, they breach, we build anew, they breach anew, and on it goes. That one by the garden gate is a bit of a brute, not above cuffing the youngsters, and not impressed by your poodle."

Lucia emerged from the high grass into an open space a hundred yards distant, bounding toward a man in work clothes with arms extended.

"Who's that?" asked Lyle.

"We call him Brother Francis. Let's slow a bit if you don't mind."

The workman was scratching Lucia's ears with both hands.

Lyle said, "I don't recall meeting him."

"I'm not surprised. He keeps to himself much of the time. He came to us two years ago, asked if he could reside in that hut by the hives in exchange for inspiring our bees. We'd seen our colony drastically reduced, and as he seemed an honest enough chap, I accepted his proposal."

Seemed an honest enough chap? Knowing his uncle hadn't done any checking on this beekeeper, Lyle said, "Weren't you concerned about a stranger on the grounds?"

"I know what worries you, Frodo. I'm the book's caretaker but my vocation is to serve. He's conscientious with the bees and playful when he has a mind to be. Told Brother Jerome he'd been a bell ringer at Notre Dame."

Abbot Henry's response didn't allay Lyle's apprehensions about strangers on the monastery grounds, and his uncle's reference to the book prompted him to say, "When did you last view the manuscript?"

"Last autumn, as is my custom. All was well."

Lyle said, "That book is beautiful, isn't it?"

"As I insisted when it was stolen."

"I had to see it for myself," Lyle continued, watching the beekeeper and dog having fun together.

Abbot Henry went on, "One would be hard pressed to notice the sewn pages, or they would conclude the stitches had always been there."

When the book was stolen, the thief had cut out the pages and placed filler pages between the covers to delay discovery of the theft. Lyle said, "Your Brothers did a masterful job of rebinding the book. I saw no other damage when I examined it."

"Unmarred, but for the cut pages. You told me Noel was the only person to have handled it, and he desired to protect it for sale."

Not lost on Lyle was that Abbot Henry said Noel Dekeyser had *handled* the manuscript rather than had *stolen* it. "And Dekeyser was inspired to steal it by Caroline Desrosier," Lyle said. "I envy the man who brought it here, the years he spent with it."

Talking about the book without being able to see it wouldn't make him feel better, any more than reading about a site he yearned to explore himself but couldn't visit. "I must go, Uncle Henry."

The abbot put a hand on Lyle's shoulder. "Shall we fetch Lucia so you can say goodbye?"

As the beekeeper and the dog were still romping together, Lyle said, "Let her be. I have to return to town. I'm glad to see her play."

"Won't you take something from the refectory before you go?"

"No, thank you, Uncle."

"You have light in your future. I know you do" were his uncle's last words as Lyle made for the car.

Instead of giving his Uncle Henry his full attention, Lyle had been preoccupied with the stranger and the book. He couldn't let it go, even now, with Lucia safely lodged and the flight to Africa imminent. And if they identified Beatrice's killer? If the disposition of that villain was within his power, he would seek a heavy retribution.

That's how it works when amateurs go on crusade…a sting-and-die mission! Sam had said that to him in the pub, suggesting the killer might be beyond their reach.

What little energy Lyle could summon was expended on obsessions—finding and punishing Beatrice's killer, that book hidden away in his uncle's monastery, what he had said to Sam in the pub—"Agnes's centipede, get it up close to the bloody bastard."

Beatrice's killer might never be identified, and Lyle might never see the book again, but he could go to the archives and retrieve that creature's name.

Lyle had explored many ancient temples where questions that possessed, beviled, and tormented men were set forth, where oracles foretold fate, where glory or doom was meted out. The

Oxford Consolidated Archives possessed that oracular quality for him, because in that archive on the day when he had pieced together the clues in Agnes CurLio's nineteen-twenties diary and decided to ask Beatrice to marry him, she had announced her decision to return to Kampala, leading to her death and his devastation, their mutual doom.

Scolo...what? He started the car. He would consult the oracle again.

APRIL 16, 2019

London

IN A ROOM WITH NO LIGHTS ON, after midnight, the streetlamp outside Sam's third-floor window scarcely mitigated the darkness in his apartment while he prepared for this solemn undertaking.

At one time he'd had a fashionable flat, a woman named Fatemeh, and money to burn. Tomorrow, he'd embark on a mission that terrified him, while his brother believed matters were well in hand. This was his occupation, wasn't it, bringing evildoers to justice, setting things right?

Yes, certainly! He'd made everything sound easy when his brother requested entry to the archives, but admittance had been touch-and-go when he'd approached The Firm for clearance. "Don't ask again, Sam," he'd been told.

They hadn't sacked him for want of evidence. "Not the man you once were" the PM's words to him on termination day. He remembered the last binge with two of his old mates. "Drinks on me," he had said, and in short order they'd had to shift him into a cab and accompany him home. Put to bed by his friends, he had muttered, "Laugh's on me too."

Arthur Russell had offered him a king's ransom the night that man had perished. "You may not have another chance to alter a bleak future, a near future, when you will no longer be useful to your country." If Sam had known then what he knew now, would he have taken Russell's offer? Not with Lyle's life in jeopardy so long as Russell lived.

He could have used that big sparkler of Patrick's, and he briefly wondered what had happened to it. Done up properly, no telling what the diamond was worth.

Could he lift himself one more time? His brother needed him. He walked to the window and leaned on the sill. He could sleep on the plane.

APRIL 16, 2019

Oxford

THE BIN GATE CLANGED SHUT, Lyle standing in place until the tap-tap of the guard's shoes faded away.

He was locked inside a fenced enclosure within a dark, silent building, determined to retrieve Agnes CurLio's diary and the name of the centipede—resurrect something of that day two years before when he'd decided to propose to Beatrice. An obsession he hadn't been able to resist.

High above, a bird darted from rafter to rafter, the only stirring in this vast archive, once side-by-side university lecture halls.

Pendant lamps illuminated the fenced area where Lyle stood. Perhaps a hundred boxes of material, once the property of a man who sometimes went by the name of John Hill, were stacked on shelves in this twelve-by-twelve-foot enclosure designated Bin 421. On his first visit, Lyle had been tracking information about the stolen manuscript, but now he was seeking the diary that had helped him understand how Adler Alembert, Agnes CurLio, and Arthur Russell were connected, and the entry where Agnes had identified one of the most dangerous creatures on earth.

Lyle hadn't come empty handed, having brought with him the Autochrome plate he had first viewed in the Alembert Archive at the Sorbonne, almost certainly depicting Adler Alembert and Agnes CurLio in evening dress—Agnes with straight hair covering

43

her ears, a small mouth and nose, almond-shaped eyes. Made in the nineteen-twenties, the image was still clear enough to reveal her clandestine glance at the man who would kill her. So many similarities between this woman and Beatrice struck Lyle, both indomitable, courageous, generous, both having taken lives, and having their own lives ruthlessly snuffed out.

Lyle located the *Odds & Ends* box and rifled through the contents. He found everything he remembered—except the diary. Had someone moved it to one of the other boxes? Had a family member claimed it, or had someone authorized to scour this bin for commercial purposes thought it might be valuable?

He searched other ambiguously labeled boxes that might contain the misplaced or re-filed diary, discovering nothing. If someone else was interested in the diary, why now after so many years had passed?

Frustrated, Lyle was ready to summon the guard to let him out when he decided to go through the *Odds & Ends* box one more time. Of course, the diary wasn't there. He wasn't so dazed as to miss something he'd held in his hands and examined more than once.

Without warning, the creature's name popped into his head, and before it faded away, he exclaimed, "*Scolopendra letalis*—lethal centipede. Of course!" The creature lived in the heart of a cactus. Though he hadn't found the diary, the bin had evoked the name and its habitat. Obsession or not, he wasn't about to lose the memory again, recording it on his phone.

He wondered what *Scolopendra letalis* looked like. Maybe someone at the university had heard of it. "You already have a mission," he told himself.

LYLE'S HOUSEKEEPING HAD DETERIORATED. Not resulting in squalor, but in something well below his former standards. Checking his phone, he saw the note: *Scolopendra letalis*.

Lyle Stuart, nutter!

He made a circuit of the flat to ensure all was buttoned up per his standard pre-expedition list and opened the letter he'd received in the post, expecting it to be another worthless circular:

The King's Watchtowers paired side by side on the main-landers' western coast, one housing sailors and soldiers, the other for captains, seeing stones, armories, treasure and astronomical rooms. Impregnable towers at major ports, never breached by mainlanders. Replicated in the Southern Kingdom after the Kataklusmós. Dismantled by the Guild over ten thousand years ago—forensic evidence destroyed. To honor the Gods of the West, Egyptian pharaohs built paired granite obelisks, miniature versions of the Watchtowers.

An unsigned letter with no originating address, a fabulist of the sort who sought out newsworthy archaeologists, as groupies did music and film celebrities. Exerting intellectual energy on the theories of these fabulists was a waste of time. How many such letters had Tolkien received when he published his story?

This one was more erudite than most, but Lyle had learned long ago that erudition, in and of itself, didn't signify scholarship.

He read it again. What was a *Kataklusmós*?

APRIL 17, 2019

☻-☻-☻

Kampala

DESPITE THE URBAN HAZE, Lyle had a good view of the city on the plane's approach to the airport: rolling hills, a few taller buildings in the central city, small green oases among the predominant browns and reds, Lake Victoria to the south.

His brother's eyes were closed. Sam had said very little since they'd left London. What was he thinking? What would he do here?

"How is my Sam?" Beatrice had asked Lyle on Christmas day.

"Rather glum since he was sacked."

"That's a harsh way to put it. You're taking time with him?"

"Sam is an unconventional lamb. He kicks when riled."

"His training, I suppose. Shall we have coffee?"

"Most certainly. I'm packed." He didn't want to leave, feeling the visit was far too short.

"Promise me you'll return soon," she pleaded. "It's beautiful here in the spring."

Memories barreled in, whether he invited them or not—a word, an image, though her voice was becoming harder to retrieve.

Lyle and Sam exited the Kampala terminal under a hot sun. Lyle had seen more than a few expeditioners looking like burnt offerings after working outside for a few days in such a sun.

"The flight must have been awful," said Maria Azira, after Lyle and Sam were seated and a tray of refreshments had been set out

46

on the low table, including the kind of honey cakes Lyle hadn't been able to resist when he'd visited Beatrice, and iced tea.

"Plenty of turbulence," said Lyle. "Sam slept most of the trip."

"Amazing what a bottle of gin can do," Sam said, prompting nervous laughter from the two women seated side by side on a sofa.

Why had Sam said that, when all he'd had to drink was water and coffee? Sam wasn't a jokester, so he must have said this for a reason. Or the other troubling possibility—his brother was as broken as he was.

Of the two women, Cornelia more favored Beatrice, physically and temperamentally, though lacking the warmth that had regulated her older sister's fiery spirit. Possessing a radiant beauty, Maria was the smallest of the three sisters, with a malleable personality. Both today wore African attire, Maria's less fashionable than her sister's.

The pair had heard little about Lyle when Beatrice was at Oxford, though they'd been friendly and gracious on his first visit to Kampala. But as they came to understand his relationship with Beatrice, they had grown more cautious, especially Cornelia, making him wonder if they thought he was good enough for their sister.

English was commonly spoken in Uganda, and Beatrice had seen to it that her sisters spoke the language proficiently. Cornelia and Maria were young girls when their family had to flee to Kampala to escape the rebels, and speaking fluent English helped them adapt to the big city.

"Grayson is away at the moment. South Africa," Cornelia said. "Ministry business."

Not too many years prior, Grayson and Cornelia Serwanga had struggled to make ends meet. They now lived in a nicely appointed five-room apartment, luxurious by Kampala's standards. They were only ten minutes from Beatrice's modest apartment—former apartment, that was, with nothing left of it now.

"*Delicioso*," said Sam, munching on his second small honey cake like a hibernating bear that had suddenly come awake, the only one of the four who looked comfortable.

Cornelia said, "We didn't expect you to come. We knew how hard you would take her..."

She was speaking to Lyle but she wasn't looking at him. He had steeled himself because he knew how difficult the conversation would be. "I had to come," he said.

"How long are you staying?" Maria asked.

"A few days. I want to visit her gravesite."

"It's across from the cathedral," Maria said. "A flat stone."

"We have beer if you'd like," Cornelia told Sam.

Lyle wanted to say, "We're talking about your dead sister," but bit his tongue.

Licking his fingers, Sam answered, "I guess not." He looked at Cornelia steadily. "May I ask a few questions?"

The two women glanced at each other. Cornelia said, "Beatrice told us you were a policeman."

After a big swallow of tea, Sam said, "I'm on the dole now, retired. Who's leading your sister's investigation?"

"ISO, the Internal Security Organization, because of the bomb," Cornelia said.

"Do they suspect terrorists?"

"They haven't said," Maria replied.

"Grayson has a South African Syrah you might like," Cornelia suggested politely to Lyle, as if they were casual acquaintances. He had met Grayson Serwanga on one of his trips, a man wary of Englishmen. Lyle knew Cornelia and Grayson couldn't have children, settling for the Siamese perched on the windowsill.

Cornelia returned with a glass of wine for Lyle and a smaller portion for herself.

"What have the police told you?" asked Sam.

Maria folded her arms and looked at the floor, or her feet, a cocooning Lyle had seen once before when an acquaintance had mentioned Maria's dead husband.

Cornelia said, "Someone set off a bomb that..."

"Why?" Sam asked, interrupting.

He'd shaken her. She didn't immediately answer. "Maybe retribution for what happened when the rebels raided our village."

"How long ago was that?"

Cornelia's mask was back on. "Sixteen years, six months."

That seemed to startle Sam. He looked past them, as if calculating something. "October 2002. Tell me what happened."

"We barely survived," Cornelia replied. "Beatrice saw us through. The rebel *commandanté* was killed inside our house. She didn't do it, but they may have thought so. Then, she killed one of their scouts on the river...she had to!"

Beatrice had related that experience to Lyle in a Mainz café.

"You think this bomb was payback?" Sam questioned.

With furled brows, Cornelia said, "What else? Let me answer, Maria. No one hated Beatrice. People loved her...her students, the vagrants she helped...everyone."

Sam kept pressing. "Was anything bothering her?"

"Is this why you came?" Cornelia asked Lyle. "You should ask the police."

Lyle recognized that she was perturbed but he wasn't going to put a bridle on Sam. "I want to know the truth, Cornelia."

"The truth is Beatrice is gone. Violence is a way of life here, vengeance for something real or imagined. She's gone. There's no making sense of it."

The distress in Cornelia's voice stirred the cat. It leapt from the windowsill, crossed the room and filled the small space between the women.

"Tell me about how she seemed the week before," Sam said doggedly, as if he hadn't heard Cornelia's explanation.

When Maria started to speak, Cornelia put a hand on her sister's knee and asked, "What do you mean?"

"Did anything out of the ordinary happen? Did she seem especially bothered?"

"Everything was fine, normal. She was...happy."

Sam shifted his gaze to Maria.

"Normal," said Maria, in a hushed voice.

"Do *you* think the rebels are responsible?"

"Give me another explanation," Cornelia said. "A thief wouldn't have used a bomb."

"Can you think of anyone in Beatrice's apartment building we might speak to?"

Cornelia shook her head. Obviously, the sisters wanted to put this tragedy behind them—and why wouldn't they—having learned this coping mechanism a long time ago. They only tolerated Sam's questions because he was Lyle's brother, and Lyle would soon be out of their lives, with no hope of finding her killer and dreading the trip back to England. In her grave, Beatrice didn't need him. Even his aimless brother had better things to do than nanny him.

Eyes fixed on Cornelia, Sam said, "I know people in ISO. Maybe I can learn something."

Sam and Lyle waited for an answer but neither woman responded. Lyle said, "Was Beatrice worried about the rebels?"

After a moment, Cornelia spoke. "If she was, she never mentioned it. I prefer to remember the courageous woman who saved us from—"

Lyle said, "Why didn't you wait for me for the funeral?"

"I'll tell you why," Cornelia said, in a griping voice. "What was left of her was *ghastly*. We didn't want you to remember her that way. We may have escaped the rebels, but all of us were scarred by the experience. Something happened to Beatrice before she escaped the village. Our mother never recovered from Paul...all those gunshots she heard as we ran. Our father was never the same either. Maria and I suffered from nightmares."

"Still?" Sam wondered.

"Yes, if you must know!" Cornelia went for her wine glass and finished her drink.

"Do you know why I'm asking these questions?" Sam said gently.

"That's what policemen do," responded Cornelia with vigor.

"I want to prevent who killed Beatrice from killing anyone else, and I want to help my brother find some peace."

Maria put her hands over her face.

"How is Veronica?" Lyle asked, trying to distract the woman from her sorrow.

Maria looked up at Lyle as if he were the only person in the room and dried her eyes with her sleeve. "You wouldn't believe how she's grown since Christmas."

Veronica Azira was a bright-eyed, happy girl. No wonder Beatrice had loved her so. That Christmas day, Veronica wore a blue dress and shiny white shoes, with a little yellow bow in her hair. She'd addressed Lyle. "*Maama* says you dig for treasure."

"That's right."

"Can I see?" the girl asked, hopping up and down.

Lyle produced an oval drachma with an effigy of Athena on one side and an owl on the other, making it disappear, then reappear behind Veronica's ear, the girl laughing and clapping her hands.

"May I see Veronica before I leave?" Lyle asked Maria.

"She would like that. How is Lucia?"

Though Beatrice's sisters had never met the poodle, they'd heard Lyle speak about her and had seen videos.

"She keeps me going."

Now, the cat made a detour in Lyle's direction on its way back to the sill, just close enough to confirm it would be pleased to see him go, the same impression he'd received from these sisters.

BEATRICE ALWAYS RESERVED A ROOM FOR LYLE at a small hotel near the university where she taught rather than at one of the international hotels. Though he was traveling light on this unscheduled trip, he had made room for the dozen matchbook-sized boxes that Foy in Entomology had asked him to bring should Lyle encounter beetles of any size, shape, color, or disposition. Hundreds of thousands of beetle species had been discovered and catalogued throughout the world, but new species were always turning up, and Foy was eager for a piece of that action.

Lyle had used the opportunity to ask Foy if he could identify the earliest scholarly articles about Agnes's centipede.

"It's not an insect, Stuart," the entomologist had told him, as if the request were a grave imposition.

At dinner, Sam said, "What's your impression of Beatrice's sisters?"

"Devastated, especially Maria. She relied on Beatrice."

"That's all?"

"What else? I know how they feel."

"No wine for me, thanks," Sam said to the waiter. "The big one didn't want the small one to say anything."

"Cornelia's always been cautious...suspicious. Do you think they're holding something back?"

Sam poured Lyle a fresh cup of coffee. "Probably."

"Why would they? She didn't have anyone else in her life, if that's what you're thinking."

Sam didn't respond to that, and Lyle wondered why not. "Tomorrow, we're seeing Joseph Mutesi," Sam said.

"Can he help us?"

Sam nodded. "If he can't, no one can."

PART II
Suspicions

APRIL 18, 2019

Kampala
(morning)

LYLE AND SAM WERE ALONE IN THE CATHEDRAL CEMETERY. The small flat gravestone read: BEATRICE ADAMS 1981-2019. No memory words.

Sam stood several paces to the side, head bent. Below Lyle's feet was an ossuary rather than a casket, as Cornelia had explained—a graphic declaration of what the bomb had done.

The flies were bad here. Thunder reminded Lyle of what their driver had said on the way to the cemetery: "It's going to rain very much."

Stepping back from the grave, Lyle collided with Sam, causing both men to stagger.

"I know you loved her, but did you trust her?" asked Sam.

In the face of Lyle's look of outrage, Sam said, "I'm not talking about another man. I mean the choices she made."

"Like her decision to return to Uganda?"

Sam said, "She didn't know what would happen, but she was convinced coming here was the right thing to do. She told me so. Beatrice thought life had meaning, that choices meant something."

Lyle shook his head disdainfully. "There's no meaning. What she did, what I do, none of it amounts to a damn thing."

Scanning the darkening sky, Sam said, "We should go inside and call our driver."

"In a minute."

"In a minute we'll be drenched. I'll wait for you inside."

The day not half over, and Lyle was already feeling its weight. Two years after surviving the bombing of the Mainz café, the residual effects were a weak leg and stabs of panic at times like this, but despite what had been done to him when he was pursuing the manuscript, he had never felt himself capable of violence. He certainly did now.

He smashed a big fly that was digging into his arm. He wouldn't contact Cornelia or Maria before he left the city. Why burden them with more distress than they were already experiencing? Without Beatrice, what did an Oxford archaeologist and two Ugandan women have in common? He felt anger too—he could feel it stirring—that they hadn't received him as he'd deserved.

Gray sky above, gray stone below, gray outside and inside. Funny—terrible!—the thoughts that invaded his mind these days, such as Ahmad Jamal's mysterious jazz piece: "I Came to See You/ You Were Not There."

The old anchorage was gone. Time to move on, schedule the next expedition, immerse himself in his work—in essence, revert to being the person he'd been BBA—before Beatrice Adams.

A gold beetle was crawling over the wet gravestone in a steady rain. Absentmindedly, Lyle removed one of Foy's beetle boxes from his bag, scooting the docile creature into the receptacle. "You'll be in the dark for a long while, old fellow," he said.

Loud thunder reminded him Sam was inside the cathedral. He trotted out of the cemetery onto the deserted street where all the artists and vagrants had been driven off by the downpour. Rain and all, someone was singing a lively tune. People with nothing sang in Uganda, loudly and joyously, something Lyle could never fathom.

Inside, Rubaga Cathedral looked larger than it had from the road, the only light coming from red votive candles in the rear and dim ceiling lights over the altar.

Sam stood a few steps from the candles. "I lit one for you and Beatrice."

Water pooling at his feet, Lyle wiped his face with a sleeve. Still full up with grief and anger, he said, "You think those candles do any good?"

"Who knows? It made me feel better."

Sam's observation recalled that nerve-wracking late night drive from their Mainz hotel to Arthur Russell's university office, when Lyle had asked Sam, *Do you go to church anymore?...Not since Mum died, but I went to confession a few times. I'm in a messy business.*

"I'll light one too," said Lyle.

"Don't forget the shilling," Sam returned. "What's wrong?"

"Nothing." Lyle's eyes moved to the front of the church, to the container, the coffer, to which Beatrice always bowed. "If you're *there*," Lyle silently mused, "*do something*.

"Did you contact the driver?" he asked Sam.

"He's down the street having tea. I told him to take his time."

Inside the drafty church, the flickering candles threatened to go out any second. Lyle knew how that felt.

APRIL 18, 2019

Kampala
(afternoon)

O N THEIR WAY FROM THE CEMETERY to Ugandan Internal Security Organization headquarters, Lyle had insisted on a detour to Makerere University where Beatrice had taught. Afterward their driver negotiated the central city, with its scores of trucks and boda-boda taxis, and the gridlock on narrow streets lined with barbed-wire-surmounted walls, as well as packs of pariah dogs. At a busy intersection, one man was pushing a large wooden wheelbarrow full of bananas while another herded goats, both oblivious to horns and shouts. *Her* city, where AIDS was a scourge and clean water a treasure.

"I understand you were her betrothed," Joseph Mutesi said to Lyle after Sam had introduced them. "My condolences."

Someone must have told him this. Cornelia? Was that how Beatrice had referred to him?

"You're wet. We like a good watering but these spring storms come on suddenly. May I get you a towel?"

"No, thank you," Lyle said, though he was dampening the man's visitor chair. Sam declined the offer too.

"What are you doing with yourself these days, Sam?" asked the burly man in olive shirt and chinos with a charcoal face and cherubic features.

"I'm a private inquiry agent. People tell me that occupation has a noble tradition."

Mutesi smiled. "You should take up golf. Leisure isn't a bad word in Uganda. We'll go to my club before you leave town."

"I won't be here that long, Joseph."

Mutesi's eyes narrowed. "A business trip."

"That's it."

"Bad business, I'm sorry to say," the Ugandan murmured, glancing at Lyle, whose already unsettled stomach was aggravated by the strong scent of the man's cologne.

This tidy office mixed fine furniture—Mutesi's desk—with metal cabinets and a sprinkling of photographs on the walls. Sam had said enough to suggest Mutesi was a man of note in the ISO.

"She was a wonderful girl," Sam said. "What can you tell us?"

"Nothing officially, but how could I turn down a request from Ratty? You'll have to keep this to yourself. I hope you haven't forgotten how since you retired."

"Like a clam, Moley."

A little laugh rumbled through Joseph, and even Lyle cracked a smile at these dangerous men's pet names. Though the room wasn't warm, beads of sweat dotted Mutesi's clean-shaven face. "Are you up to hearing this?" he asked Lyle.

"I'm not sure, but I'm staying."

Mutesi folded his hands, leaning toward them. "She entered her apartment after work on March 26. The bomb was detonated by the door, or a trip plate on the inside threshold. Everything was blown to pieces."

"How bad?" asked Sam.

"As bad as you can imagine. Splintered wood everywhere, windows blown out, sprays of blood on what remained of the walls, everything charred…the smell of death. Ghastly."

The same word Cornelia had used.

"You saw it yourself?" Sam inquired.

Mutesi nodded. "Damage to other apartments too, though no one else was hurt."

"A professional op," said Sam.

"Most certainly."

"How professional?" asked Sam.

With each passing day, Sam seemed to gain strength. Had the hunt reinvigorated his brother?

Mutesi ambled to the door and looked out the small glass panel, pushing the door to make sure it was fully closed before returning to his chair. "The perpetrator used X85ZL for the incendiary. Amateurs avoid it because it's so volatile. If you don't know what you're doing, you can blow yourself up," said Mutesi, obviously for Lyle's benefit. "The ZL postscript is an Israeli enhancement, radiates the blast broadly and uniformly, leaving no gaps where targets might survive. Favored by the Mossad. Their agents know explosives. How much of this are you already aware of?"

"Some of it," Sam said. "You're filling up the dossier."

Mutesi wagged a finger at Sam. "You're retired. Why do you need a dossier?"

"Call it a hobby."

The Ugandan frowned. "Don't let your hobby interfere with the ISO's business, Sam."

Sam extended open hands. "My brother wants to learn as much as he can. I won't make any trouble."

"See that you don't, old friend. We wouldn't have tested for that incendiary without you prompting us. May I ask why?"

Sam said, "When you've been in the business as long as I have, you have hunches."

Lyle didn't think Mutesi was satisfied with Sam's answer. The man shrugged, and said, "We're suspicious devils, you and I. Do you have time for a sip of Scotch at our special place? Nothing has changed there, I'm happy to say."

"I'd love to, but it will have to wait. Business. You interviewed the victim's sisters?"

Mutesi hesitated. "Of course."

"Were they helpful?"

"Not particularly. Cornelia Serwanga did all the talking. By design, I suspect. According to her, the victim was beloved by everyone."

"You took blood samples?"

Joseph removed a cigarette from the pack on his desk, tapping it on the surface. "Of course."

"Did you have the sense they were holding something back?"

Lyle was surprised by how hard Sam was pressing his friend, though Mutesi seemed to be taking the questions in stride. "I'd rather not say."

"What do you suspect?" asked Lyle.

"I'm not allowed to speak about the details of a criminal matter, Dr. Stuart."

What had this man been doing for the past half-hour? Lyle was formulating a response when his brother broke in. "When did you take up golf?"

"Three years ago. A membership came with my last promotion."

"Does the ISO need an experienced agent?"

"You can't run fast enough anymore, Sam."

"Neither can you."

"I don't have to. I'm the boss," Mutesi said, with a wide grin.

The loud yapping of voices in an adjacent office distracted the Ugandan, who put an end to it by banging on the wall with his fist, the photographs rattling and shaking.

"Do you expect to find her killer?" Lyle said.

"A week ago, I would have said it was likely, but that incendiary makes the killer especially hard to catch."

"Why would they target Beatrice?" asked Lyle, wearing down.

"If you have any ideas, Dr. Stuart, please let me know."

"Cornelia said it may have been connected to the rebels who attacked their village."

Mutesi shook his head. "We've never associated the rebels with a crime involving this incendiary."

"They may have recruited the bomber," suggested Sam.

"Not their fashion. They like to handle executions themselves." For Lyle's benefit, he added, "When rebellion and terrorism were at their worst, the rebels held villages and besieged cities, performed assassinations every day. A group of young ISO recruits made a pact, no serious relationships or children so they couldn't be blackmailed or intimidated by the terrorists. They would have a free hand—a hard hand—because only their own lives were at stake. Some in the ISO were afraid to work with them for fear they were reckless."

"Did they survive?" asked Lyle.

"All but two. When conditions improved, those men abandoned their pact. Several have retired, and one of them now has a desk job, but he remembers those days and his hand can still be hard."

Mutesi was relating more than history; he was telling Lyle that everything possible would be done to apprehend Beatrice's killer.

Sam said, "Do you think the killer is still in Kampala?"

"I doubt it, because of the incendiary. The Kenyan border was the likely escape route if he left the country on foot or by motorcar."

"By any chance, did she have an intel role here?" asked Sam.

"That's ridiculous!" exclaimed Lyle.

Sam ignored his brother, and Mutesi said, "Nothing connected to the ISO. Do you know something?"

Sam shook his head. "I know you're a busy man, Joseph. I appreciate the time and information."

"Not too busy for Sam Stuart, or golf. Do you need anything while you're here?"

"Nothing. Next time, we'll have that Scotch."

Sam tapped Lyle on the shoulder. Both rose and shook Mutesi's hand.

"May I speak to you, Ratty, a confidential matter?" Mutesi asked Sam.

Bewildered, Lyle stepped out of the office, closing the door and taking a seat in the waiting area. He'd learned little from Mutesi, only that the bomber was an expert at his trade and that the rebels weren't high on the ISO's list of suspects.

Exiting the room a few minutes later, Sam shook his head and said, "Women! Joseph is the last person I expected to have that kind of trouble."

"Is he married?"

"In a way," Sam said.

For a security operation, the ISO grounds didn't impress Lyle, and seemingly most of what Mutesi knew had come from information Sam had provided. That didn't bode well for a speedy arrest of Beatrice's killer. Crossing the courtyard, Lyle said, "How do you know him?"

His brother halted, gripping Lyle's arm. "Do you remember that terror attack on the bus station in Manchester?"

"That must have been ten years ago."

"Thirteen. We connected one of the terrorists to a Ugandan Salafi cell. I led a team of vipers here to make sure those people didn't cause any more mischief in England. Joseph was the ISO's point man for the op. Nothing like mortal danger to bond men."

"Did the Scotch have something to do with that mission?"

"Everything to do with it. Not all of my men, or his, survived."

"How about the cell you were after?"

"*None* of them survived," Sam said, an edge to his voice. "Not one. We got all thirty-six, including the three who broke out of the cordon we set up. They deserved it, every one of them, for what they did to those people in Manchester...and the girls we found in their camp. They would have done it again if we hadn't eliminated them."

Thirty-six men killed by teams Sam and Mutesi had led? "They were *all* guilty?" Lyle asked.

Not a trace of dissipation or sloth in Sam's voice came through when he said, "As guilty as the Nazis who didn't pull triggers but signed death decrees, or ran the trains to Auschwitz."

Lyle was tempted to ask his brother whether a guiltless man, or boy, might have come into the camp at the wrong time, a son or brother. But he couldn't make himself ask it. Not after everything Sam had done for him.

"He called you Ratty."

Sam relaxed a little. "I don't remember who started it. I was Ratty, Joseph was Mole, Nero—I don't remember his real name—was Badger, a tall gray-haired black man killed in the firefight. Thus, the ceremonial Scotch."

Lyle said, "Is Mutesi good at his job?"

"What he lacks in technology, he supplies in courage. If Joseph has your back, you needn't worry."

Lyle knew Sam had his back, but who had Sam's?

They had spoken to Beatrice's sisters, seen her grave, and consulted with the man who knew the most about her murder. What more could they do? "It's time to go home," Lyle said to his brother.

"We're not going home. You heard what Joseph said about the bomb. We're going to Israel."

APRIL 20, 2019

Jerusalem

EXHAUSTED BY EMOTIONALLY TORTUROUS DAYS and a travel day to Israel, Lyle would have gladly spent some time in bed, but Sam was having none of it, waking him up from a short nap and ordering him to put on his best clothes.

Tired as Lyle was, he couldn't help being impressed by the La Regence Restaurant inside the King David Hotel or, for that matter, by the man who greeted them at a corner table separate from the rest of the diners: Zvi Eitan, a government official according to Sam.

The rubicund fellow with shaggy, white hair who embraced Sam and shook Lyle's hand looked as if he belonged in a wilderness lodge rather than an elegant dining room.

"Sit, sit. The food here is excellent. Asian, kosher, continental...Dr. Stuart, one of your colleagues has made quite a splash in Jericho, if I may mix my metaphors."

"I'm sorry to intrude on Shabbat," Sam said.

"For Sam Stuart, an exception must be made. Say no more about it."

"How are you, Zvi?" asked Sam.

"Approaching my utmost, even if I use a different measuring stick these days." The booming voice Zvi Eitan employed to welcome them descended the register when he said, "You were the last person I expected to hear from, Sam. The matter must be serious."

When all of them were seated, Sam explained, "A friend was murdered in Kampala."

Eitan nodded. "A dangerous place. Entebbe comes to mind. A drink, gentlemen?"

"Nothing for me," said Sam. Lyle declined too, worried he'd fall asleep at the table if he had any alcohol.

Ordering Bourbon, the Israeli said to Lyle, "Do you know Dr. Fitzgerald?"

"She's a colleague at Oxford, a fine archaeologist and friend."

"This may be an antique land packed with ancient cities, but to discover a settlement hidden for six millennia in a region teaming with archaeologists—I call that impressive. I saw her on television. What a stunner—brains and beauty."

Lyle said, "I'll provide an introduction if you'd like to see the site."

"An ancient town on my doorstep, why wouldn't I?" Eitan took an olive from the bowl next to him and held it up. "Some of our trees are two-thousand years old. The leaves are bitter, but good for the blood, they tell me."

"Still holding court at the *Da-veed*. Some things never change," said Sam.

"Don't you believe it. Talk to my doctor—as if *Anno Domini* isn't stalking all of us. Are you in a hurry?"

"I'm retired," Sam said, absent the lethargic delivery Lyle had become accustomed to.

"So I've heard. Then let's enjoy our food, and if you meet my doctor consider everything we eat and drink to be confidential. He grew up in Italy and won't say I eat too much: 'O Eitan, *sei proprio una buona forchetta*'...means I have a *good fork*... the devil!"

In spite of himself, Lyle enjoyed the meal and the Israeli's company. Eitan's voice rose and dwindled according to the

contents of the stories he told. Though he left much to the imagination, the humorous parts were always crammed with details.

Looking about the room, Eitan said, "My father wouldn't
have been comfortable in a place like this. He worked up telephone poles in Lvov until he was seventy, and he warned me you
shouldn't have the best of anything or nothing else ever satisfies."

Was he speaking to Lyle? How could he be, as they had just
met, Jerusalem a last-minute decision.

Plates cleared and coffee served, Eitan folded his hands, and
said, "Now, Sam, for the matter that brought you here."

Sam nodded. "Seeing and talking to Zvi Eitan should have
been excuse enough."

"Good Lord, retirement has made a courtier of you. So, give
me the details, what you can."

After Sam filled him in, the Israeli gave Sam a hard stare. "My
friend, if you weren't Righteous Among the Nations, I wouldn't be
speaking to you about such matters. As it is, I'll tell you everything I know."

Lyle was stunned to hear Eitan's words about his brother.

Sam said, "*Almost* everything, to be precise."

"Oh, and I suppose you've told *me* everything. We know each
other too well, that's the problem. As it is, I have nothing definite,
merely ideas."

"Your ideas are better than most men's facts."

"By God, is this the Sam Stuart I used to know? I'd love
another Bourbon, Jacob, but I must decline." He waited for the
young waiter to leave and cross the dining room before saying,
"Bari Malkin may be your man."

Sam thought a minute. "I don't know him."

"That's for the better. He was dismissed from the Sayaret
Matkal ten years ago. *Kompromat* was gathered on him by the
Russians, nothing conclusively proven, but enough to retire him.
As for his professional skills, he was the mandarin behind that
business at the Beirut munitions compound. If he's involved, you'd

better keep your eyes skinned."

"A soldier of fortune?" asked Sam.

"That's putting it generously."

"Have you met him?"

The big man nodded. "I always thought he had a slate loose, though it didn't affect his work."

"Where might I find him?"

Eitan pouted. "Who knows? He shows up on our radar occasionally. Not Malkin himself, his operational fingerprint. He likes bombs, though he's capable enough with a gun or knife. Your friend made a powerful enemy if they turned Malkin loose on her. He commands a king's ransom. He never fails, he doesn't talk, and unless someone like Mutesi is engaged, he doesn't leave any evidence behind. When it comes to assassins, Malkin is the *crème de la crème*, I'm sorry to say."

"Would your people be willing to help me find him?" asked Sam.

In the blink of an eye, Eitan's face went cloudy. "As black a mark as he has next to his name, certain people in high places would be enraged if I helped bring him down. Malkin was a fair-haired boy at one time. His uncle was essential at Entebbe. I've given you what I can, and more. I'll say it again, Sam, be careful. Even if it's not Malkin, this one is a pro."

"So am I."

"I know this isn't your first rodeo but you haven't been on a bull for a while."

Sam said, "You sound like some people I know in Whitechapel."

The two men shared a laugh. Sam, Mutesi, and Eitan hailed from different cultures and had different loyalties, but in all of them Lyle sensed the same cat-watching-the-bird look.

Lyle excused himself, and in the lavatory mopped his face with a wet towel. The mirror depicted a wretched-looking stranger. A conversation that should have stirred him to righteous anger had elicited the opposite effect. He believed Sam knew what he was doing, but the more he heard from men like Mutesi and Eitan, the more skeptical he became about pursuing Beatrice's killer. Even if they were successful, retribution wouldn't bring her back. As for what Sam had said to Beatrice's sisters: "I want to prevent the person who killed Beatrice from killing anyone else," what difference would that make in a world with so many Malkins?

Returning to the table, he overheard Eitan say, "He needs darning. Ah, Dr. Stuart, are you a beer connoisseur?"

Lyle said, "I like beer but I wouldn't call myself any kind of an expert."

"Sit. What can an archaeologist tell me about beer making?"

Eitan was doing his utmost to ease Lyle's misery.

"Beer was brewed in Egypt's Old Kingdom four millennia ago," Lyle answered. "And beer making goes back further than that, to villages that pre-date Egypt and other ancient civilizations."

"I ask the question for a reason," Eitan said. "Someone told me beer is being brewed from ancient yeast. Could such a thing really be accomplished?"

Lyle nodded. "We know dried yeast can hibernate for thousands of years, so it might be extracted from ancient pottery and reactivated."

"As simple as that?"

Lyle had little interest in such questions anymore, but he'd be polite to Sam's friend. "I don't know what the extraction procedure entails, but the process would be delicate, and the extractors would have to be able to distinguish ancient yeast from modern yeast."

Eitan's eyes lit up. "So brewing Old Kingdom beer is possible?"

"Something similar, perhaps," Lyle said.

"You could sell such beer for hundreds a bottle. King Tut Ale…hah! You offered to connect me with your colleague in Jericho. Let me return the favor and recommend Constantinople as a field of study."

"Thank you, but my specialty is the pastoral nomads of south-east Europe," said Lyle. "Sorry, the *tribes* that traversed those lands thousands of years ago."

"Of course, but don't ignore Constantinople. Keep me posted, Sam, and if I learn anything more, I'll let you know."

BACK IN THE CAR, Lyle asked Sam what the *Sey-ret Mack-dal* did.

"Israel's elite fighting force executes long-arm missions, hard and fast strikes behind enemy lines. Like Entebbe."

"You've known Eitan a long time?"

"We often cooperated with the Mossad. He and I worked together on many sensitive ops."

"He said you were Righteous Among the Nations. How?"

Sam shrugged.

"Tell me, Sam."

His brother was staring through the windscreen with a faraway look. "I put my nose where it didn't belong, kept a plane of Israelis from being blown up. They awarded the medal privately because of my occupation."

That was the last thing Lyle expected to hear. "Isn't that what you're supposed to do?"

"You'd be surprised. Raised some eyebrows in Whitechapel. *Not your patch, Stuart.*"

APRIL 21, 2019

Jericho
(Oxford Archaeological Compound: Zeta2)

DESCENDING FROM JERUSALEM INTO THE JUDEAN WILDERNESS, Lyle and Sam passed Bedouin tent camps with herds of goats and sheep, crossed landscapes littered with millions upon millions of big and small stones. The Jordan Valley town of Jericho was a green postage stamp in the midst of the drab desert, and to the east rose the hazy Mountains of Moab.

Lyle had a longstanding interest in Jericho, with its ten-thousand-year-old watchtower, perhaps the oldest continuously inhabited town in the world. As with all living historical cities, the old rubbed shoulders with the new. A market selling dates, figs, and apples abutted ancient sites, some as small as a street corner. An oasis fountain helped to water palm and sycamore trees. Cars and tour buses maneuvered down narrow ancient streets where armed Israeli soldiers patrolled, mindful of passions aroused over changing borders on the West Bank of the Jordan River.

The last mile was an unpaved trail along a dry ravine, a wadi, accompanied by the sound of crunching stones, like firecrackers beneath the wheels of their creeping, lurching Hyundai.

"I'm not sure the car hire considers this customary wear and tear," said Sam, who was driving the truck, having convinced Lyle that they might spend their layover day at Zeta2. Was Sam hoping to distract him, knowing they had little hope of bringing Beatrice's killer to ground?

"I thought my stations were colorless," remarked Sam, pointing to an enclosure several acres in size, fencing topped with rolls of barbed wire.

A man seated beneath an umbrella rose from his folding chair and raised a hand. Rolling down the passenger window, Lyle said, "Would you inform Dr. Fitzgerald that Lyle Stuart is here?"

Stocky, with a carefully trimmed beard and curly hair so black it looked blue in the bright sun, the man said, "Doctor Fitzgerald not here."

Lyle hadn't bothered to check. How distracted he was. He should have known the peripatetic Andrea could be anywhere. "Is Dr. Marks in camp?"

The guard nodded vigorously.

"Tell him Lyle Stuart is here."

The man retrieved his phone and after a brief conversation fetched safari hats and safety glasses from a shed immediately inside the gate, saying, "Wear please. Not go inside ropes."

Another hot site, the truck thermometer indicating the temperature was close to one hundred degrees. Scanning the compound, Lyle noted a typically busy archaeological excavation with roped-off work areas in the rear. Along the gate-side fence were two ten-foot-square concrete buildings, one metal roofed, the other concrete roofed. Three larger tents lined the fence to the right of the gate. Along the far fence to their right, the shower tent had been erected next to a fiberglass water tank, with three smaller tents in a row adjacent to the work areas, one bright yellow.

Lyle admired the high-profile site, and wondered if he should he take Andrea up on her invitation. He could let her garner the acclaim, while he assisted Marks with the dirty work—the work he loved. That might burn and sweat the pain out of him.

Striding toward the car was a spindly man in camp attire, black work boots, and a broad-brimmed hat.

"Stuart, what a pleasant surprise," said the man, proffering a hand. "What brings you here?"

"I was in Jerusalem with my brother. Sam, this is Dr. Marks, the leader of the expedition."

"Kind of you to say so, but we know the hen rules this roost," Marks demurred.

As Marks didn't seem troubled by the pronouncement, Lyle answered, "And we know who's looking after the henhouse."

Putting a hand on Lyle's shoulder, the resident archaeologist said, "Damned sorry to hear about Beatrice. Dreadful. What were you doing in Jerusalem?"

Without hesitation, Sam broke in. "Visiting an old friend of mine."

"How long can you stay?" Marks wanted to know.

"Only a few hours. Jerusalem was a quick detour after Kampala. We fly home tomorrow. I thought Andrea was in camp," Lyle said.

Marks looked disappointed. "Too bad you can't stay. Something sudden came up and off she went. Let me show you around, though. I'm delighted you looked in. I'm rather short on the company of colleagues. Friends," he clarified. "The BBC depiction is one thing. Not bad for its type, but precision isn't their forte, shall we say."

"I thought that was what Andrea was for," said Lyle, both men fighting back a grin.

"She does what she can I suppose."

"Where is she?"

"Filming at the Dead Sea. Viewers like that sort of thing. Gorsey's with them."

Once Lyle's doctoral student, Gorsey had a nose for the main chance. So he'd left Lyle and Lido for Zeta2.

"Showers and latrine against the fence?" asked Lyle.

"The water and sewage trucks needn't come inside. They hook up from outside the fence. Gorsey makes sure they connect to the proper flange. Can't be too careful out here." Pointing to the concrete buildings, Marks said, "Artifacts in the one with the concrete roof. I have the only key. My tent's to the right of Andrea's—the canary yellow. Gorsey and the Israeli archaeology student occupy the one on the left."

"How about the tent between the latrine and commissary?"

"Lodging for overnight workers. The rest commute from nearby towns."

Compared to Lido, Zeta2 was a bustling metropolis. They'd used the small stones that littered the terrain to good effect, marshaling them to make interior roads. The site also looked secure with its tall fence and barbed wire.

"A tribute-taking city or an outpost?" Lyle inquired.

Marks removed his hat and mopped his brow. "Evidence of both, a large outpost for its era. We're unearthing artifacts every week, dating them as quickly as confirmation protocol permits. We discovered a bronze Pazuzu a few weeks ago, wings, scorpion tail and all—reptilian teeth but distinctly human male genitalia."

"Mesopotamian influence?" Lyle wondered.

"Or outcasts, a rebel princeling. I'm applying myself to the walls to determine if they were defense against attackers or protection from flood waters."

"Floods in this desert?" asked Sam, who looked hot and bored.

"We're standing eight-hundred feet below sea level. In the era we're studying, the region was wetter and greener, Mr. Stuart. Speaking of water, I'm sure you'd like something to drink. Let's go to my tent. Stuart, you'll be interested in what I've learned about the mortar those people used."

Lyle might as well have been chloroformed for his lack of interest in Marks's spirited description of the mortar in his excavated walls.

The inside of Marks's tent wasn't much cooler, but at least they

were out of the sun, and the screened openings, a generator-pow-
ered fan, and iced tea afforded some relief.

"Kindly secure the tent door, Stuart. Scorpions by the peck in
these parts. Had a big 'un under my cot last week."

Out of nowhere, Sam said, "You have a gun?"

"Never have," Marks replied. "We may be more secure than
you think. I suspect our young Israeli is here under false colors."

"Why do you say so?" asked Lyle.

"As you know, in camps secrets are hard to keep. Joshua has
an archaeological veneer, but it isn't very deep."

"Israeli security?" Sam said.

"I suspect so. To protect us, protect the antiquities,
maybe both."

"It's beastly hot," observed Lyle. "How are you holding up?"

Marks had dropped into a camp chair. "We hire locals to do
the heavy lifting. If it isn't pressing, you won't find me out in the
open when the sun's up."

Lyle could readily believe it. Even those few minutes in the
sun seemed to have sapped the man. He said, "Are you happy with
the progress?"

Lyle's question produced a spark. "We think this fortress
predated our earlier estimates by five-hundred, maybe a thousand
years. Imagine that! Andrea indulges those production people, but
she's dead serious about the site, obsessive about observing each
new lift. We started without her once and she had a temper fit."

"Hot sun, days waiting for Andrea, fifty miles from a decent
restaurant. Hard duty, Oliver."

Marks refilled their glasses. "Not the way Andrea and the BBC
tell it. To hear them, we're on the cusp of unearthing the Ark of
the Covenant. And with just enough excitement to fan interest. We
had a stir back in February—no, early March."

"What kind of a stir?" Sam inquired.

"We call them camp stories, Mr. Stuart. I visited the latrine
about two a.m. Andrea's tent was backlit, and I heard voices,

so I walked over to make sure she was all right. I couldn't hear what they were saying, so I assumed she was talking to one of the assistants."

"A row?" asked Sam.

"The volume didn't suggest it. The next morning, I asked her about it. She was reticent at first, but finally admitted a man had gotten onto the site."

Sam jumped in. "Through the gate, over the fence, *through* the fence?"

Marks swabbed his face with a wet towel. "Why is that important?"

"Whether he got in on his own or had help, whether he came on impulse or planned it all out. Was anything stolen?"

"The artifact building was secure. Nothing was reported missing. We endure the odd artifact thief, usually one of the workers, but that's the extent of it. Andrea never told me how he came in. I doubt if she knows."

Sam frowned, all seriousness now. "The barbed wire wouldn't be easy to breach, unless he was an expert with the right tools and clothing. Had anyone tampered with the fence?"

Marks looked from Sam to Lyle. "My brother's a policeman," said Lyle. "He can't help it."

"No one told me the fence was ruptured. One of us would have noticed."

"Then the guard must have let him in, or someone else did," said Sam.

"No, Mr. Stuart. I spoke to the night guard. He insisted no one went through the gate." Marks shrugged, then said, "I'm going to make myself a cocktail. Would you care for one—no?" He poured a generous dram of whiskey into a glass before going on. "According to Andrea, the man claimed to be an antiquities broker. Said unless she shared what was discovered unfortunate things might happen. She sent him away with a flea in his ear. Say what you want about that girl, but she has grit."

"Did you speak with the students?" asked Sam. "Their tent's next to hers."

"Gorsey and Joshua were in Jerusalem that night. A research trip."

Sam raised his eyebrows. "Who sent them to Jerusalem?"

The drink had invigorated Marks. He grinned at Sam. "I don't remember. Everyone knew. They always do."

"Were the police contacted?"

Marks glanced at Lyle. "Andrea said she'd handle it. Back to normal the next day."

If Marks was bewildered, Lyle, on the other hand, couldn't care less about a camp thief who hadn't harmed anyone or stolen anything.

But Sam kept at it. "Anything suspicious happen since?"

"Your brother's a thorough chap," Marks said to Lyle. "That's the extent of our excitement. Unless you're an archaeologist."

Lyle concluded that Marks had fielded enough questions from Sam. "When is Andrea expected back?"

"She thought a week, but the director sets the schedule. Not enough drama here."

Lyle reached into his pocket for a handkerchief to swab his forehead and found the small box he had stowed there. "See many beetles about? For Foy in Entomology."

Marks snorted. "A biblical plague of 'em. Burrowers mostly, big, small, you name it. Take as many as you'd like, a bucketful. Andrea will be sorry to have missed you. Resetting the Bronze Age in the Adriatic zone, are you? What a feat, old man. Solid archaeology."

These few minutes with Marks had revealed something that couldn't be papered over with bright talk or whiskey—the difficulty of managing this demanding project with Andrea gone most of the time, and trying to keep the peace when she was here, not to mention the peril in this part of the world.

Lyle knew Marks had undergone a tumultuous divorce and had left a young paramour back in Oxford. Likely he was worried about her affections wandering while he was gone. And Lyle observed that Marks was getting rather old for these long stretches in such an enervating environment. The spectacular discoveries at the site may have been rippling through the archaeological community, but for a lonely fifty-five-year-old man, life was different on the ground, hot day by hot day.

"A bite in the commissary? Pure water?" Marks offered.

"No, thank you, Oliver."

"Your brother a policeman. Who'd have thought it?" Grasping Lyle's hand with uncharacteristic vigor, Marks said, "Good to see you, Lyle."

The visitors took advantage of the latrine tent. Then, on the way to the truck, Lyle veered toward the excavation area where a woman was at work on her knees.

"No side excursions," his brother said.

"I'll be just a minute," he told Sam.

"A minute? I'll wait in the truck."

Some of Lyle's happiest times when he was a young archaeologist had involved dirtying his hands, discovering and learning things that would have bored the man on the street but had made him ecstatic. The young woman looked up as Lyle approached, and said, "I'm honored to meet you, Dr. Stuart. Everyone knows you're here. No secrets in this little village."

"How do you do..."

"Miriam...Hanna."

She removed her hat, revealing braided hair and dark eyes.

"You're an archaeologist?" asked Lyle.

A momentary frown accompanied her response. "An excavator. When I learned they were looking for workers, I signed on."

In an adjacent work zone, Lyle recognized the tops of carefully excavated walls, Marks's pet project. Out of the corner of his eye, he saw movement. Why was Sam walking the fence line?

"Dr. Marks wasn't expecting you or we'd have known sooner."

A closer inspection of the work area had seemed a good idea

but Lyle was running low on energy again, something he'd never experienced before at sites of this prominence. "My brother and I were in Jerusalem for a short stay. Are you reading archaeology?"

Miriam smoothed the space where she'd been working with a hand broom. "My father has a small farm near Jericho. Medjool dates and figs, but the crop has been poor, and our little farm must compete with prosperous Israeli farms. Dr. Marks lets me take the bus to Jerusalem every Wednesday so I can listen to the public program at the university. Last week, the speaker described investigating a tomb on Crete. How exciting!"

Holding back a smile, Lyle said, "In the classroom, I call archaeology a *cryptic* challenge. You might be surprised to learn how many ungrateful tombs we dig or bore into before we find items of significance."

Two others were at work in a different section of the excavation, so protected from the sun Lyle couldn't tell if they were men or women. "Dr. Marks told us an Israeli student is here."

She took her time answering. "Joshua. He keeps to himself." This supported Marks's speculation as to the real reason the "student" was here.

"How long have you been on site?"

"Almost two years. From the start." She seemed pleased with her answer.

"May I ask your age?"

"How old do I look?"

"No more than eighteen," he said.

"Twenty-seven last month."

He liked her spunk. Lyle spotted Sam on his knees at the back fence.

"They told me he's your brother," she said. "What is he doing?"

"Your guess is as good as mine." Lyle took a minute to observe his brother before he said, "Do you plan to keep working here?"

"Oh yes. I love the work, and the money helps my father. I'll stay as long as they need help. My time to read archaeology has passed, but I can learn from books, the public programs, this fortress town, undiscovered until Dr. Fitzgerald and Dr. Marks arrived." Putting her hat on, Miriam added, "I wish we could talk longer, but this lift must be finished today. May I have your card, Dr. Stuart?"

He found one and handed it to her. Miriam secured it in her expedition blouse as if it were a precious relic of a long-ago age. He saw a lot of himself, his former self, in this inquisitive and determined woman.

They exchanged a few more words and walked a portion of the excavation. Sam had begun tapping on the horn.

He hadn't realized how warm he was until he shut the truck door and felt the cooler air.

"A minute, eh?"

"I was quizzing an excavator."

"That kid?"

"That *kid* is twenty-seven and propping up her family. Hold still." Out came his bug box. Then Lyle plucked a red and black beetle from Sam's shoulder and put it away.

"I think I have one in my ear too."

"You can keep that one. What were you up to at the fence?"

"What comes natural, mate. Did you notice the two-foot plastic barrier at the base of the fence? The guard told me it's to keep out vermin. No clipped fence and no cut wire."

"Then, what's so important about the fence?"

"What's important is the water gate."

The truck was creeping toward the entrance. After taking back the hats and glasses, the guard waved them on.

They were almost to the paved road when Sam said, "At the back of the dig is a low spot where water collects when it rains. A four-foot section of barrier panel can be removed to let out the water."

"We have to be engineers too," Lyle said.

"A padlocked dog door in the fence behind the barrier can be opened in case debris collects and backs the water up. Big enough for a man to get in, if someone admits him."

"Other than professional curiosity, what's your interest in that man and how he got in?"

"Casting a wide net. Beatrice was killed by a pro. A few weeks before she died, Fitzgerald was visited in the middle of the night, and no one knows how the man got inside. You're acquainted with both women, and you once had in your possession an extremely valuable object, something people were willing to kill for. Is Fitzgerald the consorting type? Is she known to entertain men? At night?"

"Preposterous!"

"How sure are you?"

"If that's how he got in, one of the lodging workers, a family member, or friend must have opened the gate. I've seen such things before. I know Andrea. She's fond of the spotlight, but no fool."

Sam said, "Think of that water gate as a hidden door. Whoever let that man in is no fool."

APRIL 22, 2019

☻-☻-☻

Tel Aviv

SAM HAD STEPPED AWAY FROM THE BOARDING AREA when a
family—an older couple and twenty-something man and
woman—sat across from Lyle, the old man, carrying a cane and
displaying symptoms of having suffered a stroke.

The old woman said, "Can you imagine? Genevieve's on
her way to Istanbul. Of all places for an eighty-year-old woman
to travel."

Lyle's ears perked up, his mind, rather. What about the
woman's comment rang a bell? Something recent—Eitan had used
Istanbul's outdated name: Constantinople.

Sam took the chair next to him. "You look deep in thought."

"I haven't had a deep thought in weeks. People talking
about Istanbul reminded me of your friend insisting I investigate
Constantinople."

"He didn't insist, and what does one have to do with
the other?"

Lyle said, "Constantinople was re-named Istanbul after the
Muslims conquered it."

"You don't say."

"Do you think both Beatrice's and my being targets of bomb
attacks was a coincidence, Sam?" Lyle asked, his brother staring
at the Departures display.

"What?" Sam turned back to Lyle. "Your bomber in Mainz used an incendiary with gaps, and you were lucky to be in one of them. You heard about the incendiary in Beatrice's bomb. We know Russell provoked the Algerian who tried to kill you, but it wasn't his style to dictate means and methods. As for Beatrice's bomber, he was hired because he's an expert at means and methods." Sam paused a moment. "Did you fill all your bug boxes?" he questioned.

"Not all of them. Why do you ask?"

"They'll survive all this moving about?"

"Foy gave me instructions. He said, 'Follow the prescribed program.'"

Sam's eyes were back on the Departures display.

"Our flight's on time. I checked," Lyle said. Sometimes, his brother's behavior irritated him. "Assuming Malkin is the killer, how do we find him?"

"By moving one piece on the board at a time and not worrying about the end game, not yet."

"He sounds like a dangerous man."

"Extremely."

"What if he finds out we're after him?"

"Then, he may come to us. Wipe that horrified look off your face. I'm not as naked as you think."

APRIL 12, 1931

Basra, Iraq
(88 years earlier)

T HE HEAT WAS SUFFOCATING, but Agatha forced herself to observe and experience everything in the dining room so she could consign it to her journal when she returned to their room. She would endure the heat and the flies because they would fill in the story she was writing with a depth of authenticity.

Even within the shaded and ventilated confines of the Piccadilly Hotel, diners' brows and hands were moist. Nonetheless, tea was served, as it was every day, regardless of weather or tribal uprisings, though the next-door British barracks might have had something to do with the Piccadilly's bravado.

Most of the dining room tables were occupied, British officers comprising a couple of handfuls of the patrons. Fan blades turned overhead. Bleached and starched tablecloths shone. Servers in white jackets wafted about the room like ghosts. These being the hottest hours of the day, the street fronting the hotel was empty except for the trio of British soldiers stationed outside the entrance.

Agatha had an excellent memory. This room would come alive again in the manuscript on her dressing table.

"Thank you for coming, Thomas," said the gnome-like man at the end of the table. "And you look lovely, Agatha. No small feat in these parts."

A party of four: the gnome; Thomas, a slender tieless man; Agatha's husband Max, a big, mustached man; and Agatha in her pale-green frock. Though the two younger men had dispensed with jackets, the gnome wore a gray suit and necktie. How could he stand it? More fodder for her story.

With their server at his shoulder, the gnome said, "Three whiskeys, tea with fresh cream for the lady. Fresh, my man."

"Yessir, Mr. Carlton. Straight away," said the waiter.

"Glasgow whiskey, thank God, not a local concoction," averred the gnome, a sun-baked man who might have been fifty or seventy.

"Are you digging in the area, Max?" Carlton inquired of the big man.

"A few promising sites, awaiting Agatha's blessing," said Max.

Exhibiting a sly grin, Agatha said, "Surface-of-the-sun heat in the wilderness. I told Max I'd signed on to be Apollo's wife, not Vulcan's."

"Very droll, my dear," said Max.

"And you, Thomas?" Carlton inquired.

"This and that."

"More of the same, you might say," the gnome observed.

Their drinks arrived, along with a tray of half-sandwiches and another tray of figs, dates, and pecans.

"What do you make of Hitler?" asked Carlton.

What an odd topic of conversation. But as it happened, this was a subject that interested Agatha too, and when no one else answered, she said, "He's dangerous."

"He will destroy himself sooner rather than later," observed Max.

"You think so?" said Carlton. "Our contingent in Germany insists his supporters are uncommonly devoted. Instability is his ally." Carlton turned to Thomas in an offhand way, "You know Alembert, I think."

Thomas looked into his glass. "Perhaps I've met the fellow. What's the Foreign Office's interest?"

"At the moment, we'd like to know more about him." Carlton seemed to abandon the topic. "Sample the pecans. They're striped with honey. Max, your story?"

Max took a drink before answering. "No need for the drawn-out version. I met Alembert hereabouts several years ago. Introduced himself as a paleo-historian at the Sorbonne, asked if I'd look at a goblet he'd acquired. A unique specimen."

"The goblet, or Alembert?" asked Thomas.

Catching the server's eye, Max raised his glass. "On both counts. Alembert wouldn't leave the goblet behind, so I had little more than an hour to examine it. I don't mind admitting the man made me nervous."

Agatha said, "You didn't recognize the runes, though they put you in mind of early Mesopotamian clays."

"Yes, my dear. Thank you."

Agatha had a talent for filling in gaps. Unless she missed her guess, such was the reason Carlton had pressed to have her here. Men, including her husband, often required prodding to reveal what mattered. She said, "Max told me nothing about the man in a physical way or anything he said would evoke dread."

"Indeed," agreed Max, no doubt fortified by the fresh drink. "Then not much time passed before I crossed paths with a chap by name of Pfeiler with a P, antiquarian and likely tomb raider. He knew Alembert. Told me a barmy story about a high-stakes poker game, a trick story, like one of Agatha's, all the players except Alembert and Pfeiler soon expiring under suspicious circumstances."

"What was Pfeiler's take on it?" Thomas inquired.

Though Thomas tried to hide it, Agatha thought his interest was piqued.

"He'd had a few drinks before he related the story. Afterward, gave me the impression he regretted talking about it, closed up like a clam. Like he'd seen a ghost. Within days, he was murdered."

"You suspect Alembert?" said Thomas.

"*We* do," Carlton asserted.

Thomas put his empty glass on the table. "Then he's a man to be scrupulously avoided. Or eliminated."

"I've insisted Max avoid him," Agatha interjected, delighted in the turn this conversation was taking.

"Has he tried to contact you?" Thomas asked Max.

"Thankfully not, as of yet."

Carlton said, "We don't want to avoid *or* eliminate him."

Agatha was poised to swat a fly on the tablecloth when she realized it was a hornet. Thomas swept it away without fanfare.

"What do you have in mind?" Agatha said to Carlton.

The gnome surveyed the room before he responded. "We're seeking a cooperative relationship with Alembert. We'd like Thomas to act as liaison."

Thomas sat perfectly still, his expression and posture revealing nothing. "Alembert and I are not on those terms," he said at last, in a low voice.

"An intermediary, not an agent."

"I've learned to avoid unnecessary danger, learned the hard way, Carlton. On what business are you looking to cooperate with Alembert?"

Agatha had been observing Carlton carefully. If the gnome had imbibed any of his whiskey, he had taken no more than a sip. "On a matter of national defense, a preventative mission."

When Thomas rose and stepped back from the table, an attendant approached him with a wide-brimmed hat. Thomas accepted the hat, inclined his head to Agatha, and said, "I'm expected at Government House. I will ponder your proposal, Carlton."

APRIL 23, 2019

☺☺☺

Istanbul

"ZVI MENTIONED CONSTANTINOPLE because he wants us to go to Istanbul," Sam had said to Lyle in the Tel Aviv airport. "An old spy's way of dropping a clue while keeping his hands clean. I'll book a flight this afternoon. We'll be bankrupt after this business, changing tickets at the last minute."

"Let's go home, Sam," Lyle said, as their flight to London was announced. "I've seen and heard enough."

"Zvi wouldn't send us somewhere on a lark."

"This mission is a lark. I'm surprised you went along with it."

"Remember when I asked you if you trusted Beatrice?" Sam said. "Do you trust me? I want you to pretend you do, for a few weeks anyway. Let's change these tickets."

Lyle and Sam had found a coffee house in the Eminonu District of Istanbul where coffee had been brewed and served for hundreds of years. For all Lyle knew, portions of this building—the end of an alley, cramped and smoky—might have dated from those early days. Not an establishment the ordinary traveler would frequent.

Lyle counted twelve tables, with Lyle and Sam the only patrons in Western attire. They'd been served a copper *cezve* of coffee, from which the proprietor carefully poured a fragrant frothy brew into their small bone-white cups.

Lyle found the coffee bracingly strong and slightly sweet, erasing some of the fogginess produced by travel and long days in hot places. Sam said, "You're to drink the froth, but stay away from the *telve*—the grounds—they'll sour your stomach."

Wearing a thin cotton jacket and open-collar blue and white striped shirt, the man who approached their table appeared to be an ordinary Western businessman. Virile looking with a wide handsome face, the man was so tall that the low ceiling forced him to dip his head as he made his way to their table.

Shaking hands with Sam, but paying no heed to Lyle, he introduced himself as Brett Jones.

"I remember you, Jones," Sam said. "How long have you been here?"

"Two years. I have a full schedule, Stuart. How can I help you?"

The man rankled Lyle. How could Sam not notice his rudeness? When the proprietor came to the table, Jones said, "Another pot, and baklava."

Not too full a schedule for baklava at Sam's expense. Out of the corner of his eye, Lyle saw two mice scurrying along the wall, one behind the other.

"Who's this?" asked Jones irritably, not looking at Lyle.

"My brother. He's involved."

Jones said, "Why should that make a difference? The kind of thing that had you sacked, Stuart."

Lyle flinched, the first intense emotion he'd felt in days.

"Perhaps you'll make an exception," said Sam.

"I don't have to kowtow to you anymore. Quite the opposite," Jones said archly.

As weary as he was, Lyle had to beat back the urge to put this man in his place. Sam stretched his hand toward the baklava, changed his mind, and said, "I wasn't aware I leaned on you, Jones."

"Didn't take *any* notice," the man said.

Sam said, "Most of the juniors preferred it that way. I'm looking for an Israeli named Malkin."

After finishing his second piece of baklava and cleaning his fingers with a warm towel, Jones said to the waiter, "Be careful with that pot, damn you! You'll mark the suit." Then, he whispered to Sam, "Why are you interested in Malkin?"

"A private matter. We think he was involved in an assassination."

"Here?" Jones sat a little straighter.

"Uganda."

"Malkin has a reputation. I assume you know that."

"We were told he might be in Turkey. Can you tell me anything?"

Jones sipped his coffee, set the cup on the table, and shook his head.

The expression of pique on Sam's face seemed to please the young man, who said, "Perhaps we hear a word now and then about commissioned assassinations, things we don't care about."

Lyle felt Sam's hard grip on his knee.

"…unless a British citizen is involved, and only if political or media pressure is brought to bear, especially in countries like this. But I'm telling you things you ought to have learned years ago."

"Who's head of station these days?" Sam asked, still pinching Lyle's knee.

"That's privileged information. You've been disavowed, Stuart."

"Retired."

"If you say so. You knockabout sorts are out of fashion."

Sam said, "I'm not asking you to *do* anything. The fact is, Malkin fights way above your weight class."

The man's face reddened. Maybe he'd been looking for an excuse to start a ruckus with Sam. Now, he stood up, rubbed his fingers vigorously with the towel and tossed it into Sam's face.

Would his brother respond in kind? Jones gave the impression he expected—welcomed?—a belligerent response. He had backup and diplomatic privilege here while Sam had no one.

Sam never stirred, letting the towel fall to the floor. As for Lyle, he wasn't letting this prig walk off without a word. He stood and glared at Jones, provoking a disdainful grin. "I've met men like you at archaeological sites, *worthless* when something important needs doing. My brother saved a plane full of people and hunted down the Manchester bombers. Have you *done anything*?"

The man's smile evaporated. Lyle had gotten to this lout, and the angry-faced liaison officer stormed out of the building.

"Most helpful," Sam muttered to Jones's back. Then to Lyle, he said, "Good to see a little red in your cheeks. I don't have any sources in this country and The Firm's people here won't give me the time of day once Jones talks to them. Not your doing. He'd already made up his mind when they sent him."

"What did you do to him?"

"Nothing. I barely remember him. Maybe promotions didn't come as promptly as he desired and he needed someone to blame. Let's finish the baklava and be off. Maybe we can catch a flight. He's not the only one who wonders if I'm up to it."

"He's an idiot, Sam."

Incensed by Jones's behavior, Lyle didn't notice the other patron until he had seated himself in the chair vacated by the liaison officer. A physical contrast to Jones, short and bald, middle aged, with ivory skin, dressed in a well-worn brown suit, like somebody's stuffy uncle.

The proprietor came to their table with a fresh pot and clean cups. "You won't be charged for this pot," the proprietor said, indicating the stranger.

"We've had enough, thank you," Sam responded.

Living and traveling with his brother for weeks, Lyle recognized Sam's caution.

"I suggest you try it," the stranger said. "I drink it with cardamom. May I?"

They let the man pour before he filled his own cup. He took a long sip. "I'm Orhan Genç," he said, pronouncing it 'gench.'

"I heard you've retired, Mr. Stuart."

"That's a polite way of putting it."

"As you are no longer on active duty, may I ask what your countryman wanted?"

"To abandon us as soon as propriety permitted."

Genç took another sip. "The cardamom must be brewed with the coffee, not added like milk or cream."

Sam tasted the beverage. "Very good."

"I'm glad you like it," Genç said. "What did you do to become a *Righteous?*"

When Sam held back, Lyle said, "Kept a plane full of Israelis from being murdered."

"Saving lives is always a worthy pursuit. As you know, we publicly revile the Jews. Though in private...well..."

"Are your people concerned about my brother and me, Mr. Genç?" Sam asked, still shuttered.

Holding his cup in both hands, the man said, "We keep track of high-impact subjects who cross our borders. I came here to meet you, and to learn what interests you in Istanbul."

Sam answered right away. "We're looking for an Israeli freelancer, name of Malkin."

"Ah, another high-impact subject." The Turk glanced in both directions. "I won't waste any time waltzing with you about your interest in Bari Malkin. He was here until two weeks ago, in a fifteen hundred-Euro a night suite at the Ciragan, next door to the old Palace—under an assumed name, of course. Why are you seeking him?"

Again, no hesitation on Sam's part. "We think he killed a friend of ours in Uganda. The bomb had his fingerprints."

"Have you spoken to anyone there?"

What would Sam say to this man they'd just met? "We've spoken to someone in Uganda. Then, another someone in Israel helped us attach a name."

"Knowing a few someones helps. Malkin still has friends in

Israel. Was the person Malkin killed a colleague?"

"A civilian, a close friend."

So bloodless an explanation in comparison to how Lyle's stomach lurched every time her death was mentioned.

"That fits our profile of Malkin. I wish I had known sooner. I told him he wasn't welcome in Turkey."

Lyle's head was spinning. Here was another someone. With Sam's intelligence knowledge, maybe he had known this since Genç identified himself.

"Can you say any more about him?" Sam inquired.

"As it happens, I can. Malkin flew from Nairobi to Istanbul. When he left Turkey, his destination was Hungary."

"Thank you, Mr. Genç. If he killed our friend, his likely escape route would have been to Kenya, and the timeline fits."

"Who sent you here?" the little man asked.

"The someone in Israel who attached a name."

"How is Zvi these days?"

"You must mean Zvi Eitan. In good spirits and healthy, last I heard."

"Does your brother have anything to say?"

Lyle was drawn to the genial Genç, but he had just met the man, and if the Turk was in Sam's business... "The best coffee I've ever tasted, Mr. Genç."

"We take our time with coffee. By the way, Dr. Stuart, don't fret about the mice. They keep the roaches under control and the cat keeps *them* under control. Not so different from how we deal with men like Malkin. I told him if he didn't move on, I'd have to turn the cat loose, and he understood perfectly. Sadly, in Turkey we have too many roaches and too few cats."

"This land is steeped in history," said Lyle.

Genç made a little bow. "And we have had our share of rascals. Are you familiar with our ancient Three-Headed Serpent Column? Many believed the column was a talisman against vermin. The last of its heads toppled long ago, and since that time the vermin have run wild, including the two-legged kind."

Sam nodded. "At one time, I thought men like you and I could scatter the vermin."

"Yes, I remember, Stuart. But we were too few and too human."

The two men clasped hands. Sam said, "How do I get coffee like this in London?"

"The Afghan Home. Tell Noori, Genç sent you, and he will treat you well. I helped his family during the Soviet occupation of Afghanistan—as best I could, you understand. Scattering vermin. Tell me something, Stuart. Is Operation Latrine a fable? Some say you were escorted all the way to the border."

Sam smiled broadly. "And a cozy escort it was, Mr. Genç."

APRIL 23, 2019

Istanbul

LYLE AND SAM HAD ESCHEWED THE HOTEL RESTAURANT for one Genç had recommended, a five-minute walk from the hotel, encompassing seven streets and alleys.

Though the sun had set, the air was still warm, the sun-baked buildings radiating heat, with loud voices and music permeating every lane, the vitality Lyle used to crave.

"No coffee," said Sam to their waiter, a small man with dark hair and moustache. "Our friend recommended the *kuzu tandir* and *ayran*." Lyle had heard about *ayran*, a yogurt-based drink.

From the appearance of the place he wouldn't have expected the food to be anything special, but Genç had been effusive about it, especially the lamb—the *kuzu tandir*. Recently painted, the walls were bare except for an inscription above the door: *Allahu Akbar.*

Their drinks arrived and Sam had a swallow. "We're not going home empty-handed," he told Lyle. "We've learned this was an expert hit, a Mossad connection. The person we're after might be Malkin, in Kenya and Turkey until recently."

"Do you think Cornelia and Maria are in danger?" Lyle asked him.

"I don't think this was a revenge strike, but I don't have enough information to proclaim them safe and secure. Joseph's keeping an eye on them. We can't do anything more."

The roasted lamb arrived on a silver platter.

"Smells delicious," Sam said. The waiter refilled their water glasses from a pewter jug.

Lyle had an appetite. Taking a serving of lamb with onions and rice, he asked his brother, "Who can we trust?"

"Besides each other? Joseph, Zvi, and Genç, though they each have higher loyalties."

"How hard would it be for one of them to deceive us?"

Sam chewed a mouthful of lamb slowly, then swallowed. "Joseph pointed us toward a Mossad incendiary. If Zvi wanted to deceive us, he would have pushed back, but he gave us a name, then Genç confirmed Malkin had traveled from Kenya to Turkey. They'd have to be collaborating, and their countries aren't known to collaborate unless the matter involves national security. The lamb's good, isn't it?"

"Delicious!" Lyle said. His brother wasn't much to look at, but how many could have associated the incendiary with Israel, how many had access to someone who could connect the incendiary with a name, and how many could have convinced that someone to provide the name? Identifying Malkin had occurred so naturally the realization hadn't dawned on Lyle that such a feat would have been impossible for an ordinary person, even an ordinary policeman.

Scooping another helping of meat onto his plate, Sam said, "Genç didn't steer us wrong with this place." Then a moment later, he remarked, "You'll be glad to see Lucia, I wager."

"The flat won't measure up after the monastery." Lyle was thinking about touchdown at Heathrow, the lonely flat and the new normal. "If Malkin is as lethal as Eitan makes him out to be, have we come to a dead end?"

Between bites of lamb and the curried rice, Sam said, "Not a bit of it. Still early days. Have another helping. You could use it."

How recently had Lyle fretted about becoming flabby?

"You won't find lamb like this in your grand university town."

"You sound like Mum. What aren't you telling me, Sam?"

A jovial expression suffused Sam's face. "You know everything I do, Frodo. Seen the same things, talked to the same people."

If Sam's *Frodo* had been meant to reassure, it had rung false to Lyle.

"We have to get you back into circulation," insisted Sam.

"I don't care about that. My sofa's still empty."

"Time for you to fly solo. I promise I won't disappear."

The next day, Lyle would be back in England, the idea of long stretches alone terrifying him. He said, "I'm not up to flying solo."

Glancing at the bottle of wine at the next table, Sam said, "A lot of that about. Let's go back to the hotel. Early flight tomorrow."

"The captain instructed us to serve you dessert," said their hovering waiter. "Will you have coffee?"

"One cup, if you please," replied Sam. "Is there thyme in the lamb?"

The waiter winked at Sam and put a finger to his lips.

Lyle waited for the man to step away. When he'd embarked from England, broken and enraged, he'd given little thought to the risk his brother was taking, something that couldn't be ignored after hearing Mutesi, Eitan, and Genç. "You said you have no backup. Eitan and Genç paint an ugly picture of Malkin as ruthless and resourceful. If he's our man, maybe we should just let it go."

Sam pushed back his chair, a different man than the one who'd departed England with Lyle. "Letting it go is not an option. For the same reason we couldn't let those Ugandan terrorists go. Who says he's finished? Maybe you're next. I've been thinking about that water gate at the Jericho dig."

"What could that have to do with Beatrice's death?"

"What I said in Jericho. You knew Beatrice and you know Marks and Fitzgerald."

"No one's been murdered at Jericho."

"Not yet. As I said, early days."

Lyle ate the last of the lamb, swallowed, and said, "You think Beatrice was killed because she was connected to me?"

"I haven't concluded anything."

The waiter set coffee and caramelized cakes in front of them, saying, "Haider will escort you to the hotel."

"We know the way," Sam countered.

"Captain's orders." The waiter pointed to a huge man in the corner of the room, a man with one eye, a scar on his cheek, and a cup in his hand that looked like a child's toy.

"Bring that good man some dessert," said Sam.

APRIL 24, 2019

Istanbul to London

W HEN THEY WERE CHECKING OUT OF THE HOTEL, the clerk handed Lyle a matchbox. "With the captain's compliments. No, sir, do not open it here, if you please."

LYLE WAS SITTING IN A WINDOW SECTION. He was on the aisle, with an empty seat between him and a woman by the window. Sam had moved to a deserted row and promptly fell asleep—no ear or eye cover, just an airline-issue blanket he'd folded up and wedged behind his head.

No wonder Sam was that exhausted, as on more than one occasion Lyle had awakened in the night, observing his brother sitting in the dark, gazing out the hotel window, like a desert owl, a solitary predator, watching and waiting.

The big plane was only half full, Lyle and the woman alone in their aisle, a seat between them. He was tempted to put on his headphones and listen to one of Andrea's lectures on Zeta2 until he noticed the Makerere University logo on the woman's e-pad.

"Are you connected to the university?" he asked her.

She was about fifty, probably as tall as Lyle, with plenty of gray in her shoulder-length hair, and wearing an olive suit with a white silk blouse. "I teach in the biology department. Ornithology."

He was tempted to tell her about Beatrice, but couldn't summon the energy.

"Business in Istanbul?" she asked him.

The easy answer was to say yes and retrieve his headphones—which he wanted to do. "A few days in Kampala with my brother. My girlfriend died. She was at Makarere too."

"Not Beatrice Adams!"

Once her words registered, he said, "That's right."

"My God!" She seemed as distressed as he was to have the subject broached.

They stared at each other. "She was a dear friend. I'm Nancy Evans."

Nancy Evans? The last time he saw Beatrice, putting his arms around her from behind as she scrubbed dishes, he'd whispered in her ear, "I wish you'd come back to England."

"Maria needs me. She's still hurting."

"Cornelia..."

"Shh. We've been down that road. Next time, stay a bit longer. I want you to meet Nancy."

"You're Lyle Stuart. Archaeology, Lido, Lucia," Nancy exclaimed. "What were you doing in Istanbul?"

His head was still spinning. "My brother wanted to stop in."

Her confused look prompted him to say, "The snoozing chap across the aisle."

As she was obviously British, he asked her, "How did you find your way to Uganda?"

"I've loved birds since I was a girl. I read biology, then ornithology, took a specialty in East African species. Only natural to teach there, so close to Lake Victoria habitats and preserves."

Lyle had spent some time with Beatrice on university grounds, a far cry from the comforts of Oxford, Makerere having motley buildings and potholed roads, and only the deans with window air conditioners.

They hadn't been in the air long when the plane started

rocking. The woman gripped both armrests.

Nancy said, "I study birds, but I'm no flyer."

"It's sea turbulence. How long have you been in Uganda?" he asked to distract her.

"Fifteen years. I'm from a village in Wales."

The turbulent air wasn't bothering Sam, because Lyle could hear him snoring. The woman had noticed too. "What does your brother do?"

"Commercial traveler" was Lyle's automatic response. "He came along for moral support."

"I'm so sorry," she said, her eyes brimming. "I imagine you hear a lot of that. She talked about you often. I feel I know you... Ohh, this turbulence!"

"May I offer you a drink?"

"The sooner the better."

Rather than waiting for their stewardess, Lyle sought her out and returned with two glasses of Bourbon.

"You're as good as she promised. Excuse me," Nancy said, taking a big gulp. "How did you like Istanbul?"

"Sam has a friend there. Marvelous coffee."

Wide-eyed, she went on. "God, this flight is my worst nightmare!"

"We're dodging angry clouds, I'm afraid."

"I'll take your word for it. I don't dare look out the window."

"Same again?" Lyle pointed to her empty glass. He started to rise, but Nancy reached across the empty seat and grasped his hand. Grimacing, she said, "Wait a minute!"

He had to admit the flight was rocky, and he noted confirming expressions on the faces of several passengers.

"I'm sorry," she said, sitting ramrod straight. "I just met you and I'm holding your hand." She resumed her iron grip on the armrests.

She was seeking solace, too, for their mutual loss, but except for Beatrice, they were strangers. Someone had to take the first step. He grasped her hand and squeezed it.

"You must have seen Cornelia and Maria," Nancy said, though she still seemed distracted by the roughness of the flight.

Lyle said, "I'll be right back." A few minutes later, their stewardess followed him to his seat with fresh drinks.

"Drink it down. Doctor's orders," Lyle told her.

Within seconds, Nancy had consumed the additional Bourbon. He waited a minute. "Better?"

"Much."

The captain's voice told them the worst was over, and he was doing his best to locate more comfortable air.

Lyle said, "You asked about Cornelia and Maria. They didn't know anything except for the location of the grave. We talked to…" He bit his lip. After two Bourbons, he'd been on the verge of telling her about Mutesi, but with no legal standing and Sam a *commercial traveler* how would they have had access to the ISO?

"We talked to her sisters for less than an hour. I didn't want to add to their bad memories."

Nancy said, "If we're not careful, a few bad memories can crowd out a hundred good ones. When I heard what happened to her, I didn't sleep for nights. So bad that when I saw someone in the cab next to mine who looked like her, I embarrassed myself by calling out to the woman."

Lyle said, "I wake up every morning expecting her to be alive. I go to bed as blue as…Did you sense she felt threatened?"

Nancy thought a minute. "No. But the week before, she seemed withdrawn, not like Beatrice."

The air wasn't smooth by any means, but Nancy looked more comfortable. The pilot's disembodied voice said, "I'm afraid we're in for a few more bumps. Stay seated please."

"Shit!" Nancy said, glancing at the empty glass.

"Shall I?" he asked.

"Definitely not. Another one and they'll have to carry me off. That's if we manage to land in one piece. You'll find this hard to believe but I often go weeks between drinks." She forced a smile.

"Here's a good memory. I claimed a stone turtle Beatrice kept on her office shelf. Beatrice's people admire the turtle. It's patient and carries its protective house on its back wherever it goes. When I look at the turtle, I think of her."

Whether due to this unexpected camaraderie with Nancy, the Bourbon, or their happy memories of Beatrice, he felt more alive than he had in weeks, almost human again. He told her about the bomb in the Mainz restaurant, how Beatrice had nurtured him back to health.

She said, "I know about that."

"How can the same thing have happened to her?" he asked.

She took hold of his wrist. "I have another good memory for you. I talked her into sharing a tent with me on a birding expedition, three nights in the wilderness. The first night, after we secured the door and turned on the lamp, a scorpion scuttled across the floor and went under my cot. You should have heard me howl. Beatrice sat in her camp chair, insisted on waiting and watching while I went to fetch the backcountry guide. When we returned, the dead scorpion was on top of my field book, like a trophy. Do you know what she said? 'A game Paul and I played when I was a girl. We had our share of scorpions in the house. Whoever *done it in* was relieved of the dinner dishes.'"

"Paul was her hero," Lyle said.

"He was, but she didn't love anyone like she loved you."

"I could never figure out why."

"Now that I've met you, I can guess."

He had to change the subject before his emotions took over. "I can't top scorpions, but what would you say if I told you I have a gross of beetles in my bag?"

"Dead or alive?"

"Yes… I collected them for an Oxford entomologist. I'm suspicious it was a scheme to distract me from grief."

"Did it?"

"Here and there," he admitted.

"A friend who goes to such trouble to relieve your misery? We should all have such a friend." She looked toward the window. "Where are we anyway?"

The plane was bouncing again, though not as violently as before. "Germany. He could land here if we were in trouble. What's so funny?" he asked, seeing her grin.

"Beatrice told me when she moved back to Uganda she traded one digger for another, and here we are, side by side on the same plane."

His confused expression prompted Nancy to say, "I'm interested in transitional fossils between tree dwelling raptors and flying dinosaurs. The best sites are in China, but Africa has promising sites too."

"Isn't that the paleontologists' bailiwick?"

"Makerere is more flexible that way than Oxford or Cambridge, so I'm able to do both."

Could anyone at Oxford have imagined a Tuberculosis Control Centre on campus or wire and platted-steel fences around university buildings? His long-conditioned chauvinism couldn't admit a second-rate institution might outshine Oxford in anything. Yet, Beatrice had taught there, and Nancy.

"You and Beatrice were birds of a feather," he said to her.

"God, I miss her, Lyle."

"Would you care for something to eat?" interrupted the stewardess. "We have a vegetarian plate and a lamb plate."

Nancy declined. "Do you serve cardamom coffee?" asked Lyle.

"Not Old Town quality," whispered the woman, "but quite good."

He suggested two cups, and Nancy concurred. Another voice said, "Coming through. Make it three cups."

Taking the seat between Lyle and Nancy, Sam requested the lamb.

Nancy Evans took one look at Sam and shifted to allow him more room.

"I thought you'd gone into a coma. We passed through a hurricane and you didn't stir. My brother, Sam," Lyle said to Nancy. "Professor Evans teaches at Beatrice's university. Ornithology."

Sam said, "My eyes aren't what they used to be."

Lyle shook his head. "Ornithology. *Birds*."

"What brought you to Istanbul?" Sam asked Nancy.

"An end-of-term conference," she said, in the sort of professorial tone Lyle himself adopted when he wanted to keep someone at arm's length. "You have a friend in Istanbul?"

"A policeman," Sam said.

How long had Sam been listening to their conversation? Lyle knew his brother didn't like coincidences. This woman claimed to live in Kampala and to have known Beatrice. She'd been in Istanbul at the same time they were. In Sam's mind, what was the probability that Beatrice's friend would be sitting next to them on this flight?

"What's your specialty?" Sam inquired, tucking the napkin brought with the meal into his shirt collar.

"East African Mousebirds. Rather drab looking, like me."

"You don't say. Do you carry a card?"

She retrieved one from her bag and handed it to him.

"Your card?" she said to Lyle's brother.

"I'm between jobs at the moment."

"*You don't say.*"

JULY 7, 1931

Bilbao, northern Spain
(88 years earlier)

"H OW DID YOU FIND ME, THOMAS?" Agnes CurLio asked. She was trembling and her eyes were full. A friend in her time of need?

"I'm a resourceful man, and I've always esteemed you. You know that."

"I thought that was over when I left him," Agnes said to the slight, narrow-faced man in a leather jacket, corduroy pants, and riding gloves.

He frowned and wagged his head. "I'm not so fickle as that."

"Did he send you?" She had heard his boots on the steps as he made his way up to this tiny room on the top floor of a boarding house for transients. The space held only a cot, a washstand, a toilet, and a light bulb suspended from the ceiling.

"You know I'm a freelancer, and he's accepting of my peregrinations so long as I deliver the goods."

Agnes knew that Alembert valued Thomas's skills, the reason this man was given such a long leash. "Am I the goods this time?"

Thomas displayed a dramatic pout. "He doesn't know I'm here. I happen to be freelancing."

"Your heart is pure, Thomas."

"Let's not go overboard, my dear. More than a few lice inhabit this soul."

How long had it been since she'd seen Thomas—two years, three? His corn-colored hair was thinning. He looked weary from travel, or was it age and the hardships he'd endured? Sitting cross-legged on the floor, Thomas said, "I have information that may be helpful."

"How did you get here?"

"By aeroplane and the Brough, wheeled it down the ramp and followed the river till I found you."

The roar she'd heard on the street along the river had been Thomas's Brough Superior motorcycle. "Does he know?"

"I have no reason to believe it, but we both understand he gets what he wants. He has extended his arm into the Middle East. I say this to warn you that escaping him is not so easy as changing geography."

Thomas could say little that would make Alembert any more intimidating than she knew him to be. "Where did you learn about his extended arm?"

"A small gathering in Basra. They aimed to recruit me, Agnes."

"To do what?"

"To convince Alembert to do their bidding. But enough about that. I'm here to save you from his clutches."

She started pacing, three steps in any direction bringing her to a wall. She wasn't trembling anymore. "He won't get me."

"How can you be certain?"

"He may find me, but he will not *have* me."

Thomas lit a cigarette. "I've never forgotten our nights dancing in Paris, our conversations. Even then, he didn't have you as he did the others."

"You've said nothing about my appearance," Agnes said.

Thomas took her face in his hands and gazed into her eyes. "What is there to say?"

"You could say I'm stout, that my hair is a mess, that I'm not your Paris nymph."

"Such things don't matter to me, but I hate to see you living like this. I heard you had a mystical experience," he said, closing his eyes and opening his hands Buddha-like. "I'm too Cartesian for mysticism, or so Ali tells me."

"I wasn't expecting it, Thomas," Agnes said, trying to reconcile this man with the Augustus John portrait. She noted a resemblance, but she thought he exerted more effort to be that person than he used to.

"Now, listen to me, Agnes. I can't stay long. You know why. He's a searchlight that sweeps the landscape. But before I go, the information I came to deliver." Then, he told her the real name of the man Alembert was pursuing, the *John Hill* who had something Alembert craved.

"As for Gregory..." he went on.

She was startled. "How do you know I'm seeking him?"

"As for Gregory, he's imprisoned in a sanitarium near Paris, Port d'Ivry. He'll never get out. Destructive defiance, as I hear it. Dead butterflies—need I say more? Stay away from him. He may be bait. Alembert knows you and Gregory are close. You'd be playing into his hands."

"Has he consulted you about me?"

"He wouldn't, because he knows how things lie between us."

He looked so solemn she couldn't resist. "How do things lie between us?"

"Mutual esteem, friendship. To the death," he said, taking her fingers in his desiccated brown hand, and kissing them.

"You are just the tonic I needed," she said. "When I was in Algiers, someone left a message in my room informing me Gregory had been taken away."

"A person who could never have found you in Algiers without help."

"I left as quickly as I could."

He went to the window and looked down on the street, then turned back to her. "You're as good at the game as he is, in your way. A woman came to see me, an entomologist named Rosman. She wanted to know about Alembert's grandfather, and the thing Alembert craves."

"Does she work for Adler?" Agnes was the only person who called Alembert by that name.

"I'm sure she doesn't, and a fool to be meddling in his affairs. She asked about you. She's looking for you. I suspect for the same reason she sought me out. Information about Adler."

Agnes said, "Something is going on that's bigger than fortunes. I've sensed it for quite a while. The Oxford teacher is involved, and now this Rosman woman."

"Can you guess what it is?" he asked her.

"I don't care about that anymore. I'm going to free Gregory, or else."

"It's the *or else* that worries me, my dear."

The moment he'd revealed where Gregory was being held, Agnes began to entertain an idea. Her altered appearance was part of her plan to stay hidden, but if she went after Gregory, she'd need to be better disguised. How far could she push Thomas? If not a man she trusted, she would have to recruit a stranger. "Will you do something for me?" she asked.

"You need only name it."

When she told him, he said, "Good God! How can you ask such a thing?"

"You know I cannot resemble the woman who deserted Adler."

"Your appearance is greatly changed. Please don't ask."

"Please do as I beg you, Thomas. If you're a friend."

"You know I am!"

"The damage will be done. Will *you* do it or must I rely on a stranger?"

"Agnes, think again. Stay away from Gregory. I have friends in Provence who will shelter you. Say the word and I'll round up Ali's bandits and attack Alembert, bring him down."

"You silly fool. Do what I ask. If you love me."

When he'd finished, he removed his riding jacket and tore off a shirtsleeve to staunch the blood.

"You should know I'll never forgive myself," Thomas said.

"For your courage in protecting me?"

"My courage should be applied to destroying Alembert. Ali's band…"

"Never, Thomas. That's nothing but a death wish. Promise me. Do you know where Adler is?"

"In Europe somewhere…his giant, Niiri, too. Beware!"

"Adler wants whatever that Oxford teacher has, and he wants me. You had better be off before the searchlight finds you."

He made a courtly bow. "I shall remain as long as you command."

Her Arthurian knight, heroism and warts, metal steed at the ready. "Then, I command you to go…immediately."

In another life, she could see herself in Paris or London with him. Or she could have, before she found something better. "Where are you going from here?" she asked him.

"Back to England by way of Provence, a good time of year for the Brough."

He had always been reckless. "Is it safe?"

"Is anything safe?"

Would she ever see Thomas again? Agnes said, "A Cartesian posing a metaphysical question?"

"A practical question, as we have learned, my Agnes. A few days on the Côte d'Azur before I make for Le Havre."

"Mind the lice, my dear friend," she said, kissing him tenderly.

From her window overlooking the river, her nose still bleeding, she watched him mount the motorbike and speed away.

AUGUST 6, 1931

Port D'Ivry Institution pour le Dérangé
(one month after Bilbao)

A GNES CURLIO HANDED THE DIRECTOR THE LETTER. "The request is urgent. Read it for yourself. You are to deliver Gregory immediately, and I will escort him to the professor."

What wouldn't she have given to have Thomas at her side, but never once had she considered it. He had done what she needed him to do, her broken nose still swollen and sore.

"Yes, Mademoiselle, immediately," the director replied. "Guy," he said to the man at the desk. "Bring the patient here without delay."

She expected to be outside the gate in five minutes. The letter was so convincing—the insignia even more so—that the director hadn't bothered to telephone to confirm it. But she told herself that now was no time to relax her guard. When she'd attacked the viper's den, she had overlooked a serpent in the back of the pit. It had come at her, and she'd barely avoided being bitten.

The attendant returned, followed by something that barely resembled a man. She was reminded of Edmond Dantès, the Count of Monte Cristo, after the Chateau d'If. The man was hunched over, his bare arms and hands ivory white, and his matted hair shaggy. He hadn't been shaved in at least a week. He was dirty, and a stench hung about him.

Agnes couldn't imagine where his clothes had come from. They were ridiculously small, probably relics from another inmate. She needed tremendous self-control to prevent a wrathful outburst. Was this the bright and happy boy she had once known, had played and laughed with? And how could any man, even her adversary, do this to his own brother?

She couldn't resist saying, "What have you been doing with Alembert's money? Obviously, you've spent nothing on this man. Come, Gregory. Move smartly now."

The director gave her a strange look, and said, "This was the care the professor specified."

She should have known better than to make an intemperate remark. She took Gregory's arm and turned toward the door. The director and assistant were already halfway down the corridor that led to the patients' quarters.

She was considering the train schedule when a booming voice said, "Hello, Agnes."

The voice seemed to her disembodied, as the foyer was empty. Then she saw the cyclops seated in the alcove room, his scarred face familiar except for the missing eye. He was hatless and wearing something like a military uniform but without decorations—not quite fighter's fatigues but definitely not parade dress. And how much grayer he was. "Come in," he said.

"I'm afraid I don't know you. My name is Jane—"

"You are little Agnes CurLio. Come in. Leave that wretch in the foyer."

"Wait for me," she said to the man on her arm. Gregory didn't want to release her—he was shaking—but she lifted his chin, looked into that dirty, hopeless face and smiled at him. "Wait for me."

The room held three chairs and a small table. Christopher Niiri was sitting in the chair closest to a door that was invisible from the foyer, a door that probably opened to the outside. A lamp sat on the table. The room, without windows, was dim. Good, she thought.

Was Christopher's being here a coincidence, or did Alembert know everything? She'd never believed that Charlotte had sent the telegram, but had Alembert been following her every move since Algiers?

"I'm surprised to see you here," the man said. "Alembert will also be surprised. He wonders what has become of you."

"I've been searching," she said.

"It appears that you found someone, or something." The man looked past her at the creature in the foyer. "But what you found is none of your business."

"He's my friend."

"He's no one's friend. Do you know why that worm is here?"

How much more malevolent he looked with that hole where an eye ought to be, and no less threatening.

"No."

"And still you came for him. You used to be so reliably practical. I will tell you, since that knowledge cannot harm us or help you. The fool introduced a brown recluse spider into the terrarium."

In spite of herself she said, "Why?"

"He left a note suggesting he'd produced in miniature what his brother produced in the world at large."

"I see."

"What do you see? It was an absurd act, signifying nothing, and costing the fool his freedom, not to mention other indignities." That one eye looked past her at the slumped figure in the foyer.

"Gregory always had a gift for the dramatic."

"And where has it brought him?" Christopher asked. "Look at him. Look at you. When was the last time you bathed?"

"I'm dirty, but I'm cleaner than I've been in a long time."

"You are a filthy, ugly pig. Let's be candid."

"Candid? You don't know the meaning of the word. Power, that's all you understand."

"Now you are a philosopher. Is that what all this is about? You disappoint me, Agnes. Let's settle this business."

"We'll settle nothing, Christopher. We're just compounding something that started a long time ago."

"Enough talk, woman. Give me your bag. You wouldn't attempt this adventure without a weapon."

"If I give you the bag, you'll kill me," she said. For years, Agnes had collaborated with Christopher. She had never seen him smile, but she could tell when he was enjoying himself.

"You made that decision when you betrayed us."

"I left Alembert's employment. I haven't betrayed anyone."

"Yet you attempt to spirit away a man we want punished. The bag. If you're prompt, I'll do it quickly, for old time's sake."

He had always been a liar, and he was lying now. He would make sure her death was miserable. She handed him the bag.

After removing the gun and pointing it at Agnes, Christopher emptied the remaining contents of the bag onto the floor. The objects came out in a jumble, even the matchbox from the side pocket. He felt the inside of the bag with his free hand.

"A clean shirt for that worm. How considerate. I will take the wire cutters and scissors. I don't want you tempted to do something desperate." He picked up the matchbox and shook it.

"I wouldn't open that if I were you," Agnes said dramatically.

He smiled at her. "You open it, then. You will notice, dear Agnes, that my finger is on the trigger." Then he slid the matchbox along the floor.

"Open it."

She bent over and picked it up. She had always obsessively choreographed her assassinations, but now, this desperate situation demanded a desperate act. She tried to clear her mind of peril and focus instead on the one thing that was necessary. The matchbox exercise she had so diligently practiced would help, but good fortune—something she had never relied on—would count far more.

Curiosity getting the better of him, Christopher leaned forward, and in an instant, Agnes flicked open the matchbox and threw it in his face.

Reflexively, Christopher pulled the trigger.

"It's not loaded," she said.

He lunged at her while swatting his face and neck. Just as suddenly, the giant shivered, staggered back into his chair, and in a series of spasms more and more violent, he toppled to the floor.

She didn't know where the centipede had gone— *Scolopendra letalis*, discovered in the heart of a cactus in southwestern Mexico—and she didn't have time to find out. She shook the spare shirt to make sure the creature hadn't hidden there, replaced the scissors in the bag, and led Gregory out of the compound as quickly as she could without arousing suspicion. They hid behind a large bush while she changed his shirt.

The subway was five minutes late, and they caught it just in time. Arriving at the train station, they quickly boarded and found empty seats in a car with few passengers. Before the conductor came for tickets, Agnes cut Gregory's hair. She made a bad job of it, but he submitted passively. He was drugged, or something worse, she concluded.

"Having quite a day, aren't we?" she said to him.

APRIL 24-25, 2019

☻☻☻

St. Hugh's Charterhouse

W HEN LYLE LANDED AT HEATHROW, he had a phone message from Abbot Henry asking him to come directly to the monastery.

Heart racing, he immediately rang his uncle. "Is something wrong with Lucia?"

"Not a thing. She'll be glad to see you."

"What's so pressing?"

"That must wait until you're here."

"Should I bring Sam?"

"Not so pressing as that, but bring an overnight bag. I promise you a good meal."

"Let's not lose touch, Lyle," Nancy had said to him when they parted company in the terminal, but what did they have in common except Beatrice, who was dead and gone?

Past exhaustion, the alcohol imbibed with Nancy contributing to his fatigue, Lyle stopped in Oxford to shower and change clothes, and then took to the road in the roof-down Spider Lusso to help him stay awake and alert.

Lucia was waiting for him at the monastery door. He had thought about her often while he and Sam were traveling, more than once his brother saying, "Henry's lads are taking good care of her."

"Hullo, Luce," he called out, the poodle bounding to him. He dropped to his knees, cupping her face in his hands, trying to dry his tears without his uncle noticing.

She rolled over and stretched her long legs high in the air: the Princess Lucia pose signifying the time had come to commence rubbing her belly. Abbot Henry didn't hurry Lyle, filling him in on her adventures at the monastery while he was away.

As suppertime was near—his body didn't know what time it was, only that it needed food—Abbot Henry showed him to the guest room, inviting him to join the Brothers for evening meal—still giving no word about the reason for the summons.

Lyle having been under duress and on the move for weeks, the silent simple meal with the Brothers was the best sustenance for him—a small mercy. Afterward, Lyle's uncle took his arm and asked if he was up to a digestive walk on the grounds.

"Put this jacket on," said the abbot, and Lyle gladly complied, England being much cooler than the locales where they'd been traveling.

The sun was falling and the wind had been freshening since his arrival. The sky was clear, with birds on the move. Lyle and his uncle hadn't gone far before Lyle caught the sweet scent of the monastery's budding fruit trees. Their beekeeper, Brother...—the name escaped him—would soon be busy.

Lucia stuck close to Lyle as they made their way toward the pond at the back of the property where the grounds drained. Lyle detected a moving haze near the hives adjacent to the hut where the beekeeper resided. The vegetable garden was further in, along the path to the pond, the brew room and grotto on the opposite side of the monastery.

Lyle broke the silence with "*Der Feuersturm* will not relent. Every morning, I wake up expecting her to be alive."

"And so it will continue for a long time," his uncle observed. "You can do nothing about it, nothing healthy, I mean. That's what love does. You learned that with your mother, my sister."

Was it Lyle's imagination, or was his uncle less buoyant than when Lucia had arrived at the monastery? "Does knowing that help me?"

"Only if you accept the promise of a larger life, an elevated state of being, if you will. Otherwise, life... *'is a tale told by an idiot, full of sound and fury, signifying nothing,'* no matter how much or how little we accomplish."

His uncle's words from *Macbeth* evoked frustration rather than solace. "I'm supposed to trust an unseen someone that allowed her to be obliterated, and beg for a morsel of kindness—what you call a larger life?"

"Or act as if you trust. What Beatrice did when she left Oxford to help her sister."

"What exactly do you mean by a larger life anyway?"

Lyle detected an odd mixture of distress and glee in his uncle's expression. "As if I can do justice to such a mystery. Well, I shall attempt to answer you, but I fear it shall be a feeble effort. All the potential God created in us shall finally be realized. Without surrendering our freedom, we shall be everything we were meant to be."

Who else could Lyle converse with like this, bare his soul to without frightening the person or breaking windows? "I wish I could believe. Believing would make even this smaller life easier."

"Is that what you think?" his uncle said. "We should be suspicious of faith that gives us easy answers to every grief. As for Frodo Lyle Stuart, reverting to old patterns and priorities might be easier for him, but I don't think he will succumb. He's on a journey now." The setting sun and stiff breeze made Abbot Henry zip his coat all the way up. "You can still talk to her, you know."

"You'd have to believe in a *larger life*," Lyle said.

"Or hope to believe. Life consists of arrivals and departures."

His uncle was like the monastery's rabbits, darting from subject to subject in a flash. "Are you talking about Beatrice?"

Abbot Henry was shaking his head at Lucia's attempts to find a passage through the hedge, the dog squeezing in and scuffling back out when she found a space too tight. "All the hard departures in life. We try to make sense of them."

Lyle said, "Why do you think sense is there to be made?"

"Perhaps you shouldn't get me started on that subject immediately after your exhausting travel."

"I'm game, and if I topple over, you can continue when I wake up."

Lyle's uncle grinned at him. "You were talking about meaning, and since the Enlightenment the vanguard of science has tried to reduce everything to physical laws and numbers. But in the late twentieth century, this belief collapsed under the weight of quantum mechanics, where things at the sub-atomic level are and are not, here and there, all at once, upending the belief that if we can measure we can know everything. Einstein had already demonstrated that time and space aren't fixed dimensions. If that wasn't mind-bending enough, quantum mechanics and the Big Bang made the material world even more mysterious. A fixed laws-and-numbers universe, it is not."

"So you hope, Uncle."

"Hope? So I *hear* from my brother physicists, even those who cannot imagine a creator."

They walked on and were back at the monastery door when Abbot Henry said, "Something inside us insists these wrenching departures aren't the way it's supposed to be. You've felt it more keenly, certainly, than most. Why would we feel this way when arrivals and departures are all we know, when we've been conditioned to them our entire lives? Now let's get you to bed before you topple over."

LYLE SLEPT AS WELL as he had since receiving the news about Beatrice. He may have heard chanting during the night, or perhaps that was a dream.

Lucia slept on a mat next to his bed. Eventually, Lyle woke to a knock on the door and an invitation to breakfast, much of the food coming from the monastery garden, and honey from the hives.

"Are you fit for another walk?" asked the abbot. "Good. Let's go, and I'll tell you some things." This reminded Lyle that his uncle hadn't yet broached whatever matter had been pressing enough to bring Lyle directly from the airport.

When the question came to walks in any weather, her humble servant didn't have to ask Lucia twice. Low clouds and a stiff breeze greeted them, and Lucia bounded off. The two men passed the fenced garden and a pair of Brothers hoeing and weeding. Heaps of steaming compost were piled behind the plot.

Lyle strained to read the new placard someone had attached to the fence: CAVE CANEM—Beware of the Dog—a friendly warning to the monastery's rabbits?

Lyle and his uncle were nearing the pond when the abbot cleared his throat, and said, "You're wondering why I summoned you so insistently." He hesitated for a few seconds before going on. "The repository was invaded again…no, nothing stolen. In fact, this invasion was so expert we wouldn't have known about it but for the company that monitors our security system. They say that a week ago the alarm program was compromised. Someone was in the monastery and secret room. We were told that only good fortune was responsible for identifying this rabbit's breach, that's how expert the business was."

"You said nothing was stolen," Lyle interrupted.

"Nothing was there to be nicked. Every time you pick up a newspaper you hear of a secure system that's been compromised. I went along with what the experts recommended, then took matters into my own hands."

They had reached the stand of oaks on the banks of the pond, a dozen or so, with one towering over the rest. Abbot Henry pointed to the pond, and said, "It's at the bottom of the pond, the container and the manuscript. You see, Frodo, I had an informed faith that the container is impermeable, so I built an assembly to raise and lower it, using a mechanism in the crook of the big tree. The container is inside a wire basket on the bottom of the pond. Sensors on the pulley and the basket link up when I decide to fish it out."

"You verified it had no leakage?" said Lyle, trying to sound calm but hearing the panic in his voice.

"Not a drop, or a molecule. Of course, I tested the empty container beforehand, but I was confident it was absolutely gas and watertight, or else it couldn't have kept an ancient manuscript in like-new condition for millennia. Let's see a thief get his hands on it now."

Lyle said, "Yesterday a physics lecture and now this."

"*Fides et ratio*. You understand?"

Lyle said, "Have you seen Lucia?"

"My head would have to be on a swivel to keep up with her. Probably at the hut looking for Brother Francis."

"The beekeeper, what's his real name?" Lyle asked.

"Do I detect suspicion? He calls himself Petros."

"Greek?" Lyle probed.

"Nothing to suggest it."

"A *nom de guerre*?"

Abbot Henry made a dismissive noise. "One gun-toting cynic in the family is plenty, thank you. Brother Francis has a healing hand. He applies it to our animals, domestic and wild. He has doubled our colony and quadrupled our honey."

"He lives here year-round?"

"He comes and goes, but when he's here he lives in the hut. I've seen him about in the dead of winter with his ear to the hives. Don't get any ideas about annoying him. If he leaves and we lose our honey, I'll have the devil to pay with the Brothers."

"You can't be too careful."

"Lucia isn't suspicious. She often romps with him, as you witnessed last time."

Considering the theft of the manuscript and the recent monastery invasion, his uncle was far too casual. "Does Brother Francis know about the underwater repository?"

"I didn't reveal what I was doing to anyone, out of prudence rather than want of trust. The Brothers are used to my mechanical tinkering. If I may say so, the invention is a rather ingenious idea, but we both know it isn't the solution to our problem."

"A permanent solution, you mean," said Lyle, his eyes on the little waves the wind produced in the pond.

Abbot Henry said, "Nothing in this world is permanent, not pyramids, or even mountains, as our friend John Hill well knew when he brought it here. Tell me why we keep this thing hidden."

"Thieves, like Dekeyser."

"But we know he was manipulated by those with darker aspirations."

Thinking about the manuscript stirred him, and Lyle said, "The container alone could make a thief fabulously wealthy."

"But the greatest threats are men like Russell, having ample treasure already but pining for more than an artifact."

Lyle said, "Why not give it to the British Museum and let them worry about protecting it?"

"Wash our hands of the matter, you mean."

"The monastery is only a safe repository if no one is aware of the location of the manuscript. Once the location is known, as it now is, the book and coffer might as well be where they're better protected."

"Your logic is sound," Abbot Henry granted. "But then wouldn't a box in a bank vault accomplish as much, while keeping it secret as the donor desired?"

"I don't know how secure any bank would be if someone knew where the manuscript was. We have another option—the Oxford Consolidated Archives, converted lecture halls guarded by the government. If the manuscript were moved to an obscure bin—that of a long-forgotten Oxonian—it might be as safe as we can achieve.

I'd need to do some research and we'd want help in acquiring access to the building and bin." Left unsaid was the desire for a bin Lyle alone, and no one else, could access. He needn't remove the book, but he thought of the hours he could spend with it.

Abbot Henry said, "You've given me an idea, but let me ponder for a bit. A logical solution for Hill was to have given the manuscript to the museum. He seems a wise man, yet he brought it here and asked my predecessor to '*keep it secret, keep it safe.*'"

Lyle said, "It would be secret and safe in the archives."

The abbot smiled, not committing himself. "Now then, what were you and Sam doing in Africa, and don't tell me nothing apart from paying your respects to Beatrice's sisters."

Lyle was annoyed at having been diverted from his idea for securing the manuscript. "We saw Cornelia and Maria...and the grave. We're after the truth, Uncle."

"Ah, and did you find it?"

"Some of it, though not enough for either of us."

"Is this business connected to the book?" Abbot Henry wondered.

"I don't see how it could be."

"I see how it might be. Beatrice knew as much about the manuscript as you and I do. Maybe someone figured they could find the book through her. Sam would have thought of that." The abbot cleared his throat. "Is he sober?"

"If he's drinking, he's keeping it well hidden. He had opportunities in Kampala, Jerusalem, Istanbul..."

"Jerusalem? Istanbul? You *are* serious."

"Something we learned in Kampala led us there."

The abbot gave him a piercing look. "What are you going to do next?"

"I'm seeing Sam in a few days. I expect he has something in mind." Lyle shrugged. "Would you rather I retreat into misery?"

"That's a false dichotomy," Lyle's uncle returned equably. "Like choosing between faith and science. I can think of other ways to remedy misery, healthier ways." Bending over, his uncle moved his forefinger across the surface of the water, tracing a figure over and over again. Lyle recognized the mathematical symbol for infinity. His uncle said, "Life where you cannot see it, bees inside a hollow tree, fish beneath these waters racing like wet comets." He stopped and stood up straight again. "I don't need to remind you to be careful, do I?"

"Too late for that. We're both all in."

"All in what?" his uncle asked.

"I'd better not say. If your reason for Beatrice's murder is correct, the outcome may be a matter of who gets to whom first."

Henry seemed roused to alarm. "Nonsense! What can I do to talk you out of this?"

His blood rising, Lyle answered, "I don't want to be talked out of it. If Sam and I have anything to say, someone's going to catch it hot."

Not often did Lyle see his uncle's jaw set hard. "That gun-toting cynic ought to know better."

"Stay out of it!" growled Lyle.

Lucia had meandered back to them and her head came up smartly, no doubt knowing what that tone of voice meant.

In a softer tenor, the abbot said, "Can I do anything for you?"

Lyle was tired of hearing that question—his uncle, Agnese, Andrea. At least Sam knew better. No one could do anything for him. Or could they? Hadn't the thought been on his mind since he'd left the flat earlier? Andrea had rekindled the idea before he and Sam left for Africa, and his uncle had provided an opening by informing him about the invasion and the manuscript's new hiding place. Never had an artifact beguiled him so. When would an opportunity come again to make a compelling case, and yes, to trade on his misery? He said, "Would you let me borrow the book?"

Abbot Henry made for an acorn on the ground but came up short with a groan.

"I need to be distracted, and frivolous things won't do," Lyle said. "The manuscript would command my attention, take my mind off..."

"Did anyone suggest this to you?"

Uncanny how this man could see inside him—first, the intimation that Beatrice's death might be connected to the manuscript and now this. Indeed, the idea of working on the manuscript with Andrea excited him—and why shouldn't he experience a respite from misery?

"You said the choice between misery and retribution is a false dichotomy. Very well, I choose the book. I'm taking your advice, and I'd be very careful with it," insisted Lyle more ardently than he'd intended.

"I don't doubt that. You recovered it, and you were its guardian for a while, but hasn't the time come for you to let it go?"

Can I do anything for you? Unless it puts me out? Is that what his uncle meant to say? "How can I let it go when I don't possess it?" Lye complained.

"We set our sights on things we don't possess, then can't let go."

"I'm not in the mood for platitudes," Lyle snapped. "I'm accustomed to handling ancient artifacts. You need not fear the manuscript will be damaged."

The abbot made a small sound of amusement. "That's the least of my worries. You may have it for as long as you'd like. You have earned that privilege. I've said what I needed to say, with the exception of '*en garde.*' That is surely understood by a man whose life was repeatedly threatened on account of this thing. As matters stand, I'd consider having you with me in the coming months a grace."

"Sam and I won't be away for long, Uncle Henry. Do you need something from me? Is that why I'm here?"

Abbot Henry looked him in the eye. "Just your presence now and then. My doctor tells me I have less than a year. I'm dying. Don't look so agog. Didn't I tell you departures are so common it's a wonder we mark them?"

That stomach-lurching feeling rose in Lyle yet again. This man had been more of a father than Lyle's own father and was still guiding him through rocky waters. This couldn't be possible, not so soon after Beatrice's death. But his uncle wouldn't make such an announcement if the case wasn't so. Lyle put an arm around the man so dear to him. "You're a scientist...*ratio*. Saving lives is what science does."

The abbot shook his head "Saving this life is beyond science. *In morte veritas*."

"Then, extending it. *Do not go gentle into that dark night*," Lyle said, fishing for Dylan Thomas's contrasting words.

Abbot Henry gave Lucia's ears a friendly scratch. "The poet's words are *'good night*,' and I'm not giving in."

"Then, what do you call it?"

"Living well. Each day that is given to me. And trusting. Seeing you and you your brother now and then on my Vesper days."

"How long have you known?" Lyle felt like a toppled turtle, aware but unable to do anything.

"Rather sudden. What the doctors call a routine check-up where they usually tell you that you shall live to a hundred."

"Are you comfortable?"

"As may be for a bloke my age. I should prefer to scamper like this curly-furred brown rascal once more before I go but shall settle for walks of this sort with dear friends. I love these grounds as Frodo and Sam loved their Shire. You wouldn't think loafing about this little plot of hills, beetles, and butterflies would give me glimpses of God, but so it does."

Lyle was reminded of the chore he had performed for Foy. "I filled matchboxes with beetles from Uganda, Israel, and Turkey," Lyle said. "Not a beetle in this world would put me in mind of God."

His uncle said, "We can have no butterfly until the caterpillar is transformed, but first it must participate in the transformation, though all it does is inch toward a branch, or curl up in a matchbox like your beetles."

A gentle rain was wetting their heads and hands, the low sky relieving its burden.

Lyle said, "You call that *participation?*"

"The inching may be long and tedious. Do I have what it takes to become a butterfly? An essential question."

"I've been asking essential questions too, and receiving no answers."

"Keep asking. Keep listening. Keep inching," Abbot Henry said, apparently oblivious to the rain, as water was running down his neck and beneath his robe.

At the monastery door, Lyle announced, "I won't be needing the manuscript, Uncle, and I'm sorry for the needles."

"Let not my illness inhibit our passionate conversations. That would grieve me, and deprive me of the bright spark that follows in your wake."

"Not anymore, I'm afraid," said Lyle.

APRIL 25–26, 2019

St. Hugh's Charterhouse

STILL WEARY FROM HIS TRAVELS, Lyle accepted his uncle's offer to spend another night at the monastery. Weary *and* apprehensive about going home with no Sam in the flat, having to do all the little things that felt overwhelming: shopping for groceries, preparing meals, tending to Lucia, not to mention his teaching and scholarship responsibilities.

Not long after supper, he went to his room and promptly fell asleep.

He awoke to chanting in the chapel down the corridor from his room, the Brothers' melodious voices gradually bringing him to consciousness.

Lyle had agreed to let Lucia spend her last night at the monastery with Brother Albert, so the mat next to Lyle's bed was empty. He felt forlorn enough that he would have retrieved her if he had known the location of Albert's cell.

These days, getting back to sleep after he'd been awakened by a dream, or anything else, could take hours. Oh, for the days when he could fall asleep soon after his head touched the pillow or before the plane left the runway.

Someone had tried to steal the manuscript again, but had been thwarted by Abbot Henry's underwater repository. Lyle didn't believe for a minute the thief, or the person who'd commissioned the theft, was unknown to him, so who knew a priceless artifact was kept here? Caroline Desrosier had learned where the manuscript had been kept from the thief, Noel Dekeyser, formerly a Brother here, and she must have suspected that Lyle had returned it to the monastery.

Andrea had been informed about the manuscript by Desrosier, had questioned Lyle about it two years previously. But he had witnessed how close-mouthed Desrosier was about Russell's obsession, so why would she have told Andrea any more than necessary to make trouble for him?

Arthur Russell had told Leonidas Romanov that the manuscript had been stolen from a monastery, but why would Russell have enlightened the Russian any more than needed to lure Lyle to the consulate?

The bishop and several monks knew about it. Had one of them communicated this knowledge, intentionally or inadvertently, to someone who was determined to obtain the book?

The manuscript had been unmolested from the time it was conveyed here by John Hill until two years before when Noel Dekeyser made off with it. So the person behind this most recent attempt must have been connected to the dead Dekeyser.

The termagant Desrosier was the key. She knew about it. She had enticed Dekeyser to steal it. She had been determined to deliver it to Russell, that grand master of manipulation, who was dead— wasn't he? Russell's death had been widely reported and Sam had confirmed it at the time, but could that man have faked his death because they were hemming him in? Arthur Russell—Arthur Alembert—certainly had the brains and guile for such a scheme.

Lyle had requested more time with the manuscript, that illuminated book of books, but what would he do if he had more time with it? Collaborating with Andrea or Agnese, what could non-linguists accomplish apart from admiring the art and speculating about the runes? As to the story his mother had read him, he strongly suspected the expert linguist's informed and imaginative insertions were prominent in the saga because that scholar had no comparative texts for this prehistoric language.

In the beginning, Lyle was convinced the book was a fraud. Two years later, the last word on this subject was much less certain. The boy hearing that wondrous story at his mother's side, the archaeologist steeped in a creed that ridiculed the notion of a prehistoric literary masterpiece, the realist rapturously examining the book in a Paris hotel room, and the man who knew the brilliant Arthur Russell—he now accepted its authenticity. He was still straddling the fence in some respects, however. Not a fraud, but how ancient, how historical was it?

Checking the clock on the table for the third or fourth time, Lyle admitted he was too restless to sleep, and so climbed out of bed and put on his dressing gown. He hadn't brought his house shoes, so he embarked in his bare feet. The chanting had ceased, and the corridor lamps were dialed back to points of light like a line of stars on the walls. He padded about for some time, eyes half open, hands in his gown pockets, his feet cold. All better, he reflected, than lying in bed with his mind running a mile a minute.

Using the wall for support, he slid down until he was seated on the floor. He'd fallen asleep in stranger places, the crook of a tree in Greece for one. He was almost asleep—this close—when he jerked upright. He must have heard something; not chanting, as he was too far from the chapel. He stood and looked up and down the hall, seeing nothing and hearing only silence. He was tempted to return to bed. Instead, he continued down the corridor, passing several closed doors and an alcove with a statue of a saint, those little stars guiding his steps.

At the junction of two entry area hallways, he glimpsed a robed brother taking the branch toward his uncle's office. Was insomnia affecting his uncle, or one of the other monks? But this person's movements were too fluid for the man to be his old uncle—so, someone else—a sleepless brother walking his rosary, or a breaching rabbit?

His uncle's office door was closed and the other person had disappeared. If Lyle had remembered what his uncle told him about the monastery invasion, he wouldn't have barged in, but he was a far cry from the rational, measured Lyle Stuart of a month previously.

The office window admitted enough moonlight that Lyle could make out the shapes of his uncle's desk and bookcase, and then of a person wearing monk's attire with strange-looking glasses on, crouching behind the desk in front of an open drawer.

Immediately aware of Lyle, the intruder bounded to his feet, the face behind the glasses inky black.

"Who are you?" demanded Lyle. "What are you doing here?"

"You!" was what he thought he heard. The person produced something from beneath his robe and a puff of some substance struck Lyle's face, burning his flesh and eyes as if they'd been set on fire.

In agony, Lyle dropped to his knees, covering his face with his hands, and wondering if he would be beaten or killed by his assailant while in this vulnerable state.

A bell clanged, in close proximity if not in the office, a hand bell by the sound of it—but whose hand rang it? Why would his attacker or a confederate draw attention to himself?

Silence fell again, with nary a stirring. *Don't rub your eyes*, he warned himself—easier said than done. How stupid he'd been to confront this person. Hadn't he learned that those who were after the manuscript would stop at nothing?

He raised his head and opened his eyes. They were still painful, but not the stinging pain he'd experienced in those first moments.

The office door and desk drawer were open. He stumbled to his feet and shuffled to the washroom at the front of the monastery. There, he bathed his face and eyes with cold water. The mirror revealed pink flesh and eyes, but no blemishes or any evidence of the disfigurement acid would have produced.

Even if he could clear his vision, searching for the intruder would compound his stupidity in entering the office. As far from the Brothers' cells as the office was, the bell wouldn't have been heard. Knowing Lyle would sound the alert once he'd recovered from the spray, the intruder would have made his escape as quickly as possible.

His eyesight still impaired, Lyle slowly traversed the corridors leading from the office to the cells, noticing a ribbon of light beneath a small door in the wall.

This time, he was more circumspect, but he couldn't make himself walk past without investigating. "Stubborn, both of us," Beatrice used to say. He turned the handle and flung the door open so hard it slammed against the wall, pale light bathing the hallway.

He stood still, a vice-like tensity gripping his neck and shoulders, his eyes still smarting. He heard nothing, and counted to thirty before peering into the room.

The light he had seen from the hallway was emitted by a bulb suspended from the ceiling, with a string to turn it on and off. A small storage closet, the room had shelves on the sides and back wall with cleaning supplies, work gloves and tools. Had the light been on when he'd passed on his way to his uncle's office? He didn't think so.

He reached for the string, seeing through cloudy eyes something like wet varnish on the doorframe—or were his eyes playing tricks on him?

The chapel was empty when he went in. He took a seat in the rear pew; he was better off sitting here than sleepless in his room. The sanctuary candle took him back to the Kampala cathedral. His heartbeat had almost returned to normal again, while his eyes were clearing, and his face was dry and drawn rather than painful.

Why hadn't his attacker eliminated the eyewitness rather than merely incapacitating him? Who had been ringing the bell? Who had the nerve to invade the monastery, or was the invader someone who knew the building and grounds well?

Frenetic travel, wearying sadness, sleeplessness, and now this attack.

The next thing he knew he was sitting on a log, his legs and feet in the water, surrounded by dozens of singing turtles, the tune making him so drowsy he was afraid he'd fall off his perch.

He opened his eyes to find robed men seated on his right and left, and light from the stained-glass windows coloring the room.

After Prime, Lyle tapped his uncle on the shoulder and asked if they could talk. When he related what had happened, Abbot Henry was reduced to wide-eyed amazement and vague murmurs.

Lyle said, "Let me know if anything was taken."

He wasn't sure his uncle had heard him. "I'll ask Brother Francis if he saw anyone on the grounds last night. He keeps odd hours, walks the grounds when he can't sleep. Perhaps the time has arrived to give it up."

"Give it up?" Lyle asked, not understanding his uncle.

"The book, dear boy. What good is my hiding place if these invasions persist? An attack on my son in this sanctuary of prayer? By God, I won't have it!"

FEBRUARY 24, 1990

German Democratic Republic
(29 years earlier)

"WHERE ARE YOU?" asked Sam.

"On my way home from Uncle Henry's. I stopped at Mum's grave. You won't believe what I saw. He's there, Sam!"

"Who's there?"

"Our father. Next to Mum. I saw the stone. Do you know anything about it?"

SAM REMEMBERED THAT DAY AS IF IT WERE YESTERDAY.

He'd been called into his section leader's office. "Sam, the foreign minister called me today."

What could that have to do with a field agent awaiting his next assignment?

"He wants to know if you'll accompany an East German agent to Leipzig."

Wants to know? Why not assign him—order him? Sam knew more was coming, so he waited.

"We made a trade, one of theirs for one of ours."

"When do I leave?" asked Sam.

"Tomorrow. You'll be accompanying a casket on the return trip."

134

"One of our boys?"

"Have a seat," the officer said.

Sam never sat until superiors were seated. "No thank you, sir."

"It's your father."

He steadied himself. "Yes, sir."

"Are you sure?" the officer said. "You don't have to go."

"Yessir, I'll go." If this was some kind of test, Sam wasn't about to fail.

"We couldn't think of a better honor guard, Sam."

"Are they sure it's him?"

"We're sure."

"Where was he?"

"A plot outside Leipzig. They exhumed him and put him in a new box."

Sam could feel the heat in his face. Stay on mission, he warned himself. "Who am I meeting in the GDR?"

"The East German assigned to the transfer is Johann Kasper, a Stasi colonel. Everything will happen at the military airfield. No fireworks. Sure you're up to it?"

"Yessir. Who's traveling with me?"

"Their spy, our pilot and copilot. That's all. One day, start to finish. No drama. Events are developing in a rush over there. Ever since the Wall came down some of their people are seeking goodwill with the West. Then, they have the Kasper types, up to their hips in the mire of the dying regime. I'm surprised he was chosen for the transfer."

"Maybe he volunteered," Sam said.

"If he volunteered, you had best be on your guard. Kasper's a bad actor. Remember, Sam, no drama."

"Yessir. Who's my cargo?"

"His name is Ronald Foster, a House of Parliament custodian. Been on the GDR's payroll for twenty-five years. Surprising what a custodian can uncover when too many of our MPs and their aides are incautious. I wish we were sending Foster back to the *old* GDR, would have served him right. Here's the mission—flight from our airfield to a military airport near Leipzig, deliver Foster, load casket, fuel up, and fly home. You won't be entering any buildings and they won't be entering the plane. None better than the Stasi at concealing bugs."

As they taxied down the runway, the small terminal came into view, also, a gray-metal barracks-like structure a quarter-mile behind it, and a hangar on the opposite side of the airport, all inside the security fence.

Sam and the traitor hadn't exchanged more than perfunctory words. The man appeared tranquil enough, but Sam suspected a lot was going on in his head—what kind of reception would he receive, what would his new life entail?

A dingy, drizzly day and a dingy site. Approaching the terminal, Sam saw six men, five in uniform, standing beneath an overhang at the building entrance. In front of the overhang, unprotected from the rain, a wooden casket sat on the tarmac. Adjacent to the box, an image of the GDR flag had been painted on pavement bordered by embedded lights, and a sign that said: *Der verkehr verboten*—entry prohibited.

An older man in a dark business suit and hat accompanied by a uniformed man hoisting an umbrella made his way to the plane.

Sam came off first, followed by Foster.

The Stasi colonel, Kasper, said to Foster, "One of my men shall escort you inside."

Sam barely heard the German, so enraged was he by the sight of his father's coffin exposed to the elements.

No drama.

"You may remove it and depart," said Kasper, a bulky, coarse-featured man, well over six feet tall, still virile looking though he had to be in his sixties—a grayish man whose aide was getting wet while not a drop found Kasper.

"I'll need several of your men," Sam said.

"They shall not lift a finger," Kasper answered in a cigarette voice rife with malice.

"Do you expect the three of us to load it?" asked Sam, darkening.

"Is your coming unprepared my fault? There it is. If you can load it, it's yours. If not..."

As a manifest identifying all the passengers had been submitted to the East Germans, Kasper knew who Sam was. He had no bargaining chips—not one, and he wasn't going to beg. Had something personal transpired between Kasper and Nestor Stuart, or did venom come naturally to this man?

Sam went inside the plane, returning to the tarmac with the pilot and copilot. At least they had hats, while Sam was bareheaded. By then, Kasper was beneath the overhang with the soldiers, and Foster had disappeared.

The copilot opened the storage space, then the three men pushed the casket to the door. All were drenched as the rain was coming down harder now.

Kasper and his men were enjoying the show—laughing and trading crude insults in German that the colonel didn't discourage, taking all of Sam's resolve not to fire back.

How were they to lift the casket inside the hold with just three sets of hands? The copilot had the idea to stand it upright, flip it against the opening, and push it up and in.

Sam heard Kasper's loud voice: "He will be in pieces when you are done with him."

Finally securing the hatch, Sam said to the pilots, "I have good news and bad news. The bad news is we won't be fueling here—the good news is we'll be unloading ballast."

The pilot said, "We won't go far without refueling."

"Then we'll have to stop in West Germany, or France."

"You know unscheduled fueling isn't allowed."

"I'm allowing it this time," Sam declared.

"On whose authority?" the pilot demanded.

"We're not fueling here, Geoff. And I want you to do something."

He didn't say a word to Kasper. The cabin door was secured, the plane's engines already warming up. A man in a fuel truck parked next to the plane shouted something at the cockpit.

"Ignore him," said Sam.

Instead of taking a straight-line route down the tarmac, the plane veered to the right, taxiing over the GDR flag.

"Now," Sam shouted. "Open it."

As the plane reached the center of the emblem, the pilot opened the latrine valve, the contents spilling on the image of the flag, splattering Kasper and his aide.

Down the tarmac and onto the runway they went, as swiftly as possible.

"They're instructing us to return to the terminal," said the pilot.

"Turn off the radio. Crack on, Geoff. They'll have to shoot us down."

"That's what worries me." The pilot was trying to light a cigarette but his hands weren't steady enough, so the copilot lit it for him.

Within minutes, they were buzzed and threatened by three MIGs.

Sam was more angry than frightened, still shaking with rage over the desecration of his father's remains, but not so enraged that he didn't remember the section leader's admonition of *no drama*. If they made it home, what would his chief say when he learned what had happened? Or would he learn? Kasper wouldn't admit to the humiliation, and the pilots who had participated, wholeheartedly or not, had no reason to reveal what had occurred on the tarmac.

He knew the men in the cockpit were under duress. He was glad he'd ordered them to turn off the radio. At moments, the MIGs were no more than a few feet away, the turbulence they produced rocking the British plane.

Wouldn't it be ironic if they came down the hard way, father in a wooden box, son in a metal one?

Just outside West German airspace, the MIGs peeled off with loud roars.

"We're almost out of fuel," said the pilot.

As for Sam, he had plenty of energy.

APRIL 27, 2019

☻-☻-☻

London

THERE IT WAS, an email from Foy with a 1936 article by an arthropodologist, listing Professor A. Alembert and A. CurLio as the discoverers of *Scolopendra letalis*, extracted by CurLio from the *Mammillaria Matude* cactus in Oaxaca, Mexico—Lyle's obsession with recovering the centipede entry in the lost diary satisfactorily concluded—like seeing his father's tombstone where it belonged.

A wet procession of rainstorms had soaked the city since midnight. After forgetting his Macintosh at home, only good fortune allowed Lyle to scamper from his car to the tearoom without a drenching. He hadn't said a word or asked any questions when Sam suggested they meet here, though he had his suspicions, as no alcohol was served.

Sam took a seat while Lyle read the email a second time. They were the only men in the Sweet Afton Tea Room on the Oxford side of London, surrounded by a dozen middle-aged women too busy with each other and their scones and jam to notice the two.

Lyle had ordered the pot of tea before Sam arrived. His brother was better groomed than he'd been in some time, with a new shirt and slacks, mown hair, and smooth face.

"That's not the proper way to lift a teacup," said Lyle.

140

Sam had other things on his mind. "I visited The Afghan Home. The coffee was as good as advertised. Too bad it's not open this early. Did you know birds evolved from dinosaurs?"

Lyle spoke without thinking, all too common these days. "Everyone knows that."

"Pardon my ignorance, Dr. Stuart. You're always telling me to broaden my horizons, and when I do, you queer me."

"Sorry, but why birds?"

"Why not? How much sense did that poodle make when you took her in?"

Lyle said, "Here's something I didn't know. Centipedes are arthropods. *Scolopendra letalis*, *Mammillaria Matude*, Oaxaca."

"The same to you!"

"The centipede I told you about in the pub before I smashed the window. It lives inside the *Mammillaria Matude* cactus in Oaxaca, Mexico."

"And that's important because?"

He liked having Sam on a line for a change. "The discoverers of the centipede were Adler Alembert and Agnes CurLio, the father and mother of Arthur Russell. One sting is deadly."

"Russell or the centipede? So, what did Henry want?"

"He wanted to mend me, but that's not how it turned out. Trouble, Sam."

"What kind of trouble?"

Lyle told his brother about the security system breach and where the container and manuscript were now concealed.

"I have to give the old buzzard his due in the mental department," said Sam. "That underwater scheme of his—no leaks you say?"

"That's not all. He's sick, Sam...cancer."

"How bad?"

"Bad."

Cup rattling against his saucer, Sam said, "I'll see him while you're with what's-his-name at the dig."

"He'd like that. He always asks about you. And you should know something else," said Lyle.

Sam's face hardened.

"I followed an intruder in the monastery. He attacked me with chemical spray, and escaped."

Sam examined Lyle's face. "I'd say you're the one who escaped. How the hell do I protect you when every time you're out of sight you do something stupid? Drive a man to drink. When did this happen?"

"Yesterday, after midnight."

"What possessed you to confront him…don't bother answering. You're an idiot. We established that a long time ago. What did Henry say when you told him?"

"Deeply troubled, can't protect his nephew in his own house— that sort of thing. He suggested disposing of the manuscript."

"Did you tell him you'd take it off his hands?"

"Listen Sam, something strange happened when we returned to England, but I didn't think it amounted to anything until Uncle Henry told me about the security breach, and after what happened to me in his office last night."

"I'm listening."

"When I went back to the flat, I noticed a book had been moved."

Sam erupted with a word that turned heads. "You lost Beatrice. You were jerked out of your job. You traveled to three countries in a week. You hadn't had a proper night's sleep in weeks, and you noticed a book had been moved?"

"I can explain. Beatrice gave me some books. I kept them side by side because they reminded me of her. The day before we left for Kampala, I remember standing in front of the shelves. They were exactly where they always were. When I returned, one had been placed on its side, on top of an adjacent stack. I conducted a search. Nothing was missing, as best I could tell."

"Who else has a key?"

"Just you. I think someone was looking for the manuscript, or clues to where it might be. Maybe the same person I found in our uncle's office. They moved books and misplaced one."

Sam thought for a moment, and said, "That doesn't surprise me after Beatrice, and then you being attacked. This person is deadly serious about putting his hands on the manuscript."

"So, what next?" Lyle asked his brother.

"We're going to Paris to see Desrosier and Lourdes."

Desrosier and Lourdes had worked together at the Sorbonne when Lyle was on the trail of the manuscript, and Lourdes was responsible for the Alembert Archive. "Do you think they're involved?"

"Nothing suggests it, other than what we already know about Desrosier."

"Have you contacted them?"

"We're going unannounced, and we're going in blind. This isn't like the old days when I could snap my fingers and have a dossier or a safe house in a few hours. When I call in favors, I have to be selective. I'm not ready to spend my goodwill chips yet."

"Why unannounced?" Lyle asked.

"I don't want her to have time to prepare, tie up loose ends. Lourdes may be able to tell us things about Desrosier we can't learn from anyone else, and if it turns out she was away from the Sorbonne when Beatrice was killed, I may cash in a chip or two. We know she has killed before, her own cousin, in fact, in cold blood."

"Maybe that was Russell's doing," said Lyle, lowering his voice to match Sam's quiet speech.

"The woman I interrogated after Russell died wasn't brainwashed, not traditional brainwashing anyway."

Lyle said, "Russell wasn't a traditional brainwasher. I don't want to waste time, and what makes you think they'll talk to us?"

"Lourdes has no reason not to, and Desrosier won't be able to resist lording her freedom over us." Sam grinned. "As for wasting time, yesterday I was summoned to an audience with the home minister."

Maybe Sam's luck was turning. "Are you assisting him with something?"

"Quite the contrary. Remember Jones in Istanbul? He convinced the station chief to lodge a complaint. I was cautioned about mucking in The Firm's business."

Lyle lifted the teapot, but Sam waved him off. "What did you tell the minister?"

"I listened and made polite noises, but if he thinks I'm going to let a tick like Jones derail us, he doesn't know your brother very well. When you're finished with Lido, you can meet me in Paris."

"I won't be long. Popa's closing up shop." Lyle had been thinking about one of his monkey-brained ideas that night in the monastery. "Could Russell be behind all this? Are you sure he's dead?"

Sam stared into his teacup. "I'm sure."

If the women were listening, Lyle saw no evidence of it, their voices a perfect cover so long as Lyle and Sam avoided any loud outbursts. "How sure?" he pressed.

"I saw the body. No disguising it was Russell."

"And you've settled on Desrosier because she was his protégée...or successor?"

"I haven't settled on anyone, except Malkin, and I don't think he's the prime mover, just the executioner. Speaking of Malkin, I wouldn't be surprised to learn he was behind the security system hacking at the monastery. The Mossad are experts at cyber warfare, and to hear Zvi tell it, Malkin learned the trade well. As for the assault, I can't see a man like Malkin leaving you alive, any more than Joseph and I let an enemy escape our cordon."

"Maybe the bell frightened him off," Lyle suggested.

Sam shook his head. "With you defenseless on the floor, Malkin wouldn't have needed more than a second to finish you off before he fled. You didn't see anyone else?"

"Not a soul. If we keep on with this, aren't we bound to run into Malkin, or Malkin into us?"

"That's the idea, isn't it?" Sam said.

"You told me you have no backup."

"Neither does he, according to Zvi and Genç." Sam lowered his voice further. "In the old days, we had a motto for every mission. I'm appropriating one from the Aussies. *Invenimus et Delimus*. That means *Find and Destroy*. I've been looking for an excuse to use it for years, but Downing Street always vetoed it. An advantage of being a free agent. I give myself permission. *Invenimus et Delimus*. I like the sound of that. Will Malkin have bums with him if he comes for us, will he bring confederates? I don't think so. That doesn't sound like the man Zvi described. He'll come alone, and he'll be prepared. So must we be. We might need one of Agnes's scorpions."

"Centipedes."

More than at any time he could remember, Lyle felt a synchronization of purpose with his brother, a destructive purpose, accomplishing what no other interest or affection had succeeded in doing. Why did this surprise him? Hadn't archaeology taught him that men banded together more often for destructive rather than creative enterprises?

Sam said, "I heard from Zvi. Fitzgerald's giving him a tour of the site. We know the old devil has an interest in archaeology. He also has an interest in handsome women. Why aren't you listening?"

"Henry, that's why. I can't believe he's sick." Ever since the long ordeal with his mother, Lyle had considered himself an expert at recognizing the cancer complexion. Thankfully, his uncle wasn't exhibiting that condition—yet.

Sam said, "We need to stay focused on the mission. That's the best medicine for a lot of things."

Lyle wasn't convinced, recalling how his uncle had pushed back when the abbot learned what Lyle and Sam were up to. "Does finding Malkin matter?"

Sam leaned in. "Take my word for it, it matters."

"Do you think he knows we're after him?"

Voices raised, the women rose from their seats, collected their bags and umbrellas, and made for the door.

"Horrible weather."

"May I give you a lift?"

"So he says, 'Can't say fairer than that.' Imagine the cheek!"

The door closing behind the women meant Lyle and Sam were the only remaining patrons, their waitress observing them from the kitchen door.

"Are you curious why we're here?" Sam asked him.

"Not particularly."

"It's not why you think. My earliest memory is Mum bringing me here for my first cup of tea, or cream and sugar with a dash of tea. She was wearing a summer dress that had red and yellow flowers on it. She was happy and laughing. We ate biscuits with blue glaze. It's my best memory of Mum."

"How old were you?"

Sam shrugged. "Just a tyke, but the memory took."

"What do you remember about our father?" Lyle asked.

"I remember that whatever he did, he gave his full attention."

Hadn't Lyle had this sense too when his father read the Greco-Roman myths and tales to him? He said, "I convinced myself I took up archaeology because of the story Mum read us but our father played his part as well with the myths and histories he read to me when he was home."

"Mum said, 'Boromir will be gone a while,' when he left on one of his business trips," Sam remarked.

"Did he love our mother?"

"As well as he could, I suppose. One night, I heard them arguing about children. Mum wanted another. He said—I can still hear his voice—'They need a father too, and I'm the wrong sort.'

"She said, 'You're a good father.' And he said, 'How can you be a good father when you're not here?' That was a few months before he went off and never came back."

"Then where did the gravestone come from?"

"How am I supposed to know?" asked Sam.

"You were there when I needed you," Lyle said.

"Are you kidding? I should have been, but in those days I was in Africa and the Middle East for long stretches."

"I remember your school visits. I couldn't wait to hear your stories."

"Henry's the one you should thank. He was your advocate with the school. I'll call him today. What's the prognosis?" wondered Sam.

"A year or less."

Sam spanked the table, rattling the cups. "While I'm at it, I'll interview him about the invasions. Every bit of information matters. At the bottom of a pond...He's a ripe one, always been. Doctors can be wrong."

"Like they were wrong about Mum?"

"She lived three years when they predicted one. Well, that day comes for all of us, but a damn shame about Henry."

PART III
Speculations

APRIL 29, 2019

Oxford

I N LOOSE-FITTING TROUSERS AND A PALE-GREEN BLOUSE, Agnese Leone looked drab by her colorful standards. "You've lost weight," she told Lyle.

"A few pounds," he admitted, though the scale suggested closer to twenty.

She dropped into Lyle's visitor seat, and said, "You and I must have dinner soon."

"I'd like that, Aggie."

"The Lawrence makes a liver plate I can't abide, but I know it's a favorite of yours. Fatten you up, my lad. Hmm, reminds me of an email from a woman at the Sorbonne who said a friend of hers wanted to surprise you with your favorite dish? I had to suggest liver. Not even *paté de foie gras*, ordinary calf's liver."

Lyle's mind immediately went from idle to hyperdrive. "Do you remember the woman's name and when she contacted you?"

"A few years ago. You were on the Continent at the time so her request made sense. French, as I recall."

"Does Des-Rose-E-A ring a bell?"

"Ding dong."

"Any further correspondence with her?"

"Not that I recall. Liver on a dinner plate isn't something I care to imagine." Agnese gave him a strange look. "I haven't seen you this excited in weeks. Are you up to some mischief? Oliver Marks said you visited him with your brother, a policeman."

She had a mind like a steel trap. What did she suspect?

"Sam's retired. Thought I could use some company on the trip."

"Marks said he asked a lot of questions about a midnight intruder."

"Professional curiosity, and keeping his brother's mind off his woes."

Agnese said, "I won't ask how you're doing, too soon for that. I'm available for a chat or silent company any time, day or night. I've been thinking about something, your algorithm, a work of genius, but even genius can be improved. Take a fresh look at it. Test a few outliers, Kemper's work at Çatalhöyük. I'm sure he'd cooperate. Algorithms and the like can be things of beauty, my boy, but the problem is overreliance on them to the exclusion of a critical eye, experience, whatever you want to call it. Without such checks and balances, we have rubbish in, rubbish out, for all the sophistication of the model."

"Of course, you're right," Lyle agreed. "The algorithm has been misapplied more than once. I'll think about it."

"Can I do anything for you?" Agnese asked him.

"I'll be on the Continent for a week. Would you mind taking on my PreCiv lectures?"

"Gladly. When do you depart?"

Lyle hadn't mentioned the trip had little to do with archaeology, and she hadn't asked. Or maybe she had asked in her own way, and taken the cue.

"Soon. I'll send you the syllabus."

Preparing to leave, she stopped in her tracks and stared past him. "Do you have a crack in your wall?" she said.

"I patched it but the crack came back."

Lyle received a knowing nod from his friend, who said, "That's because they didn't properly plaster the door."

She was up to something and he wasn't about to deny Agnese her sport. "What door might that be?"

"The door to the maids' alley," she responded with evident glee.

"We're on the third floor, Aggie."

She said, "There's a narrow hallway between these offices and the outside wall. In the nineteenth century that's how the maids serviced the offices without disturbing the sanctity of those learned men's work, like little mice coming in and out when the offices were unoccupied."

Andrea Fitzgerald looked over the older woman's shoulder, and said. "Lyle, would you pop in when you're free?"

After Andrea whisked away, Agnese said, "Her Majesty couldn't wait till we were finished?"

Well aware that Agnese and Andrea were fire and water, Lyle said, "You've seen this hallway?"

"The doors to the offices and the access door to the main hall were removed over a hundred years ago. I discovered old architectural drawings and took measurements to confirm the passageway. Archaeological sites are often under our very noses."

"Of course they are. A Roman road or a Celtic shrine could be beneath this building."

"That's conventional archaeology. What I'm talking about is *unconventional* archaeology. The proof is the window you can see from the yard. You can't look out of it because the passage is walled in."

She ambled to the back of Lyle's office and rapped on the wall. "A subculture once existed behind this wall, their tools, society, legends about the gods of Oxford."

"What's back there now?"

"How should I know?" She made a face dismissing the question. "When shall we dine?"

With Agnese as a companion, he could look forward to a stimulating evening keeping the ghosts at bay for a few hours, and he'd been yearning to sample The Lawrence's menu.

He followed her out and then walked to Andrea's office, a much tidier space than Agnese's. Never one to appear rumpled in public, Andrea had installed a wardrobe against the back wall and hung curtains on the window that faced the lab so she could change her clothes without leaving the office. Maybe Agnese had referred to Andrea as Her Majesty because she was attired today in a tailored blue and white pantsuit that couldn't be purchased at H&M.

"I won't keep you, Lyle. I'm leaving for Jericho tonight but I wanted a few words."

"You just returned," Lyle protested.

"I'm going back with the film crew. I'm heartbroken to have missed your visit to the site."

"I'm sorry I missed you too. I should have called ahead. We didn't have much time, but Marks showed us around."

"He informed me your brother was with you."

Recalling he'd told Andrea he was making the trip on his own, Lyle said, "At the last minute he insisted on coming, didn't trust me on my own."

"I wouldn't have worried so much if I'd known he'd come along," she said.

"I'm sorry I didn't tell you. Everything happened in a rush. After Kampala, Sam suggested a stop in Israel."

She gave him a wry look. "Your Israeli friend is a piece of work."

"He's Sam's friend. Don't blame anything he said or did on me."

"He didn't *do* anything. It's what he wanted to do that worried me. By the way, what *does* he do?"

"He's a policeman."

"Not the kind that gives traffic citations, I bet." She started to reach across the desk, changed her mind, and said, "Lyle, I'd like you to join me at the site. I'll give you a proper tour. We'll be filming for several weeks."

"Thanks, but I'm off to Lido."

He could tell she wasn't happy, and her next words reinforced that impression. "I thought Popa was wrapping things up. You saw what we're doing at Zeta2. It's now the premier world archaeological site and I want you to be part of it. How are you holding up?"

"As well as can be expected." He owed Andrea more than this, but what else could be said that wasn't self-deception or a lie?

"I'd say I'm here for you but we both know I'm away as often as I'm here. That doesn't mean I'm not thinking about you."

"People say I'll be myself again someday."

"Of course you will. Remember what I said about productive work."

"You're a special person, Andrea. I can't wait to see the BBC series."

"I'm lecturing today on Zeta2 before I leave."

"I hear they had to move you to the hall to accommodate the crowds."

She laughed. "Archaeology plus drama. I don't mean archaeology isn't dramatic but ours isn't the public's kind of drama. I'll send you the audio—yes, to entice you."

"You're doing what Sagan did with physics."

"What I care about is luring you to Zeta2, so if you change your mind you have a tent and a bed, a warm one. Can I say it any more plainly? Think about it, won't you?"

BACK IN HIS OWN OFFICE, Lyle pondered her offer. If he were to join Andrea at Zeta2, he'd have to act quickly. And why not join her? He had traveled to Kampala, Jerusalem, and Istanbul. He was supposed to meet Sam in Paris on a mission that would probably be a waste of time, or worse if his uncle were to be believed. Could he say they were any closer to resolving Beatrice's murder than when they'd embarked for Uganda? He recalled a restaurant in Corinth en route to the Pylos site, the *polis*, city, of the mythical Sisyphus. A wall-length fresco had depicted Sisyphus straining to push a huge boulder up a hill. Lyle had laughed at that tragi-comedic figure, the face especially, eyes bulging and tongue extended. Was that who he'd become, pushing the boulder of his anger and despair up an endless hill?

His phone beeped. Another interruption—no, just a reminder of his appointment with Danielle Nguyen that afternoon. Could he cancel at this late hour?

"I'm going, dammit," he said.

APRIL 29, 2019

Oxford

"THANK YOU FOR SEEING ME, DOCTOR NGUYEN."
The small woman across the desk from Lyle in whites and golds said, "Beatrice was my colleague, my friend."

"She respected you. That's why I'm here." Lyle could tell he sounded a lot calmer than he felt. The poodle was sitting next to him. "I appreciate your letting me bring Lucia. She's been with my uncle a lot since..."

"She's well behaved."

"The credit goes to William, her former owner. He died, and I took her on."

"Lucky you."

The room was spotless, dustless. "Poodles don't shed," he said.

"I know. What do you want to ask me?"

His hand went to Lucia's head. Putting what he was feeling into words was impossible. Every time he tried the words seemed empty. "How long will I feel like this?"

"Like what?"

"You can guess."

"I'd rather not," she said. "Take your time."

Why meet with her if he was going to hold back? "Bitterness. Rage. Cursing-out-loud anger. I threw a bottle through a pub window."

Her eyes widened. "When was that?"

"The day I learned. Twenty-three days ago."

"You're keeping track. You're angry at the person who killed her?"

"Why wouldn't I be?"

"Who else?"

He didn't need long to answer. "Her sisters, for making her return to Uganda."

"Cornelia wasn't to blame, was she?"

"She and her husband live in Kampala. They should have helped Maria and the baby."

Danielle Nguyen couldn't have been more than five feet tall, but her posture, the compact chair and desk, made her seem taller. "Didn't Beatrice tell you she was going because she had to?"

"Because of Maria and the baby."

"Did Beatrice do anything simply as she was expected to? Do you think she babied Maria?"

For a moment, Lyle was taken aback. "Not excessively. That wasn't her way."

"Who else are you angry with?"

Was this supposed to make him feel better? She was dead, and he was angry about it. "Do you think I'm angry at her?"

"If she hadn't made the choice to go to Uganda, she'd be alive."

"She didn't have to go."

"If she loved you, you mean. Loneliness and sadness are normal feelings so soon after her death. Anger too, but anger can be debilitating. You're an acclaimed scientist and a man of the world. You know what I mean."

He stood, walking behind the chair, using it to support a painful leg he suspected had as much to do with his state of mind as his leg.

"Why wouldn't I hate her killer?"

"I'm not concerned about that, and I'm not concerned that you're angry at her sisters."

"Then what?"

"Who else are you angry with?"

"No one I can think of. Isn't that enough?"

She wasn't recording anything. "Do you believe in God?"

"What does that have to do with it? No, I don't."

"Because you don't think God exists, or because you're angry at God?"

"I told you I don't believe in God. My father disappeared when I was eight, my mother died of cancer when I was thirteen. Now this."

"Who else could have saved Beatrice?"

"The police might have prevented it," Lyle said, but did he believe it?

"You're not angry at them, are you?"

He recalled sitting across a desk from Mutesi, that man of action, so different from this woman who mended minds. Lyle said, "I don't think so."

"Who might have saved her?"

Nothing distracted him in this office: no ticking clock, no music, no street sounds. He knew what she was getting at. He was sweating, as if he'd walked miles with Lucia. She was at his side, so close he could feel her against his leg. "I might have," he said quietly.

"You might have prevented her from going to Uganda. You might have prevented her murder if you had been with her. You might have been able to convince her to return to England."

"Yes, but I'm not God."

She gave him an affirming nod. "Lyle Stuart may be an inspired archaeologist and a good man, but he's not God. Whether you believe in God or not, you don't have divine powers. You're a fragile human being. Darkness uproots us."

"I can't help how I feel."

"You can affect how you feel, though, the volitional part. Cognitive awareness and willful acts can help. The mind is an ocean. It can be a place of wonder and delight, a place for hard rowing to a worthy destination, or it can be a realm of terrible storms."

"So I've learned."

"You have to remind yourself you're not to blame for Beatrice's death. Say that out loud, if it helps."

He sat again. His leg hurt. He'd told himself on his way across town that he wasn't here for emotional displays, but these days easier said than done. "I try not to think of her."

Lucia had propped her head on Lyle's leg.

"She can tell when you're distressed."

"Yes."

"Lucky you. I mean it."

"Lucky me."

"What have you been doing since Beatrice died?"

"Working."

"How's that going?"

"I used to love it. Now, working is hard."

"What else?"

What had consumed most of Lyle's days since her death? "Traveling."

"Alone?"

"With my brother."

"Is he a good companion?"

"He's a retired policeman." Should he say it? Wasn't that why he was here? "We're hunting Beatrice's killer."

He expected more of a reaction but all she said was "Where?"

"Kampala, Jerusalem, Istanbul."

She gave him a studied look. "How long do you plan to keep it up?"

"Till we catch him."

She tapped softly on the desk, the first action he'd seen from her. "Psychologically speaking, that's not therapeutic."

"I don't expect it to make me feel better."

"Then, why are you doing it?"

"Stay, Lucia. I don't know. Closure."

"Retribution won't do that either, even if you drive a stake through his heart."

Lyle straightened up and said, "You won't talk me out of it."

"I'm letting you know it won't heal your rage. Would you rather I pretended it would?" She gave him another long look, and then said in a sharper voice, "Does your brother know what he's doing?"

"Oh yes. And if I'm killed, it won't be much worse than it is now."

"Beatrice would be sad to hear you say that. If you must continue, try to make it about justice, not vengeance, hatred. If you honor her, you'll remember that. She wouldn't want to see you destroyed. I'd like for you to consider something, that you could have done nothing to change what happened to Beatrice."

"I don't believe that."

"I'm not insisting it's true. I'm saying it's possible, perhaps likely, that nothing you could have said or done would have prevented that bomb from killing her."

"You're taking away the little I have left."

"If all you have left is guilt, I can't take it away fast enough."

Lyle had been shattered into a thousand pieces, and she couldn't put those pieces back together. No one could—he'd been foolish to come here.

"Nothing you could have done. Her death wasn't your fault. You want it to be your fault because you want to believe you can prevent bad things from happening."

"You're wrong about that. I don't care about the future."

"Beatrice would want me to help you care. Do you have close friends?"

"Not like Beatrice."

"That means you had a true love. Other friends?"

"My brother, uncle, several colleagues. Lucia, when it comes to baring my soul."

"Bare your soul. You don't have to do it every day, but that's how it's supposed to be with friends."

"I'm going out of town. She's staying with my uncle."

Danielle said, "Excuses, excuses. Look for opportunities to be generous and act on them when you can. At some point, you must let her go."

This soft-spoken, relentless woman was boring into him like a carpenter's drill. "I *have* let her go," he insisted.

"There's letting go and letting go."

Lyle had never learned how to let go as normal people did. Hadn't his uncle suggested the same thing with the manuscript? He'd been turned inside out long enough. "Thank you for seeing me, Dr. Nguyen."

"Are you sleeping?"

"Sometimes. Not like I used to."

"I can prescribe a sleep aid, short term."

"I'll let you know."

She said, "You and Lucia are welcome to come back. Do you have any more questions?"

"I guess not," he said, but on his way to the door, he stopped in his tracks, and asked, "Am I salvageable?"

Her expression told him she liked this question; maybe she'd been waiting for it. "It's only been a month. With time, healthy interests, and inspiring work, certainly."

"How do you know?"

"The desire to be salvageable has to come from you, so I don't really know. But I do know that others who have suffered as you're suffering now were more than salvageable. They were repaired."

APRIL 30, 2019

Oxford

LYLE WAS STARING AT HIS COMPUTER when he heard a soft tapping at his closed office door.

On his computer screen was *An Algorithmic Approach to Migratory Patterns of Adriatic Zone Neolithic Pastoral Nomads*: Lyle Stuart, Cornel V. Popa, Josip Kruge, Eva Liss. Before Beatrice's death, Lyle had volunteered to draft the paper. Progress was now painfully slow.

"Come in," he said, though the moment he said it he wished he hadn't.

The man who entered was unknown to Lyle. His medium height, tousled dark hair, fair skin, and attire—neither Savile Row nor secondhand—said nothing about him.

Lucia bounded out of her office bed. Before Lyle knew it, her front paws were propped against the visitor's chest.

"Down, Lucia!" said Lyle. He grasped her collar and led her back to her cushion, muttering, "I'm sorry about that."

"Raphael Leary," said the visitor, extending a hand, an iron grip like many Lyle had experienced in the field.

This stranger had no appointment and had given no advance notice of his visit. "What can I do for you?" Lyle inquired, perfunctorily. "I'm engaged at the moment."

"I want to talk to you about Atalantë," said the man, who had

163

already presumed to take a seat.

A lyrical *Ata-lanta*—Atlantis? Thinking about Andrea's connection with the BBC, Lyle said, "Does this have something to do with television?"

"Nothing whatsoever," the man responded.

"I'm an archaeologist, not a fabulist. What leads you to believe I have any interest in that subject?"

"Someone I trust suggested as much."

"Your informant was mistaken. I have no interest in Atlantis."

"After what you have seen and experienced?"

What did this stranger know? To whom had he been speaking? After all Lyle had been through, how could his suspicions not be aroused?

"I don't know what this person told you, but I'm a serious scientist. Now, if you'll excuse me." Lyle bent his head and commenced writing on a notepad, hoping the man would take the cue.

On her bed, Lucia was sitting upright, quite alert.

"A wonderful animal," Leary said.

Still staring at the paper in front of him, Lyle said, "I think so too."

"How long have you had her?"

"Two years."

While Leary's eyes were trained on Lucia, Lyle tipped the phone on his desktop and snapped a picture of the man.

"Poodle, yes?"

"Is there something else, Mr. ...?"

"Leary."

Dropping his pen on the desk, Lyle said, "What do you do, Mr. Leary?"

"I'm well, thank you."

"I said *what* do you do?"

"I'm an antiquarian."

The man was as slippery as an eel. "What do you do for a *living*?"

"A variety of things," Leary said.

Bats of course, exactly what Lyle had feared. He'd met his share of crackpots haunting archaeological sites and had done his best to expel them as quickly as possible, indulging them being a never-ending enterprise.

"Are you familiar with Tolkien's myth?" the man asked.

Lyle did his best to conceal his surprise. What could be gained by answering, extending this foolery? Only satisfying his curiosity about this man and why he was here. "My mother read me the stories when I was young."

"What if I were to tell you they're true? That is, mostly true."

Did Leary know about the manuscript? Was he familiar with the story John Hill had related to Abbot Henry's predecessor? Ridiculous! Leary wouldn't be the first delusional fan of that dense mythology to have embraced it as truth.

"I've come to tell you about the part he got wrong."

"I'm afraid I'm too busy to hear it," Lyle said in the practiced tone he reserved for those he wanted to move along.

Leary said, "Listening will be worth your while, I assure you."

Decidedly, wasting time with this man would not be worth his while, but Beatrice's voice in Lyle's ear said being generous wouldn't cost him anything, just a few minutes of his afternoon.

Leary got up and closed the office door before taking his seat again, another worrying sign.

"Gortho was behind it all, but that's another tale. Tolkien's depiction of the destruction of Atalantë described two factions— those loyal to the latter-day kings, and the Friends of the Great Ones who remained faithful to the *ONE*. In point of fact, a third party existed. The Physical Philosophers Guild constructed a hall on a remote corner of the island where they experimented with time and space."

Good God, said Lyle to himself, so much for Beatrice's voice.

"When the waves and earthquakes battered Atalantë, the King's Men were destroyed, and many of the Friends escaped by sea. The Guild used the science they had mastered to transport their hall out of those dimensions. Thus, they were neither destroyed nor did they escape."

The best comic stories had a veneer of truth, and so did this one. Dare he risk making this man's thick agenda even thicker? "What happened to the Guild?" Lyle inquired.

"The Guild had several thousand members at the time of the cataclysm, about the same number as those who escaped by sea. Most Guild members managed to reach the hall before the waves descended and the island was overwhelmed. Though three-quarters of the land was lost to the sea, they survived the *Kataklusmós*, reestablished themselves on the portion of land that survived in this world's dimensions, and lived a desperate existence—for several hundred years—until they were able to rebuild."

Kataklusmós! Leary was the author of the nutter letter about Egyptian obelisks! Lyle stared at the man in amazement—a head full of bugs, as his advisor, Katravesis, used to say.

Leary pushed on. "As talented as they were, those Physical Philosophers were mortal. They died, but their descendants are alive and well."

If Lyle was an Atlantis skeptic, the idea that Atlanteans still roamed the Earth was as outrageous as discovering a live dinosaur. He was too stunned to interrupt.

"In the days of the cataclysm, Atalantëans were amazingly long lived, with Genesis-like lifespans, stronger and more virile than mainlanders. Even today, they live far longer than long-lived mainlanders."

Agnese was at his window pantomiming something.

"Is someone observing us?" asked Leary, without turning around.

"My colleague." He could invite her in, and had a suspicion if he did Leary would make himself scarce.

Agnese must have thought she'd delivered her message because she vanished from view. He could tell Leary she would be back in a moment, but instead, he said, "A few thousand survivors. Science tells us the gene pool would have been exhausted long ago."

"Indeed, Dr. Stuart, why they needed breeding stock—mainlanders—though this has shortened Atalantëan lifespans."

Lyle had to give it to Leary, or whatever his name was, the man was better than most at crossing t's and dotting i's. Or he'd been well trained.

Leary kept on. "An Atalantëan unites with a mainlander to produce a child from carefully chosen breeding stock. A rare event, only when absolutely necessary."

"Why do you refer to this breeding stock—to us—as mainlanders?"

"Because for all practical purposes, you are a different race, an inferior race, or so the Guild believes."

The *you* wasn't lost on Lyle. He had set out to get rid of this man. Now, he was determined to trip Leary up. He said, "How do they convey mainlanders to the island?"

"Through a door to the dimensions where they reside," said Leary. "You see, the entire island—what remains of it—was moved out of your dimensions several thousand years ago."

How convenient, invisible to satellites, planes, and ships. "Mainlanders selected as breeding stock become Atlanteans?" Lyle said.

"Nay. When their procreative function is complete—child producing for males, childbearing for females—they are eliminated. I told you this breeding program shortens lifespans—*contaminates* the gene pool—so only prescribed children may come from mainlander stock."

"You say Atlantis still exists in other dimensions, if I can use that term."

"As good as any," Leary agreed with an encouraging nod.

"May I ask how you know all this?"

"I happen to be one of them."

Predictable, and Lyle was ready for it. "I know plenty of main-landers stronger and smarter than you."

"You think so?" said the man on the other side of the desk. "I'm no Aragorn but I've kicked a few human orcs around in my time."

Whoever he was, like Arthur Russell, Leary exuded a presence that had nothing to do with his physical appearance or his words. Drawn in by the architecture of this man's illusion, or lie, Lyle said, "As you tell it, they're doing everything they can to conceal their existence, yet you're revealing their secrets to a complete stranger. Why are you telling *me* these things?"

"Because you know far more about Atalantë than is good for you."

Lyle immediately thought of Beatrice. If this man was connected to her murder, what would Sam say about running him off without learning as much as possible? In a split second, his attitude toward Leary flipped from ridding himself of the man to uncovering as much as he could.

"If they want to remain concealed, why didn't they prevent the publication of Tolkien's story?"

"Excellent question! That story represents the conventional view that Atalantë was destroyed in the cataclysm, that all survivors merged with mainlanders."

In happier times, Lyle might have heaped praises on Leary's fantastical simulacrum of Tolkien's story, but these weren't such times. He was having to work too hard to expose the man, and that frustrated him.

"The truth is, I'm a renegade," Leary said. "There aren't many of us. Most renegades desire to carve out empires in this world. As to why I came here, years ago I met someone who convinced me that my people are bankrupt when it comes to things that matter. Have you heard the name Alembert?"

Should he answer, or feign ignorance? Sam would surely be interested in what Leary had to say. "Perhaps I've heard the name."

"That would be the renegade's grandson, Adler. His grandfather was one of us, until he bolted to establish the criminal empire Adler inherited. Few have gone renegade for reasons akin to mine, to lift rather than rule mainlanders. Long ago, in your reckoning, one of us came as the Friends of the Great Ones came in ages past, to teach mainlanders to use power for good. His name was El-Arcturus, and he was killed for his trouble. Mainlanders call him Arthur."

"That's quite clever," Lyle said.

"History is occasionally clever. In the years preceding the *Kataklusmós*, thousands upon thousands of years ago, the King's Men saw mainland primitives as fodder for exploitation, but the Friends, mindful of the nurturing they had received when Atalantë was young, assisted mainlanders until the king prevented them. Meanwhile, the Guild advanced its science while pretending to be unworldly fools."

Lyle couldn't help himself. "What you are telling me defies science, reason."

"Yet twentieth century science gave us the astounding fact that time and space are not absolutes, but dependent dimensions. At one time, men couldn't comprehend atomic energy, much less liberate it."

Still trying to trip up this nimble-minded man, Lyle said, "Before this dimensional sleight of hand, Atlantis was an island in the middle of the Atlantic Ocean?"

"Yes, as the world was then. I don't have to tell an archaeologist the advantages of living on a large island near the equator in that era."

Leary was implying they were protected from the ice age that dominated much of the latter third of the Paleolithic Period, a time that had hindered the development of mainland tribes.

"You said they sometimes interfered with mainland societies."

For the first time, Lyle thought he detected reticence. "My people think of mainlanders as bees to be domesticated, useful when needed for procreation, but intruding in a more deliberate way when a mainland empire becomes too powerful, pitting drone against drone, queen against queen. They prefer political and social turmoil. Have you heard of the Roman general Varus?"

"I suppose he was one of your people," said Lyle.

"On the contrary, two Atalantëans were sent to organize the Germanic tribes, luring Varus's legions into a death trap, with twenty-thousand casualties. Afterward, Augustus Caesar obsessed over protecting rather than expanding Rome's borders. A textbook case of manipulation when I was in school."

"Tell me how your people traveled from an island in other dimensions to a German forest."

Leary looked over his shoulder at Lyle's office window before he said, "A doorway is the most convenient means, or they construct one as they did in that forest, applying a thin line of constraining plasma to the interior of the portal frame to focus the conveying force. They used science that's quite advanced compared to mainland science, though your work with quantum mechanics, dark matter, and the like is closing the gap."

Their conversation about Alembert prompted Lyle to ask, "What do you know about Rosman?"

Leary's eyes widened. "I know something."

"Tell me about him."

"One of us. I have reason to believe she pressed Tolkien and his friend Lewis long and hard. She's still about I hear."

So, Leary had Rosman's gender correct. "Those men have been dead a long time. She'd be in her hundreds."

"Precisely." Leary's expression was that of a magician who'd produced a rabbit from the hat of someone in the audience.

Lyle said, "You admit your story is fantastic."

"I do, by your lights."

"You admit you offer no evidence."

"What do you call that illuminated *biblio*, if not evidence?" Leary countered. "And you'll find suggestive threads in the historical record if you examine them in the right light."

Lyle was testing Leary as he would a gifted student he suspected of bluffing his way through an exam, probing for the weakest column or beam in the student's architecture, applying greater and greater loads until the edifice toppled. He said, "The cataclysm was a Malthusian collapse?"

"My time is running short, and we ought to be talking about the *biblio*. Neither the Guild nor I believe Atalantë fell because of overpopulation, wars, ecological excess, major disease vectors, any of the Malthusian factors, but we differ as to the true cause. They attribute the *Kataklusmós* to a Vesuvian type of event, the island volcano erupting in concert with volcanoes in the ocean, submerging the land beneath massive waves. I believe what was recorded in the *biblio*—that the destruction of the island was precipitated by a full-scale assault on the Great Ones by the last Atalantëan king. *The Straight Way* was a dimensional path the Great Ones had made accessible to men. After the *Kataklusmós*, the path was barred."

What would Sam want him to ask? "Have you heard of Beatrice Adams?"

A moment's hesitation before Leary answered. "What I heard I was sorry to hear."

Lyle required all of his resolve to say, "Do you know why she was murdered?"

The sneaky Lucia had crept over to Leary's chair and was lying at his feet.

"You won't like my answer. If the person you call Rosman was involved, you had best divorce yourself from the book."

"Turn it over to you, you mean."

"You'd be safer, and I'd be in no more danger than I already am."

"How have you managed to elude them?" Lyle asked, still trying to confound the man.

"Confinement in these dimensions is misery for most of them. Over a century of your time, Rosman may not have resided here for more than a few decades. And she had the bad fortune to come up against some of the most clearheaded and resolute men of the past century."

"Why do you care what happens to me?" Lyle probed.

"Why did El-Arcturus care about his people? I read a story about a spider that saved the life of a pig. If you'll pardon the comparison, perhaps I can be that spider to you. Stay clear of the book and I'll do what I can."

Leary stood. The voice in Lyle's ear was Sam's now. *Detain him, keep him talking.*

"How can I get in touch with you?"

"You can't. And don't try to find me. Salutations, and farewell."

How quickly Leary bolted out of the room! No more than a handful of seconds had elapsed while Lyle pondered what to do. "Stay, Lucia," he said, making for the lab exit door.

Did Leary sense what Lyle was up to? Did he fear Lyle had managed to sound an alarm? Looking down the hallway in both directions, he saw no one. Leary hadn't wasted a minute. How could the man have gotten to the elevator or stairs so quickly? Lyle's mind was spinning with what he'd been told. Was *anything* Leary said true? Could this man have been Malkin on a reconnaissance mission? If he'd had this suspicion earlier, Lyle could never have summoned the composure to engage Leary as he had.

He jogged back to his office and called Sam. After Lyle related as much of what Leary had told him as he could remember, Sam said, "A tactic so common in my business we were coached by psychologists how to recognize it, how to react."

"Common to spin mad fantasies and expect them to be taken seriously?"

"Are you going to listen, or aren't you? The primary narrative is something the teller doesn't expect the listener to believe. The storyteller is conditioning the listener for the secondary narrative, who put the teller up to this, and why?"

Lyle said, "I wondered if he was Malkin."

"So do I. I received a description of Malkin from Zvi. Describe Leary."

When Lyle complied, Sam said, "Nothing contradicts physical factors that can't be altered."

"A disguise?" said Lyle. "BBC drama stuff?"

"I knew a Yank who could transform American agents in Moscow from buttoned-down businessmen to old women in shawls—convincingly, in less than a minute. You can bet this has something to do with our investigation of Beatrice's death, or the book, maybe both.

"Your motive for listening doesn't matter. He needed time to deliver the primary narrative so he could embed the secondary narrative in your psyche. That's what we were told, to prevent us from succumbing to the secondary narrative. Fortunately, you had me to alert you. Otherwise, you might have made a beeline for the book and he wouldn't have been far behind. A sophisticated murder and a psych op. Russia, China? He may return. He'll want something next time, and it will be connected to the book."

In came Agnese, leading Lucia back to her bed, kissing her on the nose before reminding Lyle of their dinner and then exiting. As preoccupied with Leary and Sam as he was, Lyle hadn't noticed that Lucia had gone wandering.

"Sorry, lost dog" he said to his brother. "I took Leary's photograph when he wasn't paying attention. Anything else I should do?"

"Nothing you aren't already doing, keeping your eyes open and your mouth shut about what we're up to. Send me the photo. If I could, I'd talk you out of Lido."

"You can't, so don't try. A day with Popa, then I'll meet you in Paris."

"You'd better," Sam grudgingly acquiesced. "I don't need a lost brother."

MAY 2, 2019

Oxford

L YLE WAS PREPARING A SANDWICH from his meager pantry when the visitor alert sounded. The halting voice at the other end said, "Jeremy Conway," sounding like a schoolboy when the teacher takes attendance.

Jeremy was a middle-aged Down's man with an elderly and crippled mother whom Lyle and Beatrice had met in Mont-Saint Michel, an amphibious town on the coast of France. Could Lyle handle Jeremy today? But he couldn't very well turn the man away, no matter how he felt.

Lyle pressed the intercom button, and said, "When the door sounds, open it and come in. I'm on the third floor, Flat 33."

No response. Lyle thought a minute. "Jeremy, I'm coming down to get you."

On his way to the door, he passed the letter from Zvi Eitan on the foyer table:

Dear Doctor Stuart:

The Zeta2 site is everything you promised.
The cenotaph lifts ones heart to the heavens.

Eitan

Lyle hadn't seen any cenotaphs—monuments—at Zeta2. Had the Israeli confused his sites?

Hair neatly combed, a pack strapped to his back, Jeremy looked grayer and more stooped than Lyle remembered.

Before Lyle could say anything, Jeremy extended a hand. "I'm sorry about Miss Beatrice."

Since Lyle hadn't informed Jeremy of her death, how had he found out?

"I rode the bus to say I'm sorry."

"How did you learn about Beatrice?"

"Sam," said Jeremy, repressing a smile.

Lyle had looked in on Jeremy shortly after Sam was sacked, having convinced his brother to motor about southern England for a few days. To his surprise, Sam had hit it off with Jeremy. "Come upstairs," Lyle said. "You must be hungry after that long ride. We'll have something to eat."

Lyle had three days until his trip to Lido and plenty of work to do in the meantime, but he had no intention of hurrying Jeremy, not after this man had ridden the bus all morning to express his condolences. He recalled Danielle's advice: *Look for opportunities to be generous, and act on them when you can.*

"You have a nice house," said Jeremy. "Can I say hello to Lucy?"

He'd missed her by a few hours. Brother Albert, who helped out at the Oxford Oratory Church of St. Aloysius Gonzaga, had picked her up in the monastery's Volkswagen.

On several occasions, Lyle had included pictures of Lucia with letters he'd sent Jeremy. "She's staying with my uncle for a bit. He has a big yard where she can run and play. Sam and I are going away."

Jeremy said, "Is Sam here?"

"Not at the moment. He lives in London."

"I know. Mr. Cuddy gave me money for the bus."

Lyle had never met Cuddy, but according to Jeremy, the man was a friend of his with a propensity for finding trouble. "Last time I saw you, he was in jail."

"He's home now. Being good."

"How about a cucumber sandwich and a pear?" suggested Lyle, making for the kitchen. "Did you like the postcards?"

Raising his hand and counting fingers, Jeremy said, "Kam-Pa-La, then Jeru-Slem, then...ah...In-Stan-Ball... Mum helped with that one. Then Jeri-Ko. No. Jeri-Ko, then In-Stan-Ball. I put them on the door."

One cucumber and one pear. He'd have to make do. "How did you get here from the bus station?"

"Walked."

A long walk. Lyle was glad the weather was good, but was surprised Catherine had let Jeremy come by himself.

"Here," Jeremy said, handing Lyle an envelope. "Open it."

Lyle put the knife down and removed a religious card from the envelope.

"Priest is going to pray for Miss Beatrice."

"Tell your mum thanks."

"Oh, she doesn't know. I never told her about Miss Beatrice, Mum being so low."

"Then, thank *you*, Jeremy. Here's your sandwich and pear. Tell me about your mum?"

They made their way to the table, where Jeremy removed his backpack.

The sandwich halfway to his mouth, Jeremy stopped, and said, "Hospital lady comes to help."

"Every day?" asked Lyle, apprehensively.

Jeremy nodded. "Mum can't go out anymore."

He had to strain to hear Jeremy's soft voice. "Are you sure your mum said you could come to Oxford?"

A shrug of the shoulders meant Jeremy had probably schemed this trip with Cuddy, so Lyle moved on. "How is Loretta?"

"Good."

"Are you still riding the bus to see her?"

"Thursdays."

"Do you want to call your mum and tell her you're here?"

Jeremy thought for a while, taking a bite of his sandwich while he deliberated.

"Better not," he said.

"Today is Thursday. Maybe she thinks you're with Loretta."

Jeremy grinned at Lyle. "Bus leaves at four."

"When you ride the bus to see Loretta, when do you come home?"

"Dinner time."

"But you won't arrive in Salisbury until seven or eight. Won't your mum be worried?"

The look on Jeremy's face proved he hadn't done the travel math.

"Can your mum still make dinner?"

"Sometimes I do. What are you teaching?"

Jeremy wasn't keen on the subject of his sick mother, and who could blame him, especially as she didn't know he was here. "Buried cities," said Lyle.

That caught Jeremy's attention. "Who buried them?"

"They're so old they sunk into the ground and dirt covered them up."

"Are people in those cities?" the wide-eyed man asked.

"Not living people. Skeletons, tombs."

"Ever found a..." He screwed up his face. "Mummy?"

"Several."

"I saw one on the telly."

The bell alerted Lyle that someone else was in the lobby. He wasn't expecting anyone—a delivery?

"Just a moment, Jeremy... Yes?"

"This is Harold."

Harold? No colleague by that name. Then he remembered the wizened man with the walker, the man whose name he kept forgetting who took five minutes to walk from the side door of the senior apartments to the front door.

"Harold Binker. May I come up?"

Jeremy was gazing around the room and still working on his sandwich and pear slices. "Do you want me to come down?" Lyle said.

"No need. I'll be right up, if you don't mind."

Now what? "A man who lives across the street is coming up," he said to Jeremy.

"Is he your friend?"

Lyle was embarrassed to admit Harold was barely an acquaintance. At the knock, Jeremy trotted to the door, stretching out his hand before Harold could come inside.

"I'm Jeremy Conway."

"How do you do? Harold Binker," said the man, in a falsetto voice.

The old man's face was hard to see when he was moving because he was bent over like a praying mantis. Pushing his walker to the side, he took the straight-backed chair Lyle offered him at the table.

Head now erect, puffed out by his labors but jolly enough, Binker displayed small features and penetrating eyes. "Do you live hereabouts?" he asked Jeremy.

"My mum and me live in Salisbury. I rode the bus to say I'm sorry about Miss Beatrice and to see Lucy."

"Well, what do you know? I came to see Lucia too."

Par for the course: two visitors who had come to see his dog.

"Is something wrong with your lady friend?" Harold asked Lyle.

"Died," said Jeremy, relieving Lyle of the need to say it again.

"My deepest sympathies, Professor. William and I shared a few words with her. A fine lady. I'll let the others know, if you don't mind."

More people ringing the bell? "I'd rather not have any fuss," Lyle said.

"No one will bother you. We old nags keep to our lanes."

Lyle had gotten good at moving off that topic. "Lucia's not here. I'm leaving town, so she's lodging with my uncle."

Looking crestfallen, the old fellow said, "I see you walking her but you move too fast for me. William would be cheered to hear how you two are getting on."

"And surprised," said Lyle.

"Hardly. Near the end, he said you'd take her."

"Me? We never spoke about it."

"Told me, 'She'll go with the Professor. I'm not worried about her.'"

What a story. At Harold's age, maybe something he'd imagined was converted into a memory. Lyle had heard of such things.

"An interesting bit of art on your wall, Professor," Harold said.

"It's a map of tribal reaches ten-thousand years ago, different colors for different tribes, the deeper colors near the tribal centers and the lighter shades at nomadic limits." Lyle had brought the map out from under its glass on more than one occasion to modify tribal borders with colors as closely matching the print as he could find.

Harold said, "An elegant depiction. Note the pen-and-ink relief lines."

"I have a girlfriend. Loretta," said Jeremy.

"In Salisbury?" Harold inquired.

"Southampton. With her aunt. I ride the bus. Loretta sends me letters."

Lyle said, "Harold, can I make you a sandwich?"

"Don't trouble yourself. I have lunch waiting at home. The gang's expecting me."

"Where do you work?" Jeremy asked Harold.

Turning his body wasn't easy, but Harold did his best to face the person addressing him. "I don't go to work anymore. After the war, I was at the National Gallery for forty-two years, cleaning up the paintings when they got dirty."

"My mum used to paint pictures. Gave me paint and brushes."

"What do you draw?"

"Animals. Send them to Loretta."

"You sent me one too," Lyle said, not remembering where he'd stashed it.

"Does your mum still paint?" Harold asked.

Jeremy frowned and shook his head. "Did you have a gun at the war?"

This was the first time Lyle had seen distress on Harold's features and his high-pitched voice went even higher. "You better believe it. We came in on the beach guns a'blazin'. Awful business."

"Did people get killed?" Jeremy asked loudly.

"Too many, sad to say. Friends, comrades."

"Sorry, Mr. Binker."

Harold put a hand on Jeremy's shoulder. "Why don't you call me Jimmy? That's what my comrades called me. Harold James Binker, and in those days I preferred Jimmy."

"You were at Normandy," Lyle said.

"I was."

"Do you have the gun?" Jeremy asked.

"They made us give them back when we were finished with them. I was glad to."

"Then you cleaned the pictures."

"That's right. Forty-two years. We worked in a little room off the visitors hall." Harold's face, sagging with age, had a faraway look. "Plenty of light, perfect for restoring pictures. Before we went to work, the curator examined the painting and gave us instructions. We solved mysteries, discovered secrets. We worked on the Wilton Diptych from the Middle Ages! How time flew when I was working on a painting. How good I felt to see it fresh again, back in its gallery. The pictures that passed through my hands...my, oh my.

"Ever heard of a Brough?" he asked Jeremy.

Jeremy shook his head. Something stirred in Lyle's memory.

"An old motorbike I bought when I came home from the war," Harold told them. When I rode in the rain, I was reminded of being soaked in the war, so I sold her."

That was it—an entry in Agnes CurLio's diary where she had recorded a visit from a man named Thomas who rode a Brough.

"You married?" asked Jeremy.

"Almost, once," Harold replied.

"How old are you...Jimmy?"

"I'm ninety. Proud to be." He smiled broadly. "Better be getting back. I'll look for Lucia before I cross the street again. Pleased to meet you, Jeremy. Pleasure to see you again, Professor. So sorry about..."

"Can I post you a letter?" asked Jeremy, retrieving a pen from his backpack.

"I'd look kindly on that, but only if I can send you some."

"Yes, please! Write down your street number," said Jeremy, pushing a notepad to Harold.

Harold once again exhibited that broad smile. "I bet Loretta's a sweetheart."

"Yes, she is. How do you know?"

"Because I know *you*, and you wouldn't have a girl who wasn't a sweetheart. Or you, Professor."

Harold was up on his walker, creeping toward the door, when Lyle said, "How did William know about Lucia and me?"

Harold abbreviated the tedious effort of turning around. "Because she preferred you. That's what William said. When she saw you, she'd tug at her leash. That's how he knew. If you'll get the door, I can see myself out."

Normandy, the National Gallery, William's premonition, Harold's and Jeremy's élan sparked Lyle. Jeremy said, "I like Jimmy. Did you know your brother is a spy?"

Lyle was still pondering what Harold had said about William Horrigan. "Who told you that?"

"Sam did, when you were with Mum." Jeremy ate as slowly as he walked. He was still working on the sandwich.

"Do you like pie?" Lyle asked him.

"What kind?"

"Peach."

"I like apple best."

"Sorry, no apple pie. Can I cut you a piece?"

"Yes, please. When it's three o'clock, I'm going to walk to the bus station, so I don't miss the bus."

Jeremy would be late and Catherine would fret, maybe go without supper. Lyle said, "I have a better idea. We'll go home in the Spider."

"What's that?" Jeremy shouted.

"A sports car," Lyle said. "We'll put the roof down. The Spider goes faster than the bus and it's more fun. When we arrive in Salisbury, we'll pick up dinner and some things for your mum."

Jeremy's globular face radiated joy. "Yes! Yes! Where does Lucy sleep?"

"On a dog bed in my room."

"I like dogs. We can't have one because Mum is old."

"I'll pick you up sometime so you can visit Lucia."

"Really, Lyle?"

"Really. As soon as I get back from Europe with Sam."

Jeremy soon had piecrust on his chin and a huge smile on his face. "He's a spy. Has a gun too."

LYLE ARRIVED HOME after midnight, automatically checking his postbox. After Cornelia's letter, retrieving mail felt like putting his hand in a den of vipers.

Going well beyond the call of duty with Jeremy and Catherine, he ought to have felt good about himself, but the long ride home had sunk him. Every day seemed to be an emotional war.

How was he going to help Jeremy and Catherine when he couldn't help himself?

"You won a *battle*," her voice said.

He'd try to win one tomorrow too. "I don't remember a cenotaph," he said.

MAY 3, 2019

☉-☉-☉

Oxford

"WE'RE GOING TO HAVE FUN, whether you like it or not," proclaimed Agnese Leone.

The Lawrence was an intimate fifteen-table restaurant with a tentish décor, complete with wall drapes, hanging lanterns, and Arabic scents and music. As it happened, Agnese was sympathetically attired in a tent-like frock speckled with leaping frogs of many hues.

Lyle wondered if she would initiate the conversation with a eulogy to Beatrice, but after they were seated and ordered drinks, she merely said, "What's cooking at Lido?"

"Popa's wrapping things up."

"Grand grand archaeology, Lyle." In so many words, what Marks had said.

"Means a lot coming from you, Aggie."

"And next?"

"Maybe I'll pick up where old Lefebvre left off, expound an archaeological heresy."

Her eyes lit up, meaning an eruption was imminent. "What they did to Lucas Lefebvre was criminal. The lot who disagreed should have said so, and furnished evidence. Witch burners— and a man of his stature. I told a few of those scoundrels so to their faces."

Her defense of Lefebvre wasn't the first time he'd witnessed her priestly devotion to fair play, often at the expense of her own reputation. "That's why you're so popular," he said, with a smile.

A doyenne of thalassocracies, specializing in Phoenician and Minoan maritime civilizations, Agnese was currently investigating a site near Cadiz, on the south coast of Spain. She didn't publish much, wasn't a sought-after interview or speaker, didn't seek the limelight—and her raiment provoked snickers and raised eyebrows. But when she produced something, the work was meticulously researched and reasoned. Her students loved her, as did Lyle, who had recognized her authenticity soon after they'd met.

Brushing breadcrumbs off her sleeve, she said, "Bought this dress in Cadiz from a street vendor. The fool almost gave it away."

He'd give that subject a wide berth. "Cadiz is hot in June."

"You don't have to tell me. Another round, my dear," she said to the waitress. "We'll be rubbing shoulders with anthropologists from the states."

"Human remains?" he asked her.

"Enough to interest Berro. She sent me a note promising to play nice."

He gave her a skeptical look. "I'm sure you'll play nice too."

"We were there first," she said with that penetrating look of hers. "I won't have her flapping around like a vampire. Berro has a reputation."

"So do you, Aggie, but I love you anyway." As to *flapping around*, he didn't mention the weasely-looking creature Agnese kept, an animal she'd befriended in Spain, said to be from North Africa. On one occasion, she'd brought it to a lecture hall, letting it perch on her shoulders like a shawl.

Agnese said, "Have you thought about my suggestion for the algorithm, diving back into the formulas and stretching them?"

"I have, but I haven't made up my mind." Though the subject of the algorithm had been in Lyle's thoughts.

On anyone else, Agnese's dress would have appeared

ostentatious, if not ridiculous, but if Lyle detected eyes and shaded smiles directed at his companion, he knew that Agnese, as unselfconscious as she was, was oblivious to the room's mirthful attention. But should the game get out of hand, he told himself, they'd have him to answer to.

"Have you been to Bilbao?" he inquired.

"About ten years ago we were on the north coast. Spare pickings but we came away with a few amphorae for storing Tyrian purple." Holding up a silver-plated saltshaker, she said, "In those times, Tyrian purple traded for one hundred times its weight in Iberian silver ore. Why are you interested in Bilbao?"

"Your work in Spain reminds me of a diary kept by a woman who took refuge there in 1931. Someone was hunting her. They caught up with her a year later and killed her."

Agnese jerked to attention. "You don't say so. Reading a woman's diary can be a dangerous occupation unless you're certain they're dead, and even then it's bad form. Bilbao was a vastly different place then, or so our local guide told me. The river is a high rent region now but it used to be an industrial drain. The destitute lived along the river in those days because of the pollution, bad smells, dung beetles, and the like."

Dung beetles? Lyle said, "By any chance do you know Foy in Entomology?"

That sly grin of hers told him everything he needed to know—his creative schemer. She knew he couldn't turn down a request from a fellow Oxonian and she knew beetles could be found everywhere. The question was, how many matchboxes could be foisted on him.

"How's that hound of yours?" she asked, assuredly to change the subject.

"Lucia's well, thank you, and with my uncle until I return from the Continent."

The waitress at Agnese's shoulder prompted her to ask him if he was ready to order.

"No surprise," Lyle told his companion, then addressing the waitress, he added, "liver and whatever the chef serves with it."

"Have you spoken to Dawson lately?" she asked him once the waitress had left, referring to their department head.

"He's kept his distance since Beatrice."

Dawson rarely brought good news, but he was excellent at surrounding his messages with agreeable words so the message in between—the words that mattered—didn't alarm the hearer until they'd sunk in, by which time Dawson had gone to ground.

Agnese said, "How about a wager on how long he takes to mention her name? A pound to keep it sweet? I say a month."

"You don't think much of our fearless leader," Lyle remarked.

She made a disparaging sound.

All of the tables in the small room were filled, only a few feet separating the two of them from the nearest diners. That didn't faze Agnese. "Rumor about says that Fitzgerald has set her sights on you."

He laughed softly. "Is that bad?"

Gazing into her empty glass, Agnese said, "What cobras do before they strike."

"She's been kind to me, Aggie."

"Don't let your grief or glands get the better of your brain."

Agnese was one of the best eggs he knew, but everyone had their blind spots. He had changed, so why couldn't Andrea? If anyone should have been reluctant to forgive that tornadic archaeologist he would be the one, after her harsh words two years before. Besides, he hadn't spent any time with her, nor was such likely, considering their schedules.

Agnese surprised him when she didn't launch another broadside at Andrea. "I think we are sufficiently aglow for the story I promised to tell you about the old secretary desk in my office. Sir Max left it behind when he retired. Then came Smythe-Bonet who had it for years before I happened into it. You know how I can't resist digging and a few months ago I found something remarkable inside it."

"You found something after all these years...decades?"

Their food arrived, and Agnese took one look at Lyle's dinner plate, saying, "I'd rather eat a bowl of worms, but don't mind me. The desk—I found a secret compartment. Not so rare with old secretary desks, a decorative filler piece between filing nooks. With your fingers exactly so"—she dropped her fork on the plate with a loud clank and pantomimed the action—"the piece can be pulled out to reveal a small *cachette*.

"Hidden inside was a letter to Max from a fellow named Carlton, dated April 15, 1931, posted from Jerusalem. Same year as your diary, imagine that. Max was a working archaeologist in those days. Carlton mentioned a gathering involving Sir Max, Agatha—yes, that detective novelist—and a man he refers to as Thomas. The four discussed a creepy character by name of Alembert."

Lyle had never spoken to her about Alembert. She even pronounced the name properly. How could this be a coincidence?

"How does the liver measure up?" she asked him.

He was taking his time with the food. He wasn't about to let Alembert spoil his meal. "Quite good. Your eggplant?"

"Predictably satisfying. Care for another tipple?"

"Might as well, if you're game. What did Carlton have to say?"

"Well, here it is. See what you make of it. I don't want you influenced by my interpretation. I couldn't resist holding on to the letter. I'm devoted to Agatha's stories, have a first edition of *Murder in Mesopotamia*. There she was with those three men somewhere in the Middle East. She loved archaeology and mysteries. This letter concealed in a secret compartment is a ninety-year-old mystery."

"Is it a cipher?"

"You shall see for yourself. You look a bit gray."

Though Alembert and his son were dead, Leary had talked about him, and now Agnese. Not a day had passed without Lyle wondering about Leary, who he really was, and why he had engaged Lyle—the secondary narrative Sam had warned him about. Why not see what Agnese thought about it? In spite of her slapdash manner, he trusted her judgment. He said, "One good story deserves another. I met a man who claims tribal ancestors of our most ancient civilizations had commerce with Atlanteans."

She snorted. "That tops my *cachette* story. Is he an archaeologist?"

"Not credentialed. A gilded amateur."

"Then he need not worry about the opprobrium that was heaped on Lucas. How many times did you trip him up?"

Loath to admit that *nutter*, or worse, had sidestepped all his mines, Lyle took his time answering her. "He had a nimble mind and a surprising depth of archaeological knowledge," he said, then relating some of the most preposterous things Leary had told him.

"Except for the dimensional mumbo-jumbo, his story corresponds to Tolkien's myth," Agnese observed. "He knew about your attraction to the story."

The question was, how did Agnese know about Lyle's attachment to the myth, since Lyle had been careful not to discuss the story with his colleagues.

Dessert arrived with fresh drinks. "Just tuck in," she instructed him. Agnese wasted little time herself. "What is this fellow up to, I wonder?"

He told her about Leary's linking Atlantean coastal towers and far-seeing stones to Egyptian obelisks and oracle stones. He'd been keeping his voice low but it hardly mattered, as they might have been invisible to the festive crowd.

"He *is* good," she said. "What did you say he called himself?"

"Raphael Leary. How did you know about my interest in Tolkien's story?"

"I've read it, and a little bird told me about your mother's fascination with the story."

Beatrice! That also explained Agnese's knowledge of Alembert. Of course, those two would have hit it off after he'd introduced them in the days when Beatrice was in Oxford. He wanted to tell her about the manuscript, how it had been stolen and recovered, Alembert *pere et fils*. He trusted her. Surely, such a spirited defender of Lefebvre would give him a fair hearing.

"I...uh..."

"You've hardly touched your pudding. The blueberries are to die for."

"I..." He bowed his head.

"We don't have to talk about her tonight. We're having fun, remember? Have you considered a memorial?"

He hadn't, though his uncle had informed him they were offering Masses for her.

She dusted her sleeve again, despite the crumbs being long gone. "Goodness knows my kids are always strapped for one thing or another."

Her confession about helping to care for and educate a throng of poor children was the closest she had ever come to bringing him into her philanthropy. "Amazing work you're doing," he said to her.

"Do you think so?" she asked, her eyes suddenly wet. "I'll tell you something no one at the university knows, would ever guess. When I was quite young, I had a baby girl. I was something of a goer in those days, you see. All hush-hush. A family friend had moved to the States, wanted a child but was unable. We arranged a private adoption, and I handed her off at Gatwick. I'd named her Elizabeth...never learned what name they gave her. She was thirty-nine in February. I think about her every day."

The table next to theirs erupted into several verses of *Mademoiselle from Armentières*, each *hinky-dinky parlez-vous* sung with particular gusto. Lyle waited for them to finish and the clapping to subside before he said, "I'm sure you did the right thing, Aggie."

"So I've told myself. Doing the right thing can be damned miserable. So you see, under the circumstances, my *kids* are more than philanthropy."

"Elizabeth found a good home and you're mothering a big brood."

She looked into her empty glass. "I've been wanting to tell someone for a long time, someone who understands loss. I go on with as much cheer as I can muster, and so must you. We need Lyle Stuart *mussin' up his white tie* again."

Lyle recalled the Fred Astaire lyric from *Top Hat*.

At the end of her pronouncement, Aggie stood. "Kindly lend me the favor of your arm, Dr. Stuart. I'm a bit tipsy."

HE HAD TO READ THE LETTER BEFORE HE WENT TO BED.

April 15, 1931

Dear Max,

You have met my friend, Drake, as he likes to be called. Bit of a bull in a china shop but good instincts and an iron backbone. He and some others have been kicking around the notion of recruiting Alembert to eliminate H, ER, and GS. Setting one pack of jackals against another. Drake claims he can make it worth Alembert's while. If His Majesty's Government makes direct contact, and Alembert declines and informs H's crowd a nasty howling will ensue. Thus, an intermediary like Thomas is essential, especially if Alembert trusts him. Both Agatha and Thomas being in the literary line, might she broach the subject with him? In the form of—shall we say—a literary inspiration?

Cordially yours,
Carlton

MAY 4, 2019

Oxford

THE DAY BEFORE HIS TRIP TO LIDO, Lyle was pacing the flat, circling each room.

"What a feat...solid archaeology." "Grand grand archaeology." How Marks and Agnese had described Lyle's accomplishments. So why did he feel so conflicted about his work? The easy answer was Beatrice's death, how it had dragged him down and sapped his curiosity and vigor. But what if her murder had turned a mirror on *him*?

Agnese's confession about her daughter provided another mirror, how she'd been tortured by it all these years. She was prodding him to reexamine the algorithm that had made him famous in the archaeological community, the map on his wall that had attracted Harold Binker, his exploration of the Nis Neanderthals that propelled him from obscurity to worldwide recognition, scholarly articles, a glowing piece in *National Geographic* and a *Time* magazine sidebar.

He had taken the Nis publicity in stride, not being overwhelmed by the notoriety, but like Agnese, he had consigned something to the shadows, hadn't he?

Since those heady *NatGeo* and *Time* days, he'd been searching for something Nis-like when Lido came along quite by chance, like a champion racehorse offered to a sidelined jockey. Popa had reached out to him, a perfect fit for the algorithm and in Popa an archaeologist who shunned attention and honors. As for Lyle, though he didn't chase honors, he didn't turn away from them either.

He knew what he'd consigned to the shadows, in the beginning having rationalized his ownership of the algorithm over and over until he believed it.

When Katravesis invited him to assist with the algorithm, Lyle had realized that the tense meeting with the university examiners, when Katravesis had referred to Lyle as an "intellectual minnow," had been consciously calculated to arouse Lyle to take his studies more seriously, as he had done after that summit. Less than a year later, Lyle's graduate advisor had introduced the idea of the algorithm to Lyle, and they had worked together on the groundbreaking concept, first developing the model then testing it on Katravesis's and other data-rich research.

One day, a spirited discussion about when to announce the algorithm and with how much fanfare, the next morning Katravesis dead from a massive heart attack.

With Lyle sworn to secrecy, and no one but Lyle aware of the project, he had considered what to do. Wasn't he an equal partner, even a co-inventor? He'd been troubled by this reasoning but the more he assessed his role—the significant refinements he'd made before and after Katravesis's death, the tedious data testing he had conducted, the hours he'd invested that far exceeded Katravesis's labor—the more convinced he was that the algorithm was at least as much his as his advisor's, and with Katravesis gone, wasn't it his exclusive property?

He remembered the day and where he was when he'd accepted this logic, a country ride in that battered Fiat on June 13th, the queen's birthday, three months after Katravesis's death, how relieved he'd felt when he returned to the car park after dark.

Something Danielle said had sparked the kindling of his memory. "Who else are you angry with?" Did his years-long disparagement of Katravesis, the cold caricature of the man he had manufactured, have as much to do with his claiming the algorithm as it did with his advisor? Katravesis had trusted Lyle, and Lyle alone, and even if the teacher would garner most of the acclaim, Lyle would have shone in Katravesis's reflected glory.

And how many years had gone by since he'd resolved this question to the degree that he could now use the algorithm without any unease? Why was it surfacing now, like a corpse from the bottom of a lake?

"We all rest on the shoulders of others," Lyle said out loud, more or less as Newton had said in regard to his own discoveries.

Not good enough. Lyle had used the algorithm at Nis and the algorithm was the only reason for his involvement at Lido.

"It's settled," he muttered.

Could he sit here all night with Katravesis's ghost prowling the flat? His bag was packed and standing against the wall. The matter was decided when he heated up an egg roll in the microwave, practically burning his tongue off with the first bite and spitting it into the drain.

He drove the Spider from one end of town to the other, settling on a block favored by his single colleagues and entering the first bar he saw, the place empty except for a trio of earnest young men in the corner. As for the establishment itself, if he'd seen the inside before he entered, he wouldn't have, but he didn't have the energy to keep searching.

He took a seat at the bar, figuring he might as well have a drink and a sandwich for his trouble.

"Bourbon, neat," he said to the bartender, a burly man with dark eyes and a bushy moustache.

He was examining the bottles of spirits behind the bar when a voice said, "Mind if I join you?"

Her lips parted in a playful smile. He guessed she was about twenty, wearing a black-leather skirt and lavender blouse that revealed the margins of a lace bra. Though the post earrings she wore were costume, they looked good on her.

"Holly," she said. "You don't mind?"

This time he noticed the accent.

"Be my guest," he said.

She crossed one leg over the over, hiking her skirt several inches, showing off attractive legs. "What's your name?"

"Lyle...Stuart." She hadn't provided a surname, but she'd drawn one out of him.

Her scent was subtle, expensive. As if on cue, the bartender strolled over.

"Pink gin," she said to the man, and as he stepped away, she said to Lyle, "You live in town?"

"An archaeologist at the university."

"Lovely." She smiled.

Her arrival out of nowhere, her forward friendliness, the bartender at the ready...but so what? She opened her purse, removing a compact, looking into the little mirror. A photograph fell to the floor. Automatically, he reached down to retrieve it, observing the face of a young boy.

Snatching the photo from his hand, she said, "My brother."

Their drinks arrived. The picture and compact back in her purse, she lifted the glass to her mouth and drank half the contents.

She wasn't timid about looking him in the eye. Not until then had he realized how well made-up her eyes were—feathery lashes, carefully drawn brows, golden auroras at the corners.

"Archaeologists dig things up, don't they?"

"I've been on expeditions in Eastern Europe, Greece, Turkey, Russia, the Middle East."

"Lovely...Lyle." Without warning, she reached over and straightened his collar, so naturally he wondered if she realized she'd done it.

"What do you do?" he asked her.

"Modeling. Mind if I have another?"

He needed a few seconds to realize she was talking about the drink.

"Have you found anything special?" she asked.

"Just the oldest book in the world."

"That's funny."

She traded glasses with the bartender. "I'd love to hear more. I don't live far from here, just around the corner."

There was the pitch. Though she was pretty, he had a hard time believing she was a model. On closer inspection, she was nearer thirty than twenty. When she lifted the glass to her lips, she reminded him of something—a film clip of a famous actress coming off the stage after a demanding performance, how her face and frame had sagged with fatigue.

She put a hand on top of his, the second glass already consumed.

How much of what she'd told him was true hardly mattered. He had plenty of money, and he wasn't so muddled as to believe money wasn't her motivation—though he might play along with the fiction that she was genuinely interested in him. After what he'd been through, who could blame him?

Uncle Henry didn't know Lyle as well as he thought. Reverting to the man he'd once been would be easy.

"Ready?" she asked. If what he suspected was happening, wouldn't she want to move things along? Wasn't that the genius of the most capable practitioners of her trade?

He finished his drink and paid the bartender. The woman was holding Lyle's hand again. The street was busier than when he'd arrived, and Lyle was afraid that someone he knew would recognize him. In the light of day, what was going on here wouldn't be much in doubt.

Holly was waiting for him to answer her. Too apprehensive about being seen with her to listen to what she had whispered in his ear, he'd nonetheless smelled the gin on her breath. An amount—a number—might have been mentioned.

She was a well-traveled stranger, he with no protection. But the threat barely registered. Just before they turned the corner, however, Lyle noticed the ancient oak in the middle of the city park where he and Beatrice had picnicked on their second date. The two of them had tried to guess the age of the tree, speculating about what the town had been like when the oak was a sapling.

"Across the street," she said, pointing at one of the row houses.

He wasn't a bad person. Neither was Holly. Just lost.

"I'm sooo happy we met, Lyle."

Why not an hour with this girl? Who would it hurt? He'd have his hour and she'd have her money.

He reached into his pocket and put a fifty-pound note in her hand. "For that brother of yours." With a sigh that was a combination of relief and regret, he nodded an adieu.

On the way to his car, knocked off stride by the near thing with Holly, Lyle felt Katravesis's ghost return full force. He could run but he couldn't hide, not from a ghost. Revealing his advisor's role in the algorithm wouldn't do anything for the man because he was dead. Only Lyle would be affected by the disclosure, and how couldn't be predicted.

LYLE HAD ALL NIGHT and a mind to put the car roof down and find a country road, but instead, he drove to Olives Delicatessen on High Street, miraculously finding a space in front of the green façade.

He left the deli with a tray of sandwiches and a relish tray, delivering them to the front desk attendant at the Waterloo Creek Apartments.

"Jimmy...I mean Harold Binker can share these with his neighbors," Lyle said, turning to the door.

The woman who had looked tired and bored when he walked in called to his back, "Harold's in the game room with the others. Why not bring them in yourself, Professor? They'll enjoy seeing you."

Professor? He'd only traded words with a few of these people and one of them, Lucia's former master, had died.

"Would you care for a sandwich?" he said to the woman.

"I'm meeting a friend later," she replied, pointing to a half-open door down a dim and narrow corridor.

What he'd expected when the Olives inspiration came to him was an easy act of charity that wouldn't cost him much in either money or time. How long would he need to extricate himself from these people?

A tray in each hand, Lyle pushed the door open with his shoe and took in the room, which was bigger and brighter than he'd expected. A billiard table and card table sat at one end with a dart board on the wall opposite the door. A table full of people stared in his direction.

"Professor!" Harold's childlike voice called out.

He'd expected old but he hadn't expected this. "Let me set these trays down, and I'll be on my way," Lyle said.

"These look like Olives trays," observed a man wearing all black, including a black cowboy hat. "Very kind of you, sir."

"You know Olives?" Lyle asked the man, who'd either recently traveled or spent time under a sunlamp.

"We're old, but we don't have bars on our windows."

"I didn't mean…"

"Crewe says whatever strikes him," a short-haired, ancient woman at the head of the table told Lyle.

A tiny bright-eyed woman motioned him to an empty chair between her and the ancient one.

"I'm traveling to the Continent tomorrow," Lyle said. "I can't stay long."

Another cowboy-hatted fellow sat at the table, a white hat across from the black-hatted Crewe. White Hat said, "You can't run off without proper thanks. The vino, Marvin."

Black Hat and White Hat were contrasting specimens in more than the color of their headwear. Crewe was short with a wide, whiskered face like a cat. White Hat was big boned with a long, furrowed face.

Lyle looked to Harold, who shrugged and said, "This gang introduces themselves. We won't keep you long."

"Let me pour you a glass of wine," boomed a bent-over giant sitting next to the bright-eyed woman.

"No...really." But an empty glass appeared out of nowhere, was filled and placed in front of Lyle.

As the bent-over man filled other glasses, Lyle gave the room a second going-over. Prominent were the chipped paint, chipped tables, chipped wooden floor with no rugs, the billiard table fabric split in several places, the window past the billiard table looking out on a garden of colorful flowers.

The bent-over giant extended a hand, deftly avoiding the woman and two full wine glasses. "I'm Marvin, and this beautiful woman is my wife, Millie. Our vino may not be up to college standards, but it's potable." He cawed like a crow at his observation.

"You're a good neighbor," said a soft voice across the table from Lyle, a round-faced man wearing a black bowler hat with a colorful feather in the band, a powder-blue coat with yellow pocket-handkerchief and bow tie. A cane hung from his chair. How did this man know Lyle was a good neighbor when they hadn't spoken a word to each other?

Wait! Lyle had seen this pear-shaped fellow from his window ambling up and down the sidewalk, cane tapping the pavement, sometimes half-an-hour of pacing until a car pulled up and the man ducked into the rear seat.

"My friends call me Joey," the man said. "You took in Lucia after William died. I see you walking her."

The ancient woman, wearing a faded blue and rose dress, said, "I'm Ruth, been here the longest, some say too long. William used to talk about you. We miss him, but we're happy Lucia's with you... all the long walks and such, her preening up and down the street."

Was that enough to make him a good neighbor?

"Made William walk her in the rain, that poodle did," said Marvin. "Had his hands full keeping up with her. Hah!"

"So I've learned for myself," Lyle said.

Crewe raised a hand to speak. Harold caught Lyle's eye and put a finger to his lips. All the others were grinning, even Joey.

There once was a hound from Manchester
That no one presumed to pester
She stood on a corner
And bayed at all comers
Till thunder and lightning repressed her.

"Makes them up in the moment," Millie whispered to Lyle.

"Please eat," Lyle said.

Hands were extended, trays passed around, and a bottle topped off his wine glass. Between Holly and this crowd, he'd be pickled.

"We heard about your girl," White Hat said. "Deeply sorry."

By their expressions, evidently White Hat spoke for all of them: the ancient one, Joey, Harold, Crewe, Marvin and Millie, and the so-far-silent woman on the window side of the table whose eyes were pinned on Lyle. He said, "She was a psychology lecturer." Could he say more? "She went home to Uganda to take care of her sister. A bomb blew her up less than a month ago."

No comforting words were expressed by the gang, just sad looks, Millie's small hand enveloped by Marvin's. Lyle asked her, "How many years have you been married?"

"One year and ten days," Millie said.

"A glorious year," added Marvin.

Millie spoke. "When our children were young, we lived on the same street. Then, Harry and I moved away, our children grew up, Harry and Betty died. One day, I received a letter from Marvin. We corresponded by post for a year, then we spoke on the phone for six months, then we met for dinner in Dover where I was living. When we decided to marry, I came to Oxford. The house was too big for me, for both of us at our ages."

"She cleaned things up when she moved in," Marvin said. "Out with the old."

"Do you miss the house?" Harold asked her.

"At times—so many beautiful memories—but that's over."

"I had forty-two wonderful years at the gallery," Harold said.

"And the theater," the ancient woman said. "Designing all those sets, watching from the wings, watching them acting against my props and property."

"Tell the Professor, Ruth," Millie said. "Please!"

Ruth waved her off.

"Please! It's so exciting."

Ruth's eyes quickened. "Olivier once sought me out. He told me I had 'a genius for wood and plaster atmosphere.' Those were his words."

"Laurence Olivier?" Lyle said, impressed despite himself.

"A few words in the wings. We weren't friends. Don't think that. We did a production of *Busman's Holiday*. No, *Busman's Honeymoon*. On rehearsal day, I sat in the front row with Dorothy Sayers. She wore the most elegant green beret, a lovely woman. What an eye for set pieces she had."

"When would that have been?" asked Harold.

"Let's see—the early fifties. She died near Christmas fifty-seven. I remember because...well, I remember."

They were eating and enjoying Olives fare. With one baguette left over Lyle took it. He was famished.

The black-hatted Crewe said to White Hat, "Benson, I'm going to take you down tonight."

"Both of them dart champions in their day," whispered Ruth.

"Ever been inside Waterloo before, Professor?" asked Crewe.

"Not until today."

"The Last Stop Lodge," Crewe said.

"Don't!" said the woman to Crewe's left. She wore a dark-blue scarf with tiny flakes of gold. She also had an accent. German?

Crewe said, "He should be prepared for what's coming, Irma."

Irma pointed a finger with a blood-red nail at Crewe. "I was prepared a long time ago. I don't need to be reminded."

Crewe said to Lyle, "The Last Stop Lodge if you're lucky. We can stay at Waterloo so long as we can do for ourselves. If you can't do for yourself, you're out, on a slow carrousel to extinction."

"In God's hands," Ruth said.

"God didn't seem to mind when I lost everything in town, when those crooks stripped me bare," Crewe said, loudly.

"What do you teach, Professor?" Millie cut in.

Lyle said, "Archeology...paleo-archaeology, tribes before recorded history."

"Like Atlantis," Joey said.

"Not like Atlantis," Crewe countered. "That's a fable, a made-up story. He studies cavemen."

"Is Atlantis made-up, Professor?" asked Joey. "I have a picture book about Atlantis."

"A made-up story," Crewe said. "Pure fiction."

"Joey, your people are coming soon," Ruth said.

"Is it time?"

"It is."

"You're a good neighbor," Joey said, rising from his chair, tipping his hat, and exiting the room.

Harold said, "A long time ago, someone knocked Joey on the head with a piece of pipe. He soldiers on but the blow didn't do him any good."

"How do you *know*?" Irma said.

Lyle thought the question was meant for Harold, but Irma was looking at him.

More about Atlantis? "How do I know what?"

"How do you know she was killed?"

How do you know she was killed? Irma was talking about Beatrice. He could feel resentment rising.

"That's enough, Irma," Ruth said.

Lyle said, "The police told me. They confirmed it."

"The *police*," Irma said, scornfully. Everyone was looking at her. Irma abruptly stood, and said, "Thank you for the food, Professor. I must go now."

She was barely out the door when Benson whispered, "Irma's a suspicious girl, her childhood in Austria with the Nazis, and then those damn Russians. Doesn't trust the police, can't help herself." His hand and forefinger turned into an imaginary pistol. "Bang bang," he said.

"Thank you for being gentle with her," Millie said to Lyle. "I didn't think I could be happy again after Harry. Marvin felt much the same when Betty died. You can be happy too."

"So people say," Lyle answered.

"This little garden can't hold a candle to my house garden," Millie said. "But I have more time to observe buds emerging, changing colors, the rhythm of the growing months."

"She's the gardener and I'm the pack mule," Marvin explained. "Compost, trellis, rock borders, whatever she likes. I used to be a builder. You should see what I've hauled on this back."

Turning to Ruth, Lyle said, "Tell Irma I took no offense, won't you?"

"I'll tell her."

"I will accompany you to the door." Harold labored to his feet.

Lyle raised a hand. "No need. I can see myself out."

Harold already had a hand on his walker. "A demonstration that I can still do for myself."

Passing the entry desk, now occupied by a different woman, Harold waved briskly at her, and winked at Lyle.

Looking out the glass, Lyle was surprised it was already dark. He'd been with them longer than he would have guessed.

"What did you think of the gang?" Harold asked him.

"You ought to be on the stage."

"At our age, we have plenty of time to think and observe—not always clearly, mind you. At the tolling of any hour from midnight to five a.m., I daresay half of us are wide awake, in our beds, in a chair, sipping tea or something else, looking out the window, watching the telly."

Lyle said, "Where did those cowboy hats come from?"

"Benson and Crewe are rivals for past glories, and both are sweet on Irma, though that she-falcon wouldn't roost anywhere near those two. Benson came from Texas decades ago, adopted a British accent but wouldn't part with his hat. One night, we all watched a Western film and Benson went on about it like a school-boy. A week later, Crewe started wearing that black hat. Benson never said a word about it in my hearing. Must have been five years ago, and the hats are so natural now we don't notice unless someone asks. I guess Crewe enjoys his hat as much as Benson does. As for Irma, she has a good heart and sparkling wit, until the old memories drag her down."

Lyle said, "When did she leave Austria?"

"After the war sometime, when she was old enough to decide for herself. She's almost ninety but looks fifteen years younger. We added up the gang's ages. We're going to have a party when we top seven hundred."

When, or *if*? Lyle thought.

A humorous expression suffused Harold's features, as though the old man could read Lyle's mind. "I hope your trip is successful, Professor."

Lyle wasn't sure what success meant anymore. "Call me Lyle. I live across the street, so when I return, let me join the gang and we'll have that party."

MAY 6, 2019

Bosnia-Herzegovina

O NCE OUTSIDE SARAJEVO, Lyle navigated two-lane winding roads toward the Adriatic Sea, following the Neretva River valley, a frequent pathway for ancient pastoral nomadic tribes. As he drove west, he watched the Sarajevo haze dissipate, portending a pleasant day.

John Coltrane's *A Love Supreme* was the first jazz Lyle had listened to since he received the message that changed everything. He'd chosen Coltrane because it wasn't the kind of straight-ahead jazz she had favored, or tolerated because she knew how much he loved it. If Coltrane's doleful saxophone brought back memories of his former life, he forced himself to persevere to the last note, the music reminding him that even the greatest jazz performers relied on sidemen. That's what he was, Sam's sideman, complementing his brother's investigative music.

He passed through Konjic, a valley town on the swift Neretva surrounded by tall green hills and mountains. On the other side of the town, he had to lean on his brakes to avoid a fox crossing the road, using the close call as an opportunity to pull off the road, rest for a bit, and let his mind wander.

Talking to Danielle, dinner with Agnese at The Lawrence, and his time with the Waterloo Creek Apartments gang made him wonder if he had crossed a small bridge. His students deserved his best effort. Sam, his uncle, and Jeremy needed him. Lucia deserved a better master than he'd been of late. He could hear Agnese Leone's voice clear as day. "We need Lyle Stuart *mussin' up his white tie* again." Though he couldn't imagine that, for the first time he glimpsed a way out of the storm.

Prior to leaving town for the airport, Lyle had motored to Boars Hill in the Spider Lusso, looking down on a lambent Oxford in all its splendor—domes, spires, walls, gates, everything he could see from the peak—trying to recapture something of the love he'd once had for the university and his work.

He now put the rental car in drive but kept his foot on the brake. He hadn't allowed himself to entertain the possibility that the manuscript Leary had called the *illuminated biblio*—damn his eyes!—was anything more than an extremely ancient collection of legends, a remarkably valuable artifact but hardly true history. To go further was to cross a wider bridge, and he could no more expect counsel from Sam on this subject than Sam could expect his help with the nitty-gritty of an op.

Only Andrea, Agnese, or Cornel, archaeological scholars and close confidantes, could help Lyle, and only face to face. He was wary of broaching the subject with Andrea, though, for fear such a conversation might dredge up that hot argument they'd had. He'd lost courage with Aggie at the last moment. Now, he had an opportunity with Cornel Popa. Posing his questions might be humiliating, but if the manuscript was something more than he was willing to admit, and if it was connected to Beatrice's death as Sam suspected, humiliation was a small price to pay. He would talk to Cornel if his courage held out.

That word—*courage*. Although he respected and admired Agnese Leone, deep down Lyle wasn't convinced he could abide the ridicule that had been directed at Lefebvre, and to a lesser extent at Agnese. He hadn't recognized this deeply rooted attachment to his reputation until Beatrice's death laid everything bare. He'd meant it when he told Sam in the pub that he didn't care about his work, but he knew Sam had been correct in saying he would care again one day. Hadn't his soul-searching about Katravesis answered that question? Could he stand being ostracized from the archaeological community, even if he was certain he was right?

Recovering the manuscript had been different, because he had kept it at arm's length from his professional reputation, never admitting it was more than an ancient book. This was different, talking with a colleague about it as if it were much more—and then what, other colleagues, the archaeological community?

His leg hurt from the pressure he was putting on the brake pedal. Cars were racing past. He hadn't allotted any time for lollygagging.

Mostar was another picturesque Neretva River valley town, packed with minarets, domed churches, and red tile roofs, displaying more pastels—mostly pinks and greens—than Konjic, the hilly terrain browner and rockier. This was a town he wished he had time to explore, but a tight schedule dictated he forge ahead with the meat pie he'd purchased at the airport.

Traffic stalled next to a church and Lyle watched a long-bearded cassocked priest, a bent old woman wearing a babushka, and a pretty shop girl walking past.

"Time for archaeology, Lyle. That's why you're here," he told himself.

To the casual traveler, this was a European backwater, but DNA testing demonstrated this land had been a primary migration route for three great waves of *homo sapiens* that populated Europe: hunter gatherers from Africa, and later pastoral nomads from modern Turkey, and then tribes from the eastern steppes. At Lido, he and Popa had backdated the onset of the Bronze Age in the Adriatic zone, though Lyle and Popa had more in common than backdating innovations, both of them also interested in the metabolism of ancient towns, or settlements like Lido—how such experiments in proto-urbanism lived, worked, and faltered.

He caught sight of the expeditionary camp as he rounded the last of the tall hills encircling the ancient settlement, spotting a familiar figure moving about. Conditioned by years of flitting from site to site, Lyle gripped his expedition bag as he exited the car. A minute later, Cornel Popa gave him the bear hug he had come to expect.

"Better weather than your first visit," observed Popa.

That time, Lyle had barely managed to get the Spider Lusso through the snowy hills. Now, the fence that once enclosed the team's work area had been removed, with just one bare worktable beneath a three-sided tent.

"Are you alone?" Lyle asked Popa.

"Josip is tidying up. I sent Eva ahead to the Azerbaijan site for advance scouting. She extends her warmest regards."

"When are you going to the new site, Cornel?"

"Two months. Things to do in Sarajevo first, paperwork. You know how it is."

Lyle knew how it was, three pages of paperwork for every page of actual research.

"Do you still think the Azerbaijani tribe is related to our Lido tribe?"

"I suspect it. Why not join me?" Popa posed, a question packed with more than just collegial courtesy.

"Intentional bronze, an earlier Bronze Age than anyone expected, the inspired work of Cornel Popa," said Lyle.

"Without Lyle Stuart's algorithm and experience, where would I be? And Eva and Josip. One couldn't have asked for more conscientious assistants."

Lyle Stuart's algorithm! "*You* inspired us—me, Cornel."

Popa put a hand on Lyle's shoulder. "How are you, my friend?"

The inevitable question, and Lyle never prepared for it. "*You* accept life...and death, Cornel. I fight it."

"Fighting death is a losing battle. I have never known a clock to run backward."

The *Anno Domini* Eitan had joked about in Jerusalem. Lyle said, "I remember the day I learned of my appointment at Oxford. Leaving the grounds, never had the world been so vivid to me. Since she was killed, I couldn't tell you what I've seen or heard on those grounds. Nothing! I'd do it differently if I could. More trips to Africa, less pressure on Beatrice to return to Oxford, more time for her sister and niece. Why should I need her death to teach me?"

"I don't know," Popa said.

"Are you acquainted with someone who does know?"

"I am, but he hasn't given me all the answers either. I know this—how can we insist our limited intellects and senses are capable of judging everything? How can we say with certainty that Beatrice has ceased to exist?"

"Perhaps you know something I don't," Lyle said.

"I know what I'm incapable of knowing."

Lyle recalled reading how Tolkien, Lewis, and their friends had discussed such weighty matters in an Oxford pub, as he and Popa were doing now in the middle of nowhere.

"Don't ask me to describe that existence," Popa said, "and don't ask the atheists to prove she doesn't exist. They can't."

"She's gone from me. You can't deny that."

Popa displayed the broad grin Lyle had come to know so well. "Our minds and senses may not be the last word. When I was a boy, my grandfather took me to his cottage on the sea, not far from where we stand—so many joyful memories. A humble place his own father had purchased, taken away by the communists and given to an *apparatchik* who coveted it, restored by an enemy of this *apparatchik*. I often watched a woman going up and down the beach, filling pail after pail with shells.

"'What does she do with them?' I asked my *deda*.

"'Pails are stacked at the back of her house by the hundreds.'

"'Why, *deda*?'

"My grandfather made a sign suggesting madness. Our chasing

knowledge for the sake of more knowledge can be like the effort of that foolish woman on the beach unless one also brings a sense of wonder and humility, seeking what is behind all knowledge... or behind collecting shells for more than just filling pails. Or worse, just filling pails out of pride at having more shells than one's neighbors."

Popa had taken a dozen steps before Lyle commenced walking. How different the site looked in May than in winter, the browns and grays replaced by wispy verdant fescues and a riot of wild-flower color. Birds darted about the fields in search of food.

Popa led Lyle to the top of a hill with copious purple clover and a bare crown, like a monk's tonsure. A walking path had been scythed through bee-laden clover, and Josip was waiting for them on the summit, a wicker basket at his feet.

Lyle had taken to this sturdy fair-haired young man on previous visits to the site. Opening the basket, Josip set out bread, cheese, bottles of beer, and sipping glasses on a red-and-white checked tablecloth. Despite being miles from the nearest town and with plenty of work to do, they'd spared no effort on hospitality.

"Josip, are you taking good care of this old man?"

"Of course, Dr. Stuart."

"And keeping him out of trouble?"

"That is more difficult." Smiles broke out all around.

Amid a lively conversation about their experiences at Lido, Josip finished his beer, and said, "Will you excuse me, Dr. Stuart? We're completing our restoration and packing."

Lyle stood and shook the young man's hand. "I am very...sorry about...Beatrice," Josip stammered, his eyes moist.

Lyle watched the young man walk down the hill, recalling the days when his own expedition directors had to worry about grants, permits, and paperwork. Now alone with Cornel Popa, a man Lyle respected and trusted, was this a moment to muss up his white tie? Already, reservations were creeping in as they had at The Lawrence. It was now or never.

"Cornel…"

Popa leapt to his feet. Something in Lyle's manner must have put the man on alert because he said, "You may say anything to me, my friend."

A galvanic moment for Lyle. "What if you were to learn of a masterpiece of a book produced thousands of years before the earliest known civilizations?"

Popa's eyes shone. "You yourself have examined this book?"

The moment for courage. "Page by page. The runes, colors, illustrations, maps, embellishments, all of it."

"The language?"

"Unfamiliar, advanced."

"The condition of this book?" This was the way Katravesis used to pepper Lyle with questions.

"The pages, the parchment, are unlike anything I've seen— thin, supple, strong, not a trace of pigment bleed. The coffer where the manuscript was retained is made of something like silver, but not elemental silver, engraved with complex geometric etchings. Cornel, the thing opens and closes without detectable hinges, noiselessly, seamlessly. My physicist uncle found it to be absolutely watertight and airtight—how the manuscript stayed in pristine condition for thousands of years."

"How many thousands?" the man pressed, not a trace of skepticism or jest on his features, but rather, a look of delight, like that of a child on Christmas morning.

Lyle was sorely tempted to hedge, but he said, "Twenty thousand, thirty?"

"How could such things have been produced two-thousand years ago, much less twenty thousand?"

"A question I'm not competent to answer," Lyle admitted.

"Unless a high, high civilization existed in that era. Oh! You cannot know what this stirs in me. Do *you* have any doubts?"

Lyle had never been asked this question. Wasn't he a man of doubts? What probability would he place on it, what confidence did he have? He put himself back in that Paris hotel room with the manuscript, turning pages, understanding not a word of the text and understanding everything.

"No doubts," he said. "None."

Popa put a hand on Lyle's shoulder. "I studied your work before I contacted you about Lido—not just the algorithm, the way you examined the Nis Neanderthals with a fresh eye, a probing eye, putting aside preconceptions. I believe in quiet voices that bring people of goodwill together. When such gentle voices move us—as I was moved to reach out to you—we shouldn't harden our hearts. I mean we should not put such promptings aside because they're not sufficiently *scientific*."

"After hearing such a story, I was afraid you would rush me off," Lyle said.

Popa smiled. "A woman calling herself Madame Filion came to me a month ago with a veiled bribe to pry you open on the subject of a 'spectacular ancient artifact'—her words. I listened, asked questions to learn as much as I could about her game, knowing I would see you soon. She offered a startling 'research stipend,' as she called it, confident a man like me would jump at the offer."

Lyle was stunned to hear this. "What did you tell her?"

"I said I would seriously consider her offer. I said that in order to keep her talking. Do you know this woman?"

"Describe her, if you please," Lyle requested with trepidation.

"In appearance, regal, but no light in her eyes. Haughty, though she tried to hide it."

"Have you communicated with her since?"

"Several times. She underestimates me, and I encourage it."

Popa's brio astounded Lyle. "She knows I'm here?"

"I thought it necessary to reveal your visit since she could confirm it with the university."

"I'm sorry you've been drawn into my troubles, Cornel."

"I now understand why she offered such a princely stipend. I will tell you something I've never revealed to another soul. Have you ever heard of Lefebvre, the archaeologist who claimed to have discovered a great prehistoric road?" Popa said.

"I have heard of him," Lyle said.

"Do you hold conventional views about the man?"

"At one time I did. Now, I'm not sure."

Producing a spoon, Popa rescued a bee drowning in Lyle's beer glass, casting it into the clover.

"Madame could not have known about my father when she offered her bribe or she would have been more careful. He was an archaeologist of Lefebvre's generation. Later in life, my father had an experience similar to Lefebvre's. Quite by chance, he discovered building remains where they didn't belong, in Alpine Germany—a castle or tower, judging by the foundations, with dungeons in the depths."

The bees evidently preferred beer to clover, but Lyle and Popa scarcely noticed, shooing the bees with their hands as unconsciously as horses' tails ward off flies.

"Why didn't your father reveal this discovery?"

"Because his conclusions were unconventional, unbelievable. The foundation stones were so ancient they had lost their spatial integrity. Only an archaeologist with an unconditioned eye would have recognized them."

"Have you seen this yourself, Cornel?" The same question Popa had asked him.

The little archaeologist inspected his glass for bees before he took a drink. "The site is unknown, unexplored, a harrowing descent from the mountaintop. You will never guess what I found."

"Artifacts?"

"Shackles, now merely veins of metallic ore with suggestive forms. I speculate this fortress is so ancient our Lido inhabitants are moderns by comparison. You've seen such caverns, my friend, dark and dangerous. The entrance is a tight fit, opening into a cave I illuminated with my lamp. I spent a day and night inside and I saw the evidence of the dungeon my father described, with shackles and vertical and horizontal bars."

Lyle said, "What would conventional archaeologists say?"

"What they said about Lefebvre's discovery. Fortuitous mimicry, iron veins made straight like bars by seeping water or circular, like shackles forged by air currents. Or sloppy archaeology."

So drawn in, Lyle had forgotten where they were—outside, in the bright sun, on an island in a sea of clover heaving with bees. "How did your father discover the site?"

"He was an avid mountain climber, those German mountains a favorite destination. He didn't care about the tallest or most difficult peaks, seeking unexplored heights instead."

The swarm of bees on the hill reminded Lyle of Leary, who had compared mainlanders to bees Atlanteans desired to domesticate. Should he tell Popa about Leary, when he'd told himself Leary's story was a fabrication?

He polished off his beer, wiping his mouth on his sleeve. "A man visited me who claimed the box and book were produced by a culture descended from Atlantis."

Popa grinned at Lyle. "Even Lefebvre would not have gone that far. Do you think he is connected to this danger, connected to my Madame Filion?"

"My brother and I suspect it. Why else would he have come to me? Sam said it's a psychological trick to steer me to the book, so he can put his hands on it."

"I remember the old days, the communists and their tricks."

"I'm used to trouble," Lyle said.

"Artifact thieves and hoodlums, not such men as I have known."

Lyle was all too familiar with such men and women—Russell, Desrosier, and Malkin. "Let me help you carry these things back," he said, gathering up the beer glasses.

He scanned the terrain, and descried Josip moving around the formerly fenced compound. Popa produced a pistol from the back of his pants. "I've never had to use it, but in these parts, one can't be too careful. Are you flying back to England?"

Lyle said, "I'm meeting my brother in Paris."

"A holiday?"

He couldn't lie to Popa. "Hard business."

"Connected to this matter?"

"I fear so."

A magpie plucked a heel of bread from the corner of the tablecloth and took to the air. Lyle didn't pay it any heed. He was thinking about Popa's mountain when his friend said, "Perhaps this is an advent, the coming of something unimaginable."

SEPTEMBER 1963

Cambridge
(56 years earlier)

S HE APPEARED OUT OF NOWHERE. One minute, Jack was seated in his study, his eyes closed, listening to a Mozart concerto and thinking about Charles Williams and his old friend's beliefs about co-inherence, the next his open eyes beheld someone he had hoped never to see again.

The last time had been three years before, not long after the loss of his wife. This time, she was in sporting dress—tweeds and riding pants, knee-length black boots, and red gloves. All that was missing was a riding crop.

He had no doubt he was in peril. She would expect him to ask how she'd gotten through a locked door, so he wouldn't.

She kicked the turntable plug from the wall, and said, "Decrepit. Decaying," each word affecting him like a slap to the face. How *had* she gotten in?

"I am going to have it," she insisted.

He fancied himself a keen observer. She was formidable and dangerous.

She raised her gloved hand, aiming a red finger at him. "You know where he has hidden it."

"A curiosity cabinet in his sitting room, as I recall."

"Reveal the location. Now, or prepare for an excruciating death."

The clock on the wall ticked away. A dog barked—Curtis's beagle.

Jack sighed. "If it comes to it, I must choose the *excruciatus*. Did you kill Alembert?"

"I told you I'm not here to parlay."

Was she a member of a secret society? A religious cult? An unrepentant Nazi—he had heard of such people.

She said, "You're afraid. You ought to be."

Stepping toward him, Elana Rosman seemed to grow taller. Jack was paralyzed with fear, could not so much as turn his head.

Unexpectedly, she put her hand against his chest. He could feel something hard and bony inside her glove. Immediately, a wave of anxiety surged over him, such as he'd never before experienced.

"This is just the beginning. I told you it would be excruciating. You're already dying. You don't have long, I promise you. You can feel it."

He *could* feel it. Whatever she had done with that glove had crippled him.

"Did you hear me?"

He said:

"I heard in Addison's Walk a bird sing clear:
This year the summer will come true. This year. This year.
Winds will not strip the blossoms from the apple tree
This year, nor want of rain destroy the peas."

He stopped for a deep breath. Breathing hurt, but on he went.

"This year, this year, as all these flowers foretell,
We shall escape the circle and undo the spell.
Often deceived, yet open once again your heart,
Quick, quick, quick, quick!—the gates are drawn apart."

"This year!" he said to her back as she exited the room.

MAY 7, 2019

Paris

I N LYLE'S DREAM, he was sitting across the desk from Arthur Russell. Next thing he knew, Leary was seated behind Russell's miniature desk.

"Where is Russell?" Lyle had asked.

Leary's mask slipped, revealing Russell's face behind it.

He woke up bewildered by the dream. How had his mind conjoined two such dissimilar men—one old and malformed, the other hale and handsome? Was the connection their mutual dishonesty? Or the danger he associated with both of them?

The three-hour drive from Lido brought him from the remote downs of Bosnia-Herzegovina to the chaotic city of Sarajevo. The four-hour flight to Paris conveyed him to one of the cultural and culinary capitals of the world, a quick transition from the wilderness to an urban mecca in the same day. How many times had he awakened in tents or camp dormitories and retired at night in London, Paris, or Rome?

Sam was waiting for him at the airport. As they pulled away from the curb, his brother said, "Discover any lost cities?"

"We drank beer on a barrow."

"A what?"

"Weren't you paying attention when Mum read us the story?

218

A mound the ancients built over human remains. Don't drive that way. I don't want to see a damaged Notre Dame. Where are we going?" Lyle inquired.

"We're meeting a man named Gérard Martin. I told you we'd come unannounced. I wasn't going to call in any favors until I needed to, but just before I left London, I learned Martin has replaced Lourdes, and that Desrosier has left the Sorbonne."

Lyle had been looking forward to seeing Richard Lourdes again. "Why bother with Martin?" he wanted to know.

Sam was negotiating busy Paris streets featuring frequent horns and abrupt stops. "It's possible we'll learn more from him than we would have from Lourdes or Desrosier. We don't have any leverage over her anymore."

"We're having supper at the Paix?"

"I'm looking forward to it," Sam replied, "but first things first."

Gérard Martin's perfunctory words of welcome, the man's buttoned-down attire and wary eyes, reminded Lyle of Dawson, his own department head, a man with little passion for the nitty gritty of archaeology, but a keen eye for ascending the academic ladder. Martin seemed a much different man than Lourdes, who hadn't earned a top-tier reputation but loved archaeology.

"I know your work, Dr. Stuart," Martin said, in accented English. "I stayed a bit late to meet you. We could use a man like you here. A lot less pomp and circumstance at the Sorbonne than Oxford. We value *liberté*."

Martin's words made Lyle wonder how Sam had secured this meeting. Had his brother suggested Lyle was interested in an academic move?

Redecorated with better furniture and carpeting, this room was unrecognizable as Lourdes's former office. Lyle said, "I enjoyed conversing with Dr. Lourdes about the department's work."

"Not on Oxford's scale, of course, though we have some fascinating research underway. Perhaps we can talk further. In the meantime, your brother suggested you have questions about

Dr. Lourdes and Mademoiselle Desrosier. I will assist where possible, though I am sure you are familiar with the rules concerning such things."

"Of course," Lyle said, still waiting for Sam to chime in.

"So, how can I be of assistance?" asked Martin.

After several beats and not a word from Sam, Lyle said, "Do you know where Caroline Desrosier has moved?"

Martin hesitated. "On the record, I can tell you she is in Mainz. Off the record, if I may?"

"If you would be so kind, Dr. Martin."

"Off the record, a rumor circulated she'd came into a considerable sum of money."

Arthur Russell had resided in Mainz and worked for the university for many decades. Lyle's meetings with Russell in that man's office were still vivid, last night's dream proof enough. "Does she work for the University of Mainz?"

"That I do not know."

Sam said, "She was a librarian there before she came to the Sorbonne."

"I regret that I know little of her history." Martin glanced at his watch.

"When did she leave Paris?" asked Lyle.

"A year ago, perhaps one-and-a-half years, during my predecessor's tenure."

"What can you tell us about Lourdes?" inquired Sam.

A hint of consternation pierced Martin's composed demeanor. He looked at Lyle, as if weighing how dear a price he need pay for the Oxford archaeologist's goodwill.

"I replaced Lourdes six months ago. He died a month later."

"Was he ill?" pressed Sam.

"Not to my knowledge."

A bad feeling came over Lyle. If the choice had been up to him, he'd have let it go.

"Suicide?" suggested Sam.

"That's not for me to say, Mr. Stuart."

Not a denial. Lyle recalled the shattered bowl and his last conversation with Lourdes, fearing Sam had hit the mark.

"Was an investigation conducted?" said Sam.

"You will have to speak to the Judicial Police about that."

"Do you look after the Alembert Archive?" Lyle inquired.

Martin shook his head. "We were approached by an *avocat*, a solicitor for an anonymous buyer, offering a very generous amount for the contents, meager as they were. We accepted the offer."

"You never learned the purchaser's name?" Sam asked.

"The buyer's solicitor handled everything. The sale wasn't a high priority."

"Would you mind giving us this solicitor's name?"

Martin's eyes narrowed, and some moments passed before he said, "A Monsieur Abed, as I recall. Let me give you my card, Dr. Stuart. Are you still working at the Lido site?"

"I just came from there," he replied, putting Martin's card in his shirt pocket. "Popa is completing his work."

"In such capable hands, Lido turned out to be a productive trove."

"Popa is a remarkable man," Lyle said.

"For a protégé, I suppose he is. Those people aren't up to our level of scholarship," Martin said didactically. "If you don't mind, I'll call you about our research."

Lyle bristled at Martin's assessment of Popa, but he acquiesced to the man's request to contact him.

In the car, Lyle said, "I'm afraid to ask what you told him."

"We learned things, didn't we? Desrosier's whereabouts, her inheritance."

Lyle was still thinking about Martin's disparagement of Popa. "In future, I'll thank you to advise me ahead of time when your schemes include me."

"You're front and center in this business, as I recall," said Sam, leaning on his horn in the roundabout.

"That's not what I meant. It's been a long day. I'm hungry."

Sam said, "I wanted a window table, but the place is so popular we were lucky to get in. I dropped a name and promised we'd keep it under two hours. Disgraceful what you have to do for good provender."

Approaching the familiar windows and green trim of the Café de la Paix, Lyle said, "A second, Sam, a postcard for Jeremy." He detoured to the newsstand outside the front door, smiling at the memory of Beatrice handing him a postcard to send to Jeremy on his first visit to Kampala—fishing boats on Lake Victoria. "He'll like this, especially coming from you," she had said. One of Nancy Evans's happy memories, the kind he hoped to rekindle in Sam this evening.

At a cramped corner table, Sam ordered a glass of wine rather than a bottle, Lyle following his brother's lead. "Sad news about Lourdes."

Sam was scanning the room, a common occurrence when Lyle dined with him. "You weren't close chums, were you?" Sam asked.

"I liked him. He didn't have to indulge me when I was hunting the manuscript, but he did what he could, and he introduced me to Desrosier. Did you tell Jeremy you were a spy?"

"I might have," said Sam. "Did he send you a letter?"

"He came to see me on the bus. About Beatrice."

"I've always wanted to tell someone I'm a spy and Jeremy struck me as a good choice. How is he?"

"His mother's failing. I've got to do something."

"That's big of you. Did you see Henry when you delivered Lucia?"

"Brother Albert picked her up in Oxford. Did you visit him?"

"Not yet. One thing after another—this business."

Lyle's conversation with Popa was still fresh, especially his friend's parting words about an *advent*—"something unimaginable." Lyle didn't believe in premonitions, but he sensed something too.

Perhaps a confrontation with the person who had taken Beatrice's life? Sam was surely propelling them in that direction.

Lyle said, "Desrosier's been pressing Popa about me and the manuscript."

"Well, well." Sam's antenna went up again.

"That's all you have to say?"

"Not all. We're fishing and so is she. How reliable is Popa?"

"He's playing along to learn as much as he can."

Their wine arrived. Lyle took a sip, while Sam set his to the side.

After the waiter took their orders—they were on the clock—Lyle said, "Our uncle doesn't bite, Sam."

"It's not him I'm worried about, it's me—what he'll ask me." Lyle supposed his brother didn't like the subject, which was confirmed when Sam said, "Guess who called me. Fatemeh. She was hard on you that night, but she had her moments."

"If you say so."

"Just because you're miserable doesn't mean I have to be too," Sam snapped.

"You're better off without her, Sam. Call Patrick. You two used to have a lot of fun."

Sam was taking his time tucking the napkin into his collar, and displaying the same worried expression as when they were talking about their uncle. "I might, if he weren't dead."

Lyle's hand started shaking, a few drops of wine splattering the tablecloth. "Patrick? When did he die?"

"October twenty-first, 2002."

"I never knew. I'm sorry. Do you know who killed him?"

"I did," Sam whispered.

Lyle reached across the table, gripping Sam's arm. "Don't say that. If I'd done things differently, maybe Beatrice..."

"*I did*," said Sam, then in a voice so low Lyle could barely hear him added, "I shot him on a roof in Albania. Left him there. Never heard what happened to the body."

Lyle wanted to say he didn't believe him, but looking into Sam's eyes he knew the statement was true. "Why?"

"The Chinese turned him. He and another man were hunting me. One of us was going to die that day. I wish it had been me. Don't say anything. I mean it. Let me tell you something. The story our mum read us—I've learned Mordor is real!"

They were interrupted by the arrival of their food, but none of the tension subsided. Sam looked at the plate as if it were a heap of garbage.

"If you did it, I know it had to be done," Lyle said.

"Maybe. Now you know what your brother's capable of doing. Let's eat."

Lourdes's and Patrick's obituaries on the same day, Patrick having been like another big brother when Lyle was a boy. Eager to change the subject, he said, "What do you make of this?" He placed an envelope in front of Sam, the letter from Zvi Eitan about Jericho.

His brother said, "When did you receive this?"

"Five days ago. Read it."

Reading and then handing the letter back to Lyle, Sam said, "Sounds like that old wag. What's a cenotaph?"

"A monument, like the one in London for the war dead. We didn't see any monuments at the Jericho site."

Sam was doing better with his food, even managing a smile. "Eitan is a trickster. The letter may mean exactly what it says, and it may not, the way he directed us to Istanbul. From what you've told me about Andrea Fitzgerald and from what I know about Zvi and attractive women, he could be referring to *her* as a monument. That's what I mean about Eitan and trickery."

"What if it's intelligence about Malkin, like Istanbul? You said a connection may exist between Beatrice's death and the Jericho site intruder."

"I'll touch base with Zvi, but don't get your hopes up. He's had a layman's interest in archaeology for as long as I've known him, so what he says may be nothing more than that. Don't hurry. We don't need to rush the sweet course."

At Lyle's signal, their waiter came to the table with small plates, each with two biscuits covered in a bright blue glaze.

"You said it's a good memory. We need them," Lyle told his brother.

Sam took a bite. "As good as I remembered. Mum always said you were special. She was right."

Sam was working on his second biscuit when Lyle asked, "What comes next?"

"We're going to find Desrosier, and we're going to apply pressure."

In the aftermath of Sam's revelation about Patrick, Lyle couldn't help saying, "What kind of pressure?"

Sam hadn't tasted his wine. "The kind that tells us if she was involved in Beatrice's death."

"How are you going to do that?"

"Watch me," Sam said.

MARCH 1998

Cairo
(21 years earlier)

S AM WAS IN CAIRO WITH PATRICK, betrayed by an Egyptian who'd been assisting The Firm for over a decade.

They were locked in a room in a sector of the city governed by the Muslim Brotherhood, all of their captors wearing federal police uniforms. No way out, execution imminent, or so Sam believed.

Naturally, their weapons, phones, wallets had been confiscated, but their captors hadn't discovered the death pills.

How long should they wait to use them, as they'd surely be tortured before they were killed?

The ferrets hadn't reckoned on Patrick, who was surveying the windowless room with its concrete walls, floor, and ceiling; long rectangular table; and two doors—the one they'd entered by and another door on the opposite wall—both locked.

Patrick said to Sam, "Here's what I want you to do, old cock."

"Then what?"

"Watch me," said Patrick.

Schemes with miniscule probabilities of success invigorated Patrick, always calculating how he could multiply the odds.

When their captors returned, they found Sam alone in the room. He immediately pointed to the door on the opposite wall, and raged, "The bastard left me behind to slow you down."

Patrick's shoes sat by the door. A ferret tried the latch. "Locked," he told the others. "No escape."

Sam wasn't fluent in Arabic but he knew enough to understand the man. "He used a pick-key," he insisted.

One of the men said, "Not possible."

"He had a tool, I tell you!" Sam blustered.

The captain barked orders, two of the men racing out the main door, two more grabbing Sam's arms and hustling him out.

Down the narrow hall was another room with half-a-dozen chairs and electronic equipment everywhere. They forced Sam to sit, the men restraining him.

"You will talk now," the captain said, as a giddy ferret attached a hinged and clamped device to Sam's hand, a Russian *krokodil*.

Despite what Sam had been taught, his muscles tensed, and he was too late for the death pill.

"Now you will give us the name of the traitor," said the captain.

"I don't know…"

The *krokodil* clicked once, twice, the pain making him gasp.

"What will you give me if…"

"A quick death, better than you deserve."

Of course, Sam knew the man's name, an informer in the upper echelon of the Brotherhood. Not a man of principle by any means, paid handsomely by The Firm.

The next click made him convulse in agony.

"Ismael al-Hamdi!"

"You lie," the captain said.

Another uniformed man entered the room, whispering something in the captain's ear, bringing him to attention.

The new arrival produced a pistol, executing all five of the ferrets with five pops from the Makarov semi-automatic.

"If we hurry, we can get a table at Zitouni," said Patrick.

ON THE PLANE, just the two of them and the pilot up front, Patrick put a finger to his lips and produced an uncut diamond as big as a cherry.

"Where did you get that sparkler?" asked Sam.

"From the pocket of the ferret whose uniform I borrowed. Damn good fortune, what?"

"Is it genuine?"

Patrick displayed that ironic smile of his. "We shall see, old cock. We shall see."

MAY 9, 2019

Mainz

THE MAN WHO WALKED THROUGH THE DOOR and surveyed the room was stooped, his hair unkempt. If his clothes weren't ragged, they were well worn and hadn't been laundered in a long while.

The man recognized Lyle, and made his way to the table cautiously, timidly.

Lyle stood, but the man's expression told him a handshake would be unwelcome. When they'd met two years earlier, Leonidas Romanov had been the Russian consulate's security deputy. That encounter hadn't been so long ago that Lyle didn't recognize Romanov's distinctive features, but since then the Russian's nose had been broken and the light had gone out of his eyes.

From across the table, Lyle detected the man's earthy scent. "Sit, please. What will you have?" Lyle said to the man.

"Coffee, that's all," Romanov replied. "I prefer to speak German or Russian."

"My German lets me down," Lyle countered.

Romanov shrugged. "As you wish."

The Russian had suggested meeting here, a biergarten without the Teutonic trappings, with few patrons at this early hour.

Lyle said, "Thank you for seeing me."

"Was there a book?" Romanov asked him, referring to their prior business.

"Yes, and I returned it to the rightful owner."

"I wondered if their story was a lie, like everything else they told me."

"You mean Russell and..."

Romanov's gray face colored. "Caroline. Yes, they used me, destroyed me."

What would have sounded like an excuse to someone who hadn't known Arthur Russell, Adler Alembert's son, made perfect sense to Lyle. He could do without ever hearing the name of that evil eminence again, but not until he assured himself no connection existed between Russell's and Beatrice's deaths. Lyle said, "Is your brother a monk, as you said in my hotel room?"

Romanov shook his head. The bright overhead lamps made the Russian squint. "He is a Federal Security Service section chief. I shouldn't admit that, but what does it matter? Look at me. What more can they do to me?"

"I wouldn't want you harmed. Don't tell me anything that will make trouble."

"Trouble? When I received your invitation, I spat on it. Do you know why I came?" The man hadn't expected an answer. "Russell and that woman convinced me to murder you, but I bear some of the blame. I accuse myself."

"You bear less of the blame than you think," Lyle responded.

"I am grateful we were interrupted that night, before I pulled the trigger. I would have, you know. Perhaps a God does exist after all. I don't doubt a devil exists, not for a moment."

Lyle hated thinking about that consulate room. He had made his way here anyway to learn what he could about Caroline Desrosier.

Romanov slurped his coffee greedily. "I come here often. I can walk from the consulate. Their vodka is cheap, and they don't bother me unless they have to. Nor have they complained to the consul, not yet."

Lyle hadn't expected such candidness, but he hadn't expected an apology either. "I shouldn't have accepted your invitation to the consulate," he said. "I should have known better."

The man ignored Lyle's admission. "We are fortunate age caught up with Russell soon after our..." Romanov began, his speaking setting off a violent coughing spell.

"Can I get you something?"

The Russian shook his head. He cleared his throat forcefully, and said, "I'm used to it. I'm a gate guard now. The shack is cold in winter, hot in summer, damp the rest of the time. They wanted to sack me after that night, but my brother saved me, if you can call it that."

"May I ask how you met Caroline Desrosier?" Lyle prodded.

The color returned to Romanov's face, like a last red ember. "When I hear that name, it's all I can do to resist a *Trinkgelage*... binge—that's the word. Sometimes, I cannot resist. In those days, I was receiving treatment at the free clinic. One day, she showed up there with Russell. He introduced her as a colleague, their way of getting her *kogti*...her talons into me. And those claws went deep, I can tell you. But regret is not the only reason I agreed to meet you. I had to tell someone what that woman did to me. She gave me nothing—you understand what I am saying? She took everything."

Lyle nodded. "That was their way."

Romanov extended his cup to a passing waitress.

"When I learned she had moved to Mainz, I found out where she lived. Having a brother with connections helps. I sent her letters, heard nothing, so I went to the building on my day off and rang up." Romanov spoke in a strained tone. "They said she wasn't there, not to bother her. I waited on the street, until suppertime. When she came out, I stood in front of that minx and asked why she had done such terrible things to me. I had to know. I was *obsessed* with knowing." He coughed again, then waited as if to be sure he wasn't going to go on choking.

"That's how I received this." He touched his crooked nose. "Her guard did it. I woke up on the pavement with blood all over my face. I never went back. I had received my answer. He must have broken something in my neck because it still hurts."

The longer Lyle observed the man, the more he saw. The Russian cut his own hair; he wore a coat too heavy for the season, patched in several places; he'd lost considerable weight since the last time; his hands trembled; he ate garlic—to mask the drink?

"If you'd like to see her held to account for her mischief, tell me everything you know about her."

"Alas, she learned everything about me. I learned nothing about her."

"Are you certain you won't have something to eat? No? Do you remember any odd incidents? Did you see her with Russell again?"

"Never. He had me hooked, and she played her part to perfection. I can't bear to think of it."

"I hold nothing against you," Lyle said to the man. He hadn't intended to. The words just came out.

Tears pooled in Romanov's weary eyes. He drank the rest of his coffee so quickly Lyle was afraid he'd have another coughing fit, but the brew revived him. "We were here, where we met when she was in Mainz. A young girl approached us, took Caroline's hand and kissed her cheek. The look on Caroline's face—horror. She shooed the girl off. Outside the restaurant, Caroline said Russell had introduced them at the clinic, one of Russell's patients, but I didn't believe her."

Another Desrosier victim, Lyle told himself. Had Desrosier been afraid the girl and Romanov would compare notes?

"Do you have anyone?" asked Lyle.

"You could say so. She has no job and a vicious temper, but I'm no prize either. I think about a new start. Argentina perhaps. Many speak German there, I'm told. My brother would pay the transit to be rid of me. My great-grandfather was an Argentine, living in Marseilles when he was murdered, his son born soon after he died. Yes, villains like Russell prowled in those days too."

Romanov reached into his pocket, Lyle recalling with a start that upstairs room where the Russian had produced a pistol. This time, two coins came out.

"You are my guest. Would a hundred Euros come in handy?" Lyle said, as nonchalantly as he could. He took some money from his pocket.

"It's not necessary."

"You must need something."

Romanov made a little bow. "You are too generous. As you see, I am down on my luck." He took the twenty-Euro notes and stashed them inside his coat.

JUNE 1938

Marseilles
(81 years earlier)

OUTSIDE THE TEN-FOOT WROUGHT-IRON GATE, the small figure waited for the house door to open. Most of the villa obscured by the stone wall, he was comparing what he had learned about the estate with what he saw through the gate bars. He knew the owner of the villa was inside and he was confident that when the owner saw him he would come to the gate. His charm would get the visitor in.

The caller put the man striding to the gate under his evaluative eye: Gabriel Marquez, age thirty, clean-shaven, fair-skinned, sandy-haired. Confident—perhaps overconfident, but no fool, nothing that contradicted what the uninvited visitor had learned from Rodrigo Marquez.

"What do you want, boy?" asked the man.

The visitor, who might have been on his way to school, was attired in a white shirt, striped necktie, knee pants, ankle socks, black Oxfords, and red beret. He was propped against a walking stick he held in his left hand, gripping a leather satchel in his right.

Marquez had addressed him in French, suiting the visitor as well as any of the seven languages he spoke with ease. "I have a message from Rodrigo. He is in distress."

The man who bent down—he was over six feet tall—wore a diamond-studded gold ring on his right hand worth tens of thousands of francs. The visitor knew Gabriel Marquez wanted for nothing, that he kept a large boat at the marina for visiting his Catalan mistress.

"How old are you? Why are you dressed as a child?" Marquez demanded.

The visitor wasn't four and a half feet tall, his legs pathologically bowed. "You will want to hear the news about Rodrigo," he said, the persuasive voice—the charm—that rarely failed him.

"Come along," said the man, peremptorily, unlocking the gate and leading the stranger through the paved courtyard, past the fountain and into the villa.

The opulent foyer was cooler than the street. "Say what you have to say," the man demanded.

The caller had hired a car to convey him close to the villa, walking the rest of the way on hilly lanes. His legs throbbed.

"May I have a chair?"

Looking down at the visitor's bowed legs, Marquez said, "If you must, but make it quick."

The man passed through an arched doorway, returning with a wooden desk chair, sliding it across the terrazzo floor.

"What's the matter with Rodrigo? Where is he?"

"Orleans, when last I saw him," the visitor said, the hard chair doing little for the pain.

Marquez said, "I'd rather he were in *New* Orleans, but better than his being here."

"*Je suis Arthur Alembert*," the young man said.

Marquez's eyes narrowed. "That name means nothing to me, little man."

Good! Marquez was unlikely to concern himself with a *little man*, and no indication that Rodrigo had informed his brother about the visitor.

Deposited as an infant at the Mortimer Russell Institute for

Advanced Eugenics, and never off the grounds until he was four-teen, Arthur Alembert had spent his last years there searching for information about his origins. Learning that Adler Alembert was his father, he had set out to accumulate as much information as he could about his male progenitor—a person he had never met or corresponded with—a mission requiring numerous invasions of the institute director's office. The *little man* had not only discovered his birth records—his mother's name scrubbed—he had come upon correspondence from Alembert himself and news articles about his father's mysterious disappearance in 1932, six years before.

Not yet twenty, Arthur Alembert possessed a perceptual sense as native and natural as keen sight to a hawk or scent to a blood-hound. With each discovery, this sixth or seventh sense told him that Adler Alembert had been pursuing something spectacular. Nothing identified the thing. Rather, the combination of records, correspondence, ledgers, mysterious meetings, suggested his father had been in search of something absolutely unique.

Since that time, a day hadn't gone by without Arthur seeking more information about Adler Alembert. When he defied the director and left the institute, he'd spent almost a year staking his claim to his father's huge legacy and information trove. That still wasn't enough for the son who desired to know everything about his secretive father. Who had killed him? Someone had.

Only three people had enjoyed ready access to Adler Alem-bert: an African male who'd died in 1931; a woman named CurLio, murdered in 1932; and Inigo Marquez, who had died in Marseille in 1934—the only one of the three to survive Alembert, presuming Alembert had died at the time of his disappearance, as the son had convinced the inheritance court he had.

The solicitor's trove revealed that Adler Alembert's brother owned a mechanic's shop in southern England. Gregory Alembert had seemed jovial and communicative until his nephew revealed the purpose for his visit. From then on, Gregory refused to say another word. So resolute was the man that not even the persuasive

Arthur Alembert could prevail on him to divulge anything about his dead brother.

Gregory had said nothing in spoken language at least, though the young Alembert had come away certain his uncle had been persecuted by Adler Alembert. Years after Alembert had vanished, Gregory still feared his brother, a feeling that was communicated by his uncle's eyes, hands, perspiration, respiration—things the young man could read as others read words in books.

As to the elusive treasure—not so much as a hint.

Stymied by Gregory, Arthur had shifted his attention to the steward Marquez, who had purchased an expensive villa in Marseilles. Arthur learned Marquez had two sons: Gabriel, the inheritor of his father's estate, and Rodrigo, a custodian in Orleans when Arthur tracked him down—a slow-witted, uncomfortably exuberant man, an embarrassment to his family.

If Gregory Alembert couldn't be pried open, Rodrigo Marquez had produced a pearl of immense value. Rodrigo may have been slow-witted, but he wasn't blind. In fact, he was as observant as a raven. Befriending him as Arthur Russell, a name Arthur used when it suited his need for anonymity, he had spent the better part of a month learning everything about Inigo Marquez and his household business.

Thus, he had not come to the villa impulsively. Arthur never did anything, in fact, without due consideration, knowing this was the domestic servant's day off, knowing Marquez's German shepherd was away to stud, knowing Marquez's guard spent several afternoon hours in town each day for drinks and a meal. Arthur had, indeed, watched the guard stroll down the hill before he'd approached the gate.

"…that name means nothing to me, little man."

The father a serf who thought himself a *boyar*, an aristocrat, one son a moron, this one a puffed-up toad. "Your father was Adler Alembert's steward, an Argentinean who looked after Alembert's affairs in South America."

The man was wary, as he ought to be. "What does that have to do with Rodrigo?"

"When Adler Alembert disappeared in 1932, your father made off with his property."

"Get out!" Marquez took several steps toward the visitor, looming over him.

Arthur Alembert's hand found the line of small pockets inside the satchel. "I don't care about the money, but I shall have Alembert's records."

"Get out, or I'll pitch you out...*little man!*"

Verbal cudgels from this man wouldn't daunt him. Before Marquez knew what was happening, a dart had lodged in his shoulder, a second punctured his chest.

The man staggered back, stunned, in distress.

Thump—a third dart pierced Marquez's neck. He swayed and crashed to the floor, smashing his jaw on the tile, blood oozing from clenched lips.

Bleak years at the institute, but the place had employed excellent scientists and psychologists. Absorbing everything like a sponge, Arthur, when he came upon Adler Alembert's unpublished treatise on the lethality of arrowheads treated with a stabilized reduction of golden frog venom, understood everything. He had been attending the University of Vienna when he decided to retrieve his father's property from Marquez and set about planning this mission.

The South American frogs hadn't been easy to obtain and the number so few Arthur's stabilized reduction was enough for only a dozen darts. Other men would have hoarded them for the mission. Not Arthur, who had expended eight precious darts on Austrian livestock and a farmhand so he knew exactly what to expect.

Arthur Alembert knew where his father's property was hidden, the raven-eyed Rodrigo coaxed into revealing everything, including the safe combination numbers he had seen once and never forgotten. Inside the safe were three ledger-sized journals. Arthur couldn't resist turning pages. New names, all to be plumbed to the utmost: Erikson, Basile, and a man named Hill.

He swept the stacks of cash, thin gold bars, and jewelry into the satchel with the journals.

From the villa's side entrance—the servant's entrance—a loud voice called. "Monsieur Marquez."

With Marquez dead on the foyer floor, Arthur was already deep in analysis of actions and outcomes.

The voice again. "Duperon sent for me. He said a boy came through the gate. Did you let him in, Monsieur?"

The guard was still at the side door, no doubt hoping for an all-clear from Marquez so he could return to the brasserie.

For someone with bad legs and a kyphotic spine, Arthur moved quickly to the foyer, grabbing Marquez by the ankles, laboriously dragging the big man to the front closet. He could have moved twice Marquez's weight with his arms—they were that strong—but his legs and back were brittle. He carefully removed the three darts from the dead man's body, cleaning the bloodstained tile with Marquez's pocket handkerchief.

"Monsieur Marquez!" Louder now.

Arthur had one dart left. He'd intended to reserve two, but Marquez's belligerence had provoked him to launch the third dart.

Arthur manhandled the body into the closet. Retrieving the stick and satchel he'd left on the floor, he went inside with the corpse.

He had to sit on the torso. But being inside a dark closet with a dead body didn't bother him in the least. The live body outside was what concerned him. If the guard opened the door, Arthur would have to use the dart, and the strike would have to be a true and deep piercing lest the guard could mount an assault. Arthur would have to puncture the neck with a stab rather than throwing the dart.

Very well. He reached into the satchel. Careful!

The intended tableau was a dead man on the villa floor, with nothing in the villa disturbed. Who else in Marseille would know about the secret safe he'd raided? Perhaps a schoolboy had been observed in the vicinity of the villa, perhaps not, the poison unlikely to be identified, the reason for the killing and the killer never to be imagined.

He hadn't envisioned personal peril! Not this.

He could hear movement—coming closer.

"Monsieur Marquez?"

He had learned a valuable lesson. In the future, convince others to do what he desired, as he had done with the doctors at the institute, classmates in Vienna, with Rodrigo. Even better, convince them the action was their own idea. Never put himself in such danger again.

"Marquez villa here. Is this the police?"

The guard was on the telephone, suspicious about what had happened to Marquez. Too late to silence the guard, even if he could manage it. The police were on their way. Weeks ago, Arthur had acquired maps from the municipal authority, maps of buildings and access doors, which was how he knew about the side entrance and rear delivery door—the only way out for him, and that far from certain with his impediments.

He closed the closet door and heard the telephone slam against the receiver.

To the rear of the villa Arthur went as fast as his burning legs could carry him, leaning hard on the stick—his best leg. The guard could cut him off at any moment, and reaching the dart fast enough would be impossible. Distracted as he was, he nonetheless wasn't panicked, noticing every room was richly furnished and appointed—using *his* money.

Releasing the delivery door latch, he went outside to the sound of a police horn. The tightly mown back yard was bordered by a ten-foot stone wall capped with a red brick parapet and with an oversized gate for deliveries from the back alley.

The gate was locked. If the key was with Marquez, it might as well be in New Orleans.

On the wall were trellises with flowering bougainvillea, thick with bees and butterflies.

No sooner had the bell begun tolling than Arthur recalled the incident at the cathedral as he'd made his way from the *Gare Saint-Charles* to the hired car.

Crouched in the shadows on the top step of the cathedral was an urchin in tatters with two crutches.

"You had better be strong and ruthless," Arthur had muttered as he passed.

Two old people were ascending the steps, he with a crutch, she carrying a large bag. No vagrants these, for the man wore a tailored suit, the woman a stylish dress.

The car waited, but he couldn't turn away.

After an arduous climb for two so old, they sat on either side of the boy, the urchin looking up at them with trepidation, not moving or speaking as the woman removed his shabby shirt and his short pants. Reaching into her bag, she produced new clothes, and the smiling old man assisted the boy in putting them on. They then removed the child's worn shoes, and supplied him with new ones—wool socks too. All the while, the woman bathed his head, hands, and feet with a washcloth.

After giving him rolls, sausage, cheese, and three small cartons of milk, she kissed his forehead.

Why would they associate with this alley creature? What could they hope to gain?

This had troubled Arthur, as did everything he couldn't reduce to a calculation. He had wrenched himself away at that point, as he wrenched himself away from the memory now.

If someone looked out a back window, they'd see him straight-away. Would they think to guard the alley? Why would they, unless the guard had discovered the body?

When Arthur Alembert reached a verdict, he was decisive. He pitched his stick over the wall, then the heavy satchel.

The trellis to his right was reinforced with wood slats, so he chose that one, the flimsy structure bowing and bending as he ascended. Something stung his arm, though it hardly registered.

At the instant he felt the brittle structure give way, he reached out and grasped a parapet brick.

Down went the trellis in a heap. Any normal man would have lost his grip, but not Arthur Alembert. All those hours in the institute's gymnasium, using weights, bars, and rings, and climbing up ropes all the way to his perch in the rafters, had produced apelike arms and hands.

The hand held. More than held, it raised the rest of him to the summit of the wall.

He dropped into the shadowy, odorous alley. The excruciating impact couldn't be helped, and there he retrieved his possessions.

No doubt the police were inside the house, searching for a young thief or vandal. Instead, they'd find a dead body, the tableau he'd planned.

He plodded down the alley in the direction opposite the street that fronted the villa. Faster, he commanded himself. When they saw the trellis, they'd know he'd gone over.

Dirty, sore, and bruised, he'd accomplished what he'd set out to do.

A narrow lane branched from the delivery alley, winding down the hill in the direction of the city. The clothes he'd worn on the train were in the satchel. He would make the late afternoon express to Vienna.

SEPTEMBER 3, 1973

Stockholm
(46 years earlier)

C OULD THIS SCENE BE MORE LUDICROUS? Arthur Russell asked himself.

Russell was seated at a battered worktable in Storeroom No. 16 of the Swedish Royal Museum of Natural History. Across the table was a woman in her eighties with short blonde hair and eyes that were rheumy, though a striking shade of violet. Her face was plastered with makeup.

Surrounding the two in the cramped storeroom were shelves filled with preserved animals, from the very small, such as hamsters and gerbils, to sizes as large as beavers and penguins. Alongside these specimens sat boxes, jars, books, and journals of all types.

Russell's back and legs hurt as they always did when he wasn't in one of his own custom-crafted chairs, and he found the musty smell in the storeroom oppressive—the smell of inattention and decay.

"This is where my research material is stored," the woman said in accented English. "It is *very* valuable."

Considering the clutter and grime, nothing in this room struck Russell as valuable.

They had made a strange pair, Russell understood, as Greta Erickson led him from the museum entrance through the main gallery to this rear-of-the-building storeroom: he a virtual midget relying on two canes, she with her own severe curve in her spine; his virility impressive from the waist up, her comical attempt to appear much younger than her years.

"Dr. Erickson, may I present you with this small token of my appreciation for seeing me so promptly?"

She gazed wide-eyed at the therapod claw in the small box he handed to her. He would do whatever was necessary to unlock her cooperation and he had judged this fine Cretaceous Period fossil would advance his mission.

"How lovely!"

"I have eagerly anticipated meeting a scholar of your standing," Russell said, though nothing could have been further from the truth. The only thing he cared about was information related to the treasure.

"Yes," she said, in distraction, taking in this shabby room as if she were seeing it for the first time. "I have asked the museum to serve us their famous herring dish." She cupped her mouth with a grotesque red hand as if others were listening, then bent forward and confided, "Their herring is not what it used to be."

Having studied her quickly to the core, Russell had difficulty imagining this old woman possessed information that would be of any use to him but when he'd learned that Greta Erickson had conversed with John Hill in nineteen-thirty-one, he knew he had to see her.

The name *Erikson* had appeared in his father's papers, which he'd retrieved from the Marquez villa many years before. Russell had intended to interview this *Erikson* after Anton and Basile, but with no additional information in those papers he had been searching for a man named *Erikson*—most likely connected to his father in some business capacity, as Basile, Niiri, and Marquez had been. He hadn't expected a woman named *Erickson* because whoever had recorded the name had left out the "c" and a first name, costing him a ten-year delay. Only after broadening his search and retaining a private investigator, had he been able to identify the retired paleontologist.

Russell hadn't been inactive in the past decade, however, applying his psychological charm to staff his department at the University of Mainz with those who suited him—and ridding the place of the rest. He had meanwhile brought down a public prosecutor as well as the head of an investment house who was cooperating with this prosecutor in an investigation of Russell's many businesses. He had conducted denser and denser searches into his father's enterprises and into the fog surrounding his great-grandfather, Gorgo Alembert. Years of work had passed, both enlightening and frustrating. Rarely, though, had a week gone by without his giving some consideration to his father's mysterious pursuit of what Russell now believed to be a written document of great antiquity.

"I was surprised to receive your request, Professor Russell."

"Of course, as so many years have gone since you spoke to Mr. Hill."

"Not that," she said. "Because I was interviewed less than a year ago by a genealogist retained by Mr. Hill's children to assist in preparing a narrative of their father's life."

Preposterous! This woman's astounding blindness; she had never connected the man she met with that famous author. Russell said, "What was the genealogist's name?"

"Gabriel...ah, something like cheery. No—Chary, a handsome and courteous man."

"Did he leave his card?"

"He did not."

"Was he English?" probed Russell.

"Perhaps, but he spoke fluent German."

"An older man?" Russell ventured.

"No, no. Perhaps forty. How attentive he was—and with lovely eyes."

Who else could be nosing into Russell's quarry's past? All the more reason to intensify his own efforts. Russell had read that author's books for every psychological morsel he could extract, and after researching the man himself, Russell had concluded he couldn't pry the treasure from him by direct means, as Russell's father had tried to do. But his quarry was an old man now—look at how easily he could manipulate this old woman.

"We met in this building," she remarked.

"In nineteen thirty-one," Russell said.

"Heavens no!" She giggled. "I was just a girl then. Much later."

Her conceit didn't matter, so he let it go.

"I was a museum director then. I dined in a private room in those days."

"One meeting, as I understand," Russell observed, reining her back in.

"Just one," she responded, wistfully. "Years later, I saw him at a café in London. He was still quite dashing. I was with Pedro. Or was it Paulo?"

"May I ask you some questions, Professor?" continued Russell.

"Questions about your psychological research?"

"Just so. Research I'm conducting on the creative urge. Tell me why the man sought you out."

"I was the prima paleo-historian in those days. Every-one said so."

"And John Hill?"

"He was composing a fiction. He probed me about prehistoric animals, human development too. He wanted to know if humans tens of thousands of years ago had our intellectual capacity."

"And your response?" Russell inquired.

"I told him they didn't have our wide knowledge, access to our collective experience, or advanced tools, but the capacity of their minds was similar to ours, and perhaps greater in matters of survival."

"Was he gratified by your answer?"

"Was he? I suspect so, until he asked about the Pteranodon."

Russell sat up. At the same moment, the storeroom door opened and in walked a young man with a tray of herring, a cup of dark sauce, and coffee.

"Is this how herring is prepared these days?" Greta Erickson barked. Then, taking in the man, her voice softened. "Have we met?"

"No, ma'am," said the waiter, a man in his twenties with long blond hair and an athlete's physique.

"What is your name?" she asked him.

"Harri…"

Greta Erickson flinched—Russell noticed such things—but she then prattled on and flirted with the waiter until a momentary lapse in her train of thought gave the young man the opportunity to hop out the door. He mumbled his hope that the food was satisfactory.

As soon as the waiter was gone, Erickson removed a soiled washcloth from the bag at her feet and commenced scrubbing her red hands.

The herring was indifferent, but Russell pretended to enjoy it, and Erickson consumed enough for both of them. From below the table, she then produced a bottle of vodka and a water glass, filled the glass, and drank it down—with not a word nor an offer to share with Russell. Seconds later, the bottle and glass disappeared.

What an interesting case, mused Russell, as he sipped his coffee. He would enjoy dissecting this woman's psyche if he didn't have a far more important mission on his mind.

"Mr. Hill asked about the Pteranodon," Russell reminded her, wondering how reliable the old woman's memory was.

In the act of gobbling up the last herring smothered in sauce, Erickson nodded. She swallowed noisily, and said, "He wanted to know if Pteranodon cells might be discovered and if living Pteranodons might be recreated from these cells. Foolishness, and I told him so. I'm more certain now than I was then. I'm sure my answer dismayed him."

How did she stay so slender eating like a cow? Could he trust her? Perhaps, if he didn't prick her vanity. He said, "You have a remarkable memory."

"For certain people and events, I do, and in those days, I kept a diary. I retrieved it when the genealogist contacted me—Albertson!" she suddenly said. "Harri Albertson, a journalist killed outside this museum while John and I were dining."

Wondering if the murder was connected to Hill's visit, Russell asked, "Who killed him?"

"Nazi sympathizers in Sweden. Albertson was harsh on both the communists and Brownshirts in print, and he paid for it. I don't remember all the details but John and I had a lively discussion about beliefs and principles. I told him I was a rational Epicurean, and I still am, Professor Russell. One must bow to science, and then take ones pleasures where they can be found. Don't you agree?"

"By all means, Madame."

"Mademoiselle," she corrected him. "As to science, producing a more intelligent and virile race is a worthy goal. The Nazis gave eugenics a bad name, but I attribute it to incompetent execution."

Her eyes roved to Russell's canes hooked to the tabletop. He didn't mind. He was supremely intelligent and far more virile than any ordinary fifty-two-year-old, in spite of his twisted legs.

Erickson said, "We could do with far fewer of those mindless brutes who occupy space and use precious resources. Let the next generation advance this mission. All the Nazi mischief will be forgotten by then." As she spoke, the woman retrieved her towel and began grinding away at her hands.

Russell said, "Did he speak about an artifact, an antiquity, something tangible that inspired his fictional story?"

"I don't recall."

"Anything that surprised you at the time?"

She slurped her coffee before she spoke. "The look on his face when I told him science can't recreate dinosaurs. I told him he needn't worry as not one in a thousand, now or then, comprehends that impediment, so he could fill his story with dinosaurs if he chose. Oh, and I mentioned that Sorbonne professor...I cannot remember his name. He was lecturing at a Berlin conference I attended. An intense man. Now what had interested John when we talked about him?" she mused.

"Do not hurry, Mademoiselle. You were in Berlin, a lively city in those times. A hall filled with rational Epicureans I imagine, and you the prima paleo-historian. This lecturer from the Sorbonne—white hair perhaps? A compelling speaker if you still remember him. He had spoken about...?"

"Atlantis," she said, a look of revelation on her face. "White hair, yes. And he asked me about spiders."

Russell knew his father would never have pursued an artifact with such zeal, no matter how ancient or valuable, unless he believed it to possess practical value, that it would enable him to do something no one else could do. Where could something that ancient and possessing such power have come from if not an advanced civilization?

"I can show myself out," Russell said at last, gripping his canes and clenching his teeth in anticipation of the ascent.

Greta Erickson's eyes were pinned on the therapod claw.

Russell limped out of the museum to the street where he could find a taxi to take him to the airport. The trip had not been a wasted one. He had sifted the wheat from the chaff. Time for action. Time to get his hands on this treasure.

At the airport, he purchased a newspaper. Front page news: John Hill had died.

Damn! Damn!

MAY 10, 2019

☻-☻-☻

Mainz

A RRIVING AT ARTHUR RUSSELL'S FORMER PENTHOUSE apartment via a limited access elevator, Lyle and Sam were ushered into a large open room by two men wearing blue blazers, both men over two-hundred-fifty pounds.

On the way there, Sam had said, "Desrosier may have been involved in the attack on Beatrice, but this isn't the time to do anything stupid. We learn everything we can. If we decide she's guilty, we take action on our own terms, not hers. Got it?"

The room was L-shaped. What Lyle guessed to be floor-to-ceiling glass walls to his left were covered with sectional shades. On the shorter leg of the L to his right was a table and chairs, straight ahead the kitchen and dining area. With the exception of a blue and white longcase clock, all of the furniture was made of gleaming chrome or dark leather, the flooring dark wood, the walls bare except for a neck-up portrait of Arthur Russell on the elevator wall.

Caroline Desrosier entered from a door near the kitchen, a Desrosier strikingly changed from the woman Lyle had met in Paris. She wore a chic black dress and her hair was artfully styled—the woman the broken-nosed Romanov had described.

She addressed the guards. "We will be discussing a business matter, but I might need you." Her husky voice sounded more authoritative than on their previous meetings.

250

Sam whispered, "Stay on your mark."

Until then, Lyle hadn't noticed the wheelchair in the alcove, not Russell's office chair, but the high-tech wheelchair Sam had described after Russell's death.

The guards were standing and watching. Lyle's eyes strayed to the portrait of Russell, the man in the painting so handsome and virile-looking one would have been shocked to see the rest of him.

"Where was he when the painting was done?" Lyle asked her.

Desrosier said, "It was made from the few available photographs. Arthur didn't like cameras."

"The artist captured more than a physical image," Lyle observed.

"Of course. I told him exactly the gist he was to display, sketch after sketch until he achieved it."

She rose up and pointed a finger at Sam. "Let me make something clear. My head is no longer on your guillotine block. Before you threaten me again with Dekeyser's demise, no tracking device was installed on the truck I rented. I was assured of that soon after the inquisition you conducted. Furthermore, no body was ever discovered, so he may be alive."

"The perfect crime," Sam observed.

"If I had committed the crime, you would never have discovered the body, nor would anyone else," she retorted acidly.

Lyle said, "A perfect crime that depended on the good fortune of a truck without a tracking device."

"I know where you stowed the body," Sam said, over Lyle's observation.

"And I know that's a lie," Desrosier countered. "How frustrating to find me living this life and you unable to do anything about it."

Sam's *Got it?* was ringing in Lyle's ears. He wouldn't say a word about Popa or any more about Noel Dekeyser.

Sam said, "The man who handled the acquisition of the Alembert Archive is the same *avocat* who represented you in the matter of Russell's contested will."

Watch me, Sam had said at the Paix.

"Such a small world." She clapped and said, "*Ouvrir étape quatre*," the shade on the section of window nearest them slowly ascending, pendant lamps automatically dimming.

Eight stories below, the street was busy with vehicles, the hazy Rhine visible a mile to the east.

"Why was Russell's will contested?" asked Sam.

She was enjoying herself. "Technical issues."

"Not authenticity?"

"The will has been adjudicated. The matter is closed. I own everything."

Was Sam listening to her? "What do you know about Beatrice Adams?"

"Nothing. Does she live in Mainz?" Desrosier immediately responded.

"Bari Malkin?" said Sam.

She shook her head, and glanced at the guards in the corner. "Do you expect this barrage of questions to intimidate me?"

The Desrosier Lyle had known in Paris lacked the resources to hire guards or mercenaries, but with Russell's wealth, this woman could have commissioned Malkin to kill Beatrice. He knew she held them responsible for Russell's death and she was stalking him via Popa.

"Have you left the country in the last several months?" asked Sam.

"You question me as if I were on the witness stand under oath. As a matter of fact, I haven't left Mainz since February. I've been busy with the portrait painter, and with business. Am I frustrating you? I hope so."

Her assertion that she'd remained here was a lie based on what Popa had told Lyle. At their last meeting, they'd had her cornered and cowed. This time, she wanted them to know who had the whip.

Sam wasn't intimidated. "I'm looking for Bari Malkin, if you happen to meet him."

Her eyes roved from Sam to Lyle and back. "What does he do for a living?"

"He's in the extermination business."

Lyle couldn't help himself. "Did you know Lourdes committed suicide?"

"What does that have to do with me?"

"He was kind to you, I think," Lyle said emphatically.

"Perhaps he was," she said. "I haven't spoken to him, nor thought of him, since I left Paris."

"You sent a message to my colleague three years ago asking about my favorite meal. At Russell's bidding?"

"Lourdes...it's all coming back."

"How convenient he's dead. You didn't have to batter Romanov. Who was the girl?"

He'd drawn blood. He could see it in her eyes. Desrosier said, "Boris, show these men out."

Grabbing Lyle's shoulder and looking at his wristwatch, Sam said, "Is that the time? *Enchantée, Mademoiselle...à bientôt.*"

Boris herded them into the elevator, Sam signaling silence as they descended. In the lobby, Lyle said, "She might have had Boris and his comrade block the elevator, trap us in the room."

"Then, we'd have made for the other elevator, the one in her room, the last place they'd have expected us to go, Russell's private elevator."

"How do you know about that?"

"Get in the car, then we'll talk. Do you see anything on my shoulder, the one Boris grabbed?"

"Nothing."

"Give it a good brush anyway."

They went to the car, and with a blast of his horn, Sam merged into traffic. Lyle said, "We satisfied Desrosier's urge to gloat and Boris's urge to bully, but we wasted our time."

"Rubbish! Haven't you learned checkmates are set up moves ahead? We learned Desrosier knows—at least has heard of—Malkin."

"How can you say that?"

"Observation. What got me off that Albanian roof in one piece. She was prepared for questions about Beatrice, but when I came right back with Malkin, I had her. He was supposed to be a secret that stayed secret."

"Then she's behind Beatrice's murder. The bitch!"

"I played one of my precious chips—Abed and Russell's will. As it turns out, Abed is a bent solicitor, just the sort Desrosier would line up if she intended to tamper with the will."

"They let her get away with it?"

"Let me finish. Abed is a murky operator *and* a German agent who keeps an eye on radicals."

Lyle swept Sam's shoulder a second time. "So, they look the other way when Abed abets fraud."

Sam guffawed. "That's how the play works. He's more valuable to them as a spy in the *banlieues* than locked up. As for Desrosier, she knows Malkin, and it's too much of a coincidence to think her knowing him has nothing to do with Beatrice. *Invenimus et Delimus*, seek and destroy."

"Desrosier?"

"This time, that fish stays hooked."

PART IV

Sensations

MAY 10, 2019

Mainz

INFORMED THE CAFÉ MARSEILLES couldn't accommodate them, they had supper at a touristy lodge near their hotel and retired to their room.

Sam said, "If you'd told them you were a survivor of the bombing, they'd have found a table for us."

Survivor of the bombing—the only words Lyle heard, and he wasn't disappointed to have avoided the place where he'd come close to a death schemed by Arthur Russell.

Sam said, "By the way, where were you yesterday afternoon?"

"You know I met Romanov."

"That was in the morning. I rang you twice."

A Mainz police detective's actions in the Café Marseilles probably saved Lyle's life, but the detective hadn't survived. Lyle said, "I called on Oscar Plug's sister and my doctor at the hospital."

"I'm impressed you don't want to avoid those bad memories."

"I do want to avoid them, but I went anyway," said Lyle, thinking about Desrosier. She and Malkin were behind all this? On his own, how was Sam supposed to bring them down? She had money and brutes to protect her, and who knew where Malkin was? In the Oxford pub, Lyle had set all this in motion but now he cared more about keeping Sam safe than finding Beatrice's killer.

Coming out of the hotel bathroom, Lyle found Sam on the balcony, smoking a cigar.

"Is this an approved smoking area?" Lyle chirped.

"Probably not, but no one's around to object. Pull up a chair."

As the sky was still light outside, the street was busy with cars, bicycles, and walkers. A knock on the door prompted Lyle to say, "Apparently, an objector is lurking. Put that cigar away before I answer the door."

Setting the smoking cigar on the balcony floor, Sam told him, "I'll see to the door."

"Think it's Boris or his comrade?"

"I don't think anything, but why would we have a visitor?"

Quickly retrieving a pistol from his bag and stowing it in the back of his pants, Sam peered through the tiny observation port, and slowly opened the door.

The first few steps of the lean, lupine-featured man who slid into the room suggested he was light on his feet, like a dancer or an athlete. He closed the door.

"No hawkers or circulars allowed," said Sam.

"What do you want?" the man in the entryway said.

Sam had taken a step back—the better to retrieve his pistol? "I'm satisfying myself that you killed Beatrice Adams. The incendiary that was used, what I learned in Israel and from Desrosier."

Lyle was torn between an urge to storm into the room and knowing Sam didn't need any distractions. He felt like a fighter preparing to enter the ring, alert to everything.

Sam said, "You didn't know her, like a lot of people you've murdered."

"That's rich coming from you, Stuart. As if you haven't done the same. Righteous—what bullshit!"

Sam inched forward. "These aren't enemy agents you're murdering, they're noncombatants, innocents."

The man was scanning the room, his eyes constantly moving.

"Perhaps the death I deal is more agreeable than what life has in store for them."

Did Malkin mean it, or was he trying to provoke Sam? "You cheat life of its tariff. That's the best you can do?"

Lyle couldn't see Sam's face, but he could hear well enough, and smell the cigar at his feet, another Russian consulate moment where he was on a knife's edge.

Malkin said, "People looking for me makes me nervous, and when I'm nervous I can't sit still until I've done something about it. Who's that on the balcony?"

"I'll let you guess."

"Lyle Stuart, boy wonder. I ought to finish both of you off here and now, and don't think I can't."

Sam didn't make a move for his gun. "You might be able to, but I have relentless friends who know what I know. You aren't aware of who they are. If I go down, so do you. They'll filet you like a fish. But you realize that."

Sam had trumped Malkin's first ace. Hadn't he said he'd be prepared?

Glaring at Lyle, Malkin said to Sam, "Tell me what you want."

"Your scalp, good and bloody, but I'll settle for the name of the person who hired you."

"Not proper business to give out information about a customer."

"I already have my suspicions, so if it's better for business, call it confirmation."

Lyle could hear little emotion in either voice, but he knew all hell might break loose any second. He was expecting it.

Malkin said, "Give me a day to think about it."

"Remember my relentless friends, all three of them. They've been at it a long time. They have a heap of scalps."

Opening the door behind him, Malkin said, "Maybe you'll hear from me and maybe you won't."

The Israeli was already in the hall, when Sam said, "If I don't hear from you, you'll hear from me, or my friends." Turning to

Lyle, who had reentered the room, Sam added, "That couldn't have been easy. Was it Leary?"

Lyle was trembling with anger, relief—whatever. Sam was trying hard to display composure but Lyle saw something on his brother's face he'd never seen before. Was it fear? Lyle said, "Not Leary. What do you think he'll do?"

Sam said, "I know what he'll do. He'll give up Desrosier. He knows I suspect she's behind the hit. I told him as much. Up till now, he could afford to be loyal, or whatever the word is that describes his business arrangements. Now that his deed is known, his decision is a matter of survival, protecting number one from me and my relentless friends."

"Do they exist?"

"Certainly they do, and they'll cut him down, one of them will, if anything happens to me. You don't get far by bluffing in this business."

Cornel Popa had said that *something unimaginable* might be approaching, and here that something was in the flesh, a merciless assassin of the highest order now bent on eliminating him and Sam. And lest Lyle try to convince himself the menace was exaggerated, he recalled the testimony of Eitan and Genç.

"We're all in, aren't we?" said Lyle.

"To the death, brother. *Invenimus et Delimus.* Did you think that was just a slogan? Quiet. Someone's at the door."

Lyle hadn't heard the muted rapping. The anxiety he'd felt when Malkin was in the room surged anew.

"Back to the balcony," Sam said. "Now!"

"He's back?"

"Maybe. Move!"

THE ELEVATOR DOOR OPENED, AND THE WOMAN STEPPED OUT. She was shrouded in a dark niqab, with only her eyes visible, afraid of tripping on her floor-sweeping hem as she had in the London airport.

Her heart was pounding like a jackhammer with the fear she'd experienced in every airport, in every car and train.

Her destination was down the corridor. A man was walking toward her, a person with an ambiguous aura. She had a sixth sense for auras, but she was far too preoccupied to bother with this stranger.

He whisked past, a man on a mission, better that than those who fixed eyes on her as if she were a venomous snake.

What she had done had been necessary, and what she was doing now was necessary. That's what she kept telling herself. She knocked on the door, counting while she waited, using the time to try to compose herself.

The door swung open. "I wondered how long you would take to find us," Sam said.

"Where is he?" she asked, the thin slot in the headpiece limiting her vision to Sam and the wall behind him.

Sam closed the door. "Back there. Watching us."

There he was, standing, observing them. She felt joy and fear, mingled in a way she'd never experienced. She walked past Sam to the balcony entrance, removing the head covering. "I'm sorry. I'll explain everything," she said to him.

Lyle fell to his knees, propped up by one hand, staring dumbly at her.

Sam had joined them, and said to Lyle, "Drink this." Sam handed him a glass.

With Sam's assistance, Lyle writhed to his feet, his hand shaking so violently Sam had to hold the glass while Lyle gulped the Scotch.

"Give me your hand," Sam commanded. "Look at me!"

Sam led his brother inside and helped him into a chair.

Beatrice removed the niqab. Beneath it, she wore jeans and a short-sleeved blouse. She sat on the floor in front of Lyle, waiting, her heart breaking with what she had done to him. Sam said, "I may have known you were alive, but it's a delight to see you again."

"How long have you known?" Lyle whispered.

"When Joseph called me back into his office, he told me the DNA didn't match Cornelia's."

She saw Lyle's eyes come alive. "You sonofabitch! You were laughing at me when you lit that candle."

"Not for a minute, a thanksgiving candle for both of you."

Beatrice said to Lyle, "Sam and I haven't communicated a word to each other, though I'm not surprised he knew, or suspected."

Sam gave her a sip of the Scotch. She wasn't used to the surge that accompanied strong drink.

No sooner had she tasted it than she lifted herself from the floor and reached out for Lyle. "Will you put your arms around me as you did Christmas day?"

Lyle's eyes moved like spotlights from Beatrice to his brother. She wasn't sure he'd heard her until jerking to his feet, he drew her near, then closer. Once or twice she thought he was going to speak but nothing came out.

I love him. How much I missed him. "Tell me you still love me," Beatrice said to Lyle.

"I love you but…"

She put a finger to his lips. What had she expected? Nothing, after she had let him believe she was dead, her bones beneath that stone. She had wondered if Sam knew, and if he did whether he'd inform Lyle or would go along with her deception. Nothing had mattered to her except keeping Lyle alive, and here he was, still alive but angry and distrustful.

Sam broke the long silence by telling her about their trip to Kampala, how he had suspected something was amiss at Cornelia's house and learned the truth from Mutesi, how they'd tracked the bomber to Istanbul and concluded that Desrosier was involved. Beatrice heard some of it, but her attention was on Lyle.

She couldn't guess what he was thinking. Sam brought her back when he said, "The bomber was just here. It's a wonder you didn't run into him in the hallway."

The man with the ambiguous aura. She shuddered. "Is he coming back?"

"I don't know," answered Sam.

"I thought you knew everything," Lyle said.

Beatrice broke in. "Listen to me, Lyle. Please! He may have set the bomb but he wasn't the one who wanted me dead. Four days before my apartment was bombed, I was visited by Andrea Fitzgerald. Yes, Lyle. She questioned me about the manuscript, did everything she could to recruit me to help her acquire it. I'm a psychologist, but I've never experienced so persuasive an appeal as hers. Money, your career and prestige, an obligation to science. When she'd exhausted every appeal, realized I wouldn't give in, she implored me to keep our conversation confidential until she returned to Oxford and could inform you herself." She breathed out heavily.

"May I have a glass of water, Sam?" She waited until he returned, drinking it all down. Her presence and exposition had obviously unnerved Lyle. How much did he comprehend? She must continue nonetheless. "I had an odd feeling, the same feeling I had when our village was attacked, so I asked my friend down the hall—you remember Beni—if I could stay with her for a few days." She thought he nodded.

"If you weren't in the room, who was?" Lyle said.

She was encouraged to hear him ask a coherent question. "What I didn't know when I moved into Beni's room was that she and her boyfriend needed somewhere else to meet, and my empty room was the perfect place. Before her boyfriend arrived at my room, she triggered the bomb. I knew the police would check DNA, but I hoped they'd keep it from the public. When I went to them, they agreed, and so did Beni's boyfriend.

"Lyle, you couldn't know the truth, or what Fitzgerald intended for me would have been visited on you. I decided your best defense was ignorance of what really happened, because I wasn't convinced you could keep my survival secret from someone who pressed me harder than I'd ever been pressed. As long as Fitzgerald believed I was dead, she had nothing to fear. She preferred to keep you alive because you were the key to acquiring the manuscript."

"You could have gone to the police and turned her in," Lyle protested.

"With what evidence? They would have ignored me. Or worse, contacted the British police, who would have informed Fitzgerald."

"Where did you hide?" asked Sam.

"A monastery outside the city. I was lonely and frightened, but I felt closer to my brother, Paul, than I had in years. When Paul faced down the rebels, he knew he wouldn't survive but he was willing to sacrifice himself to give us a sliver of hope."

"Who knew you were alive?" Lyle asked her.

"I had to tell Cornelia and Maria. Then I told the police, without mentioning Fitzgerald."

Sam said, "I've interviewed more than my share of people who have experienced the violent deaths of loved ones, and something was missing in Cornelia's and Maria's responses. Lyle told me how much they loved you, so it wasn't that. Even Maria's display of grief seemed off the mark, all making sense when I learned the truth, because her sadness was for Lyle, not her sister. When Joseph called me back, I was less surprised than he expected."

The strength that Lyle, Sam, Cornelia, and Maria saw as natural in Beatrice had come at a steep price. She said, "You can't imagine how hard this has been. For years after our village was attacked, I woke up at night terrified, fearing they were still hunting us, surrounding the house. That's how I've felt ever since Beni was killed, and how I feel now."

She could see the anguish on Lyle's face when he said, "Do you know what this did to me? Ask Sam or Agnese. Did you think

I'd have a few bad weeks and everything would be normal? This has been the worst month in my life. Everything came apart. I came apart!"

This was what she had dreaded and expected, what she had worried about in the monastery every day. How many times had she picked up a pen, started a letter, and torn it up? "I know this has hurt you. Not a day, an hour, has passed without the deception grieving me. I've been petrified since I left the monastery. Mutesi cleared my passport, but I worried the police would grab me. Stares, suspicious looks, whether Fitzgerald would learn I was on the move. By the time I arrived in Oxford, I'd run out of money. Danielle gave me enough to come here. The last leg was the worst. Wondering how you would receive me..."

"I'm going to eliminate the threat, Beatrice," said Sam. "Trust me."

With Sam at the helm, they'd have no more safe harbors— rather, mortal danger, day after day, until this business was resolved. Death was the inevitable outcome. But whose? Could she do again what she had done on that riverbank seventeen years before? Not just summon the courage, or whatever the word was, but survive the awful memories.

She put her hands on Sam's arms. He wasn't the man she'd said goodbye to when she'd left for Africa. How much older he looked. "You know your business, Sam, but I trusted our father to keep us safe until our village and home were invaded. He couldn't protect us. When we finally reached Kampala, he was a shell of a man."

Was Sam a shell of a man too? Would he lead them into more danger than he could handle? Lyle hoisted himself from his chair and made his way to Beatrice, taking her hand. Her heart leapt. He said, "I look awful. I said awful things, and my stomach feels like a volcano about to erupt, but I've never been happier in my life. God, I can't tell you how happy I am to see you!"

She kissed him and smiled at him, the best she could do right now.

Lyle gave her his chair, and this time he was the one who sat on the floor.

Sam said, "Tell me about the woman killed in your room."

Whatever was going on inside Lyle's brother, he was still relentless. Beatrice said, "She didn't have a family. She was an orphan from the Bwaise slum who had made something of herself. I told you I had an inkling of danger. After the bombing, I concluded Fitzgerald would do anything to ensure Lyle wasn't informed about the subject of her visit."

"The water gate," said Sam, then telling her about Jericho and Fitzgerald's mysterious visitor. "The man she hired is ex-Mossad. Bari Malkin entered the compound through the water gate Fitzgerald opened. The timing fits perfectly, a few weeks before the bombing. They were scheming together at a secure location where Fitzgerald was in charge. She had sent off the young Israeli and her assistant for the night. Hiring Malkin wasn't an impulsive decision. Identifying and recruiting him was long-planned. She intended to kill you no matter how you responded. Even if Malkin thinks you're dead, I don't like the idea of his being here."

She shook her head in sadness. "I told myself I would remain in hiding until everything had settled down, until Fitzgerald was convinced Lyle had no suspicions, until I could sort through my grief for Beni, who'd died instead of me—because of me. Until I could decide how to assist Maria, and what steps I'd take to bring Fitzgerald to justice without putting Lyle at risk. I was formulating a plan.

"Then, Colonel Mutesi came to the monastery to interview me again—two weeks ago. He told me you were pursuing the killer yourselves. That meant once Fitzgerald found out what you were doing—and I had little doubt she *would* find out—my hiding no longer had any value, just the opposite. My plan was in tatters. So, here I am, no plan, nothing but the clothes on my back."

Sam said, "I don't need a name from Malkin anymore, but I'm going to let him give it to me anyway, and you two won't be around when he does."

"What are you going to tell him?" said Lyle.

"I'm going to test his Latin."

MAY 11, 2019

Mainz
(same night)

"KATYA IS IN THE *HALLE*."

Boris had knocked on her bedroom door after midnight, something he'd been instructed never to do, barring an emergency.

Katya often arrived late, but not without an invitation. Was something wrong?

The woman hated the *pas de deux* the two of them engaged in every time they met, hated the guards knowing her weakness.

Could she have imagined such an attachment when Arthur was alive? Why had he introduced her to Katya's cousin, now replaced by Katya? Had anything he'd done been unintentional?

"Let her in."

"She's in the *halle*."

He would make her say it. "Bring her here, to my room."

She was already in her nightgown. While she waited, she made herself a drink, and one for Katya.

Did she have time to change nightgowns, to put a little makeup on her face, to apply the scent Katya liked?

Katya didn't knock. When Desrosier turned around, there she was, the door already closed.

"Here's your drink." No variation in their routine, the way she liked it.

How good she had felt tormenting that dirty man and his brother. She had triumphed, had seen it on their faces, until the younger one asked about the girl—the cousin. She had reported the questions about the assassin, so her final revenge on those men was at hand.

She embraced and kissed Katya.

"I'll be just a minute," Caroline Desrosier said, turning to the bathroom.

Like ice against her back, then it stung, a pool of blood at her feet, her throat full. She couldn't breathe.

Her last thought: Dekeyser putting the glass to his lips in her Paris apartment.

By the time the glass shattered on the floor, she was dead.

MAY 11, 2019

Mainz
(same night)

L YLE CREPT FROM BEATRICE'S BEDROOM where he'd been watching her sleep to the hotel balcony, too energized to sleep, too unsettled to eat, and too unsteady to walk the streets. Drunk with joy!

Beatrice sleeping in the bed, Sam on the sofa, Lyle was looking down on the street below their room, the busy street he'd observed just before Malkin, the man who had killed Beatrice, made his appearance.

But she was alive!

Part of him still refused to believe it, even after he'd seen her, spoken to her, held her.

Could Andrea Fitzgerald really be the author of all this mischief? The sympathetic woman he'd considered a friend, more than a friend? If he could have been so utterly deceived, what might he believe? Andrea was intelligent enough, resourceful enough, determined enough, when it came to what she wanted, and within weeks of Beatrice's "death" making a pitch for him to share her bed at the Jericho site.

Could the person who visited Beatrice in Kampala have been disguised as Andrea, or have pretended to be her? Not bloody

270

likely, as Beatrice had met Andrea on several occasions, not to mention having seen her BBC appearances.

Lyle had the urge to confront Andrea, to see the expression on her face, hear her explanation and try to make sense of her actions. She was a world-famous archeologist, a television celebrity. He couldn't believe she lacked for money.

Bari Malkin and Caroline Desrosier had to be connected to Andrea. What other explanation fit?

If just days before the bombing, Andrea had visited, cajoled, and pressured Beatrice, asked her to keep the conversation in confidence, who else could have hired Malkin? And with Malkin confronting Sam a few hours after they'd interrogated Desrosier, who else could have informed the Israeli that Sam was seeking him?

Before they'd retired for the night, Lyle had said, "We could confront Andrea, tell her what we know, tell her we've informed the police."

"Too late for that," Sam had responded. "But I'll excuse your fuzzy thinking after what you've been through. You're tired of this business, and you have Beatrice back—a miracle. Still, we have to take this rotten tree down, burn the stump, pull out all the roots. It's the only way."

Beatrice said, "Are you sure, Sam, or have you just become accustomed to solving problems that way?"

"I've been trained to recognize when elimination is the only way to prevent a worse outcome. Now's the time to press harder, not let up."

What about Leary, who had to be mixed up in all this, meaning he had to be connected to Andrea too? How could she afford so many professional troublemakers?

What had Sam meant when he said he was going to test Malkin's Latin, other than his brother intended to put *seek and destroy* into practice? Lyle knew next to nothing about Sam's business but he'd heard and seen enough in recent years to know that Malkin wasn't a low-grade operative. The man was deadly dangerous. Lyle had found Beatrice. He wasn't about to lose Sam.

His brother wasn't a low-grade operative either, though. In his day, he'd been a senior British agent, someone who'd earned the esteem of men like Joseph Mutesi and Zvi Eitan; Sam was also a man who had killed his best mate because it had to be done. But Lyle's brother wasn't who he once was.

Lyle ought to have been burned out now, but he was full of energy. Sam's dead cigar on the pavement reminded him of Malkin's visit. The sky was spangled with stars. Stray men and women were traversing the street below him, a scrawny dog nosing from wall to wall.

She was alive!

He had to make sure. Creeping back to the bedroom, opening the door, he was afraid he'd frighten her if she awoke.

She was curled up like a child, with a pillow under her head and another between her legs. He couldn't see her face, but he knew it was Beatrice. In the few words they'd spoken to each other, they had embarked on the slow process of sewing the pages of their lives back together after they'd been ripped from the binding and scattered to the four winds.

At Pylos, Nis, and so many other sites in the wake of a big discovery or breakthrough that energized him, he would take up his expedition journal, read and record, until he became sleepy or the sun came up. With Popa winding down Lido, Lyle had nothing to add to his site journal, but he'd tossed the Carlton letter into his travel bag in case Sam could make sense of it, and on his way back to the balcony, he retrieved it.

He had a hard time concentrating because Beatrice, Malkin, Desrosier, and Andrea kept intruding on his thoughts. He first read half the letter before realizing he hadn't comprehended anything; the second time he continued to the end without much sticking. Why not just put it away and let his mind roam, feel a bit of joy and relief?

Something kept drawing him back, though, as if the contents of this letter meant something to him. How was that possible, as it involved people and events from a hundred years before?

The third time he resolved to concentrate, and if nothing came to him he'd put it aside once and for all.

April 15, 1931

Dear Max,

You have met my friend, Drake, as he likes to be called. Bit of a bull in a china shop but good instincts and an iron backbone. He and some others have been kicking around the notion of recruiting Alembert to eliminate H, ER, and GS. Setting one pack of jackals against another. Drake claims he can make it worth Alembert's while. If His Majesty's Government makes direct contact, and Alembert declines and informs H's crowd a nasty howling will ensue. Thus, an intermediary like Thomas is essential, especially if Alembert trusts him. Both Agatha and Thomas being in the literary line, might she broach the subject with him? In the form of—shall we say—a literary inspiration?

Cordially yours,
Carlton

Alembert was clear enough, and Agnese had identified Max and Agatha at dinner, but Thomas, Drake, H, ER, and GS?

At that instant, the loud roar of a motorbike tearing down the street in front of him was accompanied by the sensation he always experienced when he stood on the verge of a big discovery. "What about that motorbike?" Lyle said.

Harold Binker's *Brough*, the bike he'd purchased after the war, and that CurLio diary entry he remembered, a mysterious Thomas visiting Agnes in Bilbao on the *Brough*.

Lyle went for his phone. T. E. Lawrence had died while riding his Brough Superior in 1935. Was that who Agnes's Thomas had been?

Carlton was associated with the British government in 1931, and Lyle knew what was transpiring in Europe in those times. H for Hitler, ER for Ernst Röhm? GS he couldn't place, but if his surmise was correct, someone close to Hitler in the era before he assumed power.

Alembert had disappeared in 1932. Eliminated by Hitler's people? Or had Carlton's scheme come to naught, been rejected by Alembert, or never proposed to him?

Had he dozed off? Still fuzzy, he closed his eyes.

Sam's loud voice came like a heavenly summons: "Are you going to sleep all day?"

MAY 11, 2019

ⓔ–ⓔ–ⓔ

Mainz

"T HE GAME'S AFOOT," said Sam, looking up from Lyle's laptop. If Lyle was beyond ecstatic to have Beatrice back, Sam's enthusiasm suggested he wasn't far behind.

"That expression's been used," said Lyle, foggy despite two cups of black coffee.

"We're staying another day," Lyle's brother said.

"You said you didn't like the idea of Beatrice and Malkin in the same town."

"Look at this."

The lead article in the English version of the online *Allgemeine Zeitung* described the stabbing deaths of Caroline Desrosier and an unidentified male.

"That's a month of murders in Mainz," Sam said.

Lyle was stunned. That black widow—Dekeyser's murderer, collaborator with Russell in how many other murders—dead? How had the killer gotten past her guards, or was one of them the dead man?

Anticipating his question, Sam said, "The dead man was killed in another part of town. Use your imagination."

"You think it's Malkin?" Lyle asked his brother.

"I intend to find out. Come, comrades. I'm not leaving you alone till I know more. Beatrice, don't bother covering up, but under no circumstances are you to give anyone your real name."

"Where are we going?" she asked him.

"The police morgue."

Lyle said, "Do you think Andrea killed them?"

"I doubt it. She didn't do the bombing in Uganda, not herself. Ten minutes and we're off."

Lyle was finishing his third coffee when Beatrice took his hand under the table. "Are you sure you should talk to the police?" she asked Sam.

In the light of day, how worn she appeared, far less vigorous than the woman Lyle remembered. Her jet-black hair was longer than before, pulled back and clasped behind her head, extending below the nape of her neck. She'd lost weight. Moreover, she'd lost the glow that once radiated like an inner light.

Sam said, "I have to make sure it's Malkin, and I have to know more about how they were killed."

They rushed out of the hotel, Lyle and Beatrice in the rear seat. Crossing town, Sam said, "You two stay in the car. Your coming with me will invite more questions than I'm ready to answer."

After Sam left the car, an awkward silence descended. This was the first time since she'd appeared that they were alone together. She was the same, and changed. He was the same, and changed too. Taking her face in his hands and kissing her gently, he felt her quiver before she leaned into him.

Releasing her, he said, "I'm where I never expected to be."

"We're not out of the woods. If we're not careful, we can lose everything. You heard what Sam said."

He was unaccustomed to a tentative, almost timid, Beatrice, but she'd been through as much as he had, soul-splitting pain. He said, "I've been around Sam a lot lately, have seen him in action, starting in Kampala. Cornelia and Maria were acting strangely, but I put it down to grief."

"They told me you were coming. I suggested the less they said, the better."

"Tell them they did a good job."

"You know why I did it."

He took a determined breath. "I'm going to call Andrea."

She grasped his arm. "You should consult Sam first."

"He never consults me first."

"If he were doing archaeology, he would."

"The longer we wait, the more time she has to make a move."

"You're not stable yet," she said.

"You sound like Danielle." Lyle had already retrieved his phone. She didn't prevent him as the old Beatrice would have done. He knew what Sam would say, but this *idée fixe* was too strong.

A long wait before Lyle pressed the speaker button. "Is that you, Andrea?"

"It's me. Where are you, Lyle?"

"Mainz."

"What are you doing there?" asked the voice, betraying no hint of concern.

"Visiting a friend at the university."

"What's his name?"

He didn't hesitate. "Clyde. A geographer, Lido archeo-mapping. Where are you?"

"You know where I am. Jericho, Zeta2. I still have room in my tent when you're finished with Cliff."

"Clyde. When are you returning to Oxford? I'm planning a special night at The Lawrence."

"That sounds lovely. I've been dying to go. We're filming for another week. By then, I'll be ready for a civilized meal."

"I miss you, Andrea," he said.

"I miss you too."

Lyle said, "May I speak to Gorsey for a moment?"

"He's helping the film crew with a set-up. Hold on."

Beatrice's questioning look prompted Lyle to put a finger to his lips. They waited in silence.

"Yes, Dr. Stuart."

"Do you remember where we put the Lido saddle querns?"

"Sorry, Dr. Stuart. I don't remember seeing them."

"I seem to have misplaced them. If you recall something, let me know."

"Did you check the Lido cabinet in the lab?"

"I should have, but it slipped my mind. I'm glad I rang you. Tell Dr. Fitzgerald I'll be in touch soon."

Putting his phone away, Lyle said, "By talking to Gorsey, I made sure she was really in Jericho."

"You've learned a few tricks from your brother. You had me believing you were excited about taking her to dinner."

"I am. To wring her pretty neck. I wasn't going to lie about being in Mainz. She's aware of my past association with Desrosier, so she must have been anxious to learn if I'd heard about her murder."

"She resisted the urge to ask you. You both played your roles." Beatrice gave him a weary look. "What have we gotten ourselves into?"

"She's smart and talented, but how did she manage to have Desrosier and Malkin murdered, if that's who the man was?"

Beatrice cozied up to him, and said, "You wouldn't believe how different Fitzgerald was in Kampala. Nothing like the woman I met in Oxford. Or saw on the telly. Her presence filled the room, no other way to put it."

"Agnese warned me at the restaurant, called her a cobra. Which reminds me, you never prepared that liver dish you promised. The proprietor of the Café Marseilles gave you his prize recipe."

"Did he now?"

He was glad to see a spark in her. "I remember it distinctly."

"I must have misplaced it."

"Beatrice Adams has never misplaced anything in her life."

"What if I told you it was in a recipe box in my apartment, my mother's recipe box? It's gone now."

Idiot, he said to himself.

Though the time seemed shorter, Lyle's brother was another hour in the police station. Beatrice didn't dwell on the hardships she'd experienced while in hiding—a shortage of money, for one thing, as she had no income apart from the few shillings Cornelia sent her. But he'd heard enough the previous night to know how difficult her weeks in hiding had been.

He said, "I want to tell you a story about someone who must be connected to Desrosier and Andrea, an Atlantean."

"As in the island?"

"Certainly. He came to my office and spun a wild yarn. I'd like to hear your expert psychological perspective."

"How long a leash did you give him?"

"The longest. *You* told me to indulge him, *your voice* in my ear. I tried everything, but I couldn't pin him down."

She said, "If he was prepared by Fitzgerald, does that surprise you? Tell me everything you remember. And *none of that* till we're back on terra firma," she added, rebuffing his caress.

Lyle smiled and hit the highlights of what Leary had said—and told her how Sam had explained it.

"Did he threaten you?"

"He warned me about the manuscript. He said one of his people will stop at nothing to get their hands on it."

"How did he know about it?"

"Desrosier or Andrea, I'm sure. The thing is, he knew about a woman named Rosman in Agnes CurLio's journal, missing from the archive bin when I went there before my trip to Africa with Sam. Andrea must have stolen the diary, but how would she have learned about it? I never talked to Andrea about Agnes or the diary."

Lyle could see that Beatrice was fully engaged. "Sam's right about that psychological gambit, but I've never heard of anyone attempting a primary story as fantastic as his. That's risky, and would have required extensive preparation for an expert like you, prep from someone like Fitzgerald. Was he unbalanced?"

"Not that I could discern."

"Did he claim to be an archaeologist?"

"He called himself an antiquarian."

"A skilled actor playing a part?"

"That's what I concluded."

"If he's connected to Fitzgerald, you haven't seen the last of him. Or he's been eliminated too. Maybe she decided to cut all the threads that lead back to her. He must have been trying to draw you out about the book. The direct approach failed with me so they went with something different."

"He returned empty handed. I didn't give him anything, not a crumb."

Sam had opened the car door before they realized he was back. "I told you to lock the door. If I were an assassin, you'd both be dead. Fortunately for you, an especially accomplished assassin is in a body drawer in that building."

"Malkin?" asked Lyle, in surprise.

Sam nodded. "A fresh corpse, still some foam in his nose. The police were so grateful for the identification they answered some of my questions. They found an arsenal in Malkin's room consistent with a professional assassin, a premier assassin."

"Did you see Desrosier?" Lyle asked.

"The first time I saw her without a scowl on her face. She may not have commissioned Malkin but you can bet she knew about it. My heart rejoiced to see those two reduced to…"

"I spoke with Andrea," Lyle announced.

"The hell you did!" thundered Sam.

"You would have been proud of him," said Beatrice. "I miss you, Andrea," she crooned.

Sam turned his head to the back seat, his eyes shifting from one to the other. "You better tell me everything so I'll know when we can expect more trouble."

After Lyle related his conversation with Andrea and Gorsey, Sam said, "We're probably safe for a few days. No thanks to you.

Can't I leave you alone for an hour? Both Desrosier and Malkin were killed by surgically precise knife strikes. That put me in mind of Albanian girls."

"Girls?" Beatrice interrupted, sounding puzzled.

"Destitute Albanian girls, purchased by the Chinese, trained to be assassins, young enough to be thoroughly brainwashed, pretty enough to come close to any target, and trained in the use of knives. No ballistic or poison evidence. I learned that a girl who fits this profile was admitted to Desrosier's apartment last night, and the perfectly placed knife wound in Malkin's back means that for all his experience, he had a weakness. Everyone does. Me too, but instead of sliding a knife under my ribs, she removed the clip from my pistol. I didn't find out until I was up against it."

"How much of this is guesswork?" Beatrice asked.

"Boris told the police the girl was Albanian. Stab-strokes in the back and through the heart wall, both in the same night. Those women are deadly with flick-knives, every one of them."

Lyle said, "Didn't I mention what Romanov told me about a young woman kissing Desrosier in the restaurant?"

Sam said, "You left that part out. I guess you were too busy with Plug's sister and the doc to put me in the picture. The only reason I let you meet Romanov was to dig out intelligence on Desrosier, and you buggered it up. I trust that poodle more than I do you."

Lyle was preparing to fire back when Beatrice jumped in. "The notations in Russell's journal proved he manipulated Desrosier like all the others. Perhaps he had an elimination strategy for her that involved this Albanian girl. He may have believed Desrosier knew too much—the manuscript, Russell's role in Dekeyser's murder, the scheme with the Russian. Russell's genius was discerning weaknesses and using them."

"Are you suggesting Russell murdered Desrosier? From the grave?" Lyle's eyes widened.

"Not two years later. If the girl Romanov saw in the restaurant wasn't the same one who killed her, Russell may have kindled a lust in Desrosier. He was a master psychologist."

Sam said, "If I'd heard Romanov's story, I would have used what Russell kindled to make Desrosier fear I'd had gotten to the girl. Fitzgerald is working for the Chinese, or she's helping them for her own reasons. Explains the Albanian assassins and how she was able to recruit and pay Malkin's steep fee."

"Will they come after us?" asked Lyle.

"With the Albanians? Probably not. Another Malkin? They don't grow on trees. By now, Fitzgerald and maybe the Chinese, know I'm engaged. If they decide to target us, they'll take their time and do it right. Oh, the police discovered a handwritten letter Desrosier kept in a locked drawer in her bedroom. They weren't about to give up evidence in a fresh murder case, but they let me read it. The letter instructed Desrosier to send all correspondence concerning *the pearls* to an address in Wimbledon."

Lyle said, "Desrosier must have told Andrea what she'd learned from Dekeyser, and we know she was working on Popa as Madame Filion. Andrea knows Henry's my uncle. She tried to trick the manuscript out of me, then hedged her bets with Beatrice and the monastery invasions."

"Could Fitzgerald have attacked you in the monastery?" asked Sam.

He hadn't told Beatrice about that night, and saw the instant alarm on her face.

"I don't suppose you've communicated with your friend, Nancy—Professor Evans," Sam said to Beatrice.

"I didn't dare. Did you meet her in Kampala?"

"On the plane from Istanbul to London," said Lyle.

Beatrice said, "I ought to let her know I'm alive. May I speak to her, Sam?"

"I'll do it. She gave me her card on the plane. You can fill her in later."

AT THE HOTEL, SAM PLACED A CALL to Zvi Eitan, informing the Israeli that Malkin had been eliminated.

"I won't lose any sleep. Who managed that marvel?"

"An Albanian girl."

"You know what that suggests, Sam. Don't put yourself in Li's sights," the Israeli said.

"You have reliable people in Mexico?"

"Of course, official and *sayanim*, our civilian network."

"Anyone adept at the biosciences?"

The delay meant Eitan was thinking or checking his computer. "A *sayan* who teaches in Mexico City. What is this about? I have covers and reputations to protect."

"This little job won't embarrass anyone."

"I don't want to cross Li. Why do you need us?"

"Something packaged in a diplomatic pouch, shipped to your consulate in Frankfurt," Sam said.

"When?"

"A matter of days."

"That's all?" Eitan said. "How much danger?"

"For an expert biologist, practically none. For an amateur, plenty." Sam took a deep breath: "Mammillaria Matude... Oaxaca...Scolopendra letalis. Deadly."

MAY 12, 2019

☉-☉-☉

Mainz/Oxford

"IT'S HAROLD BINKER, PROFESSOR."

What could he want? The old man knew Lyle was traveling. "Call me Lyle, Harold."

Harold's childlike voice said, "I'm afraid that celebration we talked about will have to wait. The gang is down a member."

"What happened?" Lyle said, Beatrice and Sam perking up at his urgent tone.

"Irma died, a heart attack they say."

"I'm so sorry. Give the gang my condolences."

"To be sure, but that's not the reason I called. I know you're on the Continent. Benson isn't convinced she died a natural death."

"What?" Lyle thundered.

"He thinks Irma might have been murdered."

Which of the people Lyle had met that night would want to harm Irma, and what could he do about it with everything else that was going on? He recalled Harold's observation as they'd made for the Waterloo Creek exit. "We have plenty of time to think and observe. Not always clearly, mind you."

The old man upended his thinking with, "This may have something to do with you, Lyle."

Beatrice and Sam were watching him. With all they had experienced, everything was suspicious until proven otherwise.

Harold said, "Benson's on the line with me. He has more information than I have."

White Hat. With raised voice, Lyle said, "I want to put my brother, Sam, on too. He has experience with criminal investigations."

"Jeremy suggested as much in his letter," said Harold.

Whatever Jeremy had suggested would have to wait. "Sam can hear us, Harold." Beatrice edged closer to the phone too.

For Sam's benefit, Lyle said, "Harold lives in the apartments across the street from the flat, so did Irma, who just died. I had dinner with Harold, Benson, Irma and their gang the night before I left for Sarajevo. Go ahead, Harold."

The man said, "Yesterday morning, we found Irma in her bed. We were worried because she never missed breakfast unless she wasn't well."

"Who found her? This is Sam Stuart."

"Ruth and the day attendant. They called an ambulance. We all went in to pay our respects."

"I told the medical people to look her over."

"Who's speaking?" Sam demanded.

"Benson."

"Why did you want her examined?" Sam pressed.

"Because I was suspicious." Benson's strong emotion could be heard in his Texas drawl. Hadn't Harold told Lyle that Benson was sweet on Irma? "I knew something the others didn't."

"Any reason for you to know more than the rest?" Sam had never met Benson but was bearing down on the man.

"Yessir," said Benson. "I was an American Embassy guard in the nineteen-sixties, and decided to stay here after my tour. Applied to MI6. They turned me down, so I did security work around London for forty years."

Harold cut in. "The night after you joined us in the game room, Irma told us she'd seen someone enter your building at three a.m. while you were in Africa, and your room light came on five minutes later."

Of course that gang of owls would know where his flat was located. Did this explain the moved books?

"When the person came out, Irma followed," Benson said. "In her bathrobe and house shoes, she told me she looked like a vagrant. If the person noticed her, they didn't give her a second look. Irma committed the plate number to memory, and her memory was razor sharp. I connected her with someone who identified the owner of the vehicle as a teacher who works with you, Professor."

Lyle and Beatrice's eyes locked. Who else could that someone be?

"What did the medical people say?" asked Sam.

Benson cleared his throat. "They treated me like a doddering old fool until I told them about my security work. Even then I had to lean in."

"They couldn't have conducted any tests on the spot," Sam said.

"I did the best I could. No stab wounds, no visible head trauma, no neck lacerations, no needle punctures. A small bruise on her chest, that's all."

Sam barely let him finish. "I still don't understand what made you suspicious."

"Let me finish, pardner. To Irma—you talk to your brother about her girlhood—anyone roaming alone at night was a murderer or a spy. The question she asked the professor—how he knew his girl was dead—she was asking herself too, and afterward she decided to confront the woman she'd seen that night. I warned her, but Irma was stubborn. I should have brought the gang down on her, but I didn't want to break a confidence. It was your fault, Professor, for bringing Olives and stirring up Irma, and my fault for not putting a bridle on her."

Harold said, "What Irma did was her decision. She had a good life after an ugly start."

Benson continued, "Two days before she died, Irma confronted the woman, who denied using the car that evening and entering the building. Irma told her she'd inform Dr. Stuart when he returned and let him figure it out."

"Lyle visited you on Monday the fourth," Sam said. "Irma went to see the woman on Monday the eleventh, and she died that night."

Benson took his time answering. "That sounds about right. I guess this is the twelfth. I lost track of time."

"I've met Mr. Binker," Beatrice whispered to Lyle and Sam. "Trust him."

Sam said, "Now listen to me. Tell the others you may be visited by someone—probably a woman—about Irma. She'll have an excellent reason to question you. Pretend to be slow-witted. Under no circumstances are you to question or confront this person. That goes especially for you, Benson."

"Who are you to tell me what to do, mister?"

"Someone who's seen the wreckage this person has wrought. If she thinks you know or suspect something, she'll crush you like bugs—all of you." Sam plowed on. "Slow-witted, hard of hearing. Whatever it takes, and not another word to the authorities about your suspicions. Won't bring your friend back, and speaking up may provoke someone to see to it that you join her."

"We'll do as you say, Mr. Stuart," said Harold.

"But we don't have to like it," added Benson.

MAY 15, 2019

☻-☻-☻

Oxford

HAVING MOVED TO HIS RESTING AND READING CHAIR, Harold Binker steeled himself. He didn't have to wait long, hearing a tapping on the door.

"Come in," he squeaked.

The woman who entered Harold's little room displayed a warm smile that ought to have put him at ease—was intended to, he told himself. She was tastefully dressed, but muted in comparison to her vigorous aura.

Harold was accustomed to pain, but today his left shoulder hurt like blazes, and dressing himself had been a severe trial. He'd had the bright idea to borrow stage glasses from Ruth, but the lenses were as thick as jam jars and he'd stashed them in a drawer. Anyway, he was decrepit-looking enough without props.

"Thank you for seeing me, Mr. Binker."

"It's a treat to have visitors," he answered.

After speaking to Lyle and his brother, Harold had gone to the apartment manager, not without trepidation, informing the woman that any inquiries about Irma should be directed to him because the others were so distraught about her death. Benson would have been the logical choice, but Harold couldn't trust the cowboy to keep his composure, and if Ruth didn't know about

288

Irma's adventures, he wasn't confident her suspicions wouldn't be aroused. So, the bullseye was on Harold's back.

"Don't get up, please," the woman said. "I can't stay long. Did the attendant tell you my name?"

"She may have, but would you mind reminding me?" he said in a gasping voice.

"Margaret White. I'm an historian."

"I'm ninety, proud to be," Harold said.

"As you should be. I'll tell you why I've come. I read about Irma Meisner's death. She and I had been corresponding about a history I'm writing on the Anschluss, Hitler's takeover of Austria. Very few are alive who have firsthand knowledge of that event. Did she mention this to you?"

Harold was staring out the window. He wondered if she'd say a word to bring him back but she sat still with her eyes fixed on him.

"Not as I recall, and none of our friends ever mentioned it."

"Does that surprise you?" the woman said.

"Oh no. Irma kept things to herself. Memories of her girlhood haunted her. Hush-hush with secrets was Irma."

"How did she die?"

Harold held up a finger, and it wobbled like a reed in a gale, as he knew it would. "Doctors always have an explanation, but truth is she died from being old, the age when things stop working."

"Is that what all of you think?" said the woman.

"Well…"

"I'd like to know. We only met once but she was a great help to me."

Margaret White reminded him of someone, perhaps because that other woman had made such a strong impression on him too. How many years ago had that been, fifty, or maybe sixty? The curator had brought her into the restoration room, a radiant woman in green who posed questions concerning ancient illuminated books. Had the restorers seen any, had any private collectors broached the subject, had they heard rumors?

His musing prompted her to repeat herself. "Is that what all of you think, Mr. Binker?"

"I shouldn't say," Harold said, grinning. Everything about this woman was inviting him to speak. He cupped a hand to his mouth in a confidential manner, and said, "S-E-X. You'd be surprised what goes on in these places."

"Oh!" said the woman. "I hardly think…"

"You didn't hear it from me. Benson says there are worse ways to die."

She was smiling at him. "Did he observe something?"

"Nothing of the sort, but Irma could be as lively as a cricket when she had the…ah…urge."

"I see."

"Heart attack," Harold said, knowingly.

"She hadn't been ill?"

"Not to our knowledge. Went out by herself a few days before she died. Told us all about it, an art exhibit at the university."

Her eyes never wavered, as if she were parsing every word he uttered. Harold discovered that he wasn't frightened. He was angry, but he had to disguise that emotion too. He turned to the window and let his jaw sag a little.

"Thank you, Mr. Binker. I'm relieved to hear Irma was healthy to the end. Tell your friends her story will survive in my book."

The woman stood and gripped the doorknob.

Harold said, "That will make them happy. Thank you for visiting me, Miss…ah…"

"Margaret."

After she'd left the room, Harold closed his eyes. He was exhausted. What had the professor said the night he'd brought the food from Olives?

"You ought to be on the stage."

MAY 16, 2019

Shanghai

THIS SHANGHAI RESTAURANT owned by one of the president's children rivaled the best restaurants in London, with real wood, Italian marble, original still-life paintings, and a lauded French chef.

Sam had come here for one, and only one, reason, to identify the *birdwatchers* the Chinese had assigned to him. Not that in the grand scheme of things knowing who was tailing him made any difference, just a matter of professional pride.

He was finishing a delicious seafood salad with Asian vegetables and chestnuts. With little expectation he would see England again, why not indulge? He wasn't about to tell Lyle their travels had beggared him. His small nest egg tapped out, on the bright side, he wouldn't live long enough to turn into an old soak.

He was having an early dinner because his body was on neither London nor Shanghai time, and because fewer people were in the restaurant, making identification of birdwatchers an easier enterprise.

He was pretending to drink a Scotch and soda that was really sparkling water with a dash of Cola. His hair was longer than it had ever been, and he was growing a beard, not a disguise or new image he was cultivating, merely a question of needing a haircut and ennui with his razor.

The other diners included a middle-aged couple, four businessmen, an old man with his e-pad, and two conversing women. His first and second choices were the couple and the old man.

Why the birdwatchers? Li Hwang had agreed to see him the next day, and Li would want to know everything, especially whatever they could use to intimidate or incriminate him. Sam had contended with his share of Kaspers. Li was head and shoulders above that lot.

He took another sip of his drink, eyes closed as if he were savoring it. This was the first May 16th since the Stasi colonel, Johann Kasper, was executed that he hadn't celebrated with a bottle or two of fine wine.

He'd meant to see his uncle before he embarked for Paris but the words Henry had spoken to him on his last visit still haunted him. "Without God—I'm not talking about ugly or self-serving caricatures of God—man can be convinced to do anything...*anything!*"

As Sam himself had done.

He removed an ink pen from his bag and wrote a number on the linen napkin, thought a minute, and added two to the total— the people he had assassinated, or participated in assassinating, a number that represented the termination of lives. Did Arthur Russell belong on the list? He hadn't done the deed, but he'd had that most dangerous of men cornered, and had told Russell he needed to see a dead body.

Lyle said the ancient Egyptians cut off the right hands of foes they'd killed in battle, piling them up so the number of vanquished could be counted and recorded by the scribes. Sam's number amounted to a big pile of hands.

If a heaven existed, how could a man like him be let in? Even if he was sorry—and he wasn't sorry for all of them—how could he ask forgiveness for something he was preparing to do again? Sam didn't know where his Righteous Medal was anymore because he couldn't face the hypocrisy of accepting such a distinction. He had gone so far as to wonder if the lot of some men was to be a Judas or Tolkien's Saruman, unremitting and unredeemable, whether such men were necessary in the cosmic order, if the course of their ships were preordained.

Sam hadn't attended Mass in years but he often went to Confession. More than once, he'd been refused absolution for things he couldn't promise he would never do again.

The scene struck him like a thunderbolt, and he couldn't restrain a pinched smirk. "Bless me father. I killed two men... maybe three."

The next time, he'd confess the same sin, hoping this priest would speak those salving words. Before he met Lyle in Paris, the priest had said something astounding—he wasn't a lost cause. "Why *can't* you get to heaven?" Sam was almost euphoric until this mission's motto, *Invenimus et Delimus*, came crashing in. How could a good God forgive such things?

He had written down what the Paris priest had told him but hadn't dared bring the list to China or leave it in the bag Lyle had brought back to England. He hadn't disposed of it either, tearing it into tiny pieces and eating it. Now, he was preparing to do something akin to vomiting it up.

The way the couple looked at each other and their loud laughter made him scratch them off his list.

He was here for Lyle and Beatrice, to make amends to his brother for his failures when Lyle was a boy. He remembered a night not long after their father disappeared when he had gone to the house and looked through the porch window, observing Lyle and his mother through the windowpane, his mother writing in a notebook, Lyle reading on the floor.

He had waited too long on that porch, feeling guilty for not visiting his sick mother more often, for keeping the boy who needed him at arm's length. In the end, he had turned around and gone back to London.

"A right cruel bastard you were...are," he whispered.

Those four men were too clumsy. They rose as one, shook hands, departing the restaurant. Others were arriving, but the original group was what interested Sam, the people who had arrived with him, or soon thereafter.

Within minutes, the couple walked out.

If Lyle could convey beetles from Africa to England, and if Zvi's people could convey the creature from Mexico to Germany, why couldn't he do the same? He removed the pencil from his shirt pocket, an unnecessary and frivolous risk he hadn't been able to resist, a simple wooden pencil with an eraser on the end. To cover up the impulsive action, he retrieved a notebook from his bag, using the pencil to scribble 'a right cruel bastard' on the last page.

Since he was in close proximity to the Chinese ministry office, a natural question surfaced. To what temptation had Patrick succumbed: greed, lust, disillusionment? Whatever had happened to his old mate had turned that man with the single-mindedness he'd displayed in everything else he'd ever done.

Patrick hadn't been kidding about the Zitouni restaurant. Despite their blown cover, he'd insisted on a leisurely meal before they made for the private plane that conveyed them out of Egypt.

Inside the Brotherhood's prison room, Patrick had labored like a beaver at his dam works, using their belts—leather for hand and foot straps, prongs designed for use as razor sharp instruments, screws on each table leg—to secure straps to the underside of the table, to which the orangutan-like Patrick would cling and make himself almost invisible. Sam's job was to distract their captors with the door and pick-key deception.

When Sam was dragged from the room, Patrick had been free to move, overpowering an exit door sentinel, appropriating the man's attire and gun, and going on to his grim work.

Had Patrick really found the diamond in the ferret's uniform, or had his possession of the gem proceeded from a private intrigue that provoked their capture and imprisonment?

In the end, what had all of Patrick's verve come to? At the Café de la Paix, Sam had told Lyle he'd left Patrick on that Albanian roof. True enough, but he'd heard something as Patrick took his final breaths—"Thy chase...beast in view"—that had haunted him until Sam identified Dryden's full verse:

All, all of a piece throughout,
Thy chase had a beast in view;
Thy wars brought nothing about;
Thy lovers were all untrue.

When he extended the fingers of his right hand, could he still feel the effects of the *krokodil*? Did he want to leave this earth like Patrick?

The old man folded his e-pad, exiting the restaurant at the same time as the two women.

The waiter, a nimble man with a blank face, approached Sam's table.

"No dessert for me," Sam said. "Jet lag."

"Many experience."

"What's your name?" Sam asked the waiter.

"Chen."

"How do you do? I'm Sam Stuart, from England."

"You have business in China?"

What had that station chief in Cairo told him? *The place you never think to look is where the quid stops rolling.*

Sam put a finger to his lips. "I'm a spy."

For an instant, the man's mask came off. *I still have it*, he told himself.

"How long do you stay?" Chen asked him.

"Maybe a day, maybe forever," said Sam, faking a wise smile.

"I bring your check, Mr. Stuart."

"A pleasure talking to you, Mr. Chen," Sam said.

THAT NIGHT, HE WOULD HAVE BEEN EVICTED FROM HIS HOTEL for insufficient funds if he hadn't referred them to Li's ministry. Sam was six-thousand miles from home and limited to the few yuan in his pocket until his next pension deposit arrived.

In bed, worn, weary, and sleepless, he pondered the question of shame. Some felt it keenly at first blush, others only when confronted by a grave personal failing, still others seemingly immune. As for Sam, in recent years, shame had loomed over him like a storm cloud.

He'd told Lyle the story about Badger, the black giant who'd lobbied hard for a place on the Uganda mission team. His being an expert cartographer had tipped the scales. Sam hadn't revealed to his brother that prior to the attack on the terrorists Badger had asked him to deliver a message to his grandmother residing in a Dover care facility if he didn't survive. "My *Gra-mere* reared me, you see. Tell her I've expunged the shame. Use those exact words, Sam. I've expunged the shame."

Sam had been too preoccupied at the time to question Badger, and only after recalling the man's request a month after that awful ordeal in the wilderness did he make the day trip to the care facility.

Helena—he couldn't recall her surname—was a woman well over six feet tall and as thin as a stick, slow in body and mind but not bedridden or senile, a game old dame, no doubt impressive in her day, receiving her grandson's message with no visible emotion.

What shame had Badger expunged and how did it involve his *Gra-mere*? Spurred by curiosity, Sam had talked to others in The Firm who'd known Badger and had nothing but esteem for their comrade.

He sat up in bed and smiled. There it was, locked away in his memory of that chaotic time, Badger's name, Jonathan Neary.

MAY 17, 2019

Shanghai

ACROSS THE DESK FROM LI HWANG, Sam should have had one thing on his mind—delivering the message and exiting Shanghai in one piece—but he had complicated a mission already fraught with danger, something he'd been warned against his whole career. Operation Latrine, when he'd picked up his father's casket, was one thing, a spur-of-the-moment inspiration; this crazy scheme, though, was planned in advance by a man who ought to have known better.

Even on the most dangerous ops, agents were taught to take precautions to protect themselves. Sam had dispensed with precautionary measures for his meeting with Li, resigning himself to prison or execution, telling himself this was his penance for Patrick.

As for Li, bad enough that he had corrupted Patrick, but the minister had compounded that grievous deed by participating in an attempt to kill Beatrice, with Lyle as collateral damage. How could Sam let such belligerence against his house stand?

Fearful that Lyle and Beatrice were in mortal peril from the next Malkin, he had sent them to his apartment in London, instructing them not to contact him for any reason, spending his remaining chips to make sure they were protected.

As expected, Li's security detail had removed every piece

of metal and every drop of liquid from his person before he was permitted to see the Ministry of State Security director.

Li said, "I hope my people didn't inconvenience you, Mr. Stuart."

He'd resolved to leave the incident at the hotel unmentioned unless Li brought it up. "One cannot be too careful, Mr. Li," said Sam to the man who had turned Patrick when Li was a field agent.

"A formality in your case," said the minister. Li was about Sam's age, graying, a few inches shorter, the fit and styling of his monotone gray suit bespeaking London or Paris.

"They let me keep this pencil and notebook so I don't forget what I came to tell you."

"We are approaching that age, aren't we, Mr. Stuart? Ginseng is good for memory, or so they tell me. It appears you have forgotten your shaving kit. I have a barber who still shaves with a straight blade. I assure you, he achieves the intended effect."

How subtly Li had reminded him of his money problems.

Second nature for Sam was to size up every room he entered. Here, Li enjoyed the best furniture, none of it made in China except for the millennia-old Song Dynasty table and tenth-sized wooden rendering of a richly caparisoned war horse. While the air had been thick with smog on the drive from the hotel, Li's office air was fresh, having a faint lavender scent.

"Do sit down. May I offer you something? G and T?"

"No, thank you, Mr. Li." Not much escaped this man—the reason Sam's plan was madness.

The requested item had arrived at the Israeli consulate in Frankfurt the day before he'd departed for Shanghai, packaged in something resembling Lyle's beetle-boxes, along with instructions for transferring the creature to the false pencil bottom, a process that involved fogging the creature as one would a hive of bees.

"Your people told me if I leave anything behind, I'll be staying too."

Li shook his head disapprovingly. Sam understood those men had done exactly as the minister had instructed.

"Your message was puzzling," said Li.

"Necessarily so. We traced two murders in Mainz to Andrea Fitzgerald. They bear MSS fingerprints."

Li's face hardened. "How so, may I ask?"

"Albanian girls."

"An unruly country."

"MSS has used Albania's unruliness to its benefit."

Sam's accusation chipped away some of the minister's urbane veneer. "You know how things work, Stuart, so why put yourself out?"

"The strong do what they can and the weak do what they must," said Sam.

"Your experience?"

"Thucydides."

Li said, "I didn't take you for a classicist."

"I'm not. An old friend was. His name was Patrick."

Li's eyes dimmed—*I still have it!* "Why is MSS sponsoring Fitzgerald?"

Li said, "We tell a fable that when our ancestors invented spears and arrows, hunting dragons became so popular those magical creatures had to transform themselves into cats. A matter of survival."

"Or conquest. Dragons will be dragons."

He couldn't allow Li to suspect he intended more than enlightenment, that Sam planned to *do* something. The idea had come to him that day in London when Lyle told him about the Mexican centipede. Zvi's biologist had secured specimens, including the one sent to Sam in a diplomatic pouch. *My people learned the hard way the creature is attracted to human hormones. Neglect to pacify it, and you will rue the day.*

He would have to leave Shanghai as soon as possible after his meeting with Li, the reason for booking the first leg of his flight to Melbourne on the Australian airline rather than traveling west over Chinese airspace.

Sam said, "Fitzgerald is playing you. She's after something, and she's using you to get it. Her mischief in Kampala and the murders in Mainz jeopardize China's relations with Uganda and Germany."

"All conjecture. Tell me what you *know*."

"We know when Andrea Fitzgerald was in Israel and Kampala, though we've found no record of her traveling on any commercial airlines. Pardon me, Minister Li, but I know more. We know Bari Malkin was in Israel during one of Fitzgerald's trips there, in Kampala shortly after she left that city—at the same time a woman was blown to bits using an Israeli incendiary. And Malkin was in Istanbul two weeks prior to my trip there."

Li clasped his hands. "I would be shocked if you have associated any of this with China. What do you want from me?"

"The artifact Fitzgerald seeks is connected to my brother. He doesn't have it, but she thinks he does, or can locate it. She'll do anything to put her hands on it, damaging China if necessary. I want her neutralized before she harms my brother."

"I followed your career, Stuart. We wouldn't have tossed you out like a bad fish."

Sam would have sworn he could feel the creature moving. "You don't know everything about me."

"I know you're still dangerous." By standing, Li signaled the meeting was over.

Sam intended to surreptitiously release the creature and get the hell out of China. Without food for over a week, confined as it had been in that small dark space, it would be ravenous once fresh air and light reactivated the hemolymph that animated its legs.

Sam was only half-listening when Li said, "We could keep you here. I'm the law concerning matters like this."

"You're receiving valuable intelligence from someone who could deliver more of the same."

"Do you want anything else, Stuart?"

This man had turned Patrick and participated in Malkin's recruitment. He deserved to die.

His mother's voice reading Tolkien's book to her boys: "*Many that live deserve death. And some that die deserve life. Can you give it to them? Then do not be too eager to deal out death in judgment.*"

Li extended a hand. He has no suspicions, Sam told himself.

Fear wasn't what prevented Sam from releasing the creature, and he had no expectation he'd be forgiven for the things he'd confessed, but he had to make a stand sometime if he wanted to stop adding numbers to his ledger.

"I wish you a tranquil journey home."

Sam was almost through the door when Li said, "I'm sorry about your friend."

Was Li being contrite, provocative, sarcastic? Was he seeking forgiveness, as Sam was seeking forgiveness? Had this man's mother or grandmother made an indelible mark on him that no amount of sin could eradicate? Or were Li's words calculated to produce an intended effect?

Something else held Sam back from releasing the creature, but why persist in the absurd notion he and Nancy had a future? Only because of those few words she had shared with him: "If Beatrice and Lyle found a way, why can't we?"

He didn't turn around or respond, passing the sentry, retrieving his personal property at the entrance door, walking outside into the busy, smoggy street. Still stiff-kneed from the long flight, he walked several blocks, certain he was being shadowed. Stopping at a busy corner, he was on the verge of letting the pencil slip from his hand and fall through the sewer grate when an idea came to him. *Don't be hasty.*

Cursing so loudly he turned heads, Sam hailed a cab.

JUNE 5, 2019

London

"LIKE IN THE PRINCESS AND THE PEA," Lyle said. "I can feel every knot in the floor."

Since the two of them had been staying in Sam's London apartment with its sitting room, kitchen, toilet and tub, bedroom, and walls needing fresh paint, Beatrice had been sleeping on the bed, while Lyle was sleeping on a bed of blankets on the floor.

He was amazed at how barren and pauperish Sam's lodgings were. The man had little to his name and what he did have was threadbare and worn. Lyle's flat seemed a palace by comparison.

Lyle had taken a detour on their way from the airport to Sam's apartment, motoring along the Thames Embankment to view Cleopatra's Needle, the Egyptian obelisk built by Thutmose III, straddled by two sphinxlike figures. Driving by, he told Beatrice about the letter Leary had sent him insisting paired Egyptian obelisks were inspired by cultural memories of Atlantean Watchtowers.

"I've never met the man, but he may have intended to inspire you to retrieve the manuscript so he could steal it."

Lyle had parked where they could view the obelisk. "That's what Sam thinks too. I wish you could have spoken to Leary. For the first hour, I was annoyed. The second hour, I felt frustrated I couldn't trip him up. By the time I decided to detain him and learn what I could, he bolted."

"If he was scheming to get his hands on the manuscript, his presentation would have been choreographed, including his exit. Do you think he's still lurking?" she said.

"Quite the contrary, I suspect he's dead. Everyone else connected to Andrea's scheme has been eliminated."

As usual, Beatrice had the last word. "Let's not waste any more time on Mr. Leary. Sam's our primary concern, then your lovely colleague."

Day after day of rain and low clouds, then foggy nights, went by, and not a word from Sam—two weeks and counting—but in spite of gloomy weather and worry, Lyle was joyful every morning he awoke with Beatrice in the next room.

They spent part of an afternoon talking about the connection Lyle had made on the Mainz hotel balcony between Agnes CurLio's diary entry and the Carlton letter. He might have impressed her, though all she had said was, "No wonder you get in so much trouble."

A clock somewhere in the district tolled the hour, interrupting an extended mending silence, Beatrice keeping busy sewing and darning Sam's garments and ratty curtains.

Recognizing the shirt she was patching as the one Sam had worn on the plane from Istanbul to London, Lyle said, "Do you know if Sam spoke to your friend Nancy?"

"He has."

"I think he's suspicious of her."

"Did she impress you as that kind of person?" Beatrice inquired, without looking up from her work.

"Certainly not, but Sam's the expert."

She gave him her look. "He's changed, Lyle. Haven't you noticed?"

Sam was often on his mind, the worry dragging him down. Rain pelted the window. He said, "This could go on forever. We have to do something."

"Sam knows what he's doing."

If Sam knew what he was doing, why had he stashed his phone in Lyle's luggage, and why weren't the contents password protected, as if Sam didn't expect to need it anymore and wanted Lyle to have access to everything.

He said, "I could always count on Sam for a G and T but I've scoured this place, and nothing doing."

"Another day of this and I'd join you, and I don't like gin. Has Fitzgerald contacted you?"

"Three texts. I responded—pleasantly and obliviously."

"Let's stay here a while longer. That's what Sam wanted."

"The time has come to do something," Lyle insisted.

Lyle and Beatrice had been together night and day for several weeks, but their relationship was a patchwork of slow repair, forward mixed with backward motion, joy and relief, bouts of melancholy, and the distress of knowing a master killer was after them.

Looking up from her work, Beatrice said, "When Cornelia informed me you were coming to Kampala, my first instinct was to conceal myself in her room so I could hear your voice again, catch a glimpse from behind the door, *do something*, until I realized I couldn't witness your grief without revealing myself and explaining everything. So, I stayed away. Tell me what you've been doing," she said to him.

"Sam and I have been hunting your killer."

"I want to know more than that. I missed our phone calls, video visits, emails, normal life. Lucia, Agnese, Popa and Joseph, your research. You haven't said more than a few words about anything that isn't terrifying."

"You know Lucia is running wild with the Brothers. She has practically lived with Henry since Cornelia's letter. The Brothers love her, especially Albert and the beekeeper."

Beatrice said, "Have I met the beekeeper?"

"I haven't met him yet myself. He's not one of the Brothers. He lives in a hut by the hives. They call him Brother Francis. I told Uncle Henry I was suspicious of a stranger on the grounds."

She frowned. "A beekeeper is suspicious? How long has he been there?"

"Two years."

"I'm inclined to trust Lucia and Henry," Beatrice observed. "Why do they call him Brother Francis if he isn't a monk?"

"Something to do with animals, as I recall. That's it—Uncle Henry said he has healing hands. Oh, Jeremy came to Oxford by bus one day to pay his respects over your demise. What a fine fellow he is. He was hoping to meet Lucia, but she was at the monastery."

"He came by himself?" Beatrice asked.

"A day trip, that's all."

"Quite a day trip for Jeremy. I'm surprised Catherine went along with it, or did she?"

"Truth is, she didn't know."

"That doesn't sound like the Catherine I met. What aren't you telling me?"

"Catherine is incapacitated."

"How do you know?"

He shrugged.

"How do you know, Lyle?"

"I gave him a lift home and stocked their larder. She's worried about what will happen to him when she's gone. I'm investigating options."

"Can't he stay in the house?"

"He'll need support. On the way to Salisbury, Jeremy told me the grocer calls him Simple Simon. I said I'd talk to the man but Jeremy said no."

"He needed to tell someone and he's comfortable with you. He trusts you. My Faramir. That's who you've become."

Faramir was Tolkien's heroic captain of a wilderness band that tried to hold back a vicious enemy with a thousand times as many fighters. Lyle said, "Don't make me laugh. Want me to tell you about Holly? Nothing happened, but it might have."

"Faramir wanted to take the ring from Frodo, but he didn't. Was Jeremy alright?"

"Right as rain. When I told him we were putting the car roof down, he said you were a lucky girl."

"I *am* a lucky girl."

"I'm worried about Harold and his gang too. Are they safe? I don't dare contact him, not until we have Sam back."

He'd been dreading the next thing he had to tell her. "Uncle Henry has cancer. After all you've been through, I've been waiting for the right moment to let you know about Catherine and Henry. I couldn't find a right moment, could I? He has the manuscript hidden where no one will find it, not even Andrea or the Chinese."

She had the look of a fighter who'd taken one punch too many. "The manuscript means nothing compared to your uncle. We're going to see him as soon as we can. Once we have Sam back, we'll visit your uncle and retrieve Lucia."

They hadn't heard much thunder earlier, but now a sudden glare of lightning lit up the room and thunder rattled the window. Lyle had to raise his voice to make himself heard over the din of the rain, but he'd been waiting a long time to say this. "I want you to stay in England, Beatrice."

She was staring out at the gray through the wet window. "I want to stay, but we'll have to see the hand we're dealt."

"This time *we're* going to deal the hand. I've contacted Mutesi, and Eitan in Israeli intelligence, and asked them to help us bring Sam out of China."

"What makes you think those men will intervene? The Chinese are in the Premier League these days."

"These are the only cards I have."

"You don't have *any* cards. Those men don't owe you anything, and they didn't rise to where they are by sticking their necks out when they don't have to."

"Don't be so encouraging. Someone has to fetch my Billy goat of a brother."

"I'm being realistic," she said. "We can't do anything for Sam, not while he's in China, except pray."

Who had Sam's back? Lyle hadn't received any assistance from the British government, no communications of any kind except for a text from an anonymous person informing him, in so many words, that Sam was on his own. He was furious at the Joneses, high and low, in Her Majesty's Government, and at men like Li who did whatever they pleased to whomever they pleased. "I'll give Sam another few days, then someone has to retrieve him."

"Who are you proposing for that mission?" Beatrice asked.

"Who do you think?"

"I'm afraid to think."

"You won't say anything against it, will you?"

She looked as sad as he'd seen her since her return from the dead. "I want to know what you're going to do when you're in China."

"I'm telling Li I'm not leaving unless Sam's with me."

"Do you know how long the Chinese put you in prison for rubbing the wrong people the wrong way? Aren't you frightened?"

"Certainly, I am. But Sam told me when something needs doing and you're frightened, you may have to do it scared. Why would Sam take that risk? He didn't have to go. He hasn't survived this long by being impulsive, rash."

"Maybe generosity, preventing Fitzgerald from harming us by confronting the Chinese. Or a death wish, putting on the war paint for one last charge. No, not that," she added quickly.

Lyle walked to the rain-streaked window. Was he expecting a new scene, or to see the sun? He didn't want to argue with her. He didn't want to go to China either, but he'd convinced himself only he could bring Sam home. When he turned around, Beatrice was trembling; then she began to shake from head to toe. He crossed the room and took her in his arms. As violently as she was shaking—now weeping—he clasped her closer than ever before, minutes passing before the eruptions subsided. And just when he thought she was settling down, a peal of thunder set off another burst of emotion.

"Thank you!" she said, her eyes red and her cheeks wet with tears. "I love you."

"Better?" he asked, his eyes wet too.

"I think so. We'll see."

The ordeal in Kampala, travel from Africa to Mainz, Sam's fate unknown, her *betrothed* on his way to China, could he distract her, even if just for a few minutes? She'd know what he was doing, but she might go along with it.

He put a finger to his lips. "I have a mysterious letter in my bag from Sam's friend, Eitan. I know you enjoy deciphering things. You saved my life by deciphering Russell's journal. Eitan's letter purports to be about the Jericho site but I'm not convinced, considering the sneaky way he directed us to Istanbul."

She dabbed her eyes with a handkerchief. "Didn't you say he met Fitzgerald at the site?"

"That's what Andrea told me."

"A man like that wouldn't send intelligence information in a letter. Let me see it," she said.

That was what he'd been hoping she'd say.

Considering the brevity of the letter, she took her time with it. Lyle was pleased to see that contemplative look on her face.

She looked up, and said, "I presume Mr. Eitan has sources in many intelligence agencies. Hand me your phone please."

"Who are you calling?" asked Lyle sharply.

"Not a soul. Research."

A few minutes later she handed it back to him.

"You know something, don't you?" he said.

"I don't *know* but I have suspicions. I was searching for the meanings of cenotaph. If I'm right, it's as personal as a message can be. The cenotaph, his intelligence sources, tells me the two sentences aren't connected. Mr. Eitan knew, and he wanted you to know too."

THAT NIGHT, SHE TOOK HIM BY THE HAND and led him to the bedroom and the maple four-poster that had belonged to his parents, too big for the room and in need of varnish.

"Hold me," she said. He lay down against her, put an arm over her, as vulnerable as she had ever been to him.

A night redolent of when the thirteen-year-old Lyle had climbed into his mother's hospital bed the hour she had died, trying to comfort her, and feeling helpless and frightened. But now, Beatrice's familiar scent and warmth comforted him. The dark room, Sam's sagging bed, the rain, and no words spoken. A low rumbling thunder came and went, like Lucia's nervous growling, but absent any flashes of lightning. Her breathing told him when she was asleep, her twitching saying she still needed him. When he was convinced she was at peace—at two a.m.—he lifted himself from the bed and made for his blankets on the floor.

JUNE 10, 2019

☻-☻-☻

Frankfurt

IF THE GODS HONORED IN EVERY TOMB Lyle had ever examined—or desecrated, as Sam's former girlfriend Fatemeh
insisted—conspired to derail him, they could hardly have done a
better job of it.

The mishaps started with Lyle tripping on an airport terminal
bench, tumbling down in a heap on top of his wheeled bag and
re-injuring the leg that had experienced delicate surgery in the
aftermath of the Mainz bombing.

He was limping about on a leg that hadn't hurt this much since
he'd returned to England after recovering the manuscript. What
had he done to it? Was the injury temporary, or would it worsen?

At the gate for his flight to Shanghai, he sat and tried to take
his mind off the pain by checking his messages, the first announc-
ing an emergency department budget meeting three days hence.
Only two such meetings had taken place during his time at the
university, and if he'd learned anything it was that those who
weren't able to attend were sorely neglected. Without a spirited,
forceful *cum* obnoxious defense of one's projects, all was lost, the
subsequent budget assigning breadcrumbs to the absentee's areas
of interest.

All about him, the terminal buzzed with voices, announce-
ments, cart and light-rail traffic, but he hardly noticed. Could he

trust anyone in the department to defend his projects? A month ago, he'd have left it in Andrea's capable hands. Agnese? She had a hard time defending her own projects, always ending up with less than the rest. "All this haggling over lucre is beneath us, Lyle. It ain't dignified," she'd once said to him, not an Agnese Leone endorsement when one was seeking a forceful proxy.

He could trust no one to fight for his receiving an average allotment, much less what he needed—deserved!

As if this weren't enough, before he'd left London, he had told Beatrice about Katravesis and the algorithm, and had communicated with the *Journal of Paleolithic Archaeology*. Whatever the repercussions of admitting the truth, he would face them with a clear conscience.

He'd been derailed and tipped over, those desecrated gods cheering his downfall.

"China Air Flight 7426 is overbooked. China Air is seeking eight volunteers to fly with us tomorrow at six p.m., or we will fly you back to your point of embarkation. Both offers include a thousand Euro voucher."

What kind of fool who had lost the love of his life—irretrievably lost her—and then had her restored would voluntarily leave her with no certainty of ever seeing her again? He had re-injured his leg and was assailed by doubts about his fitness for this mission. He was an archaeologist on the verge of confronting a man as deadly as Shelob, that giant, demonic creature, in its lair. In the meantime, Beatrice was in London, mere miles from Andrea, who would eventually discover Beatrice was alive and eliminate her, with his Uncle Henry the next likely victim. The decision was at hand, and how ill equipped he was to make it.

Lyle labored to his feet and made for the counter. He could be back in London today or tomorrow, have his leg seen to, and attend the budget meeting.

Only one person stood in front of him, and with so many flights between Frankfurt and London, he was assured of a voucher and a same-day ticket home. Sam would find his way back, and if Sam couldn't, how could Lyle hope to extricate his brother from China? What had he been thinking when he came up with this batty idea?

"Yes, sir. Are you volunteering?" asked the woman.

Sam was in China because he suspected a connection between the person who'd tried to murder Beatrice and the Chinese, because Lyle's brother was convinced he needed Li Hwang's help to neutralize Andrea. That was why.

When Sam had visited Lyle at boarding school, Lyle had never felt Sam was in a hurry or just doing his duty. Sam had done his best, always bringing him something memorable, like the Roman denarius on Lyle's artifact shelf.

Lyle held the red arrow. Who else would come to Sam's aid?

"Are you volunteering, sir?"

Lyle shook his head and limped away.

JUNE 12, 2019

Shanghai

TWO DAYS BEFORE LYLE'S FLIGHT TO SHANGHAI, he had received a special delivery letter:

Your brother is in prison for conspiracy to harm a Chinese ministry official. He will remain in custody until you deliver a certified check for one million pounds to Minister Li and witness the prisoner's written confession.

Had Li learned that Lyle was traveling to Shanghai? The ransom amount was out of the question, something Li undoubtedly knew, but this was an excuse for Lyle to meet the MSS director.

The flight from Frankfurt to Shanghai was brutal, not just because of his leg, but due to his sense that he was walking into a trap. Sure enough, when the plane landed, two armed soldiers none-too-gently removed him from the plane before any of the other passengers were permitted to exit.

He had no delays with customs or bags, but was herded into the backseat of a twenty-first century Black Maria with opaque windows and an eerie siren, a vehicle that parted traffic as Moses had parted the Red Sea.

No one said a word to him. The soldiers who'd escorted him off the plane sat on his either side, with two men in civilian clothes in the front seat, separated by a transparent panel.

"Where are we going?"

That was the third question he'd asked without an answer. They drove through a tunnel. He was led from the car past a fountain surrounded by yellow and red flowers and into a massive brick and glass building, going up in an elevator, walking down broad corridors to a corner office, his leg feeling as if someone were jabbing it with a cattle prod.

All four Chinese accompanied him into the large office, the man behind the desk speaking words in Chinese that prompted one of the uniformed men to seat Lyle on the visitor's side.

Lyle was examining the minister's three-dimensional display of art and archaeology when Li said, "Your *vitae* suggests you have nine lives and that you have used up most of them. I am a busy man, so what do you have to say to me?"

A slender man in business attire, Li would go unnoticed on an Oxford street. "You know why I'm here, Minister Li."

"I know you're in way over your head. Your brother threatened me. What else was I to do?"

Lyle said, "I know how that works in China. Words the Soviet KGB used when they wanted to do away with someone, *Show me the man and I'll show you the crime.*"

The nearest guard grabbed his neck, applying painful pressure until Li held up a hand. "You may produce the check, then we will witness the confession. After that, we shall see."

"I don't have the money and I won't be witnessing a forced confession."

"Yet, you come here where my word is law. I presume you are aware I received messages in support of your brother. I tell you they will not influence my decision."

Unaware of who had communicated with the minister, Lyle said, "You may need the goodwill of those men in future."

"China doesn't require anyone's goodwill," the minister snapped.

From Beatrice, Lyle had learned to be attentive to posture, facial expression, vocal timbre, all clues to what people were thinking and feeling. In spite of Li's dismissive words about the intercessory messages, Lyle was convinced the powerful Minister of State Security was perplexed.

The next thing he knew the soldiers had gripped his shoulders and were raising him from the chair.

"Don't you want to hear what we found in her *other apartment in Wimbledon?*" he asked, with as much courage as he could summon.

Li's features froze. While the soldiers hadn't relaxed their grip, they didn't move him along either.

As with the best bluffs, an element of truth lay in what Lyle said. Knowing Desrosier had been working for Andrea, he had guessed the handwritten letter to Desrosier about *the pearls* referred to the book, and the Wimbledon address a secret room Andrea maintained.

If Sam's visit had prompted the Chinese to search Andrea's Oxford residence, he was hoping they were unaware of the Wimbledon room, Li's expression suggesting as much.

"Release my brother, and I'll keep silent about what we found. Otherwise, the material will be delivered to the British government."

"How do I know you will keep your word?"

"The British government refused to help me. Why should I go out of my way to help them?"

"Your brother has committed a serious offense. You were informed of the conditions for his release. We have a hundred ways we could explain anything you might have found. Look at the Russians who poisoned a British citizen, yet no one has ever been brought to trial. Don't think I haven't dealt with far more dangerous men than you, and yes, more intelligent men, convinced they had backed me into a corner. Can you guess where they are now?"

"Where is Sam?" Lyle asked.

"Somewhere he can't make any mischief."

Keeping Sam front and center was the only way Lyle could say these things to Li. "You know he didn't threaten you."

"What I know is my own business," said Li, a man who oozed menace. "I didn't force your brother to come here, nor did I force you. Britain's laws don't apply in China. Your government could have told you that if you had bothered to ask."

"I *did ask*, and I didn't like what I heard."

"Then, you are a bigger fool than I took you for." Li stared Lyle down. "You want to say more but you're a coward—no hero. Have it your own way, Dr. Stuart." The minister raised a hand, and the soldiers pulled Lyle toward the door.

"If Sam and I aren't back in England in three days, I've given instructions for the Wimbledon material to be delivered to Sam's colleagues. As you don't know who has this material, you have no one to negotiate with. I have to live with my choices. So will you."

To Lyle's back, Li said, "The rice is cooked, Dr. Stuart, and *your* choices will lead to some very unpleasant experiences. Do you know why your father was killed? Because he was a meddler like your brother."

If his guards had been resolute in handling him prior to the meeting with Li, they were more aggressive on the way to the car, his throbbing leg eliciting audible groans.

They then drove for over an hour. After a while, Lyle finally found a position where his leg was a little less painful. He had eaten next to nothing for two days, but with his stomach tied in knots, he had no appetite. Out of nowhere, a surge of panic swept over Lyle, magnified by the silence of his captors and apprehension about what awaited him. Though he made no sound, the expression of the guard to his left suggested the man sensed his anguish and was gratified by it.

When the car stopped, the guards grabbed his arms, dragging him out. He had hoped Li was simply trying to frighten him before sending him home, but this wasn't the airport.

They were inside a fenced compound with a dozen single and two-story buildings, and elevated towers at two corners of the yard. The sky was thick with ominous clouds. Wherever they were, Lyle could still smell the smog, though not as intense as in the city. He was hustled along to the nearest building and a small room where he was made to deposit all his personal possessions in a bowl and change his clothes for a filthy jumper.

"Sit," said one of the guards in civilian clothes, pointing to an armless metal chair in the center of the room.

"Sit now!"

Lyle was pressed against the rigid back of the chair so hard the metal stung his spine. His hands, pulled behind the chair, were manacled together. One of the others rolled a light stanchion to the front of the chair, directing the bright light at Lyle's eyes.

"You threaten minister!" said the man in civilian clothes who had made him sit.

"I was negotiating with Minister Li…"

"Threaten! You stay here a long time." Every word shouted, the guard's face so close to Lyle's he could smell fish on the man's breath. He was completely in Li's power, too late for calculations, too late for anything. As Li had said, they could explain away anything that was discovered in Andrea's Wimbledon room, the disposition of the Stuart brothers too.

"Long time!" hollered the man as all four captors left the room.

When Lyle leaned back to relieve his wrists, the metal bit into his spine. Leaning forward pinched his wrists. His face grew hot whenever he turned to the lamp. After a while, his arm muscles began cramping, with no way to relax them.

Was Sam undergoing similar torture, or worse?

Without warning, the guards burst into the room. By then, Lyle's head was sagging and he was only half-conscious, pain the only thing that registered. Unshackling him, they pushed him down a corridor behind the metal chair room to a series of cells with slender slide panels in the doors. They shoved him into one of these rooms, the door slamming behind him and a bright-green roach scuttling under the bed mat.

If Sam knew he was here, the knowledge would shatter him. Why had Sam put himself in Li's power with a fool's hope Andrea might be cut loose by the Chinese?

Li said their father had been killed, or was that another lie intended to confuse and dismay him? Wasn't Nestor Stuart buried in the plot next to their mother?

The room was six feet by six feet. A dim light bulb was suspended from the ceiling while a straw mat sat in one corner and an open chamber pot in the other. A drain lay in the center of the concrete floor, and the cell had no windows to the outside or the corridor except for the closed viewing panel. The bad smell reminded Lyle of an animal-rendering factory near the Hattusa expedition site. A roach emerged from beneath the sleeping mat. The same one or another in an army of these creatures? He wasn't about to move the mat to find out.

Lyle had nothing of Faramir, or anything heroic, in him. Exhausted and still hurting from the chair, he dropped to the mat, succumbing to a troubled sleep, waking suddenly to the loud rattling of the metal door as it banged against the wall.

The two uniformed guards entered the cell, pulling him to his feet and half-dragging him down the corridor. As they piloted him along, he managed to catch the eye of one of the guards and was reminded of the look on Romanov's face when the Russian aimed a pistol at him inside the consulate.

They emerged into a walled courtyard, fine netting attached to the tops of the walls. Within the courtyard were three X-shaped structures made from timbers, with shackles at the apexes of the upper arms.

An execution yard? His heart began thumping so hard he forgot about his injured leg and painful arms. He heard not another sound, not even bird calls. One of the guards slammed the palm of his hand against Lyle's ear, staggering him and producing the loud buzzing he'd experienced after the Mainz bombing. The guard attached his aching wrists to one of the structures. If not for the support of the flesh-tearing shackles, his legs couldn't have held him up.

One of the guards provided three uniformed men with rifles. These men, unfamiliar to Lyle and wearing different uniforms and hats than his guards, stood in front of him, rifles raised.

Lyle's world shrank to those gun barrels and Beatrice's memory of her brother Paul's sacrifice—Lyle too had done something good, had earned the name his mother gave him.

The rifles rang out—bangbangbang.

His body jerked unconsciously, spasmodically. Except for his pounding heart and aching wrists, he didn't feel anything. He remembered reading about mortally wounded soldiers who hadn't realized they'd lost limbs, or were bleeding to death.

He tried to breathe, but all he could manage were little gasps.

The soldiers lowered their rifles. One of them was grinning at him. Another one raised his rifle again and waved it at him.

The two guards removed the shackles from his numb blue wrists, dragging him back to his cell and closing the door behind him. His clothing was moist where he'd wet himself. He vomited into the chamber pot. Nothing came out except for bile, as he hadn't eaten anything. This was one of those *very unpleasant experiences* Li had promised him. If these sham executions were repeated, would the experience become easier, or more terrifying?

Alone on the Mainz hotel balcony, he'd felt ecstatic. If he never returned home, he wouldn't have been cheated, not after those weeks with her and the night when she'd said, "Hold me."

Thirstier than he'd ever been in his life, he tried to say, "water," but the word came out as an inarticulate moan. He started laughing but didn't like the sound of it, so he made himself stop.

Lyle was in pain and he was terrified. At the same time, an inner voice told him it didn't matter if he had to stay here for a month or a year if that was necessary to free Sam. What if he was the only person in the universe capable of bringing Sam home? He didn't want to believe this, but he desired to behave as if this belief was true.

Did he fall asleep and awake hours later? The next thing he knew, two guards entered the cell, giving him a cup of broth and a piece of bread, standing like statues while he consumed the food. Then they led him out of the cell into the metal chair room where he was instructed to put on the clothes he'd worn on the plane.

A wordless trip to the airport. Lyle had no questions for these men. On the plane, he was escorted to the front cabin. He had a seatmate, and didn't recognize the man until he was about to sit—Sam.

First class seats, Beluga caviar, a bottle of Dom Perignon, accompanied by a note:

Another life expended, Dr. Jones…rather, Dr. Stuart. Must I remind you archaeology is your métier?

JUNE 13, 2019

Shanghai to Frankfurt

L YLE AND SAM HAD CONSUMED THE CAVIAR, accompanied by a better-than-ordinary meal.

Freshly shorn and shaved, Sam said, "On the way to the airport, I was introduced to a man with a razor."

Lyle was anything but fresh. The best he could do was finger back his filthy hair, what little remained, then try to clean up in the toilet, mopping his face and hands with a wet towel. Except for those few hours in the prison suit, he'd been wearing these clothes since he'd left London, soiled by days of wear. He hurt in a dozen places but was surprisingly free of severe damage. The guards had been torture experts.

Clear skies afforded a view of the plains and mountains of China's vast interior, all the migratory and acquisitive pathways on a map in Lyle's head.

The knowledge that they were on their way home invigorated him, that and the food he'd desperately needed now that he no longer faced imminent persecution or death. "This is Professor Evans kind of flying," said Lyle, setting aside his empty glass and napkin. "You informed her Beatrice is alive?"

Sam grunted an assent, removing a pencil from his pocket and examining it.

"Do you still suspect her?" Lyle asked his brother.

"I never said I did."

The hovering Chinese steward waited for a moment of silence. "Minister Li said you are most welcome to more champagne and caviar."

"No, thank you. That reminds me. Be careful what you say," whispered Sam, after the man had departed.

"Too bad Mum didn't teach us Elvish."

Sam rolled his eyes. "We're not sitting mute for thirteen hours like Henry's monks, but we can make it harder for Li if he's listening."

"Why did he detain you?" asked Lyle, in a confidential voice.

Sam was picking at his duck and sprouts. "With Li, you never know. To buy time for something he wanted to do, to reel you in, find out if I had anything incriminating, see if any of the intelligence agencies would intervene."

"Where did they keep you?"

"An apartment close to the ministry. I had to relinquish almost everything I'd brought with me." Sam tapped the side of his nose with a forefinger, meaning he'd gotten away with something.

Lyle glanced out the window, the mountains replaced by copper-colored plains.

"You?" Sam asked him.

Lyle related what had transpired in Li's office and afterward, his brother's face hardening as he went on.

"Tiger Chair," said Sam, practically spitting out the words. "For interrogations, intimidation, inflicting pain without permanent damage. Fake executions, inflicting terror without evidence." Sam raised his voice. "I should have killed the bastard when I had a chance."

Lyle tapped his nose.

"Don't mind me—Li won't. What I should have done doesn't matter in my business."

"He said our father was killed," Lyle said.

"Hold still. Got it!" Sam said, his finger in Lyle's ear.

"Got what?"

"Not a beetle—flea or louse."

Lyle wasn't surprised. "Just one?" Sam had dodged the question about their father. "Why did you leave your phone behind?" asked Lyle.

"I didn't want Li to get his hands on it."

"Is that all?"

Sam shrugged. "I'm sure you took good care of it."

"You have a lot to live for, Sam. Beatrice has been tidying your apartment, mending too." Lyle went on to tell his brother how they'd occupied their time while holed up in London.

The snoring man wasn't listening.

They had never been as besieged and broken as they'd been in recent weeks, and they'd never been closer to one another. As for Li, their suspicion that Andrea was a Chinese agent, that the Chinese directed those Albanian assassins, that Li was complicit in the attack on Beatrice, was unproven, probably never could be proved. Contrary to what Lyle had told Li, Andrea's Wimbledon apartment hadn't been searched, and as to torture—the Tiger Chair and the mock execution—what had happened was his word against theirs.

With Sam sleeping and with a full stomach, Lyle imagined what life had been like for the nomadic clans crossing the plains below them into a more fertile southeast Europe—men, women, children, livestock, and the houses they'd carried on their backs until they established settlements, while he was traveling in comfort at ten miles per minute to a destination with creature comforts those people in their wildest dreams couldn't have imagined.

Traveling in comfort, but with bruises and lacerations where he'd been shackled and slapped. He guessed he was in for some firing squad nightmares, Li counting on it.

Smooth air prevailed, the champagne glow lingered, and Lyle looked down to see a village now and then. Suddenly, Sam was shaking his shoulder. "Where are we?" Lyle muttered, fogged by his first restful sleep since he'd left London.

"Petersburg's below us."

He looked out the window. The great city and palace district were clearly visible.

"They're serving food again," Sam announced.

"Nothing for me," Lyle said.

"I've learned not to turn down a free meal when out of a job."

Lyle leaned toward his brother. "You have a job, a serious one. Should we try to get into that Wimbledon apartment?"

Sam's meal arrived, and he dug in like Lucia after a long walk. "Fitzgerald probably cleaned it out after Desrosier's murder. Not a good use of our time."

"How much time do you think we have?"

"If I were in Li's shoes, I'd verify the intel we provided before confronting Fitzgerald. We'll have the field to ourselves for a while. Not months, weeks."

Lyle said, "In the meantime, we know Andrea is brilliant and ruthless. I can't believe I'm saying that."

"When you doubt it, remember the Tiger Chair and those rifles, lad."

Lyle picked a baby carrot off Sam's plate and popped it into his mouth. "Desrosier or Malkin must have informed Andrea about our visit. Even if they didn't, she has to be suspicious that I was in Mainz. We can't count on Li keeping her in the dark either. She might know everything. I'd like to know if Leary is dead or alive."

"You're making matters too complicated, Professor. Cut off the head, everything else dies. We're going to concentrate on the big picture. When the time is right, Beatrice will have to convince the police to interrogate Fitzgerald, but not until D-day. If you're curious, that's *Delimus* day—Destroy day. In the meantime, keep Beatrice under wraps and make up for lost time. Why the long face?"

"Li's prison. I saw how weak I am."

"You didn't acquit yourself badly. Far from it. You're no Adonis, but you have redeeming qualities. And the name Mum gave you, even if you're afraid to claim it," Sam said, trying to hide a grin.

JUNE 15, 2019

☉-☉-☉

Frankfurt

"SAM STUART, PLEASE MEET YOUR PARTY at Information Station Seven."

"I'll see to it," said Sam.

"The hell you will. Li?"

"If he had something to say, he had ample opportunity, and all the leverage in the world. *Mein herr, wo ist information bahnhof sieben?*" Sam requested of an airport attendant.

As Lyle and Sam were approaching the information station, a robust young man with cropped hair headed them off.

"Mr. Stuart?"

"That's right. Who are you?"

"Mr. Eitan would like to speak with you. He will return you to the airport in two hours."

Sam waited. "*Mammillaria Matude...Oaxaca...Scolopendra letalis*," said the young man.

Sam put a hand on his confused brother's shoulder, pulling him along. What in the world could Agnes's centipede have to do with Sam and Eitan?

They climbed into an unattended Mercedes sedan parked in front of the terminal, unbothered by the ubiquitous security police. A short drive took them to a commercial zone, where they exited the car and entered one of a series of single-story metal-sided buildings, its inside in stark contrast to the utilitarian exterior, with oak paneling and a bright red bar in one corner.

"Welcome to the Red Room," said Zvi Eitan, sitting at a small table smoking a cigar.

"How did you know we'd be here?" Sam asked him.

"Minister Li sent me a message."

Their driver had vanished. Except for the bartender, an ancient man in a white coat, Lyle, Sam, and Eitan were alone.

The big Israeli stood, giving them both bear hugs. In his sweater vest and jeans, the tousled-haired man might have been preparing for an outing with his grandchildren, but this Zvi Eitan struck Lyle as less at ease than the version they'd met in Jerusalem.

Eitan said, "Pardon my sloppy posture, a bulge in my groin. To the best of my knowledge, you are the first *goyem* to enter this room."

Sam bowed. "The Red Room...the red bar. A *cozy*?"

"You could say that," said the Israeli. "Red to remind us of the need for vigilance...so Germany has taught us, or reminded us."

Eitan's words made Lyle realize that the room had no windows. Was that, and the anonymous exterior, why Sam had referred to the space as a cozy?

Eitan went on. "The news of late has been shocking, with Malkin murdered, and Sam Stuart and his brother detained by Li Hwang. Not to mention a return from the dead. But first, refreshments." Eitan raised a hand, and the bartender came to their table with a tray of smoked salmon, biscuits, and fresh fruit. Bottles of San Pellegrino were set in front of them.

"Cigar, my friends? No?"

Taking a generous swallow of the sparkling water, Sam said to Eitan, "Is this all my wine-loving friend is having?"

"If it is good enough for my friend, it's good enough for me. Then, I think of my dear mother who was fond of reminding me of the fine line between a oenophile and a dipsomaniac. She was something of a moral poet, to my father's dismay. The salmon melts in your mouth. Eat! You must be hungry."

"Li put us up front with gourmet meals," Lyle said.

Eitan appeared puzzled. "How did you secure those luxuries, and your freedom?"

Lyle expected Sam to quiet him, but his brother didn't stir. "A suggestion we had information the minister wouldn't want to be made public."

Eitan shook his head. "One would have to have a death wish to play such a hand with Li Hwang." He set down the cigar and pinned his eyes on Sam. "May I ask what became of the contents of the package? If it has been...ah, traced to any of my people?"

"Never fear, Zvi," Sam insisted. "The package is with me at this moment. You may tell your man in Mexico I followed his cargo transfer instructions to the letter."

"What is this about?" questioned Lyle.

With a reassuring smile, Eitan said, "Taste the salmon, fresh caught from Norway. If you need anything, let me know. Daniel won't leave the bar unless I summon him."

Thinking about the creature Sam had plucked from his ear, the itching that might be vermin or nerves, Lyle said, "Do you have a shower here?"

"We don't have time," his brother said. "And you don't have a change of clothes."

Eitan said, "No bath I'm sorry to say, Dr. Stuart. Sam, what do you know about Malkin's commission?"

Sam nodded. "We think Andrea Fitzgerald is behind it, that she contracted Malkin to kill Beatrice Adams, concluded we were coming too close to the truth and decided to cut bait with Malkin and a woman named Desrosier, both murdered the same night in Mainz."

"That lovely archaeologist, a murderer?" exclaimed the astonished man, training his eyes on Lyle.

"Working for the Chinese while pursuing her own agenda. She's after a priceless artifact, and she believed Beatrice and Lyle could help her acquire it. Beatrice turned her down and was targeted so she wouldn't inform Lyle."

"Sam, if it weren't you telling me this, I would take it as rubbish. If she's working for the Chinese, she knows the risk of a double game. I met her at the Jericho dig, a memorable woman, to say the least. She had to pass security screening to get into my country."

"Would you look into it, Zvi?"

"I have just the man for the job. We'll scrub her until she *gleams*."

Lyle said, "A man calling himself Leary, working for Andrea…"

"A pox on your Leary," interrupted Sam. "I told you he's small beer. When we net Fitzgerald, we'll have him too, if he's not already dead."

"Raphael Leary," Lyle said to Eitan. "I'll send you a photograph."

"Mr. Eitan is a busy man," Sam insisted in his commanding voice.

"Your brother has pluck, Sam. Proved it when he went to China for you. Send me the picture. So, where have you hidden her? Mutesi told me she wasn't the person killed in the bombing."

"My London apartment," said Sam.

The Israeli's eyes widened. He re-lit his cigar. "Since our conversation in Jerusalem, you could say I've been following your exploits from afar. I'll do what I can. Don't press too hard too soon. Li may not be finished with you. If you haven't noticed, they like control. You'll see Chinese flags on the tarmac at their gates. No other national airline enjoys that privilege."

Sam said, "I have never underestimated Li. I went to Shanghai with my eyes wide open."

"So I feared," Eitan said. "Know this, you're not friendless. I said to myself, if he has the cheek to walk into Li's den with nothing but his horn and a...pencil, the least I can do is post a gripe on his behalf. And I wasn't the only one. Mutesi let it be known he was slow-walking a Chinese extradition request until you were released. Now, we must return you to the airport. They're fussy about passengers arriving at the last minute, and it wouldn't do for you to return to London on my plane."

"One more thing," Lyle said.

Eitan looked from Lyle to Sam. "By all means, Dr. Stuart."

Lyle hadn't expected to be face to face with Eitan, and he might not have the opportunity again. "Imagine a man with intelligence sources all over the world, informed about a bombing that might have been perpetrated by a former Mossad agent, reaching out to a source in a foreign security service and discovering the victim wasn't who the public believed her to be. How does he inform the victim's...betrothed without compromising the deception his old comrade is abetting?"

"I'm all ears," said Eitan.

"One definition of cenotaph is an empty grave."

Shrouded in a wreath of smoke, Eitan said, "Pluck *and* brains! Sam, my *old comrade*, about the package, I had little doubt you'd be discrete, but you know the younger generation. For them, data is all that matters."

MAKING THEIR WAY TO THE GATE, Lyle said, "Generous of Eitan to come to Frankfurt to help us."

"Not quite," said Sam. "Didn't you hear him? He was ordered to come, to make sure I hadn't compromised Israel. Everything we said was being monitored. When he said *data is all that matters* he was informing me all devices we had on us had been hacked."

"He said he'd help us with Andrea."

"He will, provided nothing incriminating comes of the surveillance they conducted in the Red Room."

Sam said to the woman gate agent, "Minster Li intended that we sit in first class. See, here are our boarding passes from Shanghai."

The Chinese agent said, "I'm sorry, Mr. Stuart, but these are your assigned seats to London." These passes were for seats in what another age would have called steerage.

Sam's hard-edged voice suggested he had more on his mind than airplane seats. "Tell your manager Minister Li will be distressed to learn we have been treated so shabbily."

The nervous woman made for the phone. Sam frowned at Lyle. "China Air's latrine valve...where is it, I wonder."

PART V
Summations

JUNE 15, 2019

St. Hugh's Charterhouse

A S WEARY AS LYLE WAS, as soon as he returned to his apartment and bathed, he and a shrouded Beatrice embarked on a trip to the monastery for Lucia.

They were still in mortal danger. Someone resourceful enough to eliminate the Mossad-trained Malkin and maneuver past Desrosier's Praetorian Guard was capable of anything. Learning that Beatrice was alive would surely escalate Andrea's malevolence, so Lyle had convinced her to travel to the monastery in a robe and cowl they'd acquired.

Beatrice had taken advantage of the drive from London to the monastery to pepper Lyle with questions about his encounter with Li. Detecting his reticence to talk about the experience, she said, "You may not have received serious physical wounds as you did in Mainz, but you experienced a psychological explosion in that prison camp and execution yard. I should know after the last two months. Seeing Danielle again wouldn't hurt."

By the time the two arrived at the monastery, the sun was nearing the western horizon. Abbot Henry and Lucia were waiting for them in the yard, the sleek poodle bounding toward them like a cheetah. While Lyle was frisking about with his dog, Beatrice said to his uncle, "Lyle told me you had Masses offered for me. Do they do any good if I'm still alive?"

His arms encircled her, and Abbot Henry said, "A bit irregular, but I'm sure our good God is able to work it out. I will hear your story when we have sufficient time. For now, just seeing you is a tremendous grace. As for Lucia, she missed her master."

Lyle looked up and said, "I doubt that, with all the attention she's given here." He smiled for the first time since leaving China. "We can't stay long, Uncle."

A rabbit racing toward the pond caught Lucia's attention, and off she went in hot pursuit.

"That's how much she missed me," observed Lyle.

"Those long-eared rascals will be glad to see her go home," the abbot said. "We'll miss her though, the best garden protector we've ever had."

"Excuse me a moment," Lyle requested, reading a text from Dawson with a monetary amount: *All we could manage this budget cycle, Lyle*

Lyle responded immediately: *No matter, am considering move to Sorbonne, consulted with Martin while on Continent*

Dawson's reply lit up his phone: *Don't take any decisions!!! Let me see what I can do!* And a follow-on text: *What do you need?*

Lyle would let him stew a bit, a tangible benefit of Sam's intrigues with Martin in Paris.

Abbot Henry said, "I know you're pressed for time, but tell me what you can about China."

China. Could Lyle ever hear that word again without reliving those seconds with rifles pointed at him? "I was interrogated and roughed up a bit. They did their best to convince me to keep my distance."

"That's all you have to say?" asked Abbot Henry.

Beatrice had his hand. "That's all for now," he said.

"Your brother no worse for wear?"

"He's…"

A shot rang out in the direction Lucia had gone, a single crack.

All three froze in place. Where was she, behind the pond oak? Otherwise, she'd have been visible.

Lyle ran as fast as he could in the direction of the oak. Nothing to worry about, he told himself, a dead tree limb snapping off. No wonder he was nervy, after all he'd been through.

Only as he approached the pond did he see her on her side beneath the towering oak, eyes closed, the fur above her front leg wet with blood. He wouldn't have noticed if the red hadn't stained her white belly. The trail behind her revealed she'd carried herself some distance after being shot.

He looked in every direction, saw no one and heard nothing. Crouching next to Lucia, caressing her face, he said, "Lucia!...Luce!"

She didn't respond. He thought she was dead until one of her ears twitched.

Beatrice and his uncle approached and Lyle looked up at them, shaking his head. He hadn't quit rubbing her face. He had to get her to an animal hospital. Where was his phone?

When she opened her eyes and looked at him, he knew. He lifted her into his lap, her blood soaking his shirt and pants. His eyes were full and his throat had narrowed. He pressed his face into hers; her familiar smell suffused him.

How would he have made it after Cornelia's letter without this little girl? He should have been enraged, but he was full up with sadness.

"I'm sorry. It's my fault," he said, rocking her back and forth. "My fault."

SEEING LYLE'S GRIEF, BEATRICE'S HEART WAS BREAKING. She felt helpless. What could she do except wait, as she had done while in hiding?

No, no more waiting! Now, she had to be the one he could rely on.

What had he told her in Sam's apartment? Jeremy and Catherine, Henry, Eitan's letter, the beekeeper. "Give her to me," Beatrice said. "Hurry!"

"She's gone," Lyle moaned.

"Give her to me!"

Beatrice lifted Lucia and made for the little hut by the hives. As she tromped away, she heard Abbot Henry say, "Let her go. It can do no harm."

She had the same feeling she'd had in those desperate moments by the river with her father knocked silly and her mother and sisters cowed by the rebel. Doing something was better than doing nothing.

Busy attending to her footing in the tussocky grass and the ever-increasing swarm of bees, Beatrice scarcely felt Lucia's weight. The sun was descending and the air was cooling. Her robe was bloody.

She rapped on the door, holding the dog tight to her breast. The door opened; a clean-shaven gray-eyed man in work clothes stepped outside, taking in everything.

"Help me!"

A log in the hearth split in two, producing a loud crack and a flash of light that illuminated both their faces.

"Come ahead," he told her.

Inside the hut, she scanned the room, seeing plank flooring, white-washed walls, no ceiling but rafters for the sloped roof, a rough-hewn table and two chairs, a bed against one wall, a hearth against the opposite wall, a sink on the back wall, a travel bag in the corner. These days, Beatrice wanted to know everything about every room she entered.

The man retrieved a blanket from the bed, placing it on the tabletop.

Beatrice put down Lucia as gently as she could, stepping back and sweeping the cowl from her head.

He gave her a quick look, a mystified look, lifted one of Lucia's eyelids, and shook his head.

"Please try!" Beatrice pleaded.

"I can't."

"Abbot Henry said you have healing hands."

He looked down at the still animal and clutched the fur behind her neck, then went to his bag and removed something. "Leave her with me. Go."

"I'm staying. What can I do to help?"

He stopped what he was doing. "Be still."

He was holding a glove so closely matching the color of his flesh that when he put it on she couldn't tell the difference between the glove and his bare arm.

Closing his eyes, he put his hand on the wound, inserting two gloved fingers into the gash made by the bullet. When he extracted them, the bullet came out too. He reinserted one finger up to the second knuckle, standing rigidly still, sweating, though the room wasn't warm. His hand movements made shadows on the wall that looked like flitting birds and butterflies. Removing the finger, he placed the gloved hand on the wound as he had before.

"What can I…"

"Shhh."

Why had she come? The removal of the bullet couldn't undo the damage. So much blood on the ground, on her robe and hands, on the blanket. She wanted to return to Lyle, knowing how devastated he was, not wanting him to be alone.

Calm yourself. You asked him to try.

Lucia was twitching. Almost imperceptibly, but Beatrice had seen movement.

Lifting his hand from her side, the man inserted a gloved finger into her ear, holding it there as he'd done with the wound.

"Those lanterns," he said, pointing to the hearth with his free hand. "Light them for me, and bring them here."

They were oil lanterns, and she needed some time to light them from the hearth. Then she brought them over and placed them at the head of the table. For some reason, the lanterns imparted a numinous quality to the room that soothed her.

"Lie down on the cot and rest. I'll be some time with her."

She hadn't expected to, but she dozed off—all those sleepless nights when Lyle was in China. She awakened to a perfectly still Brother Francis, his gloved hand resting on Lucia's wound.

When he saw she was awake, he said, "Could I trouble you for a cup of water? There, in the sink."

Sweat streaked his face. He looked exhausted, and he drank greedily, asking for more.

"Will she live?"

"Have the Brothers bring a cushioned pallet, move her to the monastery."

"Shouldn't she be still for a while?" Beatrice asked him.

"Please do as I request. She should be watched and attended."

Who better to watch Lucia than Brother Francis? Beatrice wondered. Lucia's eyes were closed, but her tail beat once, twice. Beatrice wanted to ask a hundred questions but she hurried out the door and ran as she hadn't run in ages.

LYLE HADN'T EATEN A SPECK and had drunk only a glass of water. Distressed over Lucia, worried about Beatrice, he had fallen asleep late and slept fitfully, dreaming of swarming bees, though not at the hives but inside his office.

A knock on the door roused him from his bed, as if he were a soldier mustered to battle. Head swimming, he had to sit down and take deep breaths before he could stand again.

"She's alive!" were the first words Beatrice spoke, Abbot Henry at her shoulder.

"Not possible," Lyle said. "Don't..."

"Truly, she is," said Abbot Henry. "The Brothers are seeing to her, trying to keep her still. She's determined to worry her rabbits."

"How?" Was he asleep and dreaming?

"Lyle. Attend and listen," his uncle said.

Beatrice hurriedly recounted what she had witnessed. "It sounds impossible, but that's what I saw," she said.

Lucia was alive! He wasn't dreaming or hallucinating. Brother Francis had healed her, the beekeeper. And he'd dreamed of bees. Lyle said, "Describe him."

"What does that matter?" she asked.

"Please—it's important."

"She's alive. That's what matters. Alright, about your age, medium height, heavy eyes, an intense man, but gentle."

"What was in the hut?"

Lyle recognized his uncle's *indulge him* expression. Beatrice said, "Nothing out of the ordinary, until he produced the glove. The place was neat as a pin, except for a spider web in the corner, a big black spider working on an unlucky bee. After I came back with one of the Brothers, I went for his broom, took two steps toward it before he said, 'Don't sweep her away. Charlotte and I are on a first-name basis.'"

Abbot Henry said to Lyle, "I called on Brother Francis before we came to your room. He and his bag were gone. He was in a hurry because he left the door open. I'm sorry to see him go but I can't say I'm surprised. As compensation, we have our Lucia back."

"That's why he wanted Lucia moved, because he was planning to leave. I regret not thanking him," Beatrice said. "I was in a daze when I left."

Lyle said, "I want to see her. Let me dress. Wait, don't go yet."

Beatrice's description of Brother Francis; the bell ringer the night he was attacked in his uncle's office; Lucia's reaction to Leary in his Oxford office; Leary's reference to mainlanders as bees to be managed; and Charlotte. If Leary was working for Andrea, why would he have stymied her the night of the attack and healed Lucia?

Lyle's logic was unraveling. He retrieved his phone, locating the photograph of Leary, displaying it to Beatrice and his uncle. "Is this Brother Francis?"

They stared at each other, each waiting for the other to speak.
"You first," Lyle said to his uncle.

Lucia showed no signs of having been grievously wounded,
already romping with Brother Albert.

Observing her vigor, Lyle said, "We have to go, Uncle Henry.
Without your beekeeping sentry, you're in too much danger while
we're here. Someone was on the grounds with a gun, and I think I
know who it was. We have to see Sam."

"After all you've been through, I know you will take care of
each other, and my dear Samwise."

Beatrice took the abbot's hand and said, "How are you?"

With his eyes fixed on Beatrice, Abbot Henry said, "I am
blessing God for you. We must embrace the certainty that God
is *infiniment bon*, that he wills for us our greatest good. We must
always be happy, never unhappy, nor should we fear death because
we are hastening to meet the One who loves us and knows what is
best for us."

"Yes, Father Abbot," she said. "We love you."

"I have one more thing to say before you go. What I mean
to say is, the *thing* is gone from our monastery. Be at peace, my
dears. I am the one who sent it away, and only one other person in
the world knows where the thing is.

"I've been pondering our discussion on your last visit, Frodo.
What should we do with it? A very wise man decided to bring it
here, entrusting it to that abbot's care. Why should we not do the
same now that Hill's secret is no longer safe?"

"Your words fill me with dread, Uncle," said Lyle.

"Because you fear for the safety of the book, or because you
yourself feel its loss?"

"You have already guessed the answer. Both."

Abbot Henry said, "I did what John Hill did, conveyed it to a
house of prayer, a medieval abbey in northern Scotland that still

lives the Rule of Benedict. The abbot there is an old and dear friend. None of our communications involved electronic devices, all were written in the imaginative language we've employed for over twenty years, a game we enjoy playing. We had a lively conversation about a rare beetle and its carapace, an idea you gave me, Frodo, when you returned from your adventures with Sam. You see, a beetle must open its carapace to produce wings."

"Does your friend know about the wings?"

"John Hill decided my predecessor should know, so I did likewise. They have more than one priest's hole in Aubert's abbey. Those who constructed those hidey-holes were very good at it. Have I said enough about beetles?"

Wearing a borrowed clean robe and cowl for the return trip, Beatrice said, "How was the beetle conveyed to Scotland, Abbot Henry?"

The abbot had difficulty getting words out for his mirth. "Why, in the monastery's Volkswagen Beetle, with half a dozen crates of ale, piloted by one of our Brothers with no inkling a beetle had crept into one of the crates."

He forestalled Lyle's question with an upraised hand. "The beetle is safe, confirmed by Abbot Aubert, but a shame my greatest invention must be retired."

JUNE 18, 2019

London

S AM WAS ALONE IN HIS APARTMENT, but he wasn't lonely. This was a cleaner, cheerier place after Beatrice's lengthy residence here.

He kept reliving that long distance phone conversation with Nancy before Beatrice reappeared.

"If Beatrice and Lyle found a way, why can't we?"

"Even if we could, why would you bother with a man like me?" Sam had asked her.

"Because I know things about you that you may not know."

"You don't know me as well as you think. You can't say I'm Mister Reliable."

"Maybe I'm looking for more than that. You've suspended your own life to protect your brother and help him find some peace. I know Beatrice loved you because she told me so, and I could do worse than trust her judgment."

His inner life had been cloistered for as long as he could remember, even during the Fatemeh era. If he couldn't welcome an enlivening relationship with Nancy, what was the point of the hard changes he was making?

Perhaps that dark day when the prime minister sacked him was the best day of his life.

The table was busy with a pencil, bee-fogging equipment, a

flash device, and medicine that might or might not work if things went awry. He had to be at his best for this. And indeed, his hands were steadier than they'd been in years.

Everything on the list the Paris priest had given him was alive in his gut. This time, he was a soldier in a just cause, with an evil enemy—yes, *evil*. If he could find a way to hold his fire, he would do it, but he wouldn't let this enemy kill his best mates.

That's what his gut told him.

JUNE 19, 2019

Oxford

S HE HID IT MORE ABLY than Lyle could have imagined, but when Beatrice walked into the room Andrea's features froze. Not fear, anger, or even confusion, rather, a watchful expression, the reaction of someone scheming a way out.

Sam had passed on to Lyle and Beatrice what Eitan had learned about this woman when he scrubbed her until she gleamed. An expert patch had been applied to Fitzgerald's historical record prior to 1999. So, how had Eitan's man discovered the patch? Not by finding false records, inconsistencies, or suspicious events. The only evidence for this patch was the significant difference in the *volume* of historical data pre and post 1999. That signaled something was amiss, though what was amiss couldn't be identified, even by one of the best identity investigators in the world. As for Leary, Eitan had struck out, concluding that Raphael Leary was an assumed name, and someone who had managed to avoid any notoriety.

Andrea wore a black dress with a canary jacket, her face and hair radiant. Sam said, "We were talking about Desrosier, her murder."

Beatrice took a chair. Andrea said, "Lyle knows Desrosier and I communicated several years ago, but we never met. I don't know her. From what you've told me, I did well to stay away from her."

Andrea wasn't going to question Beatrice. She was going to make them come to her. Sam had warned them that once Beatrice appeared, Andrea would know they had connected the dots between her visit to Uganda and the bombing.

How soon would Sam show his cards, and how hard would Andrea resist when she realized he was holding all four aces? Or was he?

Sam said, "We know you hired Malkin to kill Beatrice. We know you're working for the Chinese. We know you hired the Albanians to kill Desrosier and Malkin. We know you murdered Irma Meisner because she saw you enter Lyle's flat while he was in Africa. We know you'd do anything to get your hands on the book."

"You have evidence?" she said as dispassionately as a solicitor might have done. "You don't believe this, Lyle. It's ludicrous. Why would I risk everything when I have Zeta2 and the BBC?"

Lyle had to give it to her. Her appeal had just the right tone, a combination of incredulity and earnestness. And Andrea didn't wait for him to answer. "Yes, I spoke to Beatrice. Yes, I would love to see and study the book you found. What archaeologist wouldn't? What happened in Uganda had nothing to do with me and I deeply resent the accusation."

Sam wasn't having any of it. "We know Malkin entered the dig through the water gate. You made sure Gorsey and the Israeli were in Jerusalem. No doubt you and Malkin were planning Beatrice's murder."

"Lyle, talk some sense into your brother. The law has something to say about slander."

Lyle was ready to caution Sam, she was that compelling. "The CID are on their way," said Sam. "They agreed to give me an hour. In the meantime, keep your hands where I can see them."

Lyle said, "You tried to kill Lucia. What makes the manuscript so important that you'll kill to have it?"

The look Andrea gave Lyle, writ large on her haughty features, convinced him she was an altogether different person than the woman who had consoled and encouraged him after Beatrice's presumed death—*what cobras do before they strike*, Agnese had said—but he'd been wrong to conclude Lucia was revenge. Andrea had failed to unlock Lyle via Beatrice or by endearing herself to him after Beatrice's death. The attack on Lucia was intended to unlock him by enraging or unhinging him—an emotionless calculation.

She said to Sam, "You told me the police will be here in an hour."

"Less than that. We've used up forty minutes."

"You have everything lined up, don't you?"

"More than I've revealed," Sam said. "More than enough."

"Desrosier warned me about you," Andrea calmly said.

"*Why?*" Lyle asked her.

"You already know the answer," Andrea said. "If it's authentic, it is the most valuable artifact in the world, in history."

"I never said it was authentic."

"Do you think you were my only source? You'd be amazed at what I know."

Why so candid, practically admitting she had been behind the attacks? No, they couldn't have incontrovertible evidence, despite what Sam had said. Why not continue to profess innocence, affect outrage?

Lyle said, "You're the one who attacked me in the monastery. You didn't kill me because Leary intervened with the bell."

Did she wince at the mention of that name?

Beatrice broke in. "Nothing you said or did made me suspicious you'd resort to murder. I wasn't certain of anything, but I decided to be cautious. You killed a woman who had nothing to do with what you were after."

Sam placed a capped data storage device on the desk in front of Andrea.

When I inform her about the flash drive, you are to say nothing...nothing! Sam had told Lyle and Beatrice.

Sam said, "This device contains everything—private plane flight plans, what Beatrice told us, Li's revelations, material from the Mossad, the German police, Desrosier, and Leary. Everything. The information on this device will keep you in prison for a long time."

"You want me to snatch it when you have copies of everything."

"I ought to have done, but I'm just an old knockabout, and I have you where I want you. I'd rather watch you snatch. Call it fair play."

Andrea's eyes shifted from Sam to the storage device. "You said the police are coming. You have me cornered. May I get my bag from the wardrobe? You can train your gun on me. I'll raise my hands if it makes you feel better."

"Make it quick," said Sam, his pistol on his lap.

She stood. "We could have had everything, Lyle. Do you understand? Everything!"

Andrea opened the wardrobe, exposing clothing on hangers and a black bag on the floor. Before they knew what was happening, she had leapt inside and pulled the doors closed.

"Get down on the floor," commanded Sam, gripping the gun and making for the wardrobe.

Lyle dropped to his knees, observing Sam unsuccessfully trying to open the doors.

The flash drive was gone.

Beatrice said, "Just ring the police, Sam. She's not going anywhere."

Something was troubling Lyle. Something in his memory—Agnese's maids! He shouted, "You have to get inside, Sam. Before she escapes. There's an abandoned passage behind that wall. Closed up for years. How the maids cleaned the offices without trespassing on the faculty. That's why the wardrobe's there, a way out."

Sam removed a sturdy knife from his pocket, prying the doors open in a matter of seconds.

The rear of the wardrobe was a disguised door to the passage, visible when Sam illuminated it with his pen lamp. The bag was missing. Two men with CID in prominent letters on their jackets entered the office and made their way toward Sam, now in the maids' alley.

Backing out, Sam said, "A window at the end of the passage. She's on the roof or in the yard."

The CID men and Sam raced out of the room, Lyle starting to join them until Beatrice prevented him, saying, "Let's see for ourselves."

The wardrobe led to a narrow corridor with barely enough room for one person in the little alleyway. Dust covered everything. Shelves on the exterior wall contained pails, rags, and bottles. To their right, the corridor dead-ended after several paces; to the left, it extended some thirty feet to another dead end. Once a door to the building hallway, this was where the window to the yard was located.

Lyle said, "You can bet once she got to the window, she had the means to go up or down."

At the end of the alley, Beatrice said, "The dust on the floor hasn't been disturbed and the window hasn't been opened in ages."

"It's the only way out, unless another door is in here somewhere."

Without much light, Beatrice brought her eyes close to everything that interested her. "Wouldn't we have heard something if she exited the passageway into the lab? Wouldn't Sam or the police have seen something in the hallway if she came out that way?"

When they weren't able to manhandle the window open, Lyle told Beatrice to close her eyes, and broke the cloudy glass with a pail, sending shards into the lot below.

With twenty feet up to the roof, forty feet down to the yard, Lyle watched Sam and the policemen circling the area below.

Lyle shouted at Sam, who gave him a thumbs-down.

"What are you thinking?" Beatrice asked him.

"Andrea's convinced the manuscript is authentic. She's obsessed with having that archaeological treasure. We must have missed another door."

Stirring the dust on the floor with her shoe and wiping a small patch of grime from the window frame, Beatrice said, "I don't think archaeology has anything to do with it."

ONCE HE WAS FINISHED WITH THE POLICE, Sam tracked Lyle and Beatrice down at Lyle's flat where they'd been discussing their options.

"Nothing new," Sam informed them. "She's a wily one."

"Tell us about the flash drive," Lyle said to his brother.

"I appreciate your behaving yourselves. I wanted to see how she'd react."

Lyle said, "You couldn't have expected her to escape."

"I didn't expect her to escape. How could she, with one way out, my gun on her and the CID on the way? But if she managed it, she wouldn't leave the flash behind, and when she removes the cap from that flash, she'll find a horse of a different color. I should say a *bug* of a different color."

Lyle stared at him, remembering what the young Israeli had said to Sam in the Frankfurt airport and Eitan's interest in the package there. "What did it look like?"

"Grayish green, about three inches long, lots of legs, ugly as sin."

"Weren't you frightened?" Lyle asked his brother.

"No more than usual. Some things you have to do scared."

"You made that decision yourself?" Beatrice asked Sam.

"I made the decision about the cargo. I made the decision to place the flash drive—*my* property—on her desk. *She* made the decision to steal it and she'll make the decision to open it."

"She's wily, as you say," Beatrice remarked.

"So is my cargo. When the cap's removed, a right boisterous contest. Let's see how she does scared."

JUNE 2020

Cornwall
(one year later)

A PERFECT DAY FOR A CONVERTIBLE MOTORCAR, with bright sun, warm air, a twisty coastal road—the sea on one side, glens and the occasional town on the other.

They'd left Salisbury after breakfast and had been motoring for hours, with stops here and there to inspect the landscape, stretch their legs, and taste the local fare. Lyle and Beatrice were up front; Jeremy with his girlfriend, Loretta, in the middle row; and Lucia in the rear, the poodle's head stretched out the window.

Ten months earlier, Lyle and Sam had been waiting in the vestry of the Oxford Oratory Church of St. Aloysius Gonzaga. Abbot Henry was presiding, while Cornelia and Grayson, Maria and Veronica, Danielle, Agnese, Jeremy, Cornel, and Harold were in the front pew. Nancy was up front waiting for Beatrice. Lyle and his uncle had done all that was necessary to receive the Sacrament with Beatrice at the altar. Whatever Lyle was after that day, he was more than an earthling.

Jeremy and Loretta were wide eyed from the moment they embarked from Salisbury. As for Lucia, she'd been on her share of car rides, but nothing like this sustained ecstasy, enjoying fresh air, friends, and foreign food.

This holiday had been Lyle's idea—"Somewhere with less pestilence and more green"—and not even a second was needed to convince Beatrice. Stretches of the ride allowed Jeremy to pepper Lyle with questions. Loretta gradually opened up. Like every happy couple, Jeremy and Loretta gave one another a corrective word now and then, albeit less discretely than more socially conscious couples.

Reentering the car after a joyous romp on the beach, Beatrice had whispered to Lyle, "They're holding hands."

LYLE EXCUSED HIMSELF FROM THE BEACHFRONT COTTAGE they'd rented. Beatrice, Jeremy, and Loretta were absorbed in a puzzle, but Lucia was happy to accompany Lyle to the beach.

Beatrice accommodated jazz, not for as long or as loud as Lyle liked it, so the beach would be ideal for listening to the recorded April Lincoln Center jazz concert with a dozen quarantined performers.

The setting was just right, featuring warm air and gentle rolling waves on a rocky Cornwall beach. Since the hour was after ten p.m., light was supplied by a full moon in a cloudless sky.

Lyle sat on the sand ten paces from the lapping water. Lucia sat, too, for all of a minute, before darting in and out of the surf.

"You'll not be sleeping on the bed with wet feet, little girl." If she understood, she ignored him.

He wasn't in a hurry to put on his headphones, delighting in the beauty of the night, contemplating Popa's cave—their coming August adventure.

Lucia was fifty yards up the beach by the time Lyle noticed she was gone.

"Here, stay!" he called out.

She kept loping ahead toward a solitary figure coming in their direction.

"Hello, Dr. Stuart." He had a beard this time.

Lyle said, "What are you doing here?"

"I was told it's a public beach."

"Lucia, come."

She looked up at the man, who nudged her toward Lyle.

Raphael Leary began, "May I have a word with you? Don't worry, this will be our last. I'm going back, as Peter returned to Rome, to do what I can."

They were alone on the beach, but Lyle wasn't fearful, not after what Beatrice had told him about the night with Lucia and Brother Francis. Lyle said, "In my office, you said you were a blood traitor."

"So was Peter, in his way."

Lyle hadn't expected to have the opportunity to thank this man. "I'm grateful for what you did for Lucia, more than grateful."

"You half-believe me now?" Leary asked.

"Forty-two-point-five percent. I'm a creature of my training, Leary," Lyle said, delighted to see this man again.

"You need not be a slave to it."

He was still a step ahead of Lyle. Every once in a while, Lyle or Beatrice came up with a question they wished they could ask this man. Here was Lyle's chance, and Beatrice wouldn't be happy if he let the opportunity pass. "Why haven't we found ruins and more artifacts?"

Leary knew exactly what Lyle was getting at. "Much of the telltale was moved or effaced by my people, using skills main-landers don't possess and with thousands of years to accomplish it, to shield us."

"Your Rome is far away?" Lyle inquired.

Leary pointed to the moon, glowing like a lantern. "Much closer than our little sister and infinitely further. We are where we always were, just...up above, where you can't see us. Do you mind if we sit? I've hiked all the way from Polperro."

Lucia squeezed between Lyle and Leary, who commenced petting her. The moonlight and effervescent surf were hypnotic, a night Lyle wished would never end. This mysterious man, however, had undoubtedly come here for a purpose he had yet to disclose.

Leary said, "This beach reminds me of where I was born—the stones, the cadence of the surf. My father was Council First for most of my youth and my mother spent much of her time in First Town, so my early days' companion was my mother's aunt who lived with us. We had nothing about the legends in our home library, but my aunt told me all the stories, as history. Up and down the beach we'd walk, day and night, the happiest days of my life."

Popa's beach with his *deda*, his grandfather.

"That life ended when I began relating my aunt's stories in my parents' presence. Suddenly, my aunt was gone and I had a First Town schoolmaster."

"The damage seems to have been done," Lyle observed.

"Truly!"

"Shall we speak of Rosman?" Lyle asked him, having deduced Andrea's true nature and purpose.

"And spoil such a lovely night?"

"Where is she?" Lyle inquired.

"Not in *Rome*, so to speak, or so a little eagle informed me. That's where I'd expect her to be in the wake of all that happened. I'm quite confident she isn't there, and I can't imagine her remaining on the mainland."

Lyle wiggled fingers menacingly and said, "When she escaped, some 'thing' went with her."

"Ah!"

In a flash, Lucia bounded down to the surf, kicking sand in Lyle's face.

"What fun we had," said Leary, watching the poodle wade in the water. "She was fascinated by the bees and wise enough to keep her distance."

Lyle spit sand from his mouth, dusting his face with a hand.

"Lyle, are you all right?" called Beatrice from the cottage door. Lucia's ears went up.

Lyle looked to Leary, who said, "The fewer who associate with me, the better, for them. She is a lovely and indomitable woman."

"All's well," Lyle called back.

He heard the door close. "When do you leave for Rome?"

"Tomorrow."

"So soon?"

Watching Lucia at play, Leary said, "I settled on departing the day after I spoke to you. I want to reinforce what I told you about the *biblio*. If they believe the peril persists, they will send someone else. You must give it a wide berth, you and your good uncle, as if it no longer exists."

Lyle said, "I shudder to think how close she came to acquiring it."

"Among my people, she's known to be Council-able. That means nothing to you, but it's high praise. She hadn't created the Rosman persona when we were betrothed, which was before I went renegade and she volunteered for the recovery mission. I deciphered her Rosman role, though not immediately. She came on and off the grid—these dimensions—when she decided to act or desired anonymity. I did what I could to hinder her without revealing myself, scoring more failures than successes. Then, she disappeared for years. I suspected a new persona, undiscovered until the attempt on Beatrice. If I wasn't certain, I had grave suspicions. The reason I revealed what I did in your office when I knew she was in Jericho."

"Why didn't you warn me about Andrea?"

"I warned you *off* the *biblio*, the only safe warning. If I'd warned you off Fitzgerald she would have discerned your altered attitude no matter how hard you tried to disguise it."

That was the same thing Beatrice had concluded after the bombing. "Andrea killed an elderly woman in the apartments across the street from me because the woman saw her in my flat while I was in Africa. Irma followed her, recorded her plate number, and confronted her."

"Poor woman," Leary observed. "How could she have known the danger she was in?"

"Why wouldn't Andrea have used a portal to move in and out of my flat?"

"Of course, she could have done, but perhaps she chose conventional entry because you were far away. Using a portal saps your strength, like someone running a marathon. You pay the penalty in vigor, for a while at least. Many of the devices that magnify our capabilities are like that."

"The glove?"

Leary smiled. "The result was worth the toll," he said.

"Should I apologize for the cargo we sent to her, the thing?" Lyle said.

Leary shook his head. "She and I made our choices long ago. Before she vanished, or was vanquished, she would have killed me if she'd had me in her power."

Down the beach cruised a seabird, gray in the moonlight, mere feet above the sand. Lyle said, "If yours is a society of Rosmans and Alemberts, what do you hope to accomplish?"

"I will try to reason them out of what I can't talk them out of on moral grounds. While mainlanders may be thwarted in this or that enterprise, they are now far too numerous and advanced to be held back *en masse*. My people will be found out sooner rather than later, pursued and run to ground. We number in the thousands, you in the billions. A better—more rational—strategy is to disengage, seek even more remote dimensions. That such a strategy accomplishes what I desire on moral grounds, without resorting to moral suasion, need not be mentioned."

"They will give you a hearing?"

"They may, after their close call with your Andrea, and who better to make the argument than someone who's lived with mainlanders for over a century. Now, I have a question for you. Have you heard of Henrijk...R-I-J-K...Albertson?"

Lyle thought a minute. "I can't say I have."

"Thirty years ago, he was in the vanguard of quantum physics, and held a number of public debates about whether science proved the universe was godless. Henrijk argued that the Big Bang and quantum mechanics suggested deeper mystery, and not a naturalistic explanation for the universe."

What Leary said stirred a memory, but Lyle couldn't put his arms around it. "Is he connected to the Guild, someone in your line?"

"Heavens no! When his family moved to England, his father shortened the family name to Albert."

Lyle perked up in recognition. "That's my mother's maiden name."

"Henry Albert used his birth name, Albertson, at university and in the physics community. Your uncle was more than a journeyman physicist, and his ideas were what first attracted me to his monastery."

"You didn't know about the book?"

"I knew *of* the book. I knew Elana Rosman was after it. I knew John Hill must have had access to it, but I was astounded to learn it was hidden in your uncle's monastery. The invasions made me suspicious, then I learned about Dekeyser's disappearance and Beatrice's murder, amounting to too many connections and coincidences."

Before Beatrice, Lyle's uncle had been the most important person in his life. Here was Raphael Leary, the man who had brought Lucia back from the brink of death. Lyle steeled himself and said, "May I request a favor?"

"Yes, Dr. Stuart?"

Leary's response suggested he anticipated the request.

"Heal my uncle."

Lucia, wet and wild, had again wedged herself between them, and Leary began petting her, as Lyle did when he was distressed. "I may not."

"You healed Lucia. Henry is your friend."

"My *good* friend. Would you make me another Roman? I can say no more than that. I would go with your blessing, not in sorrow."

"Is there anything I can do for you, Leary?" Lyle asked him.

Leary turned toward the water. Was he looking for something, or was he thinking? "As a matter of fact, you can. Whenever you are tempted to talk about the book—worse yet, seek it out—remind yourself why your lady was threatened, and remind yourself why she's infinitely more important than the *biblio*."

They rose as one, dusting sand from their trousers. Leary said, "Give me your hand, if you please."

The man placed a flat octagonal object in Lyle's palm, luminous silver strung with a slender silver chain.

"Turn it over."

The object displayed a string of symbols matching those Lyle had seen in the manuscript.

"An amulet," Leary said. "A pledge of troth in the ancient tongue, returned to me when she let me go. The time has come for me to release this piece of the past, as a gift for your lovely wife. But remember this Frodo Lyle Stuart. You have your lady back. Your reputation glitters. Your future is bright. But no final happiness awaits anyone in this world. A healed Abbot Henry, one hundred years for you with Beatrice and the *biblio* would not produce it. Recall the book your mother read you. After that evil kingdom was thrown down, where was Frodo's final happiness, Elrond's and Galadriel's? Even Aragorn and Arwen came to a sad sundering. Final joy is not here, though we plan and pretend and look the other way when this truth daunts us."

Lucia didn't follow Leary as he retreated down the beach, instead sitting at Lyle's side until the visitor was swallowed up in the darkness.

Lyle remembered his troubling dream about Arthur Russell and Leary, men so physically and temperamentally dissimilar, but if Leary was to be believed, both with Atlantean blood in their veins. Did Russell know this or just suspect it? Or had he merely conformed to his genetic heritage?

The surf was tumbling harder now, the cottage dark. "Let's go inside," he said to Lucia.

A light came on as soon as he opened the cottage door—Beatrice making sure he was safe and sound.

"We're back," he said.

AUGUST 2020

Alpine Germany

"WHOA! WHOA!" the dislodged, swaying man said, as rocks clattered down the face of an inverted Alpine mountain.

Actually, the clattering came through a walkie-talkie pressed against Beatrice's ear.

"He's safely secured, Mrs. Dr. Stuart," Miriam Hanna reassured Beatrice. Into her own walkie-talkie, Miriam said, "Mr. Dr. Stuart, reel yourself in, find a new hold."

Beatrice was encouraged by Miriam, an expert climber and Lyle's new field assistant. With Lyle's sponsorship and with Lyle and Beatrice helping her family, Miriam was reading archaeology at Oxford.

Beatrice was more than weary, she was queasy, and not from fear of heights or apprehension about Lyle's safety. But that was her secret.

She knew the video cameras in Lyle's and Popa's helmets allowed Miriam to see everything they saw, and the walkie-talkie let her tell them what to do, as if she were rappelling down with them.

"Here we are," said Popa.

"Thank God," Beatrice heard Lyle say.

LYLE AND POPA WERE NINE-THOUSAND FEET UP, and two-hundred feet below the ledge where Beatrice and Miriam were perched.

Above them was a bright sun and dwarfish clouds, the climbers shaded by the mountain, the peak to their right bathed in sunlight. All around them were jagged rocks, with thick-trunked cypress sprouting from the vertical face.

Convinced the descent would be easier than Lyle imagined, it had turned out to be just the opposite. If not for Miriam's reassuring voice, he'd have panicked. As for Popa, that grandfather of twelve was meandering down the cliff face like a mountain goat.

Not infrequently, a foot or hand slipped from its niche, with an accompanying pang of terror, but the tether held. If he survived, Lyle would have to tell Jeremy all about this adventure. He could already hear his friend's response. "Really, Lyle?"

"These trees may be five-hundred years old," Popa said.

"What trees?" Lyle managed to say, seeking his next grip with trembling hands.

Miriam's voice in his ear said, "To the right, Mr. Dr. Stuart. There."

Popa's voice sounded again. "Don't worry about falling. Miriam has you tethered. No, do not look down, my friend."

No one would have guessed it, but Lyle had never been happier. As for Sam, he'd been assisting Joseph Mutesi. Comparing it to plow-horse work, Sam had accepted the position because it afforded him the opportunity to be in Kampala for extended periods of time.

Popa said, "The opening's just below us—let me catch my breath. I recall this tree."

The tree was three or four feet in length, with a two-foot diameter trunk and dozens of interweaving branches.

"Remember what I said about the branches being brittle. There—that opening."

"I don't think I can get in," said Lyle.

Miriam's voice directed him. "Head first."

He was gasping rather than breathing. "I'm liable to strangle myself with this tether."

"Then, take it off," said Popa.

"Don't! You! Dare!" came Beatrice's frantic voice.

Lyle managed to worm his way in, followed by the thinner and nimbler Popa, who said, "No more communication with the summiteers. Tons of rock between us and them."

Lyle had the same exultant feeling as when he'd recovered the manuscript. Though Popa had surely seen his public communication about the algorithm in the *Journal of Paleolithic Archaeology*, his friend had said nothing about it, nor did Lyle note a hint in Popa's attitude toward him of any reticence or suspicion. Nor had the disclosure made an iota of difference to Agnese. Dawson had lectured Lyle about scholarly norms but apparently wasn't about to risk his departure to the Sorbonne, or anywhere else, especially with Andrea vanishing into thin air.

At the rear of the cavern, Popa squatted with his lamp and eyes tight to the rock wall.

Lyle had sensed something mysterious in the works ever since they'd embarked from home. Even Beatrice seemed different, though she hadn't said or done anything strange.

He recognized a purpose in his pursuit of the book and in his renunciation of it. A net not of his own making had been cast into a sea of chaos and had gathered in Beatrice and Sam. He was at peace with everything—good and bad—that had brought him to this moment because he had pondered and accepted what Leary had said to him on that moon-bathed beach. "But remember this Frodo Lyle Stuart. You have your lady back. Your reputation glitters. Your future is bright. But no final happiness awaits anyone in this world... Final joy is not here, though we plan and pretend and look the other way when this truth daunts us."

Popa was making little noises of delight. He turned to Lyle, and said, excitedly, "You must see this!"

Lyle joined his friend at the wall, the two of them examining the embedded artifacts together. Lyle said, "Cornel, if we wrote down everything we've seen and learned about the book, this cavern,

Leary—everything! Put the weight of our reputations behind a real *Atalantë* and those who escaped to the mainland, how many would take us seriously?"

Popa's expression told him everything he needed to know, and Lefebvre's obliterated reputation spun toward him like a monster tornado.

Frodo Lyle Stuart and Cornel Popa clasped hands.

JULY 1973

☙☙☙

Oxford
The End of All Things

T HE DOOR CLOSED. Owen had paid him a visit, and oh what a conversation they'd had.

He was back in his chair, the lap rug covering his legs.

He was a man who had been in the eye of terrible storms: on battlefields, and for long years besieged by the deadliest of men. A man who had loved fiercely, joyously explored ideas and beliefs, now reduced to a name on the spines of books and this cramped existence. As for those who lauded him, few knew him, or understood what moved him.

Nine months had passed since he'd delivered the book to the abbot, never once regretting the decision, though often yearning once more to see that beautiful coffer swing open, page through the book, feel as he had felt when he was its custodian.

In his mind's eye, they were back in the Bird and Baby: Jack, Owen, Hugo, Charles, and the rest—storytelling, debating, disputing, engaging in lively conversation.

"Warble us a song before we go," one of them said. "One of your ditties."

If only they had known how hard he'd worked on those *ditties*, laboring until he'd captured the spirit of the original in his own language.

"Professor, you have a visitor," the middle-aged woman at the door said.

He was confused. "Do I have an appointment, Jane?"

"Not to my knowledge."

"Then, please tell the visitor I'm not seeing anyone."

"He's a gentleman, Professor."

After Owen's visit, he was weary and inclined to immerse himself in memory before he retired for the night.

"Will you see him?" she asked, in her encouraging tone of voice.

Whoever the visitor was, the man had impressed Jane, and the professor knew her to be made of stern stuff.

"Very well. Show him in," he mumbled.

Though this was summer and the day warm, the old man had felt the need to cover his legs. He had no sooner set the lap rug to the side than the visitor strode into the room, with Jane closing the door behind him.

The visitor stepped forward and stooped down to shake hands so the professor need not rise from his chair. "Thank you for seeing me, sir. My name is Gabriel Chary. I'm an antiquarian with information you may find interesting."

A pleasant-looking man, Chary had a full head of dark, wavy hair and lively eyes. Why had Jane referred to him as a gentleman? He hadn't identified a title or senior station.

"Take a seat, Mr. Chary," the professor said.

Chary sat down where Owen had sat. "Don't blame Jane. I can be rather persuasive."

"Hmmm. You're here to interview me, I suppose."

"I'm here to inform you."

"I'm not seeking information," the professor rebutted, immediately realizing how narrow that made him sound. Hadn't he always been a seeker, and was he going to abandon the quest in his last days?

"I promise to be brief," Chary said.

Something about this man was familiar, something in the way he carried himself. Had the old man met Gabriel Chary before? "I'll hear what you have to say."

Chary put his hands on his knees and leaned in. "You questioned whether certain things in the chronicle were historical or whether they had been invented by the authors."

The professor was on the alert now. He wasn't as resolute as he once was but he could still summon a measure of fortitude when required. The professor told himself he had no need to affirm or deny what Chary suggested. If this man was after the book and coffer, he was too late.

"To your credit, you allowed the things you suspected of being invented to remain in the chronicle," said Chary.

To his credit? A bit of cheek that. A grin appeared on the old man's face.

Chary said, "A man calling himself Hill met with Greta Erickson in Stockholm in nineteen-thirty-one to ask questions related to a literary project he had undertaken. I spoke with Dr. Erickson several months ago."

"What do you want?" the old man asked suspiciously.

"I want to encourage you, and I want to make sure the thing is safe."

Whatever the professor said to this man, he wouldn't lie. "I need no encouragement, nor do I possess anything that must be kept safe."

"Then you've turned it over to someone else. Someone trustworthy. Good!"

Chary's words stirred the professor's memory of his meeting with the abbot and what he himself had said at that time. "This is a beautiful place. Peace pervades it. Perhaps I have not erred in coming—I have with me an antiquity—I want to leave this with you." He also remembered the long walk back from the monastery to the village and the sense of loss that had accompanied every step. Like many necessary decisions, that one hadn't produced contentment, nor had he expected it to.

"Why should I trust you?" the professor said.

"I haven't asked you to trust me, nor shall I. Greta Erickson was wrong about those flying beasts. My people have discovered dinosaur remains with intact tissue and DNA. Over sixty-million-years old—mummies for all intents and purposes."

My people.

Chary lowered his voice. "Such a beastly recreation could have been accomplished by the dark being you wrote about. That's what I came to tell you. I've brought a last word of caution for you as well. Do not imagine that because a certain person is long-dead, you're safe."

The professor said, "I'm too old and too convicted of my beliefs to worry about being safe. Nor am I naïve when the matter concerns human nature."

Gabriel Chary rose quickly and was almost out the door when the professor called out. "It has not been cast into a pit of fire, but I judge it to be safe enough."

What had possessed him to say such a thing? The door closed behind the visitor. Chary hadn't pressed him about the book, not as that woman Rosman had. Who was this visitor anyway? A question many had asked about John Hill. The old man gazed out the window at the tidy little garden and the gate in the wall, watching the bees and butterflies at work, pondering what he had heard.

"The road goes ever on and on," he said.

www.ingramcontent.com/pod-product-compliance
Lightning Source LLC
Chambersburg PA
CBHW050535260626
47157CB00002B/300